Duke's Project

Sharon Lanergan

An Ellora's Cave Publication

www.ellorascave.com

Duke's Project

ISBN 9781419968341
ALL RIGHTS RESERVED.
Duke's Project Copyright © 2008 Sharon Lanergan
Edited by Helen Woodall.
Cover Design by Dar Albert.
Cover Photography by Shock, Chorazin/Fotolia.com.

Electronic book publication April 2008
Trade paperback publication 2013

With the exception of quotes used in reviews, this book may not be reproduced or used in whole or in part by any means existing without written permission from the publisher, Ellora's Cave Publishing, Inc.® 1056 Home Avenue, Akron OH 44310-3502.

Warning: The unauthorized reproduction or distribution of this copyrighted work is illegal. Criminal copyright infringement, including infringement without monetary gain, is investigated by the FBI and is punishable by up to 5 years in federal prison and a fine of $250,000. (http://www.fbi.gov/ipr/)

This book is a work of fiction and any resemblance to persons, living or dead, or places, events or locales is purely coincidental. The characters are productions of the author's imagination and used fictitiously.

The publisher and author(s) acknowledge the trademark status and trademark ownership of all trademarks, service marks and word marks mentioned in this book.

The publisher does not have any control over and does not assume any responsibility for author or third-party Web sites or their content.

Dedication

To my family, to Jennifer Crump, and to PD. And to my editor for giving my book a chance.

Chapter One
London, 1815

The shining black boot stood out among the usual rotting cabbages, half-eaten sausages and discarded bottles in the alley by The Black Swan.

"What 'ave we 'ere?" Dani called aloud to the rats in the narrow lane. Not that she considered the scurrying creatures running past her, wriggling their noses, her comrades.

In fact, when she'd first entered the alley looking for anything useful or edible she was pretty certain she'd smelled a dead rat. The stench of death permeated the narrow lane.

She licked her lips. There didn't seem to be anything edible, she snorted with disgust but the appearance of the boot was promising.

The sun was just rising around her but she had been awake for hours listening to the night sounds. She couldn't afford to sleep more than a few hours at a time. There'd be someone round to steal you blind if you let your guard down.

Dani glanced toward the opening of the alley, watching to make sure no one else came down it to try to steal her prize.

Dani pulled her tattered pale yellow shawl tighter around her shoulders against the slight chill in the air. Her shawl was one of her few possessions and a real treasure. It was one of the articles of clothing Mary and Grace had taken with them when their seamstress shop closed all those years ago. It wasn't in the best of shape any longer, but it had been well made once, and Dani loved it. Grace told her that her mother had made it herself.

A rat scurried over her foot and Dani took a quick step back, instantly feeling a squishy substance on the ball of her foot. Frowning, she raised her foot to see what she'd stepped in. She wore an old pair of shoes but they were wearing through, had been, in fact when she'd bought them from a beggar woman a few months back with a few coins she'd received from Mary. Oozing into the hole in her shoe was some yellowish brown substance. Dani thought it best not to wonder too long what it was. Later she would wash off her shoes.

Dani crept toward the polished black boot. She'd been about to move to another part of the alley when she spotted it. She could only see the foot of the boot from where she stood but she saw not a scuffmark on it. It appeared to be brand new and was glossy with its shine.

It was a man's boot, to be sure and she had no idea if she would find its mate but... "Well, who would throw away only one boot, I ask you?" They'd be too large for her feet, true but she knew a shopkeeper or two who would pay good money for boots like that.

Dani stepped around the pile she'd been standing by to move closer to the boot. More rats scurried toward her and a shudder went up her spine.

"Shoo," she yelled at the rat.

Dani whistled low in her throat. It was an expensive boot, she'd wager. How in the world had it gotten into the refuse of a seedy tavern like The Black Swan? Well, she wasn't about to let such good fortune pass her by. She reached to finger the fine, rich leather.

She backed up quickly, nearly stepping on one of the rats in her haste. The boot was attached to a leg! She was sure of it.

Dani took a breath, willing her racing heart to slow down. It couldn't possibly have been a leg she saw. No, no. Her imagination was getting the best of her on this fog-enshrouded morning that was all.

"Only one way to find out," she said. She crept toward the boot once more.

It was a leg. No mistaking it. A man's leg wore the beautiful polished boot. The leg was encased in dark brown tailored breeches. Biting her lip, Dani peered closer. Her eyes followed the line of his leg and then her gaze fell on the man's torso. His coat was the same rich, dark brown of his breeches.

Maybe he was just passed out, she told herself. He might have drunk too much at the Swan. His cream-colored fine linen shirt and cravat were soaked in something red. Her hand went to her throat. Blood. Lots of it.

Finally her gaze went to his face. He was young and handsome once. No more than twenty Dani guessed. And wealthy from the look of it. A member of London society. And quite dead.

Murder!

Dani screamed.

* * * * *

Simon Thorndike, fifth Duke of Stratford, sighed. He was headed out to see the magistrate at the request of his mother's widowed sister, Lady Penelope Norton.

Three weeks before, Aunt Pen's only son, Douglas, had been found dead in an alleyway outside a tavern by the docks called The Black Swan. Found by a doxy, Simon was told.

Devastated by her sudden loss, Aunt Pen was not satisfied with the investigation by the authorities. Killed in a robbery attempt was the verdict. She begged Simon for his assistance. Why would Douglas have been down a dark alley in that part of London? Knowing what Simon did about Douglas, he had a pretty good idea of what his young cousin had been doing at The Black Swan.

Simon hadn't been able to speak with the magistrate, but that morning at breakfast he'd promised he would go today. He could not refuse her.

Wilkins handed Simon his greatcoat and hat. A clap of thunder interrupted the brief silence in the entry hall. Yesterday's sun was but a memory. Heavy rain splashed outside the door.

"There are several invitations that need going over, Your Grace," Wilkins, his butler of more than ten years, said from beside him.

Simon grimaced and glanced at Wilkins. The silver-haired butler gestured with a long bony hand toward the side table whereupon a stack of cards lay. He hadn't had time to go through them.

"Later, Wilkins." He pulled on his gloves and opened the door.

A young woman stood there with her hand raised as though about to rap on the door. She wore an old faded brown gown years out of fashion and repaired many times. Around her small shoulders was draped a yellow shawl. Finally, perched on a head of unruly long curly hair was a lopsided bonnet in a slightly lighter shade of brown than the gown.

"Would this be the home o' the Duke o' Stratford?" she demanded, peering up at Simon with the prettiest periwinkle eyes he'd ever seen.

"Yes."

Her gaze was intent. "Would you be the duke?"

Simon blinked. "I...yes."

She grinned. "What luck! I found you me first try."

Simon shook his head, perplexed at what this woman could possibly want with him. She was clearly from the lower classes. Her cheeks were quite red as though she'd spent a long time scrubbing them. Even so a smudge of dirt streaked across her forehead.

"Of all the impertinence," Simon heard Wilkins say. He stood behind Simon, no doubt thinking to protect his employer from the girl. "Don't you know whose house you're at, girl?"

"If she's looking for handouts, send her to the kitchens. Instruct Mrs. Martin to give her something," Simon muttered to Wilkins. The rain battered down on both himself and the girl. She was already soaked through.

"Disgusting filth," Wilkins cried out. "I don't know who you think you are." Wilkins paused to sniff. "But you are in the presence of the Duke of Stratford and we don't allow…"

She wouldn't let him finish. "Well, excuse me, Lord 'igh and mighty but I 'ave some important information as it were. 'E'll want to know, I'm guessing."

Simon barely listened. He checked his watch fob. Her slightly rough accent was giving him a headache. "Wilkins, give her some coins and send her away."

"I'll take the coins, Your Grace but I won't be going nowhere until I says me piece."

Simon raised an eyebrow at the cheeky urchin. "I have an appointment."

"I suggest you cancel your appointment then," she said, glancing over her shoulder at the street in front of his house. A carriage slowed down as it passed. The occupant wondering why Simon stood out in the rain, no doubt.

"I'll handle this, Your Grace," Wilkins said firmly. "Now see, here, if you do not leave at once I shall have to call for a magistrate."

"I always did want to 'ave a proper tea in a fancy parlor. Do you think I could?" She crossed her arms in front of her and peered at Simon. "You do want to talk to me about that man's body I found, don't you?"

Dani knew she was taking a risk coming to the duke's home. The magistrate who'd been in charge of the murder investigation told her the duke would probably want to question her about what she'd seen when she found the body. She wheedled the address out of him and managed to get some coins out of him too for the information she gave him.

Some of which she had used to buy a sliver of soap to wash her face and to pay the hackney to come here.

She peered at the duke and the old servant from beneath her lashes. She knew they were looking her over. She did the same. She was surprised at how handsome the duke was. She'd never met a duke before and didn't have any real expectations about him. But he was a damn sight better looking than anyone in the East End, that was for sure.

He was dressed in dark blue breeches and the same kind of black polished boots the dead man had been wearing. He was wearing his greatcoat, which was black but she could not tell what he wore underneath. His hair was a rich mahogany shade—she'd never seen the like—and his eyes, a beautiful gold-green. He was tall too, he easily towered over both her and the old butler and the shoulders filling out his coat were broad.

Yes, he was a pleasure to look at, Dani decided. The sour-faced butler, Wilkins, was as thin as a branch from a tree, with silver, thinning hair and a hooked nose. His eyebrows were bushy and they reminded her of a dove's wings.

Dani began to get uncomfortable in the ever-growing silence and she shifted, conscious of the puddle forming below her.

"Well, what's it to be, Your Grace?" Dani asked bravely breaking the heavy silence at last.

Wilkins' upper lip curled in disdain. "Go to your appointment with a clear conscience, Your Grace. I shall take care of the baggage."

Dani opened her mouth to protest the name-calling but the duke spoke.

"No, Wilkins. I may as well hear what she has to say."

Dani smiled triumphantly. It was a big victory and it didn't really matter that the duke's voice was resigned as though he were being led to his executioner. But to Dani's surprise, Wilkins wasn't through.

"Then have the magistrate speak to her, Your Grace." The curl of his lip went higher if that were possible and Dani was tempted to stick her tongue out at the offending man. She cast her eyes at the double doors in front of her. To be warm and dry with hot food like the old days. Surely God would not allow her to get this far only to be turned away on the front stairs.

"No, I'll conduct the interview myself, Wilkins," the Duke of Stratford said. He had a nice deep, cultured tone when he spoke. Very pleasing to listen to, Dani thought.

Wilkins' glance in her direction was baleful. He snorted and turned back to his employer. "Very well, Your Grace but might I suggest we send her round to the kitchens?"

Dani was beginning to dislike the old interfering butler. "Now just a minute, Your Grace…"

The duke waved a gloved hand, not even looking in her direction. The rain pounded harder, flattening her bonnet to her head. Dani resisted a shudder that threatened to run up her spine. Normally in cold rain she would find some place for shelter. By the time she was done here, she would have to walk back to the East End. She didn't have enough coins left to take another hackney home.

"Wilkins, take Miss, er," he paused and glanced questioningly at her.

"Dani," she supplied, smiling and blinking her eyes at him as she'd seen her friends do.

The duke raised both eyebrows at her, then said to Wilkins, "Take Miss Dani back to the kitchens…"

Dani blew out a breath of disappointment. She grimaced resentfully at the now very smug butler. The old butler beamed like he'd won a hundred sovereigns.

But the duke surprised them both with the next words he said.

"And give her a bath. When she is clean have her brought to the parlor. I'll speak with her there."

"A bath?" Dani and Wilkins yelped the question at the same time. She really wasn't sure who was more appalled. Dani shook her head. "What trickery is this?"

"Your Grace, I really don't…" Wilkins began sputtering. His face was so red, Dani was sure he was going to have a fit.

"You all right, Wilkins?" Dani asked, coming closer to him. He might need pounding on his back. Grace once did that to a man who was choking. She put a hand on the old man's back.

Wilkins jumped as though she scalded him. "Don't you dare accost me, you, you, common doxy!"

"'Ey," Dani cried out, insulted. "I ain't no doxy."

"Trying to pick my pockets, were you?" Wilkins demanded scornfully. His bushy eyebrows seemed to grow thicker and fuller. Dani stared fascinated. "You see the kind she is, Your Grace?"

"I ain't trying to steal nothing," Dani said, directing her statement to the duke, who was scowling at them both. "I thought 'e were 'aving a fit."

The duke growled low in his throat and his jaw, which Dani noted, was finely chiseled, tightened. "Enough of this. Miss, er…"

"Dani," she reminded him with no little exasperation. It wasn't a common name. Was he not bright enough to remember?"

"Miss Dani," he said, nodding. "You mentioned you wanted a proper tea in my parlor, did you not?"

She agreed at once.

"If you agree to the bath you will have that tea in the parlor. If not, you might as well be on your way right now."

Put like that, Dani didn't see she had much choice. It would be her only opportunity to ever feel like she was a lady of the *ton*. If she had to suffer through a bath, then so be it.

"Well, 'ow can I refuse?"

At least the warm water felt good, Dani decided a short time later when she'd been hauled unceremoniously to the back entrance. She sank down into the large porcelain tub. Trying to freeze her solid making her walk round in the downpour.

Dani couldn't remember the last time she had a real bath. There weren't a lot of opportunities to bathe by the docks. Probably when she was still a child back at her mother's seamstress shop.

The tub had been set in the kitchen by the hearth, where a fiery blaze burned. Smelled like soup was cooking over the fire too. She licked her lips and sighed. Her stomach growling painfully, she wished she'd ask for a meal instead of just tea. She'd love a proper soup even more.

Dani watched warily while the duke's kitchen staff scrubbed her down with a pale pink soap smelling of roses. Leave it to the gentry to have something as expensive as roses. Ol' George, the flower man, would give his wife's right arm to get hold of roses. The scent always made Dani a little sad, though, for her mother had been named Rose.

The duke's kitchen staff was apparently made up of two maids, one blonde and one brunette both of them homely with faces like horses. A plump woman who stood by with her hands on her hips supervised them. Mrs. Martin, she called herself. The maids chattered the entire time about young men they'd taken a shine to.

When at last they pronounced they'd scrubbed every speck of dirt from her skin—it was nearly raw—and every bit of grime from her hair, the bathing ordeal was finished.

Dani was then informed that her clothes were being cleaned and she was given another dress to wear. The blonde maid held up a beautiful light green muslin gown embroidered all over with tiny yellow flowers. Dani wondered if her shawl would match it.

"Well," said the dour faced Mrs. Martin, "you clean up nicely." The woman pointed her toward a mirror that a maid had fetched on Mrs. Martin's orders shortly after the bath was over.

Dani was shocked at the reflection of herself. She didn't even recognize the person gazing back. She studied herself more closely in the mirror. Was that long light red hair really hers? She ran her fingers through it. Soft and silky. Next she touched the glass, where her eyes stared out. She'd seen her reflection as an adult before in window fronts and the like but she'd never lingered. She knew her eyes were blue but she was surprised how different they looked in a thoroughly clean face. Dani studied her body then. The dress showed off her breasts more than she was used to and she blushed, quickly covering them.

"'Who owns this dress?" she asked.

"It belonged to Lady Jessica." The housekeeper sniffed. She clearly thought the dress above someone like Dani but she did not comment openly on it.

"Is that the duke's wife?" Dani wondered.

"No, that's one of his sisters. She hasn't worn the dress since she got married year before last," Mrs. Martin told her. "Now, you are to go into the parlor and wait for him. Don't even think of touching anything."

Dani could barely contain her excitement. "Do you think I could 'ave some cakes with the tea?" Dani asked. She knew she probably shouldn't ask but she hadn't ever had a proper tea. Not that she could remember at any rate.

"Very well." Mrs. Martin's lips thinned. "But don't get used to it. We don't serve common trollops here."

"We don't serve trollops 'ere," Dani muttered, walking toward where a footman had directed her. I'm not a trollop. She sniffed.

Dani should have asked them to bring the mirror into the parlor. There wouldn't be much chance to look at herself all dressed like a lady. She wondered if there was some way she could get to stay here a few days. She was in no hurry to get back to the East End. Should she say she knew more about the murder than just finding the body?

She opened the door carefully and peered in. The parlor was empty. From where she stood, Dani could see the room was painted a pale green. A forest green settee sat in the middle surrounded by two matching high backed chairs. There was a large window facing onto the street. Dani crept in and closed the door behind her.

She stepped up to the settee and stroked the soft cloth of the cushions. Such luxury was unimaginable. Even with what she could remember of her mother's shop, she did not recall such fine furniture. She would remember every detail so she could relay it to Grace and Mary. Dani frowned. Mary had been missing the last few days.

The sound of the rain pelting on the glass drew her to the windows next and she peeked out of the thin, filmy curtains. They were a shade of green darker than the walls and lighter than the settee and chairs.

The door opened and a tea tray was brought in. Dani nearly clapped with delight. The servant who brought the tray snorted then left. Dani hurried to the tray and with a shaky hand poured herself a cup of the steaming liquid. She cried out aloud at the sight of the tiny little teacakes. More than she could have ever dreamed of. Not being able to count that high, Dani wished she remembered more of the lessons her mother had taught her, so she would know how many there were.

Dani glanced at the door, waiting but when nothing happened, she quickly stuffed the cakes into her mouth, one after the other. She feared they would take them away before she'd had the chance to eat them all.

The door opened again and in walked the duke. Dani swallowed the last of the cakes. She wiped at her mouth, hoping he wouldn't notice the evidence.

The duke, who had removed his gloves and greatcoat to reveal a dark blue coat and white lawn shirt and cravat, stood staring at her in the doorway for so long she began to feel self-conscious. She touched her hair, wondering if she had a bit of the cakes in it but she felt nothing. Everything seemed to be in place. He continued to stare at her intently.

"Your, er, Grace?"

He straightened, seemed to collect himself and came forward. His gaze went to the tea tray, then he turned to her, puzzled.

"I thought I'd told them to include teacakes."

She smiled vaguely.

He shrugged and sat down on a chair near the settee she sat on.

"Would you like some tea?" she asked him, trying to think of how a proper lady would behave.

His lips quirked up at the corner and Dani resisted the urge to put her hand over her heart to stop the fluttering. Lord, he really was handsome. She hadn't ever seen any man down by the docks who looked like him. Aye, he was a rare one.

"Yes, I would like some tea."

With a shaky hand she lifted up the teapot and poured the amber liquid into the cup. It splashed over the sides.

"Oh!"

"Allow me," he said, taking the pot out of her hand and setting it down. "Mrs. Martin," he called.

"Your Grace?" The servant came in at once as though waiting outside the door.

"There's been a small accident and some tea has spilled," the duke told her. "Can you get something to clean it up?"

"At once, Your Grace." Mrs. Martin glared in Dani's direction. She disappeared through the door again.

"I'm sorry," Dani said, her cheeks growing warm.

"No harm done," he assured her. Mrs. Martin came back into the room with a small cloth. She picked up the duke's teacup and wiped around the saucer. Though she did not look in Dani's direction, Dani felt the hostility emanating from the woman.

"Will there be anything else, Your Grace?" Mrs. Martin placed the cup and saucer on the tray.

"I'd asked for some cakes to be served with the tea," the duke said.

Mrs. Martin looked at the tray and then at Dani, her eyes accusing.

"I don't know what happened," Mrs. Martin said. "I'll have some brought in at once."

"Now, then." His Grace turned to Dani. "Why don't you tell me what you saw?"

"When I found the body or before?" Dani asked, holding her breath. She held her cup in both hands nervously.

The duke raised his eyebrows questioningly. "Before?"

Dani lowered her voice. "I think I might 'ave seen it 'appen."

Simon stared at the young woman for several moments in silence, assessing her. He had to admit she was much lovelier than he had even believed when she'd confronted him on his front stairs.

Her hair was a light red and fell in ringlets down her back. Her lashes, a shade to match her hair, were long and swept over her extraordinary periwinkle eyes in a graceful sweep. She had a heart-shaped face with high-sculpted cheekbones. In London society, she would be the envy of other women and pursued by rakes and marriage-minded men alike.

Simon nearly shook his head at how surprising she was. Gathering his senses he concentrated on the words she'd just said. It helped him to remember she was probably just a doxy in spite of her calculated protests otherwise.

"You saw it happen?" he asked carefully. He took a long sip of the steaming tea. He frowned into the cup. He liked cream and sugar in his cup. He set the cup down and reached for the bowl of sugar.

"Well, I think I might 'ave." Dani twisted her hands in her lap. "I-I ain't really sure."

"Maybe you'd better tell me what you saw," Simon said, making his tea as he liked and trying to ignore the pounding in his head. He was considering putting off his visit to the magistrate for another day. He felt a bit guilty for he knew Aunt Pen was desperate for any news concerning Douglas. But maybe Dani would be able to supply him with something to report.

"Now, where was I?" he asked, attempting a smile.

"You was about to 'ear what it were I saw," she supplied for him.

Simon winced at her abrasive accent. His headache was surely getting worse. He pinched the bridge of his nose.

"'Ere now, got yourself a pain 'ave you?" Dani asked, rising from the settee. She clucked her tongue and approached him. "I know just what to do for that."

"You do?" When she leaned over him he got a face full of her breasts. He closed his eyes.

"Oh, sure," Dani told him, placing the fingers of both hands on either side of his head. She started massaging his temples. "Grace taught me this trick a long time ago."

"Grace?" he murmured. Simon wasn't sure his head was feeling any better but another part of his body was reacting to her nearness. Had he no discipline at all?

"Aye, she and Mary are the nearest I have to a mother, you know," Dani said, leaning further in. Her breasts grazed his chin.

"Ah, Dani?"

"Mm?"

"Why don't you return to your seat?" Simon suggested with no little effort. He would rather… No.

"But your 'ead."

He pulled her hands from his temples gently and turned her toward the settee. His hand brushed her bottom.

"It feels much better," he assured her. She looked doubtful. Time to get down to business, he decided. He'd spent enough time being attracted to the urchin.

"Now, then. What is your name?" Simon asked.

Dani sighed heavily. "I told you, Dani."

"I know but Dani what?"

"Just Dani. No other names," she told him.

"How old are you?"

"Oh, um, eighteen…no nineteen."

The door of the parlor opened again and a maid hurried in with a tray full of cakes. She smiled shyly at Simon, curtsied, then ran out of the room.

"What about your parents?" he asked.

"I ain't got any o' them neither."

"You must have at one time."

"My mother were a seamstress. Mary and Grace, too. They all worked together in her shop. Trained by a French modiste, they were." Dani nodded. "She died when I was young. I don't know my father cause he weren't around but I remember she used to say 'e were a man of importance. A man from the gentry, I suppose."

"This Mary and Grace that you mention, do they take care of you?" he asked.

"I take care o' meself," she told him indignantly.

"No doubt you do a fine job of it too," Simon said.

"I ain't doing so bad." Dani sniffed and clenched her hands together as though she were about to say a prayer.

"Dani, I know you found Douglas' body in an alley."

Dani nodded. Now whatever she said next would be important. If she was going to convince the duke she had real information that he would pay her for she had to think carefully. She opened her mouth to reply when a loud clap of thunder made her jump. She and the duke both glanced at the rain streaked window.

He shook his head and got up to look out. "This is some storm. I think I won't go to my appointment after all."

Dani assessed him shrewdly. "Going to see a woman?"

"No, the magistrate actually. About Douglas." He turned from the window to look at her. Another thunderclap. The duke made a face. "You can't go home, wherever that is, in rain like this."

Dani bit her bottom lip and the duke's gaze lowered to stare at her mouth.

"Have you got fare back home?" he asked gently.

"No."

"I didn't think so." He leaned against the wall directly beside the windows. "You'd freeze in this weather."

"I am just getting warmed up," she said haltingly. She followed his gaze to the windows. If she could get a bit of gold out of him she would hire a cab to take her back as she had when she'd come here.

He smiled. "There, then you see, you'll stay. In fact," he said slowly. "Why don't you plan on sleeping here tonight?"

"Sleeping 'ere?" A thought occurred to Dani. The duke had been staring at her rather intently and there was that touch on her bottom. "I ain't no doxy."

"I don't consort with street women, Dani."

"Oh." She felt foolish now and stared at her hands, willing the redness in her face to disappear.

The duke crossed the floor to the doors of the parlor, his black polished boots clicking on the floor. He opened the door and called for the butler.

In a moment, the old stodgy Wilkins walked slowly in. The old man's bushy eyebrows rose disdainfully at Dani before he gave his attention to his employer.

"Shall I send her away now, Your Grace?"

"Wilkins, Dani is going to stay here for the night."

"Your Grace?" Wilkins' face turned blotchy red.

"I think Lady Jessica's old room will do nicely," Dani heard the duke say. She was shocked down to her toes. She had been sure he would have put her somewhere in the servants' quarters.

"Lady Jessica's room? But, Your Grace…"

The duke raised an eyebrow and the old butler immediately backed down. "And inform Aunt Pen we have a guest."

"Yes, Your Grace. I'll have the room prepared immediately." Wilkins exited the parlor without glancing in Dani's direction. Disappointed, Dani pulled her tongue back into her mouth. She wanted to show the old butler her triumph.

"All right," the duke said, smiling. "You found Douglas' body three weeks ago and…"

He was interrupted by the loud opening and closing of the front door. The duke went out into the hall. Curious, Dani followed him.

Dani saw a young man, perhaps a few years younger than the duke, five and twenty she would guess, standing in the foyer. His hair, a slightly lighter shade of mahogany then the duke's, was wet and sticking to his skull. Dani supposed he was a brother. With him was a young girl with golden hair, just a couple of years younger than Dani's own nineteen years and the young girl's maid.

The young man and girl were both laughing and smiling.

"We got caught in the rain!" exclaimed the girl to Wilkins, who had come into the hall. "We were just coming out of the boot makers, weren't we, Jack?"

"Hmm." The young man, Jack, had noticed Dani standing behind the duke and was staring intently at her. "Who is this, Simon?"

"Dani is staying the night," the duke said, though it didn't answer Jack's question. "Jessica's room is being readied."

"Oh?" The young blonde girl hurried forward and pulled Dani the rest of the way out of the room. The girl still wore her soaking wet cloak, droplets of the fresh rain dripping all over the floor.

Jack removed his gray overcoat and handed it absently to Wilkins. His head tilted to the side, he blatantly stared at Dani. "I don't recall seeing you before."

"Oh, isn't this exciting," the girl cried. "Are you someone Simon's been seeing? I've heard that he might offer for Miss Haversham. You're not her, are you? You are so beautiful! Am I glad I'm not having my season now, no one would even look at me."

Dani's head swam with the girl's chattering. She stepped back from the girl's enthusiasm.

"Lady Lucy, keep away from that doxy," Wilkins said, coming forward and placing his tall frame between Dani and the girl she now knew was named Lucy.

"What?" Lucy said, falling back in surprise, running into Jack. "Wilkins, how can you be so rude?"

"I'm not a doxy," Dani spoke up, raising her chin. "I'm just a girl down on my luck."

"She's a street urchin," Wilkins said derisively.

Jack smiled for the first time. A wolfish smile that reminded Dani of the way some of the customers of Mary and Grace looked. "She don't look like a street urchin to me."

Wilkins sniffed. "I'm sure His Grace doesn't approve of Lady Lucy spending time with someone like her."

Though Dani expected nothing less, the butler's harsh words hurt. She wished she'd stayed in the parlor. The duke visibly stiffened but he did not refute the old butler's words.

"Lucy, you probably ought to go upstairs and change out of those wet clothes," the duke said. "Aunt Pen is waiting for you. Dani and I have a lot to talk about."

Lucy pouted. "Well, all right." She removed her sodden cloak and handed it to Wilkins before she turned and headed for the stairs.

"Now," Jack said, rubbing his hands together. "I'll just spend some time talking to, er, Dani myself."

Dani just wanted to return to her tea and pretense that she was someone special.

"Get out," the duke growled. "I'm in no mood for your games."

"But…"

"Now," he said.

Jack grimaced but headed up the stairs.

The duke turned back to Dani and shook his head at her. "I'm sorry, Dani. Shall we finish our tea?"

Her stomach churning with shame and humiliation, Dani nodded. After the scene in the hall, the fantasy had lost much of its allure. It was impossible to pretend she was anything other than what she was—an urchin from the streets, like Wilkins had said.

Chapter Two

Dani took her seat back on the settee and picked up her teacup and a cake just to have something to do in the uncomfortable silence that descended after she and the duke reentered the parlor. She knew she was being overly sensitive. But somewhere inside her there was still a little girl dreaming of being rescued by a prince.

"Dani, why don't you tell me about finding Douglas?" The duke's tone was much stiffer and colder than it had been before his brother and sister arrived home. Another sign that her hopes of this interview coming out in her favor were to be dashed.

She stared at him over the rim of her teacup. Did he have to be so handsome? It was going to be hard to lie to him but she might be able to salvage something from this stupid trip to the proper part of London. She sniffed.

"Well, I didn't realize at first when I finded him just what it was that were so familiar about him," Dani said slowly, pausing to take a long sip. She closed her eyes briefly the better to savor the taste. Tea was a luxury she didn't get by the docks. "And?"

When he broke into her thoughts she realized she'd spent too much time gathering her thoughts. He'd raised one of his eyebrows questioningly, the left one. There was a little curl of mahogany hair rebelling against his otherwise perfectly coifed hair. She resisted the smile that tugged at her mouth.

"I was down by The Black Swan that morning…" She set down her tea. "That's the name of the tavern where I come across 'im."

"Yes, I know."

"Oh. I s'pose everyone knows the Swan," Dani said with a nod. "Anyway, they have some of the best rubbish there. First-rate." She smiled at him.

"Forget the refuse, Dani," the duke told her.

Dani blushed a little. Why had she told him that? A man like him had never had to dig through trash for a meal. "That's why I was there. I hadn't had anything really good to eat in a few days and…"

"Dani," the duke interrupted. She glanced at him in surprise. But there was no censure in his gold-green eyes, only sympathy. Or was it pity?

"What?" She asked cautiously.

"I hadn't really thought of it before." He rose from his chair and went to pull a cord by the mantel. "Teacakes aren't enough sustenance."

Mrs. Martin came in a moment later. "Your Grace?"

"Bring in some sandwiches, Mrs. Martin and some of Cook's soup from last night," the duke ordered. He smiled at Dani. "Soup will be just the thing in weather like this."

Mrs. Martin bobbed a curtsy and went to do as she was told.

Dani's stomach grumbled just at the suggestion. Hot soup. When was the last time she had a hot meal? Dani couldn't remember. Her eyes pricked with tears at the prospect. She swallowed, clenching her hands to compose herself.

The duke reseated himself and gave her a sheepish smile. "I'm really very sorry, Dani. That was completely thoughtless of me."

Dani didn't know what to say so she just shrugged.

"You were telling me about finding Douglas," the duke reminded gently.

She nodded. It was easier to look out at the rain still gushing from the sky then to lie to his face. The first part of her story would be true enough.

"I was going through the trash," she said again. "I smelled something that reminded me o' death. Do you know?" She glanced at him then to see his reaction.

His jaw tightened. "Yes."

The detached tone the duke used told Dani he had experienced something to do with death that he would rather forget. She cleared her throat and moved on.

"I thought it was rats," she whispered, then blushed. Dani wasn't sure why telling the handsome duke about the rats embarrassed her but it did. "Sometimes they die and it's an awful smell."

She was dismayed to see the pity back in his eyes. None of this was going as she imagined it. She blew out a breath and tried to calm herself. Her pulse was racing.

"The first thing I noticed were 'is boot," Dani said softly. Simon wondered why she looked toward the windows as she spoke. What a horrible life she must have. For a moment he thought about Lucy. His sister was younger than Dani by a few years but not so far off that he couldn't imagine her living the sort of life Dani did.

"I thought to myself, Dani you could make tidy sum with boots like that," Dani paused and looked at him.

Her periwinkle eyes were achingly beautiful and familiar somehow. Where had he seen eyes that color?

"Must 'ave been thrown away," Dani continued softly. "Though I did wonder why someone would do that. Maybe they were lost in one o' them card games, that sort o' thing."

"Reasonable," Simon agreed. The movement of her lips captivated him. Though the sound coming from them was abrasive, her mouth was pert and pretty. He took a large swallow of tea, heedless of the burn he'd just given his tongue.

"Yes," Dani said. "I thought maybe what 'ad 'appened was their owner lost them at the Swan and whoever won them was too stupid to know their worth." She gave an inelegant snort. "But I weren't. When I got closer I saw 'im."

There was a tap on the door just before Mrs. Martin and a maid hurried in with a cart of sandwiches and two bowls of soup.

Mrs. Martin placed the cart next to the settee. "Shall I serve, Your Grace?"

"No, Mrs. Martin, I'll take care of the duties. Thank you," he added dismissively. The housekeeper's mouth thinned leaving Simon in no doubt regarding her feelings toward their guest. Impertinent staff, the lot of them.

When Mrs. Martin and the maid had gone, he picked up a white china plate trimmed in green. There were three triangular-shaped chicken sandwiches on it. He handed it over to Dani.

She took the plate and stared at it. "For me?"

"Yes and here." Simon stood up and pushed the cart close to her. He removed the silver dome that covered the steaming bowl of cream of carrot soup. "Have some of this. Cook does wonderful soups."

Her eyes were wide with wonder and he could tell he was overwhelming her a bit but she deserved some nice times to remember, he decided. He watched her pick up the soupspoon with a shaky hand and dip it into the soup.

"It's a funny color," she said, flicking a questioning glance at him.

"It's made with carrots," he explained, smiling.

She nodded and slurped a spoonful loudly into her mouth. "Ouch!" She exclaimed at the heat.

He knelt beside her and gently pulled the spoon out of her hand and set it down. "It's hot, Dani. Let it rest for a moment. Let me see your tongue."

She stuck out her tongue, which was now a blotchy red. Simon winced. It was burned all right but more than that he grimaced because seeing her tongue had reminded him of things he could be doing with it. He gritted his teeth and was about to stand when Wilkins came into the room unannounced.

"Your Grace…" Wilkins stopped. Stared at Simon kneeling before Dani, her tongue sticking out. Simon could well imagine what an oddity it appeared.

He stood up and cleared his throat. "Yes, Wilkins?"

"I don't mean to interrupt your, er." Here Wilkins paused and frowned. "Interrogation. But there seems to be some leakage in your study from the storm. If I could have just a moment of your time?"

Simon looked at Dani and realized she would need a moment to eat her food anyway. He didn't want to treat her as though she were some prisoner being beaten into a confession.

"Dani, I'll be right back," he promised.

"Right," she mumbled, her mouth full of a large bite of sandwich.

Dani had stuffed the last bite of sandwich in her mouth and slurped down the last of the soup when the door burst open. She glanced up, expecting to see the duke but instead it was his younger brother. What was his name? Jack.

He came into the room with a broad smile and shut the door after him. "I wonder where Simon's gone. What was your name, love?"

"Dani."

"What a lovely name. A bit unusual for a young woman. But you're unusual, aren't you?" Jack glanced down at the cart. "Had yourself a meal, have you?"

"Yes."

He walked closer to her to stand by the settee. He wasn't half as handsome as the duke, Dani decided. And a lot more cynical. He moved like a wild beast.

"Are you the one who found that bastard's body?"

Dani blinked. "Bastard?"

"Couldn't stand him. Good riddance, I say." He grinned, unrepentant. "So you're from the East End, eh? Bet you've seen it all."

"Well…"

"So, then, my sister's old room being haunted, won't bother you a'tall, will it?" He drawled.

"'Aunted?" Dani's jaw dropped.

"Sure. Before my father bought this townhouse a lady died in that room."

"Died?" she exclaimed. She touched her chest. Her heart was pounding."

"Something about her husband murdering her." He smiled, shrugged. "Nonsense, no doubt."

The duke stepped back into the room. His hard gaze landed on his brother immediately.

"What are you doing here, Jack?" His tone hard and cold like steel.

"You've found her." Jack grinned.

"Found who?" The duke growled.

"The love of my life."

"Get out of here now. I'm having an important discussion."

Jack's snort was derisive. "If it has to do with Norton it's not important. But I am going. I merely came in for a book I left." To prove his point he went to the other chair in the room and picked up a book that was placed on it. "I hope to see you again, Dani."

He waved and left the room.

The duke turned back to Dani, his expression grim. "If Jack ever comes within a foot of you while you're here, I want you to start screaming."

"Is he dangerous?" Dani wondered.

"Very." He took his seat once more. "The storm isn't letting up, Dani. You're going to stay here the night for sure."

Recalling his brother's words, Dani bit her lip. She didn't want to pass up her chance to sleep in a real bed in a duke's home but still.

"Is it really 'aunted?"

"Haunted?"

"Your brother, he told me a lady were murdered by 'er 'usband in that room," Dani said, folding her arms in her lap to keep from trembling at the thought.

The duke growled. "No one has ever been murdered in this house, Dani."

"Oh." Relief washed through her.

"Although I think I can make an exception where Jack is concerned." He sighed. He eyed the empty plates and bowls of soup. "Would you like more?"

Dani would but thought he might think her a glutton if she did. She smiled and shook her head.

The duke sat next to her on the settee this time. So close in fact that his leg touched hers. Her breath caught.

"Tell me the rest," he urged.

How could she tell him anything with his hard thigh against hers? She turned a little to break the contact of their legs. Now his face was mere inches away and she was staring into his gold-green eyes.

Sitting this close to Dani had been a mistake. Simon knew that now. It would be too hard to explain moving away. Her periwinkle eyes widened, their depths momentarily causing him to lose the gift of speech. The finest courtesans had not aroused him as easily as this small street urchin.

The heavy silence that hung between them was only broken by the sound of the rain splattering against the windows. Somewhere outside the parlor a tray rattled by but these were distant noises. They didn't offer much distraction.

Simon cleared his throat to end the tense moment. "Dani, do you want more sandwiches or…anything else?"

Dani blinked, her lashes sweeping over her eyes like a shutter over a window. She shook her head, glanced at her clenched hands.

"No, Your Grace. I'm quite full."

"Now, then, you were going to tell me about finding Douglas."

"Douglas? That were 'is name?" Dani's eyes met his once more, a hint of uncertainty there.

"Douglas Norton, yes."

"Were 'e a friend o' yours?"

Simon resisted a snort. "No, my cousin, actually. We weren't close and hardly ever saw each other. I didn't run in the same circles as Douglas."

Dani blew out a breath and brightened instantly. He did wonder at that. She had returned her gaze to her fisted hands. He stared at her ears. He'd never noticed a woman's ears before but hers were small and dainty. He wondered if they would be soft between his teeth.

"Your Grace?"

Good lord, what was he doing? He stood abruptly and walked casually over to the mantel. Though her beauty would still be a distraction, from this position her nearness would not.

"Tell me, Dani," he commanded.

"I went to The Swan. That's what we locals call it. It's easier, y'know." Her voice trembled. "It were a Tuesday. The man what owns it, Old Sam, we call 'im that, but there ain't no Young Sam round that I know of."

Simon smiled.

"Old Sam dumps 'is best rubbish on Monday nights, so I like to get there bright and early the next morning. You can find all sorts o' great stuff there on Tuesdays." Dani paused and bit her lip. She took a deep breath, her breasts rising and falling in the gown.

"Go on, Dani," Simon urged. The tray rattled back in the same direction outside the parlor. A bolt of lightning lit the room and a thunderclap answered it.

"You can find bits o' eggs and sausages that ain't gettin' eaten at The Swan." She smiled shyly. "Once Grace found a bottle with a wee bit o' whiskey left in it." Dani wrinkled her nose. "I didn't like it, so Grace drank it all.

"There's all kinds o' rats what 'ang around there too. They figured out it's the best rubbish too, I suppose. I hate them. I thought it was one o' them I were smelling when I went up to the garbage. One o' them dies on occasion. But then I saw the boot." Dani shuddered.

Simon nodded sympathetically. He could well imagine the fright this little urchin must have received He noticed her cup was empty. "Do you need some more tea, Dani?"

She followed his gaze to the teapot. "No. I just want to get it out quick."

"All right."

Dani's beautiful eyes had taken on a haunted look that Simon did not care for. Finding Douglas had been difficult for her. Hell, life was difficult for her. What justice was there in the world when such a genuine beauty could spend her life wallowing in the garbage by the docks? Someone should help her.

"I think I told you I was 'appy at first to find the boot. I didn't even realize at first a leg were attached." Dani blanched. "'E were twisted round. Not lying natural-like. One leg behind 'im. And blood everywhere." She paused again and stared down at her hands.

From where he stood he could see her bottom lip trembling. He felt a cad to make her recollect that day. But she'd come to him, Simon reminded himself.

"I ain't never seen a person dead like that before. I seen someone who died but not with blood," Dani said, her voice dropping to barely above a whisper. The outside storm nearly made it impossible to hear her. "I screamed and Old Sam came running. He's the one what notified the authorities."

"Must have been horrible for you," Simon murmured.

"Oh, it were," she agreed immediately.

"Dani," Simon said slowly, staring straight at her. "Do you really know anything about the murder?" He was a pretty good judge of character and he'd been able to pick out a liar easily. She definitely found Douglas' body. Of that he had no doubt. He couldn't say the same for the rest of her claims.

"Well," Dani said softly. Her eyes shone when she looked up at him. "I...er."

"Dani?"

"Old Sam reminded me that we'd both see the man Monday night round The Swan," Dani explained. She wasn't looking at him anymore but rather at the wall behind him. "I'd thought 'e were kind o' handsome. We don't get 'is type round the docks very often. That's why I noticed 'im."

Simon moved away from the mantel, drawn strangely by her voice. Her accent still hurt his head but there was something about the tone that was melodious. It wouldn't take much to make her into a lovely young woman. The way she held herself, she would polish easily. He stood near but he didn't like looking down at her. Before he realized his own intent he sat down next to her on the settee once more. Not as close as before but close enough that he was able to inhale the rose scented soap used to wash her luxurious red hair.

"'E went into The Swan late. Don't know what time, but I was standing outside it with Mary and Grace." Dani smiled. "You remember I mentioned them before."

"Right."

"I…" Dani faltered. What could she say next? It was hard to concentrate on anything with him staring so intently at her. Could he hear her heartbeat? It sounded louder to her ears than the thunder outside. She was only making up some of it. Old Sam had told her the murdered man was at The Swan that night before. It was just a tiny lie that she'd seen him.

"Go on, Dani," the duke urged.

"Mary, she's my friend that went missing the same night."

"Went missing?" He frowned.

"Oh. Didn't I tell you about 'er?" Dani was relieved to be able to stall her fib that much longer. She pushed aside the stab of guilt momentarily to tell him about Mary. "She'd told me about a man who'd been round the docks recently what looked like the gentry. Well dressed she said 'e were. And young. I'm thinking 'e must 'ave been your cousin what got himself murdered."

"Maybe. Tell me about Mary's disappearance, Dani."

"Well, on the day I found 'im, I went looking for both Grace and Mary. Wanted to tell them everything, y'know. They're my best friends as well as being like mothers." Dani licked her lips. She wished he weren't so handsome himself. "You got friends, Your Grace?"

"A few."

"I finded Grace right quick enough but the two of us, well, we couldn't find Mary. Not the whole day or the next. Or since neither. I looked before I came 'ere. It ain't like Mary. She likes to show us her winnings." Dani blushed. She almost forgot who she'd been talking to. "Mary's a doxy."

"I gathered as much," Simon said, his lips quirking up just a little at the corners. Dani blinked and looked away.

"She…didn't use to be one. I told she was a seamstress and before that a maid for a real lady," Dani whispered. "I been thinking. It's possible that Mary and your friend's murder is related somehow, ain't it?"

"I don't think there is any connection," the duke said doubtfully.

"Well, there might be," Dani said quickly. "Maybe she saw something and 'ad to go into hiding." Dani took a deep breath. "And if she 'ad to go into hiding, maybe I should too."

He raised an eyebrow at her. He didn't look at all like he believed her. There was a tap at the door that drew their attention. The old butler poked his head in.

"Your Grace, sorry to interrupt but you were due to attend Lady Grobstone's fête tonight. It was the first event you were to attend after your cousin's passing."

The duke frowned and flicked a glance to the darkening day outside. Dani followed his gaze and realized the daylight was fading away. How long had she already been at the duke's?

"I'll skip the fête, Wilkins," the duke said. "There's going to be endless boring events to attend."

Wilkins nodded. "Very good, Your Grace. I'll tell cook you'll be dining in tonight."

"Thank you, Wilkins. Be sure a place is set for Dani as well."

The right side of Wilkins' lips curled disdainfully. It was gone nearly immediately. He bowed and quit the room.

"Dani, are you trying to tell me you are afraid that whatever happened to Mary might happen to you?" the duke asked, giving Dani his full intense attention once more.

"Yes," she said nodding emphatically. "I were getting to that, Your Grace. You see." She dropped her voice for effect. "When the man went into The Swan, I saw three men go in after 'im."

"Three men? What three men, Dani?"

Dani thought about it. "They were all dressed like 'im. Nice like. I didn't really think much of it at the time. But when Old Sam reminded me, well…" She let her sentence hang.

"What makes you think they had anything to do with Douglas' murder?"

"They looked evil."

The duke shook his head and then to her surprise, rolled his eyes. "Dani, you're a terrible liar."

"But, Your Grace!"

"You didn't see anything concerning Douglas or the murderers the night before you found his body, did you?"

"I did," Dani insisted. Grace once said if you were ever caught in a lie by someone in authority crying would get you out. She bit her lip hard. Tears sprang to her eyes almost immediately. "You don't believe me," she wailed in an accusing voice.

"Dani."

"I saw them, I did," she said, sniffing for effect. "They were three tall men. They saw me too. Looked right at me."

"Dani, all right," the duke said. He was close to her again, his muscled thigh against hers. He reached for her hands. "Don't cry."

"But you think I'm lying," she said, sobbing. She looked at him from beneath her tear saturated eyelashes to see the effect her crying had. He didn't look any more convinced but the pity was back in his eyes.

"Well, let's just say I'm not convinced the men you saw were responsible for Douglas' murder."

"But they might be."

The duke nodded. "Yes."

Dani took a shaky breath. Crying was hard work. She squeezed out a single tear that streamed down her right cheek. Her breath caught when the duke stopped it with his finger.

"I could identify them," Dani said hoarsely. "They might be looking for me right now."

The duke looked past her at the window. It was fully dark now. And the rain had not ceased. He turned to face her again. His gold-green eyes were intense but unreadable. His lips were so close she thought he might kiss her. Hoped he might. She opened her mouth to receive his kiss.

Chapter Three

෨

She bit her lip hard, desperately trying not to cry out her disappointment when he moved his head away. Had she really forgotten for a moment this was not one of her dreams?

"Very well, Dani. Describe these men to me. I want every last detail."

Details? Dani wiped her wet cheek, stalling. She had seen an occasional well-dressed man in the area. Surely she could remember a description of them. She lowered her lashes and sniffed again.

"One o' them 'ad a big scar running across 'is left cheek."

"What was the shape of the scar?"

Dani peered at him from beneath her lashes. Shape of the scar? He appeared to be completely serious too. Truth told, the duke didn't smile very much. And the few smiles she had seen, he'd never once shown his teeth. She was oddly curious about them. Would his teeth be straight like Mary's or crooked like Old Sam's?

"Er, long and thin it were, from a knife, maybe," Dani answered. "That one wore one o' them outer coats."

"A greatcoat?" The duke suggested.

"Yes, that's it," Dani agreed. "Brown it was. Not dark brown but light." She added that last bit in because she could already see the question forming on his lips.

Dani wished the old butler would interrupt them again. It would give her a chance to think but no one came to her rescue. Only the occasional distant thunderclap broke the silence in the parlor.

"I think 'is pants were brown too but I ain't really sure. I didn't look too closely," Dani said. She raised her eyes to meet his finally. "And brown 'air and eyes too."

The duke nodded grimly. "How old would you say this scarred man was?"

"Older than you," Dani said. She nibbled on her lip, trying to guess how old the duke was. Finally she decided she would ask. "How old are you?"

"Twenty-eight." He seemed amused by her question.

"Yes, older than that. Ten years maybe."

The duke nodded and shifted ever-so slightly on the settee. Hardly noticeable. Unless you were watching his every move as Dani was. The movement scooted him a few inches further away.

Dani cleared her throat. "Shall I tell you about the other men?"

"Yes."

"One o' them 'ad blond hair and 'e were real tall. And…" Dani thought a moment, trying to remember images of men she'd seen pass through the dock area. "His nose looked like it might 'ave been broke once."

The duke raised an eyebrow at that and for the first time since she'd begun her story he looked uncertain. No longer quite as skeptical.

Warming to her story, Dani continued, "And the last one, were young and 'e ad dark 'air, nearly black it were so dark and blue eyes." She realized she had given him the description Mary had given her and Grace of a man who had come by asking questions a few days before the murder. Well, he might be involved. He had been nosing around, hadn't he? "He wore fancy evening clothes and no—what'd you call it?—no greatcoat."

"Hmm."

"I was standing near the entrance to The Swan, minding my own business when your friend went in. Mary was there too." Dani laid her hand on her breast. "He didn't even look at us but the other three men did. They went in just a bit after 'im. Whispering to each other. They looked straight at me and Mary too." Dani dropped her voice. "And I told you I ain't seen Mary since that night."

"But other than seeing the men go into the tavern after Douglas, you didn't really see anything, did you, Dani?"

"Well, no," she said reluctantly. She didn't feel right about lying about what happened to the poor man. She wasn't even sure how he'd died. She knew there was a lot of blood.

"It's probably good that you didn't witness it, Dani," the duke told her with a slight curving of his lips.

Dani stared down at her clenched hands for a moment. She was glad herself. Growing up on the streets, she had been witness to a lot of nasty happenings. Even been the victim of a few. But murder was something she hoped never to know. Finding the body was nearer than she wanted.

"'How did they kill 'im?" Dani asked softly.

"He was shot."

Dani flinched at his words. They were curt and to the point. Not particularly detailed but enough to give her an image she wished she could block out.

When she heard the sounds of footsteps outside the parlor door, Dani yelped in surprise.

"It's all right, Dani." The duke stood up and grasping her hands pulled her up from the settee. "It's just the servants."

She nodded, trying to force her heart to its normal pace. "I was thinking about the murder."

"Forget about it for a while," he told her. "You've told me everything, haven't you?"

"Yes. But what if those men did kill 'im and they don't want any witnesses?" Dani asked. Telling him her tale had been so difficult it almost seemed as though it were real and she really had seen the men. She could almost believe they really might come after her.

"Don't concern yourself, Dani. Come, it should be time to dine."

In her wildest dreams, Dani had not imagined sitting across from a duke at his dining table. Yet here she was. She was tempted to pinch herself.

It didn't matter that across meant she was seated several feet from him. The duke was at one end of the long oak table and she was at the other. If she wanted to be heard she would probably have to shout. They were alone save for the servants who milled about to serve them.

The old butler, Wilkins, came into the room at that moment and didn't spare her a glance.

"Your Grace, Lord Jack has asked me to inform you that he will not be dining tonight."

"Oh?" The duke raised an eyebrow and frowned. He drummed his fingers lightly on the table. "Where is he off to, Wilkins?"

"To the club." Wilkins sneered. His voice dripped with disdain and his expression reminded Dani of the time she'd eaten a bit of a rotten meat.

The duke grimaced but did not comment. Wherever "the club" was it must be unpleasant.

Wilkins briefly shot her a superior look, then sniffed. "Lady Lucy is suffering from a megrim after her ordeal in the rain and will eat in her room with Lady Norton."

A megrim? Whatever that was. The duke waved Wilkins away. The old servant bowed and departed the room.

Dani waited impatiently for the servants to bring the food over from the side table. The odor that drifted to her nostrils indicated there was fresh baked bread.

One of the footmen started to set a plate of food in front of the duke but he waved it on in her direction. The footman walked the length of the table and placed it in front of her.

Dani blinked away the tears forming in her eyes. On the plate before her was a large helping of poultry of some kind, she was not sure what, covered in thick gravy. Next to it was a thick slice of bread slathered with creamy butter. There was also a dish of cranberries and turnips. It was a feast.

Dani started to reach for a piece of the poultry when she noticed the duke forking a bite of his own food. She licked her bottom lip and spied the fork beside her own plate. She had used one before, though it had been years ago. Her face reddened as she tried to remember and she lowered her eyes when she saw the duke glance in her direction.

"Dani."

She raised her eyes to meet his. He was holding up his fork.

"Hold it like this," he said.

Dani reached for the fork and held it in her fingers the exact way he was holding his. It felt odd but she used it to stab a hunk of the meat. She tore off a slice with her teeth.

The duke smiled. "It's Cornish Game Hen. Do you like it?"

"Yes," she said around the mouthful of bird. She didn't think she'd ever had a meal that tasted so good.

Simon entered the dark wood-paneled room, heading straight for the brandy. He poured himself a large dose. Sipping at it, the first hint of the usual burning sensation rolling down his throat, he stared at the oak desk that had once belonged to his father. He could see once again his father slumped drunk over his books. When the memory turned to his father slumped over, blood coming from the self-inflicted head wound, he shoved it aside.

Forcing his thoughts from his father, he finished off the last of his brandy and glanced at the documents on his desk that had arrived from his solicitor. He really ought to go over them but it just wasn't in him. His mind kept drifting to the street urchin sleeping upstairs.

Seeing everything through her eyes had been quite jarring. He took so many luxuries for granted. He'd heard her squeal of sheer delight a short time ago when she saw the bed she would sleep in for the night. A bed gave her so much pleasure. Truthfully he did not need to take on another member of the household, but the temptation was there and he couldn't stop thinking about it. He had a feeling she would be a fast learner. She was clever and beautiful. She'd already picked up the proper way to eat. Aunt Pen was already helping prepare Lucy for her come out. Perhaps she could help Dani too.

He set the empty glass down on his desk and extinguished the lamp.

He was only a couple of steps away from his own set of rooms when a screaming Dani flew out of his sister Jessica's old room nearby. Her eyes wide with fright, she flung herself straight into his arms.

"He's after me," Dani wailed, her tiny fingers clutching his arm hard.

"What? Who is after you?"

Dani took a huge breath and then began to hiccup. Her eyes were wild.

"Dani," Simon said slowly. "What is wrong?"

Her hand shaking, she pointed to the door. "The m-man."

Simon glanced at the door. Something had definitely frightened her. It occurred to him with a rather startling suddenness that she wore only a thin white nightdress. With her body pressed against his he was finding it hard to concentrate on whatever she was babbling about. He was obviously the worst sort of scoundrel. He gently pushed her away.

"What man?" he asked, removing his coat without thinking and placing it across her shoulders.

She clutched the coat tightly. "The man who died. The one I found."

"Douglas?" Simon asked, shaking his head. She threw herself into his arms again, trembling. "Dani, that's not possible. You've just had a nightmare."

"He's in there," Dani insisted, burying her face in his chest. "I seen 'im. Blood all over."

"It was a dream, sweetheart," he said soothingly. "Come. I'll go to the room with you and show you."

She didn't look like she wanted to go back to the room but he took her hand and led her inside. The room, still lit with a small candelabrum on the bedside table, was empty. The sheets on the bed were rumpled.

"See. There's no one."

"But I saw 'im," Dani said, her breath coming out in short bursts.

"I know," Simon said. "Listen, Dani, if it will make you feel safe, I'll sit in this chair over here." He walked to the chair by the side table. "Just until you've fallen asleep."

"I..." Dani bit her lip hesitantly.

"Everything will be all right. I promise. No one will get you, Dani." Simon sat down in the chair. "Go to sleep."

Dani swallowed and nodded, walking carefully back to the bed. "Oh, wait." She blushed. "Your coat."

He took the coat from her outstretched hand.

She crawled under the blankets and pulled them up to her chin.

"There, see, just fall asleep," Simon said with a reassuring smile. "I'll stay here."

It took a long time but Dani's eyelids finally closed. Not long after that the soft sounds of snoring came from the bed.

Simon yawned. Lord, he was tired himself. He ought to go back to his room. He imagined he'd be asleep before his head hit the pillow.

Dani woke clutching a fluffy feather pillow. Sunlight streamed through the window. It was late, that much she could tell by the cast of the rays. The storm of yesterday was over and she would be expected to return home. Unless…

She glanced toward the chair the duke had spent most of the night in. Once while it was still dark, Dani had awakened, a little afraid still and she had intended to rise but then she saw the duke sleeping in the chair. His head bent forward, his chin touching his chest.

It had been very easy to return to sleeping. She did feel very safe and also incredibly warm.

Dani struggled out of bed and picked up the discarded garments she wore the day before. Dressing quickly, Dani ran her fingers through her tangled mass of hair. She spied a brush on the table beside a mirror. Dani picked it up and ran it through her locks, giving up after a bit and tying her hair up on top of her head with a ribbon and pins.

She hurried downstairs, hoping she would find the duke. Was there still a chance she could convince him she was in danger? At the foot of the stairs, she stopped and looked around. A male voice echoed from the parlor. Hesitating only briefly she opened the doors and stepped in.

Wilkins, the sour faced butler, stood before two dogs and three cats. In his hands he held treats. The animals stared transfixed at him, their mouths hanging open collectively, in various stages of salivation. One dog was dirty white with immense paws and the other was small and black and appeared not to have eyes. The three cats looked to be relatives as they were all gray striped. But the most startling image Dani saw was a peculiar yellow and blue bird perched on Wilkins' left shoulder.

"Wilkins, what's this?"

"These are strays," he replied, glaring at the interruption. "Or they were. Now they are household pets."

"Strays?"

"His Grace is fond of taking in homeless creatures," Wilkins told her, looking down his nose at her. "Which is no doubt why you are still here."

"Well," Dani said after a moment, "I ain't no worse than this lot." She gestured to the menagerie in front of Wilkins. They took their gazes off the butler and his treats for a brief moment to study her but apparently not impressed, they returned their attention back to Wilkins.

"Who wants theirs first, hmm?" Wilkins asked the animals.

Dani rubbed the twitch in her nose and wondered if the old man expected one of them to answer. "Have they got names?"

"Of course they've names," snapped Wilkins. He fed a treat to the large dog. "This is Bernard."

"Bernard? Ain't that a strange name for a dog?"

"He's named after the duke's uncle," Wilkins explained.

Dani made a face and rubbed her nose again. "Don't think I'd like a dog named after me."

"This one," Wilkins continued, giving a treat to the small black eyeless dog, "is Snow."

"Excuse me?"

Wilkins grimaced. "Lord Jack named Snow. The cats are James, Elizabeth and William. Named after past monarchs. The bird is Molly."

Dani shook her head. "I don't understand a bit o' it."

"What are you doing wandering around here anyway?" Wilkins asked crossly.

Dani ran her tongue across the roof of her mouth and twitched her nose. "I'm looking for the duke. I wanted to ask 'im something."

"You aren't to disturb him," Wilkins informed her. "Anyway, he isn't here."

"Oh."

"He went to his club and then to speak with the magistrate. He had an appointment with him yesterday." Wilkins' bushy eyebrows bunched together. "But he was delayed." He left no doubt as to what he thought of Dani causing the delay. Wilkins sniffed. "He went to speak about Douglas Norton."

"The one what got himself murdered?" Dani exclaimed, her hand going automatically to her throat.

"He didn't get himself murdered. Some fiend did the deed without any encouragement from him," Wilkins said, scooting the bird off his shoulder.

"I was wondering when I was going back to the docks." Dani dared not say if, though she wished it were so.

Wilkins turned away from the animals and sighed heavily. The nostrils of his crooked nose flared but he said nothing.

"Well?" She demanded impatiently.

"You aren't being sent back," Wilkins told her, frowning. "You're going to be allowed to stay at least for a while."

"What?"

"I told you that His Grace takes in strays," Wilkins explained. "They become his project. He's decided to make you one."

"I'm a project?" Dani, asked, wiping her running nose with the back of her hand.

"Yes. Now, I am very busy," Wilkins told her, heading for the door of the parlor. He paused at the doorway. "Don't touch anything in here."

Dani sank down onto the settee and watched the dogs follow Wilkins out of the parlor. The three cats remained and began to wash themselves. "I ain't quite sure what a project is," she said to the felines, feeling a peculiar heaviness in her stomach. "But it don't sound very good, does it?"

Chapter Four

೫

Simon didn't want to report his lack of much progress to his mother's sister, Lady Penelope Norton. He found her sitting in the back, seldom-used parlor. Since her son's death she'd taken to sitting there working on embroidery.

Penelope Norton was a woman nearing fifty. With her golden blonde hair and vivid blue eyes, she was still attractive in spite of years of abuse at the hands of her late husband. Simon's mother and Penelope formed a sort of club of their own when both were young. The Survivors, they called themselves. Besides the two of them, there were at least a half a dozen others of their peers who were club members. Simon knew them all well and would help them when he could.

Pen, as she was affectionately known, received him in the clean pale yellow parlor. A pot of steaming tea waited on a nearby table. At the moment he wished for brandy.

"Simon, at last," Pen said, smiling wanly. He was instantly struck by how much Douglas resembled her. A smattering of gray hair mixed with her golden-blonde hair now and he cared not for the lines around her mouth. Her blue eyes were still animated but there was a depth of sorrow that hadn't been there before. Pen took his hands. She gestured to the paisley settee. "Sit and tell me what you've learned."

"Are you eating?" Simon asked, taking the offered seat next to her. He reached up and touched her white cheek. "Mrs. Martin says you are refusing food."

"I cannot eat," she admitted. "The thought of food turns my stomach."

"You must try."

"I will. But you are trying to change the topic. You did not go to see the magistrate yesterday as you promised. Don't try to tell me you were frightened of a storm." Her tone, mildly reprimanding, and her cool, assessing gaze reminded him of his own mother.

Simon reached for the pot of tea and refreshed the cup he noticed by Pen's side. He poured himself a cup. "The woman who found Douglas..." He paused. He almost said Douglas' body but somehow found it difficult to say those words to his aunt. "She came here yesterday."

Pen's eyes lit with excitement. "Really? Tell me have you learned anything?"

He had wanted to speak with Dani this morning. Tell her himself he wanted her to stay but she was sleeping so soundly.

"Simon?" Pen spoke sharply.

Simon glanced around the room, looking anywhere but directly at Douglas' mother. What could he say to her to give her spirit any ease?

"Simon, stop studying the draperies as though it is the first you have seen them," the older woman admonished.

Forcing a smile, he turned back to face her. "She said she saw three men follow him into The Black Swan. They looked suspicious."

"And?" she prodded hopefully.

Simon felt a fiend for dashing her hopes but he did not want to lie to her, even if it might offer her some small comfort. "Nothing else. She didn't really see much."

"Oh." Pen's crestfallen expression pierced his heart. She attempted a smile and patted his hands. "I know you are doing your best."

"Douglas knew a lot of people, Pen. It will take some time to question them all but I intend to seek them all out," Simon vowed. He sipped at the sweet, milky tea.

"I know. Really I know. It's just that, I know he wasn't always a good person…"

"Stop right there," Simon interrupted. He shook his head at her. "He was your only son and my cousin and that is all that matters to me." To his dismay her eyes filled with tears again. His head pounded. "I will find who did this, Pen. I swear it. It just might take some time."

"I believe you, Simon," Pen replied. "I am trying to be strong. It is just so hard sometimes. I keep remembering when he was just a little boy and he was all I had, you see and…" Her voice broke off, thickened with her tears.

"Don't." Simon tightened his hold on her hands.

She closed her eyes and pulled herself together with visible effort. "I wish the authorities would take Douglas' murder more seriously."

"They think it was just a robbery gone badly."

Her gaze was shrewd. "But you don't believe that, do you, Simon?"

Unfortunately, Pen knew him too well. He shook his head. "That's too pat an answer for me."

"If only he had allowed you to influence him." She disengaged her hands from his and rose to pace the room. "What was he doing in that…that place anyway?"

Simon blew out a breath and pinched his nose. How much should he tell Douglas' mother about his visits to brothels and gaming? "I'm not really sure, Pen."

She stopped her pacing long enough to point her finger accusingly in his direction. "It was your brother, Jack's influence, no doubt."

"What makes you say that?" Simon asked, surprised.

"Douglas told me once that Jack took him to a tavern when they were at university together," she retorted.

"Pen…"

She threw her hands up in the air. "I know what you are going to say. One little visit to a tavern couldn't have resulted in this."

"Well, yes." Simon set his teacup down and rose from his seat. "Jack and Douglas hadn't been close for years, Pen. I can't imagine Jack being any influence on Douglas."

Pen's lips quivered, then her mouth thinned and her shoulders dropped in defeat. "I know you're right, of course."

Simon understood her need for answers, the need to blame someone, anyone. He kissed her cheek. "I want to talk to you about the young woman who found Douglas."

"Oh?"

Dani had been looking for the duke all afternoon. She'd overheard Mrs. Martin say he had returned from his earlier appointments but he hadn't come by to see her since sleeping in the chair in her room the night before. Was Wilkins right? Did the duke intend to have her stay?

A maid had mentioned something about another parlor. One at the very back of the house and Dani headed there. It was one of the few places she hadn't checked. She had to keep hiding from passing servants for she didn't want them questioning why she wandered freely about the house.

Unfortunately, coming down the hall was Wilkins. She didn't have time to hide either for he looked right at her.

"What are you doing?" he asked.

"Wilkins, where is 'Is Grace?"

"He's in the parlor." He gestured to a nearby closed door.

Dani went straight for the parlor door.

"No, wait, he's..."

Whatever else Wilkins was about to say Dani missed because she had hurried into the parlor. She wished she had stopped to listen to Wilkins. An older woman sat on the settee with Simon, elegantly dressed in a black mourning gown. The woman, her hands encased in black gloves, held Simon's hands in hers. Dani hoped she could escape without them noticing. She backed up.

The duke turned, dashing all chance of escape Dani might have had. He frowned and shook his head. Mortified, Dani's cheeks reddened. Obviously she had come in on something she was not supposed to. She backed away further as he stood.

Wilkins came in the door after her. The aged butler glared at her then looked to the duke. "I'm very sorry, Your Grace."

"Dani, it's all right, come in," the duke said, coming toward her. He reached her before she had time to make her escape and, taking her hand, led her into the room. His warm fingers wrapped around her suddenly cold hand. "That will be all, Wilkins."

The widened eyes of the woman made it clear that she was as shocked to be faced with Dani as Dani was with her. The woman glanced at him.

"Dani, this is Lady Penelope Norton, my aunt."

Dani let out the breath she'd been holding. Douglas Norton's mother. Of course. It made sense now. She should have known. Her embarrassment increased. How could she interrupt his meeting with Lady Norton? Wilkins was no doubt having a fit on the other side of the door.

Lady Norton stared at Dani with renewed interest. She glanced at the seat beside the duke that had been unoccupied. "Why don't you sit there, my dear?"

Dani opened her mouth to protest but the duke sat and dragged her down with him. He still held her hand and, though she was grateful for the warmth, she had a feeling it was to keep her from making an escape from the embarrassing situation.

"Simon, who is this?" Lady Norton asked the question Dani feared she would. She cursed her own stupidity.

"Pen, this is the young woman I was just telling you about. Dani is the one who found Douglas by the tavern," he said, his tone all kindness.

"Oh." Lady Norton stared down at her own clenched hands, which she'd wrung into an odd knot. Lady Norton's smile was strained. "I see. This is the young woman you wish to make another of your projects?"

Dani stiffened and Simon must have noticed for he squeezed her hand tightly.

"Given the circumstances I don't want to send her back to the East End," the duke explained.

"Circumstances?" Lady Norton's tone was imperious.

The duke didn't seem to notice for he continued, "She's really quite clever and I think would be a fast learner."

Learner? Of what, Dani wondered.

Lady Norton glanced over at Dani. "What did Simon say your name was? Dani? That's a bit unusual for a young lady."

"Me mother named me after 'er father," Dani explained.

Lady Norton glanced at Simon, pursing her lips.

"Yes. I admit she has a somewhat unusual dialect," he said. "I thought you could help her. Her mother and friends were all seamstresses before they lost their shop some years before. Dani, do you know how to sew?"

Dani wondered where this was going. "Yes, I can do some. I mend my own things sometimes."

The duke smiled. "Can you read at all?"

Dani blinked. "Well...a little. I'm not very good at it though."

Lady Norton arched an eyebrow. "Indeed." Lady Norton stared hard at Dani for a moment. "You know, I've had nothing to keep my mind off Douglas' murder these past weeks other than spending time overseeing Lucy's lessons with her governess. I could spend some time assisting Dani to speak properly and with her reading and language skills."

"Are you quite certain?" the duke asked. "I could hire a tutor or perhaps ask the governess…"

"Don't waste your money on some untrustworthy tutor, Simon," Lady Norton said. She smiled. "You already have your hands full with paying for Lucy's education. I don't think it would be appropriate to instruct them together, anyway. Besides Dani's questionable background she might be somewhat behind in what Lucy has already learned. I shall teach Dani."

Dani didn't like the way they were both talking about her as though she wasn't even there.

"Yes," Lady Norton continued. "I need a distraction and you need a tutor for this young woman. I'll teach her how to speak properly and anything else she might need to know as a, er, member of your household. Embroidery shouldn't be difficult since she knows how to sew. Can you draw or paint?"

It took Dani a moment to realize Lady Norton had spoken to her. "Um…I've done a bit o' drawing with sticks in the dirt."

"Hmm. Not quite what I had in mind. We'll have to work on that too."

The duke looked very pleased. "Are you sure it isn't too much for you, Pen? I have plenty of money for such an undertaking."

"I want to do it."

"Well, if you are sure."

"Ain't anyone going to ask me what I think?" Dani asked, standing up. She didn't want to listen to them discussing her as though her opinion didn't matter.

The duke looked at her, as though seeing her for the first time. Then he smiled and reached for her hand again. "It's all right, Dani. Lady Norton will help you."

Dani couldn't believe it when she felt the first prick of tears behind her eyes. He found her lacking, that much was clear. She supposed she shouldn't think otherwise. What was a man like him supposed to think of a street girl like her? Hadn't he even said he didn't consort with street women?

"You don't want to learn, Dani?" Lady Norton asked, her gaze shrewd.

When the duke finally decided he'd had enough of offering her charity, it might help to know how to speak well and act like a lady. She could perhaps become a proper seamstress like her mother had been. Or even a ladies' maid as Mary had been all those years ago. It was better than living on the streets again, wasn't it?

"Yes, I'd like to learn," she said at last.

"Excellent."

Lady Norton nodded. "We can begin this afternoon over tea, if you'd like."

"That would be splendid, Pen." Simon was a little too enthusiastic for Dani. "I have to go out anyway. There's a man I must see. I'll see you later, Dani."

* * * * *

The rose garden at the duke's home was one of the most beautiful sights Dani had ever seen. She'd discovered it out of boredom, over the last few days, waiting for Lady Norton to tell her it was time for another lesson. She'd hardly seen the duke. It was strange how certain parts of the things Lady Norton had been teaching her seemed familiar.

Dani wandered into the conservatory. The garden consisted of a variety of shrubs spouting blooms everywhere, many of the bushes taller than her. Every shade of pink was represented as well as white and red flowers. Droplets of water dusted the roses and the fragrance assailed her nostrils with such wonder she could have wept. A welcome relief from the putrid smells of the streets.

Dani fingered a soft pink rose. The flower was perhaps a tiny bit softer than the material of her dress.

"There you are, Dani."

Dani froze in the act of leaning over the delicate bloom to inhale its sweet fragrance. She didn't even need to look to know who stood in the doorway of the conservatory. She swung round to face him.

"You're breathtaking," Jack said, grinning. The duke's brother wore only black breeches and an off-white lawn shirt. His cravat was undone. Around his eyes were dark circles. Dani wondered if he'd just come home. Jack walked into the rose garden uninvited. She backed away on his approach and his smile faltered only slightly.

"You wound me, don't you know." He stopped and leaned his tall frame against a small table and chair set beside one of the bushes.

"Is His Grace home yet?" Dani asked, pronouncing each word carefully as Lady Norton had taught her. She fidgeted nervously.

He covered his heart with one of his hands and moaned. "Ah, that cut to the quick. Now, Dani, please, aren't I good enough company?"

Dani shrugged.

Jack sighed. "I'm just curious about where you fit in. You're not Simon's usual sort of mistress." He flashed her a toothy grin. "I've already guessed you must be his mistress though, eh?"

"No," Dani said, shaking her head vigorously. Did that one night he spent sleeping in her chair make her his mistress? She doubted it.

"Well, anyway, I collect from Wilkins that Simon wants you to stay here for a while. I've also heard Aunt Penelope has been giving you lessons. He's never done that before. You must have something special about you. But no matter. I wasn't very nice to you the other night. I've come to apologize."

"You have?" she asked warily. Even though he did not move, she took another step back.

"You have my word as a gentleman," he said, then laughed. "All right, so I'm not a gentleman but I still apologize. I heard you were frightened the other night by my stories. In my defense, I was only teasing. I thought you would know I was jesting."

"I ain't accustomed to stories," Dani told him. She'd said that wrong, hadn't she? Jack was making her forget her lessons.

"Hmm. You are from the East End, though, aren't you?" Jack asked, crossing his arms in front of his broad chest. "You must have some experience with scoundrels."

Dani blushed but said nothing. She had no intention of telling the duke's brother anything about her past.

"I never would have imagined Simon would pick a prostitute from the docks as his next conquest." Jack looked genuinely puzzled.

"I ain't a doxy," she defended herself. "I'm not a doxy," she corrected herself.

"Well, if you aren't, how come you live by The Black Swan?" Jack nodded, pleased with himself no doubt.

"I do live there but Mary and Grace kept me away from most of it."

"Mary and Grace?"

"My friends and my mother's friends. They looked after me after my mother died. My mother were a seamstress but she had a terrible cough and my father weren't nowhere though I heard he were a member of the gentry. After their shop closed down they sometimes worked as doxies."

"I see." Jack studied her silently and then shrugged. "So these two, Mary and Grace, reared you. But if they were as you said you must have learned from them."

Dani shook her head. "They told me many times that they wanted me to have a better life than they did." Though even they hadn't been able to keep her safe from the one who had raped her.

"Still, you knew what they were doing," Jack pointed out.

"Sure, I knew. I know about that sort o' thing. But the best they could they kept me away from it. Most the time I hid at night in a little corner."

"Anyway," he said, smiling. "I am sorry that we had a misunderstanding." He stepped closer to her. "Someone like you must think you're in some kind of dream ending up in a place like this."

"Aye, it's hard to get used to," Dani admitted. She didn't like him getting closer to her. Was he like the man who attacked her once? She couldn't be sure. She swallowed a lump of fear and stepped back, colliding with a rose bush.

"There, be careful, sweetheart," Jack warned, immediately pouncing on her and pulling her away from the bush, which swayed. "I won't bite you, Dani. There's no reason to try to get away."

"I think I'd like to go back inside now," she said, her stomach lurching uneasily.

"Why don't you tell me more about your friends," Jack suggested, running a long finger across her left cheek. "Are they jealous of your situation?"

"I-I don't know what you mean."

"Or are they glad that you're staying?"

"They don't know about it. I only knew I was staying for a bit a few days ago. I came by only to give the duke information." And hopefully be paid for it.

Jack raised a surprised eyebrow. "So your dear friends don't know where you are?"

A twinge of guilt sailed through Dani. She'd given little thought to Mary and Grace. Grace might wonder if she went missing like Mary.

"There weren't time to tell Grace," Dani said, fretfully, remembering how anxious she was to come see the duke. "And Mary went missing."

"Missing?" Jack asked, frowning. He stepped back and stared at her. "What do you mean, missing?"

"The same night as Douglas Norton got murdered," Dani told him, her lungs seizing painfully, her throat clogging with tears. She had been so selfish. Grace was probably beside herself with worry. "No one knows what happened to me. I-I need to get back."

"What?" Jack exclaimed, clearly surprised by her statement. She pulled her arm out of his grasp and brushed past him, wringing her hands.

"I haven't thought about Grace. She'll be so worried about me."

He nodded and then smiled. "Don't worry, Dani. I have the perfect solution."

"You do?"

"We'll get a hired carriage and we'll go there right away," Jack vowed. "You can visit Grace."

Dani had been pacing the conservatory until he suggested she visit Grace. She stopped and stared at him, shock throbbing through her. Go to the docks with him? She couldn't do that. How would the duke feel? Dani saw no reason to possibly make him angry. He might throw her out. He was only allowing her to stay because he thought her in danger. Her heart twisted in her chest. But how could she turn down the chance to see Grace? To find out if anybody knew what happened to Mary? She was torn and she did not care for the feeling.

"I know what the problem is," Jack said, entwining his hands behind his back, grinning disarmingly. "You're worried about what Simon will say when he learns you went somewhere with me, right?"

Well, of course Dani was concerned. She didn't want him to be angry with her. Dani couldn't bear to see disapproval in his warm, gold-green eyes. Maybe the duke would take her there. But if she asked, the duke might think she was ungrateful for him taking her away and maybe see this as a reason to leave her there.

"Let's take Wilkins with us," Jack broke in to her thoughts.

"W-Wilkins?"

Jack nodded, rubbing his hands together gleefully. "Since Simon can't come with us then the next best choice is to bring Wilkins, his watchdog." He took her arm and led her out of the conservatory and back toward the front of the house. He yelled for Wilkins.

"But-but what if he won't come?" Dani asked uncertainly.

"He won't have a choice," Jack assured her. "We'll make him come with us."

Wilkins appeared a moment later. He sneered both at her and at Jack. Dani wasn't quite sure who warranted the bigger sneer.

"Wilkins, you're coming with us," Jack told the old butler.

Wilkins straightened up to his full height, which, though considerable, did not come close to Jack's. In spite of that the old butler had a way of looking down his crooked nose that made Dani feel very small.

"Coming with you? Where?" Wilkins demanded.

Jack smiled and patted his thin shoulder. "To the East End."

"To the what?" The servant exclaimed, his face turning all blotchy red.

"Dani needs to see her friend. We're going with her."

"His Grace…"

"Isn't here," Jack finished for him.

"The proprieties…" Wilkins tried again.

"Damn those too. Come on, Wilkins." Jack shrugged. "I order it."

* * * * *

Simon was surprised by Mrs. Martin greeting him at the door when he arrived home a short time later. The plump, white-haired housekeeper wrung her hands, her normally welcoming smile replaced by an anxious frown.

"Mrs. Martin? Where's Wilkins?" Simon glanced around the entry area. He reached to remove his coat.

"He's gone, Your Grace," Mrs. Martin wailed.

"Gone? What the devil are you talking about?" Simon demanded.

Mrs. Martin sighed heavily. "I told them not to go but they were insistent. Wilkins went with them."

Simon struggled for patience. "Who, Mrs. Martin?"

"Lord Jack and Dani," she explained.

He might have known. But the knowledge that Dani went somewhere with Jack caused a hollowness in his chest. Overwhelming disappointment too. Even a smidge of jealousy. Where had that come from?

"Mrs. Martin, have Richmond bring the carriage round immediately."

Chapter Five

ಎ

"I cannot believe that I have been talked into this," Wilkins complained again.

Ever since Jack had practically dragged the old butler out of the house and into the hackney Wilkins hadn't shut his mouth. Dani was getting a severe headache.

"If it will make you feel better, Wilkins, you really had no choice," Jack said cheerfully from his carriage seat.

The carriage lurched and Dani's stomach turned over. The ride today was much rougher than the hackney ride that had taken her to the duke's house. She grasped the side and prayed she would make it there safely. Between the wheels finding every rock in their path and Wilkins' endless protests, she did not feel well at all.

"His lordship will have my head over this," Wilkins snapped to anyone who would listen.

"Nonsense," Jack insisted. "He will be grateful that you are along to look after Dani."

Wilkins looked down his long nose from across the carriage. Unfortunately, Dani had been subjected to sitting beside the man. The old servant sat stiffly erect, coldness coming off him that rivaled the iciest weather she'd endured on the streets. She shivered.

"This foolish adventure is nonsense." Wilkins' hawklike gaze falling on Dani. "The duke will not be pleased when he learns where we have gone."

Dani swallowed hard. She feared the same. In fact, she was afraid he would be so displeased he would tell her to stay where she belonged. It had been a mistake to let Jack talk her into visiting Grace but she was worried about her friend and didn't want her to think she had disappeared like Mary. She stared at her fingers, marveling still at their cleanliness. To be warm, full and treated like a princess was heaven. In the last few days she'd held a paintbrush and read half a book. Almost like a real lady. Memories of the duke staying with her that first night, making certain she could fall asleep washed over her. Would memories be all she would be left with?

"The truth is, Wilkins," Jack said, yawning, leaning his head back on the back of the carriage seat, "Simon would have thought of this himself given the chance."

"And just what would he have thought of?" The ancient servant demanded, his voice heavy with contempt.

"He would have taken her to see her friends. Dani clearly misses them."

"She can return to them anytime," Wilkins muttered, glancing her way pointedly.

"What was that, Wilkins?" Jack asked. "I didn't quite hear you."

Wilkins sniffed and shrugged.

Jack smiled at Dani. "We should be there shortly." He studied her carefully, assessing something but Dani didn't know what. "You're pale, are you all right?"

"I'm just a bit nervous," she admitted.

"What in the world for?"

"Well." Dani bit her lip. "What if we can't find Grace?" She fretted. "Then I would have made the duke upset for nothing."

Wilkins snorted but otherwise made no comment.

"I really wouldn't worry about how Simon reacts, Dani." Jack grinned. "I'll take the blame for everything."

That didn't offer Dani much comfort. Misery threatened to swallow her. Finally she felt safe. It was just possible she'd thrown all that aside.

The carriage came to an abrupt stop that nearly knocked Dani off the seat. Unthinkingly she grasped Wilkins' sleeve to steady herself. He glared balefully and pulled it away.

Jack opened the door and leapt out gracefully. He leaned in and helped Dani out. Wilkins quickly followed.

Dani wondered if all retainers were as presumptuous as Wilkins was to question a member of the gentry so easily.

Dani glanced around. Nearby an old woman was selling oranges and lemons. She called out to those who passed by, "Sweet oranges, fine lemons, juicy oranges, fine lemons fine. Buy my lemons and sweet oranges."

Dani stared wistfully at the woman, knowing she relied solely on her fruit to make her living. No one stopped and bought the oranges and lemons. She longed for the money to buy some. If circumstances were different it might be herself selling half-rotten fruit.

"Let's get some oranges, shall we?" Jack asked, following Dani's gaze. He headed for the old woman and gestured to Dani to come. "Good day, love. How much for your oranges?"

Dani hurried after him, Wilkins followed more slowly, his tongue clicking in displeasure.

"I really don't think..." Wilkins began but Jack waved away his protests as though the man hadn't spoken. To Dani's surprise, Jack reached up and caressed the old woman's cheek affectionately. The orange seller grinned in reaction.

She held up a large, round orange. "They's the finest oranges in all o' London, ye know. I 'appen to 'ave one right 'ere. Want to taste it, luv?"

The woman reached into the pocket of her dirty apron and removed a section of orange for Jack's inspection. He didn't even look at it but instead opened his mouth. The old crone laughed and popped it into his mouth and waited for him to chew it. He did so slowly, as if to savor each tiny drop of its sweet juice. Jack widened his eyes dramatically and then swallowed the slice.

"Well?" the old woman asked, anxiety creasing her eyes. Dani watched him carefully too, wondering what he would come up with next. Out of the corner of her eye, she noticed that Wilkins was even studying Jack, obviously fascinated with his act.

"It's so incredibly sweet it makes my eyes water," Jack assured the woman. "How much?"

She beamed proudly and gestured to her box of oranges, which sat next to a box of much punier lemons. "Three for a penny."

"No, my dear lady," Jack said, shaking his golden brown head. He glanced down at Dani and winked. In some ways he resembled the duke so much and yet to Dani the duke would always be her idea of a prince. She could never think of Jack that way, even now when he was obviously trying to charm her she could only wish that it were the duke stood there with her.

"I meant for all of them."

"All o' them?" the crone repeated, her voice rising in shock.

Surely not. Jack wouldn't buy all of her oranges, would he? But why? Dani glanced at Wilkins who appeared as puzzled as she was.

"I'll take them all," Jack was saying. He scrunched down onto his haunches and peered at the oranges in the box. He fingered a lemon in the box next to them. He brought it to his nose and sniffed it with exaggerated slowness. "Five for both boxes."

"Five?" exclaimed the woman. "They're worth far more'n five, me lord."

Jack angled his head to look up at her. "No, my girl. I meant five pounds."

"Pounds?" Wilkins cried out, unable to be silent one more minute. The servant grimaced and shook his head. "This is insane. What are we doing here? What are you thinking to pay this old woman five pounds for a few rotten oranges and lemons?"

Jack stood up from his squat and for the first time since Dani had met him, his expression was startlingly unpleasant. She took a step backward, even though his malevolent glare was directed at Wilkins. Was this what lurked below that careless grin Jack always wore? He moved closer to Wilkins until he stood towering over the old man.

"Let me explain something to you, Wilkins," Jack said, softly, ominously. "It's my allowance to use as I see fit. If I had it my way you would have been gone years ago. I know you were with my father before Simon. I only tolerate you because you've been with the family for so many years but even my tolerance has its breaking point. You were brought along only to make Dani happy but we can just as easily lose you in the fog."

To Wilkins credit, he was not cowed by Jack's behavior. He pulled himself up until his spine was as straight as a stick and with his nostrils flaring, he looked up his nose at Jack in superiority. "Only your brother has the authority to separate me from my employment."

Jack's green eyes flashed fire for a moment longer and he opened his mouth to say something but abruptly closed it. He reached out and patted Wilkins right shoulder like one might pat the head of a dog. Without another word, he turned back to the orange seller who had been anxiously watching the exchange between the two men. He handed the woman the promised five pounds. She stared at them long and hard. Dani was sure the old crone had never seen so much money. She hadn't either for that matter.

"I'll pick up the boxes before I leave," he told the woman, who had not torn her eyes from the money she held in her soot-covered hands. "Keep them for me."

Jack placed his hand on Dani's back in a possessive gesture she didn't like at all and pushed her away from the orange seller. Wilkins followed, sniffing his disapproval.

"You'll never see that fruit again," announced the servant.

"Hmm?" Jack asked, his voice sounding distracted.

"When we return she and the fruit will be long gone," Wilkins predicted. Dani nodded her agreement. You couldn't trust anyone by the docks.

"I can't abide oranges," Jack replied, stopping in the middle of the street they had been walking along.

Dani couldn't take the time to understand Jack because she found herself swept away in familiar sights and sounds.

Her nose wrinkling, she realized familiar smells too. Frozen in time, she turned and looked around one of the streets where she spent the better part of the last several years. She could see herself as a little girl hiding from the monsters lurking in the shadows, missing her mother, while Grace and Mary tried to earn a few coins. Not far from where she stood now was the small corner she had wedged herself into as a scared child, shivering from fear and the cold. Her thin rags providing little protection.

A woman with her shoulders hunched walked past the small corner and Dani swallowed the lump in her throat. Only yesterday she looked very much like that woman. If she wasn't careful she would find herself sharing the discarded coals the woman had stopped to use as warmth.

"Dani."

Dani tore her gaze away from the frail, bony woman warming herself and stared unseeingly at Jack. These people were like her. They were all she'd known. Her eyes welled with tears.

"Dani?" Jack said again, concern on his face.

She took an involuntary step backward and stumbled into a passing man. The tall, thin shabbily dressed man grabbed her around the waist, painfully squeezing his bony hands into her.

"'Ey, lady, watch where yer walkin'," he screeched, his rotting teeth staring out at her. His putrid breath assailed her nostrils. Dani fought to keep from gagging. Her heart thumped wildly, the night of her rape came rushing back to her and she tried to push away the sense of panic.

"Come on, Dani," Jack said, peeling the glaring man's hands from her. He stared coldly at him. "Be on your way."

Dani blinked rapidly, grateful for Jack's interference.

"At the risk of repeating myself," Wilkins said, studying Dani in a manner that appeared almost to be concern, "what in the world are we doing in this place?"

Jack kept a steadying arm around Dani's shoulders and for once she was grateful. She trembled. She wanted to leave. She wanted more than anything in the world to see the duke, disappointment on his face or not.

"Dani wants to see her friend. Do you see Grace anywhere?"

Dani tried to see Grace in the throng of people milling around them. Mostly she saw the usual sort that sold flowers, fruits and vegetables. The prostitutes didn't frequent this part of the East End of London because the authorities tried to discourage it. Sometimes the rest of London came to buy the wares sold here and the merchants didn't want them put off by the sight of the doxies. They needed to look closer to the docks.

"No, she isn't here," Dani whispered. "She's usually by the docks."

"Then, shall we go?" Jack suggested.

The man she had run into still stood nearby. He rubbed his beard with one hand while the other one was rubbing a part of him that was even more obscene. Dani quickly looked away. She allowed Jack to steer her down the long street that would take them to the docks. Her stomach flipped. How was it that she grew up by the docks and now she dreaded seeing the area again?

A bedraggled child darted out in front of them with a suddenness that startled Dani. She stopped in her tracks, Jack colliding with her back. The child, a little boy, reached down to pick up a ball. He turned his dirt-stained face to Dani and stuck out his tongue.

"What in the world?" Jack protested from behind her. He stepped around and saw the boy. He scowled at the child. "Can't you watch where you're going?"

"What a disgusting urchin," Wilkins said, whipping out a swath of cloth and holding it over his nose. "We're never going to find this person," he said giving his unsolicited opinion.

"That's the spirit, Wilkins," Jack said sarcastically. "Let's keep moving."

Dani bit her lip and continued to watch the little boy as far as she could seem him. Surely a child had more right to be cared for by someone like the duke than she did. She'd never done anything in her life to deserve the kindness she'd been shown. Guilt pierced her heart. She was nothing but trouble to him. She began walking again, all the while studying the people around her. Some of them she recognized. Some were new. Families huddled together for warmth, men talking and laughing together, women averting their eyes from the leering men.

The sour smells of the East End became stronger the closer to the docks they got, including the scents of old fish and urine. The docks swarmed with sailors and prostitutes even in the afternoon as it was now. The three of them obviously made a strange sight because a number of dockside vagrants turned to stare at them.

"Where does she usually hang around, Dani?" Jack asked her.

Dani let out a heavy sigh turned her gaze away from the gawking men for a moment. "In an alleyway close to The Black Swan. She often sleeps there during the day and then comes out at night."

Wilkins lowered the cloth he held to his nose and grimaced. "This isn't the alley that Douglas Norton was found murdered in, was it?"

"Yes." Mary hung out in that area too. Dani wondered if there was any significance in that. Shrugging, she said, "I'll show you."

They hadn't gone more than a few steps when a very large man blocked their path. The man was dressed in old black rags he'd probably stolen. Dani wrinkled her nose. The stench coming from the man was very much like a dead body. On his head he wore a hat pulled low over his left eye.

"Well, if it ain't Prinny and 'is court," the man bellowed for all around them to hear. Several others around laughed in response. "What brings 'is royal 'ighness 'ere?"

"Forget Prinny," called another man, this one with a large scar across his right cheek. "I'm more interested in the lady what's with 'im."

"I knew there'd be trouble," Wilkins said under his breath. To Dani's surprise the old servant scooted closer to her.

"We're not here for any trouble, my good man," Jack told the giant looming over them. "We just want to get to The Black Swan."

The man shrugged. "You and the old man can go any time. The lady 'ere we'd like to get better acquainted with."

"I'm terribly sorry but that won't be possible," Jack said, shaking his head. He too, moved closer to Dani so that she was now between Jack and Wilkins. She swallowed, trying to keep her fear from making her bolt.

"'E ain't being very cooperative, 'is 'e, Eddie?" the second man who'd spoken called to the giant with the foul clothes.

"I guess we're going to 'ave to take care o' 'im if we wants the lady," Eddie agreed, grinning. He rubbed his hands, apparently relishing the challenge.

To Dani's horror, Eddie pulled out a wicked looking knife and seemed intent on pointing it at Jack.

Eddie froze and he and his accomplice glanced at some point behind her.

"I really wouldn't if I were you, Eddie," her savior said from just behind her. She recognized the duke's voice instantly. Relief nearly brought her to her knees.

Chapter Six

Eddie's gaze lit on the duke. Looking uncertain, he gripped his knife tighter.

"For God's sake, 'e's got a pistol," the other man wailed. Eddie growled in frustration then yelled at his friend to run. The pair took off down the street.

Dani ran to the duke and threw herself into his arms without thinking. His arms closed around her.

"Are you all right?" He asked her, concern in his wonderful eyes when he tilted her head up to look at him. He lowered the ugly looking pistol and pulled her closer.

"I'm so glad," she said into his coat. He smelled of brandy, spice and masculinity and she inhaled his fragrance. At the moment it was the most wonderful scent she'd ever known.

"Your Grace, I trust Mrs. Martin gave you the news of our whereabouts," Wilkins asked. Dani was a little surprised to hear the relief in the old man's voice too.

"Indeed," the duke said coldly. He gently pushed Dani away from him and then brushed his fingers on her cheek in a touch that made her quiver. "Wait inside the coach, Dani. I'll be there shortly."

Dani glanced behind him to see his carriage there with a uniformed driver holding the door open for her. She swallowed the lump in her throat and nodded her agreement and walked to the coach.

"I could have handled it, Simon," Jack said, glaring at his brother. He folded his arms in front of him in a defiant gesture. "You didn't need to come to the rescue."

The duke shook his head and put away his pistol. "It never ceases to amaze me how incredibly thick-skulled you can be. You put Dani and Wilkins both in a great deal of danger. I realize you don't care about yourself but Dani is my responsibility and Wilkins would hardly be able to defend himself. They are both under my protection."

Dani winced at hearing herself called a "responsibility".

"Dani wanted to see her friend Grace," Jack said petulantly.

"Yes, I've been informed of the plans," Simon assured him too furious to think clearly. Jack tried his patience more than any living creature. He couldn't begin to explain the rage he felt when he saw the situation Jack had put Dani in. "Get in the carriage and let's go home."

"I am not a child, Simon, nor your mistress. I'll make my way without your aid," Jack snapped. He turned on his heel and stalked off in the direction of The Black Swan.

Simon sighed. Jack was becoming more like their father all the time. He glanced at his carriage and knew the time had come to talk to Dani about his decision to have her stay with him.

"Your Grace," Wilkins said from beside him.

"Wilkins," Simon said, somewhat startled to realize he'd forgotten the old servant. "I trust that you aren't suffering any aftereffects from the ordeal."

"No. I would like to offer my apologies for my part in this adventure, Your Grace," Wilkins said stiffly.

Simon smiled. "I am grateful for your role in watching over Dani. She's going to be with us for a time, Wilkins. I would appreciate your assistance in looking after her and making sure her adjustment to her new life goes smoothly."

It was clear from Wilkins' pained expression that he thought little of the news. But to his credit, Wilkins straightened up, pulled his black coat down and nodded his agreement. "Yes, Your Grace."

"Stay outside with Richmond for the moment, Wilkins," Simon ordered. He didn't want Dani to be humiliated by having the old servant witness their conversation. He opened the door to the carriage, jumped inside and took the seat next to her. Her bottom lip quivered and all ready unshed tears shone in her eyes.

"I know what you're going to say," she said, her voice sounding watery.

"You do?" Simon asked, surprised.

"I shouldn't have let him talk me into coming back here." Her whole body shook with emotion. "It was only that I was worried about Grace."

"Dani…"

"I-I don't blame you if you want to get rid of me," she said forlornly. She used the sleeve of her dress to wipe at her eyes, which were now streaming with tears.

"I don't want to get rid of you, Dani," Simon assured her.

"Of course you do," she insisted, hiccupping. "I'm s-sorry."

Simon pulled her into his arms and pushed her head to his chest. He didn't mind that her tears soaked his favorite white lawn shirt. He'd had some experience with crying females. After several minutes, he cleared his throat.

"Dani?"

"Y-Yes?"

Her periwinkle eyes glistened with tears. God, she was lovely. And he was the worst sort of cad. "I'm taking you to see Grace."

"What?"

Simon would do anything to see her smile again. If Dani had mentioned wanting to go to her friend, he would have taken her himself. She hadn't had the chance because he'd disappeared on her. He was nearly overwhelmed with a need to protect her. He'd never felt that way about a woman not related to him. "I'd worry if I wasn't with you," he told her, taking her hands, "but if I come too I can keep you safe."

Dani nodded and then licked her bottom lip with her small pink tongue. Simon stared at the morsel trying desperately not to give in to the sudden temptation to taste it. Surely this was not the time.

Dani's puzzled expression made him realize she didn't understand his protectiveness and he guessed he couldn't quite explain it. Maybe it came from the fact that he had failed to protect his mother from his father. In the end it didn't matter why he wanted to keep Dani safe, he just did.

"I want you to stay by my side the entire time, Dani," Simon told her. The fog was rolling in early this afternoon. He frowned. Dani didn't even have a cloak. He shrugged off his greatcoat and handed it to her. "Put this around your shoulders."

Dani did as he said and they stepped out into the street once more. Chill air greeted them. Wilkins and Richmond huddled nearby. The fog enshrouded lane dripped with moisture.

"Wilkins, you and Richmond stay with the carriage. We'll be back as quickly as we can," Simon called to the servant. He glanced down at Dani's head. He made a mental note to take her shopping for gowns and accessories to go with them, especially a bonnet.

Simon reached for her hand and tucked it in the crook of his arm. "Stay close."

"Yes, Your Grace."

Simon frowned. "I mean it, Dani. We still don't know who killed Douglas or why Mary disappeared. And I don't want you running into any more like Eddie."

"Maybe Mary's come back home now," Dani said out loud, her voice hopeful.

He looked at her. Their eyes locked and he stared at her for a very long time. "I suppose that's possible, Dani. Let's go. The fog is getting thicker by the moment. If we are going to find your friend we have to hurry."

But she tugged at his hand, keeping him from moving away down the long cobbled street for a moment.

"I want to believe it," she said. "I know it ain't…isn't likely though. I used to hope my mother would come back even when I knew she wouldn't. I used to hope my father would come and take me away from the docks too."

He reached up and wrapped a stray lock of her hair around his finger, wanting to feel the silky softness.

Simon lowered his lips to hers. Her mouth was sweet. Dani reached her arms up around his neck, pressing into him. They both seemed to forget for a moment that they stood in the middle of the street in the East End. A shout from a nearby man startled them out of the kiss.

"You've had a harsh life, Dani," he said softly.

"Aye, I guess it was. But it isn't any different from lots of others and better than some."

His smile was strained but he tucked her hand in his arm once more and pulled her down the cobbled lane with him.

They quickened their pace. They both knew that as bad as it could be by the docks during the day it was nothing compared to the night. They dare not linger too long after darkness descended.

Simon glancèd from side to side and all around. While it was true Dani grew up in the area, she didn't look like the street urchin she did a few days before. Her appearance was that of a lady and therefore, an easy target.

Truth be told, he did not make it a habit of coming to the East End and wasn't all that familiar with where they now were. A stroke of luck was the only reason he'd found Dani, Jack and Wilkins as quickly as he had.

A man dressed all in black rags stood on a nearby corner, sneering in their direction. Simon assessed the man's threat and hurried Dani along even faster. He could handle any trouble, Simon was sure, but he didn't really want to put Dani through more than she'd already experienced.

"The Black Swan is just round that corner," Dani said. Her voice had dropped to a hoarse whisper, husky to Simon's ears. They turned down a narrow street and Dani pointed to a doorway. A yellow glow emanated from within. The worn sign hung precariously above. "Grace is usually nearby this time of the day."

Simon wrapped his fingers around her cool ones. She trembled a little. He shot her a glance. Was she cold or frightened? He was more concerned about their surroundings than she appeared to be.

He recognized the area a bit now from his visit there a few days before when Douglas Norton was found. More than the old, battered storefronts, the familiar stench of decay and feces reminded him.

Grimacing, Simon glanced behind them to ensure they were not pursued by the man in black rags or any of his cohorts. Though a number of men and women milled about, other than a few curious glances, no one had yet bothered them. He wondered if any of them had witnessed his altercation with the thug, Eddie.

He gently urged Dani forward in front of him. There were a few of the tavern's patrons standing outside the door. Two of them were men and they argued about who won the last hand of cards they'd played the night before. The man closest to them let out an enormous belch. Dani snorted beside him.

"That's Weak Willie," she told Simon.

He peered down at her. "Why do they call him that? He looks rather large." The man's stomach protruded over his dirty, brown breeches and his gray shirt was open at the collar revealing a thick mass of fur.

"Not sure," Dani said, smiling. "He's cries a lot over minor things. Maybe that's why."

Simon raised an eyebrow and was about to ask her about that statement when she put her hand on his sleeve to draw his attention.

"Over here. The alley."

Dani tugged him toward the narrow lane next to the entrance of the tavern. Weak Willie and the man he'd been arguing with stopped and stared at the pair of them. Weak Willie scratched at his stomach.

"Go about your business, Willie," Dani called bravely to him.

Weak Willie ceased his scratching and now stared in open wonder at Dani. His thick lips hung open. With his other meaty hand he swatted at a pesky fly.

"Dani? 'Ey, girl, is that you?"

"Well, it ain't the queen," Dani said, laughing.

Simon frowned, feeling distinctly out of sorts.

"Where'd you get the fancy frock and 'oo's the dandy?" Willie called after them when they started down the long thin alley.

Dandy? Simon was tempted to show Weak Willie just how much of a dandy he was. But Dani ignored Willie and his friend.

Simon turned his attention to the narrow lane beside the tavern. The uneasiness that crept through him the last time he'd been in the alley returned with new force.

A large rat scurried out from a nearby hole in the wall of the tavern. The creature wiggled its nose at them, its beady eyes baleful. Simon almost thought it snickered. It ran across his expensive Hessians and to the other side of the alley. He and Dani glanced down at his boots at the same time. On the toe of his right boot the rat had left a present.

Dani cleared her throat, she sounded amused. "Quite a bit different from what you're used to, eh?"

The low moans of a man leaning against the wall drew Simon's attention. The man's breeches were open at the waist and a woman knelt before him. Frowning, Simon pushed Dani past the couple.

Dani tried to peer around him to look.

"Dani." He gritted his teeth.

"I want to see if it's Grace," she explained, shrugging.

Simon reminded himself Dani was unlike any other woman he had known. Grimacing, he allowed her to view the couple.

The woman had stringy gray hair and from what Simon could see, she was an older woman. Well into her fifties would be his guess. He pushed away the thought of Dani ending up like this woman.

Dani shook her head. "Not her."

Grateful to move on, Simon let out a breath and took Dani's hand in his once more.

The alley was remarkably crowded. Simon couldn't help wonder at it. If he lived in the area, God forbid, the last place he could see himself hanging round would be this narrow lane.

A woman and a small child were huddled a few paces from the prostitute and her customer. The child was so dirty and so thin Simon couldn't tell if it was a boy or girl. Worrying about the rat feces on his boot seemed so trivial.

"There," Dani said from beside him. He followed her gaze. She pointed to a woman at the back of the narrow lane against the tall stone wall. The woman was hunched over. It appeared as though she had recently retched.

"That's Grace?"

Dani nodded, placing her hand on her own stomach in seeming sympathy. Already the woman's vomit mixed with the other odors from the alley. Old fish, urine, rat droppings, sex.

"Let's go," Simon urged, pulling her forward toward the woman. "I don't want to linger here."

Simon recognized the pile of rubbish where Douglas Norton had been found. Dani had been picking through it a short time ago looking for her next meal. He swallowed the bile that threatened to rise in his throat. He would never let her come back to this life.

He glanced down at Dani. She was pale around her mouth and her hand was clammy in his.

"Are you all right, Dani?"

She nodded almost imperceptibly. She said nothing, just walked directly to the hunched over woman. She released his fingers.

"Grace?" Dani called to her friend.

Grace turned at the sound of her name, a drop of vomit still rested on her upper lip. She did not straighten up but clutched her stomach. Her eyes, a murky brown, were glazed over.

"Grace? It's Dani."

Grace didn't look at Dani but rather at him. Her eyes widened in fear and she stepped away, her back butting against the soiled wall behind her.

"I don't know where she is. I told you," Grace cried out, crossing her arms protectively in front of her. "Leave me be."

"Grace..." Dani took a step toward her friend but the woman gasped, gave a strangled cry, then pitched forward in front of them. "Oh!"

Simon knelt beside Grace and turned her over. Dani was right by his side, her brows furrowed in fear. She grabbed at her friend with one hand and him with the other. She raised her eyes to his, searching for reassurance.

He shook his head. "She's not dead, Dani." He gave his words a chance to sink in and then squeezed her hand gently. "But, she's very ill." He glanced down at the ground. "Unless I'm mistaken she's spitting up some blood."

"I can't leave her. She could die," Dani wailed, tears shining in her lashes.

Simon had to agree. He could not leave the poor woman like this. He sighed and ran his free hand through his hair. "We'll take her with us."

"W-What?" Dani's expression told him she wasn't quite sure she heard him right. What else could he do?

"We're taking Grace home with us. I'll send for a doctor." Simon felt Grace's forehead with the back of his hand. "She's burning with fever."

"Thank you," Dani whispered, a single tear falling down her pale cheek. Her bottom lip trembled.

Simon brushed at the tear. She made him feel like a hero. "Let's get her out of here."

"Do you want me to help carry her?"

"I think I can manage one small woman, Dani," Simon informed her. He lifted the feverish woman in his arms and stood up.

"No, stay away," Grace murmured and then followed that with an incoherent word.

There was an old man standing close to them but he didn't seem to think it odd that they were taking Grace with them.

They'd almost passed the woman and her child, when Simon stopped. He stared down at them for a moment. The child peered up at him with large brown eyes. Simon came to a decision.

"Dani?"

She had stopped behind him when he paused by the mother and child, her expression curious.

"In my coat, there are a few coins," he said softly. "Give them to these people."

Dani didn't hesitate, though her eyes had widened in wonder. Her hand reached into his coat pocket and pulled the coins out. She quickly handed them to the mother. The woman stared at them as though she couldn't quite believe they were real.

"Thank ye, guv'nor," she said after a moment. "Bless ye."

* * * * *

The look on Wilkins' face when he saw him carrying the woman toward the coach was almost worth it by itself, Simon decided. Before then he didn't know the old man's eyes could protrude that much. Obviously his butler was certain he'd finally lost his mind. At that moment, Simon was inclined to agree with him.

"Your Grace?" Wilkins asked, stepping away from the door to the carriage when Simon and Dani approached.

Simon attempted a reassuring smile. "We're going to have another guest, Wilkins."

Wilkins blinked rapidly, looking from him to Dani. Then he straightened up and tried to compose himself. "Would this be Grace then, Your Grace?"

"Yes. She's quite ill. We'll need to send for the doctor, Wilkins."

"I'll see to it, Your Grace. Shall I assist you in putting her in the coach?"

"I think I have her," Simon told him. Dani opened the carriage door and entered before him. He followed her carefully inside and set Grace down on the seat next to her, then took his seat across from them.

"Do you think she'll die?" Dani asked, tears thickening her voice. She clenched Grace's fingers in her own.

"I don't know," Simon said softly. "But she'll get the best care she can have."

Dani turned her attention back to Grace. With her free hand she brushed the older woman's dark brown hair away from her face. "She's not breathing very well. When last I saw her she complained she didn't feel well. I shouldn't have left her."

"You couldn't have prevented her illness." Simon was glad Dani had come to see him. But there was a lot he still needed to talk with her about.

The coach rumbled over a bumpy patch of road and Dani put out her hands to steady Grace. She didn't want her friend to fall onto the carriage floor. Dani peered at the duke. She was grateful to him for so many reasons.

Sitting in the corner of the coach across from her and Grace, he wore only his thin, now damp coat. She pulled his greatcoat tighter around her, inhaling his scent. The fog had dampened his mahogany hair and one lock curled on his forehead.

Dani could barely believe her good fortune. He was bringing Grace to his home. He had no reason to do so, other than because he wanted to please her.

"Thank you," Dani said after a moment. It didn't sound good enough to her ears. Not only had he taken in Grace and agreed to get her help but the duke handed over coins to the woman and her child in the alley. Dani's throat hurt from the tears of gratitude she tried to hold back.

"Dani, don't thank me."

She was a little taken aback by his almost cold tone. He spoke sharply, curtly. Dani wondered at it. Grace moaned, drawing her attention.

"I just hope she doesn't have what my mother had. I won't have anyone if Grace dies."

The duke frowned. "What do you mean?"

"Mary and Grace were my family," she replied, ashamed her tears were flowing freely down her face.

"Dani, come here."

"What?" Dani stared at him in surprise. A moment ago his expression had almost been angry, now he was telling her to come to him. Confusion washed over her. She shook her head.

"Come sit with me," he told her and he held out a hand for her. Dani hesitated only a moment longer before she rose from her seat and took his hand. He pulled her down next to him. The duke wrapped his arms around her, resting her head on his chest. "You're not alone anymore," he promised, stroking her curls. She shivered at his touch.

He lowered his head until their lips were just a hairsbreadth away. Dani could feel his breath touching him. He dropped his mouth to taste her.

"Mm," Grace moaned from across the coach.

"Grace," Dani exclaimed a little too enthusiastically. She pushed away from him by pressing hard against his chest. She flew across the coach and back next to Grace. "Grace, are you awake? It's me, Dani."

Simon clenched his jaw and forced his senses back under control. He'd never been a rake before so why was he being one now? Her friend was perhaps dying in his coach and he was in danger of attacking Dani like some madman. The plain truth is he wanted her. He hadn't been unable to stop thinking about her since she arrived on his doorstep.

"Dani, we need to talk," Simon said. It was time to tell her of his decision never to let her return to the docks. He didn't yet know what he would do with her. Perhaps give her a position as a maid in his household? No, he wouldn't lie to himself. He wanted a far more intimate relationship.

Dani bit her lip and cast a furtive look in his direction. She was shaking. "What?" Another moan drew her attention back to Grace. "I don't think she's awake," Dani said, mournfully. She gently touched Grace's cheek. "She's still so hot."

"Dani…" He wasn't sure what he could say to offer her comfort over Grace's condition. It was probably not the best time to talk about their future, whatever that would be. Simon was, therefore, relieved when the coach came to a stop. The door of the carriage opened and Richmond stood waiting for them.

"Your Grace, Wilkins said to inform you he's gone inside to send a footman to fetch a physician at once," the unflappable Richmond said.

"Excellent," Simon said, picking up Grace from her seat.

He stepped down from the carriage and through the open door of his townhouse. He spotted Mrs. Martin waiting just inside the entry. "What rooms have we available, Mrs. Martin?"

"One of the maids' quarters is vacant, Your Grace."

Simon hesitated. He didn't feel right putting Dani's friend in with the servants, though he didn't know why. He shook his head. "What else?"

Mrs. Martin tried to contain her surprise but failed. "I, uh, well, there's the room down the hall on the second floor next to the governess's."

Simon nodded and headed up the stairs and down the long hall to the room Mrs. Martin told him about. Dani followed closely after him. He placed Grace down gently on the bed Mrs. Martin pointed out.

He stepped back and let Dani get close to her friend. He brushed at the soil on his coat and breeches and said to Mrs. Martin, "I'm going to change. See to it that Dr. Henning is brought to Grace immediately. And don't let him leave before I have a chance to speak with him."

"Yes, Your Grace." Mrs. Martin hesitated. Then she looked like she came to a decision. "A note was delivered by a young boy this afternoon."

"A note?"

"Yes, Your Grace," the housekeeper said. "It's sitting on the tray in the entry hall. He said he was to wait for an answer and was quite disappointed when I said you weren't home."

"Very well, Mrs. Martin." He glanced briefly at Dani but saw she was completely engrossed in Grace. With a nod to Mrs. Martin, he immediately went down the stairs and picked up the folded note on the tray on the front hall table.

If you want to know why Douglas was killed, come to Vauxhall Gardens on Saturday at four.

Chapter Seven

Dani noticed Mrs. Martin hovered over her and Grace as though she expected them to run off with the silver. The very notion of Grace being a threat was ridiculous. But the housekeeper glowered at them from nearby.

"What's wrong with her?" Mrs. Martin demanded from her post. The housekeeper stood with both of her plump hands resting on her hips.

Dani touched the unconscious Grace's ghostly pale cheek gently. Usually Grace's complexion was alive with freckles splattered across her cheeks and chin. Her skin burned beneath Dani's palm. "I'm not sure. His Grace says she got a fever."

Mrs. Martin sniffed but fell silent. Dani was grateful for the quiet. Her mind was a whirl with emotions she never knew existed in her.

Desire, need, longing. Thanks to the duke she now wanted something she never believed she would have. Not really. She might have been better off never knowing what she was missing. What was the matter with her anyway? Shouldn't she be thinking of Grace now not herself?

"The doctor has been sent for," Mrs. Martin told her, now folding her arms across her chest. The older woman shivered, then hesitated. "I could use a spot of tea. It's right chilly in here today."

"Go right ahead, Mrs. Martin," Dani told her. "We'll be all right for a few moments."

"Well…"

"Oh, heavens, Mrs. Martin, Grace isn't in a condition to go pilfering through the house and I've been here for days," Dani pointed out, exasperated.

Mrs. Martin sniffed again. "I was going to ask you if you might like a cup as well."

Dani's face burned with embarrassment. "Oh. I would like one, yes, please."

Mrs. Martin shrugged as if none of it mattered and headed out the door. Dani turned back to Grace. Her friend was unnaturally still but she appeared to be breathing when Dani leaned over to check. She wished the doctor would hurry.

The sound of footsteps coming down the hall told her Mrs. Martin was returning already. Expecting to see the housekeeper, she turned to ask if she needed help with the tea. Instead, the duke stood in the doorway. He had changed his clothes. Now he wore a pair of fawn-colored breeches, a beige lawn shirt and matching cravat, with a fawn-colored coat and brown boots. His mahogany hair had been tied back with a fawn-colored ribbon. The fawn breeches clung to his finely muscled legs almost indecently. Her heart raced. She wanted to please him. To be the perfect lady he deserved. She'd been working very hard on her lessons. Learning to speak properly. It hadn't been that difficult which surprised her. It was coming back to her. Memories of her beautiful mother who had spoke so gently to her.

"How's she doing, Dani?" the duke asked, coming fully into the room.

Dani moistened her dry lips and quickly looked at Grace, guilt for ignoring her friend squelching her longing for the duke.

"Dani?"

"Ah, she's no different," she muttered, keeping her eyes averted.

"Where is that damn physician?" He shook his head and knelt down next to her and Grace. He was so close warmth emanated from him. He studied Grace's matted dark hair, then her too white skin. The duke frowned, then stood up. He reached down and pulled Dani from her seat on the side of the bed, leading her over to a corner of the small room. "Dani, I don't want to say this but I don't think she's going to make it."

The honesty of his words struck her straight to the heart. He thought Grace would die. Misery overwhelmed her. If she had been with Grace she would have been able to take care of her. Tears stung her eyes but she did not fight their flow.

"It's my fault," she whispered, her throat burning from the sorrow that overcame her. "I should have been with her. I never should have left her." She'd been so selfish, only thinking of herself and her own needs.

"It's not your fault, sweetheart," the duke insisted. He took hold of her hands and linked her fingers in his warm ones.

She pulled her hands from his and hurried back to Grace's side. "You can't die, Grace, you can't," she sobbed to her friend, laying her head on Grace's chest. "I can't go on without you."

"Dani…"

"You're all I have, Grace. I won't have no one. No one."

Simon turned when he heard Mrs. Martin returning with the doctor. Relief flooded his senses. At least now the physician would do whatever could be done for Dani's friend.

"Your Grace," Dr. Henning said, nodding at Simon. He was a man of some forty years who wore a neatly trimmed mustache and beard that recently sported some gray. He went right to Grace. Seeing the hysterical woman clinging to his patient, he glanced pleadingly at Simon.

"Dani, the doctor needs to look at Grace now," Simon told her, disengaging her grip. She turned into his arms and buried her face in his chest. He closed his arms around her and sighed.

Mrs. Martin cleared her throat. "I have some tea waiting, Your Grace."

"Very good, Mrs. Martin. That'll be just the thing." Simon tilted Dani's head up until she was looking at him. He smiled gently. "I want you to go have some tea with Mrs. Martin while I speak with Dr. Henning. All right?"

She didn't appear to understand him. She shook her head, opened her mouth to protest.

Mrs. Martin came forward and took her arm. "Come on, Dani. We'll have us a nice warm cup."

Simon waited until Dani and the housekeeper were out of earshot before turning to the doctor. "Well? How bad is she?"

"Very bad. The fever rages in her and her lungs aren't functioning well." Dr. Henning shook his head. He frowned, studying her. "Is she one of your servants, Your Grace?"

"No. A guest." Simon did not elaborate.

Dr. Henning smiled. "I won't ask any questions, Your Grace. After all this time I'm quite used to your strays."

"Yes."

"I really can't say exactly what she has. The, er, streets of London," Henning said, glancing quickly at Simon, "are dangerous. She might have any number of diseases."

"I understand," Simon said. "But will she live? Is there anything we can do for her?"

"I don't know. She will need extensive care. If we can bring her fever down, anything is possible. If she makes it through the night, her chances are better but still not good." Dr. Henning hesitated. "Who was that woman?"

"Dani," Simon said simply, not bothering to pretend his didn't know who Henning referred to.

Dr. Henning nodded. "So she's part of the household now, is she?"

"Something like that." Simon didn't feel it necessary to explain himself to Henning. Or anyone else. He kept his life very private.

"Wilkins told me she's your latest project."

He was going to throttle Wilkins one day. Could he be held accountable for the murder of an impertinent servant? "If there is one thing Dani is not, doctor, it is a project," Simon said harshly.

* * * * *

"There now," Mrs. Martin said soothingly to Dani. "Feel any better?"

Dani sat at the dining room table, a cup of tea held in her shaking hands. The little cakes she treasured were placed in front of her but she could touch not a one. She had ceased her sobbing but tears still freely flowed and her chest hurt. Grace would probably die. Dani felt wretched.

"No, I don't feel any better."

Mrs. Martin, who had never struck Dani as particularly warm, now sat next to her patting her hands in a comforting matter. "His Grace will see that the best is done for your friend."

"He said she might die," Dani said, her bottom lip trembling.

"I see," the housekeeper said, nodding and taking a sip of her own steaming cup of tea. "I'm certain if anyone can see to your friend's health, it'll be His Grace. Dr. Henning has been seeing the family for years. Servants too. Grace will be all right. You'll see."

"I 'ope so," Dani said, mournfully, too upset to try to remember proper speech.

"Aye, he's a kind man, our master," Mrs. Martin assured her. "He'll see to matters." She pointed to the cakes. "Why don't you try eating one of them?"

"I don't think I can."

"I'm not usually the sort who gossips, mind you." Mrs. Martin poured herself more tea. She peered at Dani's tea but set the pot down when she noticed Dani still had a full cup. "But His Grace is prone to taking in outcasts and those not wanted elsewhere."

"That's what Wilkins told me."

Mrs. Martin nodded. "Wilkins is the only servant who came from his father's household. Been with the family for years, Wilkins has. I think he was around when His Grace was a child. Looks down a bit on the rest of us because of our circumstances."

Dani blinked. What was Mrs. Martin trying to tell her? "You don't mean you're an outcast, Mrs. Martin?"

The housekeeper chuckled. "O' course I am."

"But how? You aren't from down by the docks," Dani cried. She set her cup of tea down before her shaking caused any more to spill out.

"Heavens, no. I was a housekeeper for several other employers before I secured this position," Mrs. Martin confided, stuffing her mouth with a bite of one of the cakes. She shook her head and said around the mouthful, "I was sacked from every one."

Dani's eyes widened. Mrs. Martin sacked? She seemed so efficient. "I can hardly believe it."

"Oh, it's all true, my girl. I was horrendous. Why His Grace hired me when I had no references, in fact, quite the opposite, I'll never know. I was extremely grateful though," the woman told her. "I determined right then never to make him regret hiring me and to my knowledge he never has." Her face beamed with pride. As well it should, Dani thought.

"He's just about perfect, isn't he, Mrs. Martin?" she asked, reverently.

"You won't get an argument out of me, Dani." Mrs. Martin offered her the cakes once more but when Dani shook her head, she picked up the tray and set it on the side table. "He's no saint, though, so don't be thinking that."

Dani was struck yet again at how wonderful the duke was. Better than a prince.

"He's no rake either," Mrs. Martin continued.

Dani had heard the term before. "That's a man who beds a lot o' women?"

"Yes. The late duke was a rake and a scoundrel. Lord Jack is a lot like him." Mrs. Martin sniffed her disapproval.

"Does he have a mistress?" Dani wondered, hoping Mrs. Martin wouldn't tell her to keep her nosey questions to herself. Of course she probably didn't want an answer to that question. She regretted asking it. She opened her mouth to say never mind.

Mrs. Martin stared at her a moment then shrugged. She sat back down. "I know he's not seeing the one he did before. Margaret her name was." She made a face. "She didn't fit with his lordship at all."

"Why?" My, she was sticking her nose where it didn't belong, wasn't she?

"Well, like I said, I am not the gossiping type but she wanted more and more money and privileges from him. I heard she demanded he make her his wife."

Dani tried to ignore the sharp pain that pierced her heart. So, a mistress of the duke's never had a chance of being more. She mentally snorted. As if she ever thought different. Not that he had offered her the position. But still, if he were willing for her to be his mistress, even for a short time, she would treasure that time and hold it close all her days. Wouldn't she? If only the thought of him with some beautiful woman from the gentry didn't nauseate her.

"Do you think His Grace is done talking with the doctor?" Dani asked Mrs. Martin. She was anxious to learn what the doctor had to say about Grace's condition.

"I'm sure they'll come downstairs when they've finished." The housekeeper stood up once more and took away the pot of tea. "I've got work to see to. I suggest you stay here until they've finished."

Dani nodded, leaning her chin in her hands. It seemed an eternity before Dr. Henning and the duke finally came down. Her tea was now cold and the gloom from dusky fog outside seemed to permeate the very house. Finally the two men came into the dining room. The duke frowned, which meant the news couldn't be good but the doctor had a slight smile on his face. She couldn't fathom what that meant.

"Dani, Dr. Henning has finished with Grace for today. He'll be back in the morning," His Grace told her.

"Grace?"

"She's very ill," Dr. Henning said. "She'll need someone to look after her carefully tonight until I can come by again tomorrow."

"I'll watch her," Dani said, immediately.

The doctor nodded. "I'll see myself out, Stratford."

The duke waited until Dr. Henning disappeared through the door, then he turned to Dani. "I don't know if I want you staying up all night looking after Grace."

"I don't mind."

"You may not mind but I do." He shook his head. "I'll ask Mrs. Martin to sit with her also. When she isn't available, one of the maids will do."

"I can do it."

"No. I don't want you to become ill too." His stern expression left Dani little doubt that he would continue the argument with her. "I'll see that you are informed when you are not with her. Besides, you need to continue your lessons with Aunt Pen."

The duke took out a slip of paper from his coat pocket and scanned the contents. His frown was troubled.

"What is it?" Dani wondered, pointing to the note.

"Hmm. Someone claiming to know something about Norton's murder wants me to meet them on Saturday at Vauxhall."

"You're not going are you?" Dani didn't quite like the sound of that.

"Yes, I probably will."

"Well," Dani said, thoughtfully. She touched a fingertip to her bottom lip. "I could come with you."

"You?" The duke raised an eyebrow.

Dani knew she had to go with him. She just didn't know why. Finally she thought of something. "Well, suppose one of the men what followed him to The Swan is there. I could identify him."

Chapter Eight

෨

"No," Simon said to Dani the next afternoon, his intent to tell Dani just what he thought of the absurd notion of her accompanying him to Vauxhall Gardens. They were talking just outside Grace's door. He had gone in there to check on Grace's progress and discovered Dani sleeping next to her.

Grace's fever had broken just a bit but she still had not awakened. The doctor had been by earlier to relay the news he was concerned she had not given any sign of waking. Simon hadn't told Dani about that. He thought it better to wait and see rather than see the pain in her beautiful eyes.

Unfortunately, when he insisted she allow Mrs. Martin to stay a bit with Grace while she rested, Dani had brought up the note regarding Vauxhall again. He'd told her it wasn't a good idea the night before.

"But I could help," she protested.

"It could be very dangerous and…"

Wilkins came into the dining room. "Your Grace, the Duke of Scarborough is here. Said he'd wait in the parlor for you."

Scarborough? Simon frowned. What the devil was he doing here?

Wilkins cleared his throat. "Said he was expected. Something about an affair you were to attend."

Hell. He'd forgotten this was the night of Lady Berkeley's ball. Simon had promised his friend he would accompany him, his mother and his young sister for the first few hours.

Dani was eyeing him expectantly. Rotten timing, Scarborough had.

"We'll discuss Vauxhall tomorrow, Dani," Simon said after a moment. He thought of her. Truth told this was the first time he'd seen her all day and he didn't want to walk away again so soon. He was drawn to her. He wanted her, damn it. He could take Dani with him to the ball. Where had that idea come from? She wasn't ready for that, was she? Maybe if Aunt Pen came with her, but Pen still mourned Douglas. A mad notion, surely, but if he kept her close by his side, maybe... He turned to Wilkins, thoughtfully. "Most of Jessica's gowns are still in the room Dani is using, aren't they, Wilkins?"

"Yes, Your Grace. Lady Jessica said she thought they might prove useful to Lady Lucy one day."

Simon nodded. "Have one of the maids show Dani and help her dress properly for the Berkeley Ball."

Simon wasn't sure whose gasp of surprise was more exaggerated, Dani's or Wilkins'. They both stared at him, their mouths agape, as though they were certain he'd lost his mind. He wasn't ready to let Dani out of his sight just yet. Images of the life she had led still swam through his mind. He had an intense need to protect her, to keep her by his side. Going to the East End and fetching Grace yesterday made the instinct in him even stronger.

Taking Dani with him to the ball might be a little insane but he was going to do it. Who would dare stop him? She would stay by his side and not speak to anyone. He could make it work. He'd go and speak to Aunt Pen. Surely she would be able to help him find someone to chaperone Dani. One of the ladies from the Survivors group his mother and aunt had formed.

"But, what about Grace?" Dani stammered after a moment. Her periwinkle eyes were overly bright.

"You'll only be gone a few hours and her fever has eased," he said with a false sense of cheer. He felt a bit guilty, but Grace would be all right. "You can look in on her as soon as we return. Mrs. Martin and the maids will care for her." He gave Dani what he hoped was a reassuring smile. "It'll be fine,

Dani. Come down to the parlor when you're ready. I'll be waiting."

* * * * *

Simon had known Julian Baird, the Duke of Scarborough, for many years and counted him among his few close friends. They'd gone to Oxford together.

He found his friend sitting in a chair, leaning his head back, his fingers linked together behind his fair head, his eyes closed as though in sleep.

Scarborough was dressed in elegant black evening attire, his ivory cravat tied in the latest crisp fashion.

Scarborough opened his eyes and briefly scanned Simon. He closed them again and sighed. "You're not dressed."

"It will take me but a moment. I'd frankly forgotten all about the affair."

"Wish I could," Scarborough muttered. "I suspect you've had your hands full the last few days what with young Norton's murder."

"That's the least of it," Simon replied. "I came here to make sure you were comfortable while you waited." Simon raised a brow. "I needn't have worried."

Scarborough smiled but kept his eyes closed. "I'm never one to stand on ceremony."

"I'll be back in a moment." Simon wondered if he ought to tell Scarborough about Dani accompanying them. He shrugged and decided it could wait.

Dani wasn't at all certain the gown the maid had picked out suited her. She studied herself with a critical eye in the looking glass.

The gown was a deep violet, which the maid had enthused, would look smashing with Dani's eyes. The color was lovely, Dani agreed but the way the bodice of the gown drooped down to expose her breasts gave her no little pause.

"You look beautiful," the maid, who'd introduced herself as Maggie, proclaimed. She stood back, hands on her hips, to survey Dani.

"You don't think it's a bit much?" Dani asked, worrying her bottom lip between her teeth. She crossed her arms in front of her bosom.

"No, not at all, miss," Maggie assured her. "It really, er, how do you say it, accentuates your attributes." The maid smiled.

That was exactly what Dani was worried about. She stared down at the matching violet slippers that peeked out from under the gown. They didn't exactly fit, they were a little loose. She hoped she wouldn't embarrass the duke by slipping out of them at the ball. Or with her dancing. Would he allow her to dance? Sometimes when business was slow, Mary would teach Dani and Grace a few dance steps. Mary hadn't explained how she knew the dances and they hadn't questioned her. Dani loved to dance. They would laugh all day pretending to dance with dandies from the *ton*. Lady Norton had only just showed her a bit of it as well. She still had much to learn. Never had she thought of really going to a ball. She could hardly believe he was taking her with him.

Her heart beat so loudly she was surprised Maggie didn't comment on it. She pressed her hand to her chest to feel the racing.

Maggie twisted her mouth and gazed at Dani's hair. "Now just to do something with your locks. It's such a pretty color, miss."

Maggie came forward with a hairbrush and after a few tries bound up Dani's light red hair in a knot at her nape. She made sure a few tendrils dangled here and there.

The maid stood back and smiled at her handiwork. "Lovely. Just lovely. I only wish I had some violets we could stick in there too. Well, it's perfect anyway. Go on downstairs and show His Grace."

Dani took a moment more to view herself in the mirror. She felt almost pretty. She wistfully touched her reflection. Treasure each moment, Dani, she told herself.

Simon stepped out of his bedchamber, ready to make his way back to the parlor. He closed the door with one last order to his valet.

"I was coming to see you," Jack said, coming down the hall toward him.

Simon immediately noticed Jack's cravat was missing and his shirt torn. "What the devil…"

Jack grinned. Touched his lip gingerly. There was blood on his mouth and bruises on his face. "I need a drink."

"What happened?" Simon demanded, studying Jack's face closely. There was a large black bruise on Jack's left cheek just under his eye and another one to match on the right side of his jaw. Dried blood was encrusted around Jack's nose.

"Whatever you do, don't touch anything," Jack said. "It hurts like hell."

"You've been fighting," Simon accused.

Jack snorted. "Your gift for stating the obvious never ceases to amaze me."

"Explain yourself." Simon's jaw tightened.

"Just a misunderstanding at a hell. Man though I was cheating him and got a bit nasty."

"You're lucky to be alive."

"Something like that," Jack agreed. "Took everything I had too. Fortunately, I was able to convince a hackney to take me here. Wilkins paid him the fare. Good man, Wilkins."

"I'm glad you're so casual about nearly being killed." Simon shook his head. He surveyed Jack's arms and chest. "Are you injured anywhere else? Did he have a knife?"

"A wicked one." Jack nodded. "But no, I was able to get it away from him." He attempted a lopsided grin. "I guess I'll need a few pounds until my monthly allowance comes due."

"My man of affairs will be by tomorrow for our usual appointment. Rest up tonight. I'll talk to you tomorrow. I'm late."

Jack reached down and pulled the note Simon received from the waistband of his breeches. He waved it at Simon. "Speaking of appointments…"

Simon frowned. "That's a private note, Jack."

"If you want to know why Douglas was killed, come to Vauxhall Gardens on Saturday at four," Jack read out loud. He raised one dark eyebrow. "Very mysterious, eh? Word of warning, Simon, if you want your private notes to remain so, don't leave them lying around."

"I'll remember that." Simon grabbed the note out of his brother's hand.

Jack eyed the note dispassionately. "You're not fool enough to go there, are you?"

"You don't think I should?"

"You'll do what you want, I've no doubt and out of some absurd notion you owe it to our aunt but if you ask me, it's probably some sort of trap," Jack said. He nodded to emphasize his conclusion.

Simon had considered the possibility as well. But still, he could not back down from the challenge. "Pen is counting on me."

Jack snorted. "Of course she is. Everyone counts on reliable Simon, don't they?"

"Leave it be, Jack," Simon muttered. He rubbed his aching temples. It was time he got downstairs. He didn't want Dani to reach the parlor and run into Scarborough without him.

"If you insist on trudging off to such a boring place as Vauxhall," Jack said quietly. "Then there's no hope for it. I shall accompany you."

"You?" Simon asked, not even bothering to keep the surprise out of his expression.

"It doesn't say anything about your coming alone," Jack pointed out, with a vague smile. "It might be amusing."

"Why do you want to come?"

Jack shrugged, then flexed his shoulders, groaning. "I shouldn't move like that. Still a bit sore." He sighed. "Because I know that you are going no matter how much I try to talk you out of it. *Noblesse oblige* and all that nonsense. There's something I don't think you've realized, Simon."

"What's that?" Simon frowned.

"You're mortal. If this mysterious person who penned your note is the murderer it might be some twisted plot to kill another peer of the realm. We wouldn't want that victim to be you, would we?"

"I'm surprised that isn't just what you do want, Jack." Simon smiled a little. "You could inherit the family fortunes."

"What in the world would I gain out of your untimely death, Simon?" Jack asked innocently. "I don't want to be the duke."

"Very well," Simon said, after a moment of silence. "I suppose it won't hurt to have two of us going to Vauxhall." He hesitated. "Dani wants to come too."

"Dani?" Jack's eyes widened a moment. Then he smiled. "She's got spunk. Got to admire that. Are you bringing her?"

"I don't think so. Could be dangerous."

"With us two big strapping men to protect her?" Jack grinned. "Bring her." He crossed his arms in front of his chest and leaned against the nearby wall. "This gets more interesting all the time."

Dani stood in front of the parlor door trying to decide whether she should knock first. After all, the duke did have a guest. Another duke, according to what Wilkins said. It wouldn't be proper to just rush right in, would it?

Letting out the breath she was holding, her stomach fluttering, Dani tapped the door lightly with her knuckles. There was no answering response. Frowning, Dani wondered if they had left without her. She hadn't taken that long. Her stomach fell with disappointment at the prospect of the duke leaving her behind after getting her all excited about attending a *ton* function. Dani realized she really had no right to feel this way. At least that's what she told herself.

The only way to find out was to go in. Opening the door, she stepped into the room. Her gaze searched the room, a painful lump forming in her throat. Dani was about to turn away when she spied movement in a chair at the back of the room. She'd nearly missed the blond giant lounging there.

The same moment she noticed him, he appeared to realize there was someone in the room with him, for he opened one blue eye and peered at her. Both eyes opened, startled. He straightened, staring openly at her.

"Who the devil are you?" The blond giant demanded, somewhat irritably.

"Dani."

The man stood up to his full height, which, Dani realized as he loomed over her, was considerable. She tilted her head to look at him.

"You aren't a friend of Lucy's are you?"

Dani shook her head, still gaping at him. He was the sort of man, she figured, most women would swoon over. Large, blond and angelic looking. But to her, Simon was much more beautiful.

The man frowned, then his expression cleared. He smiled, showing perfect straight white teeth. "I know. You must be a friend of Jack's."

"No," Dani said, then thought better of her answer. "Well, yes, I suppose so. Are you the Duke of Scarbatten?"

His grin widened. "Scarborough. Yes, that would be me."

Dani nodded, taking in his elegant black evening clothes. "His Grace says I'm to go with you to her ladyship's ball."

Scarborough's frown returned. "Does he indeed? How…fascinating."

Chapter Nine

∞

"Did you say Dani was your name?" Scarborough purred. The infamous rake had Dani's hand trapped in his grasp, a fake but effective smile dazzling his face.

Simon, who'd been standing in the doorway to witness the irritating scene, came forward and smoothly removed Dani's hand from his friend's. "That's Miss Crest to you, Scarborough."

Simon had no idea where his invented name for Dani had come from, it just came into his head the moment he'd extracted Dani from Scarborough's grasp. He linked his fingers with hers, frowned somewhat darkly in his friend's direction and turned to take in Dani's appearance.

His breathing stopped, his chest constricting. Simon had thought her lovely before in his sister's discarded yellow gown but standing before her now, he couldn't remember a woman more achingly beautiful.

The violet of the gown set off the lilting periwinkle of her eyes. The bodice was very nearly indecent in the amount of her perfectly rounded breasts that it exposed, but Simon knew though the gown was from two seasons ago, it was still fashionable. It swept down past her long shapely legs, the toes of the matching slippers just barely visible.

The ringlets of her red hair framing her nibble-enticing ears were a temptation Simon fought to resist. He wanted to tell Scarborough to go to the devil with the Berkeley Ball. Bury his face in the column of her throat. And take her to bed. If he didn't stop his errant thoughts, Scarborough would be amused about the plain evidence of his arousal.

"You didn't tell me you were bringing such a delightful friend," Scarborough commented dryly.

"Miss Crest is a guest in my home." Simon sent a warning gaze in Scarborough's direction. "Under my complete protection."

"Hmm. Indeed." Scarborough's lips twitched. "Where did you say Miss…Crest was from?"

Simon shrugged, not taking his friend's bait. "I didn't say. Are we all ready to leave? We need to make a quick stop to fetch Aunt Pen's dear friend Lady Aberlie. My aunt sent her round a note while we were making preparations. She'll be accompanying us. I am sure your mother and sister are anxiously waiting for your appearance."

Simon glanced to the window as he spoke. The day had been cold, the night would be colder. Dani didn't have a wrap sufficient for the elements. He reminded himself tomorrow he would have to take her shopping. He'd bring along a maid as her chaperone. Pen wouldn't want to appear in public yet. In the meantime, he would have Wilkins fetch something suitable from upstairs.

When they were safely ensconced in Scarborough's carriage Simon relaxed a little. He'd thought to bring a maid to sit in the carriage with them. He didn't care about the proprieties but others did, so he took the extra precaution. As for Dani, he would make sure she never left his side during the evening and would speak as little as possible. He exhaled. She could be a family friend from the country. If he knew his friend, Scarborough wouldn't stay long. If Scarborough didn't stay true to form, Simon would hire a carriage home.

Scarborough shifted in his seat. He stretched out his legs in front of him and sighed rather dramatically.

Simon felt Dani's gaze. He smiled reassuringly.

"It will be fine, Dani. Stay close to me and don't talk to anyone but myself or Scarborough. All right?"

"Yes, Your Grace."

He kept his voice low. "I've meant to tell you how wonderfully you are doing with your lessons. I spoke to Pen and she is very pleased. I heard you painted a watercolor this morning."

She blushed. "Well, it was just a tree."

He smiled. "I knew you were clever and would learn fast."

Scarborough cleared his throat.

"Why don't you tell me about what you've learned regarding Norton," Scarborough said, briefly glancing out at the gloomy darkness. "Might take my mind off this insipid event."

Dani tensed beside him and Simon wondered at it. He was grateful, himself, for the distraction Norton's murder would provide him.

"Not much to tell," Simon said, shrugging. "I've learned Norton spent the better part of the evening he was murdered engaging in cards with Dresden, Pembroke and Carstairs. I'll be looking to speak with all three men."

"Lady Berkeley's ball is just the sort of affair where I would expect to find a fop like Dresden," Scarborough commented, shifting in his seat once more. "You might get your chance tonight."

Simon nodded. "Good, then it may not be a complete waste of time." Dani flinching ever-so slightly made him aware how completely jaded they must sound to her. She was, no doubt, thrilled to her toes at the opportunity to attend a ball of the *ton*. Most young ladies her age could barely contain their excitement at the prospect, let alone someone of Dani's background.

Dani shivered when the duke rubbed her thumb with his in a featherlight stroke. Ever since he'd come into the parlor and taken hold of her hand, staring at her as though he could eat her, she'd been excited and thrilled beyond any measure.

The duke acted downright possessive. Held her hand, tugged her along, all like she belonged to him.

Her decision to come to his home had been the right one, she decided. Spending that bit of blunt she got from the magistrate on a hackney had been hard to rationalize but now Dani knew, somehow, that she was fated to meet the duke.

Growing up, always afraid, always wondering what garbage she would dig up her next meal from, wondering if she would be able to hide another night from the slimy predators around her, Dani dreamed about another life. Better than even being a seamstress. One she was just certain she was destined to live. Even told Grace and Mary about her dream. They'd scoffed, not meanly but it was plain they didn't believe her.

Dani flushed with guilt. She should be beside Grace, looking after her, not attending a fancy party with the duke. Grace's fever broke overnight, but she still hadn't awakened and her color was not good. The duke said it would be all right and she had to believe him.

The carriage bumped underneath, jolting her. Her leg touched the duke's. Warmth radiated from him. An unexpected surge of desire heated her blood. After her rape she'd never expected to feel this way about any man.

She cast a wary glance at the older woman sitting primly next to her. Lady Aberlie. Lady Aberlie was a tall, thin woman with very dark hair streaked through with gray. She wore a rather severe plum gown. Apparently, Simon had told her, she was a fairly close friend of Lady Berkeley and would make the introductions. Lady Aberlie had been polite and gracious, but Dani guessed it would be difficult to say no to either the duke or his aunt.

The carriage pulled to a stop and Dani could barely contain her excitement. Her stomach flipped. She only hoped she wouldn't provide the duke with any reason to regret taking her with him. All that she'd already learned from Lady Norton filled her head.

A footman opened the door and reached a hand in to help her down. Dani stared at the oddly dressed servant. His knee breeches and matching coat were a shimmery peach. He wore a powdered wig neatly tied back with a peach ribbon. The footman appeared not to notice her stare.

The maid who had also accompanied them excused herself to go on ahead to the retiring room for maids inside the Berkeley manor.

Dani wondered at the Duke of Scarborough's blanched expression. Her own duke tucked her hand firmly in the crook of his arm, and offering his other arm to Lady Aberlie tugged them toward the long winding outdoor staircase that led to an enormous set of double doors. Next to the bottom of the stairs were two statues of what appeared to be children with wings.

Dani noted the same winged figures had been elaborately carved into the ornate entrance doors. Scarborough jumped ahead of them and headed quickly to the doors. Several others of the gentry were arriving in the queue of carriages.

A pair of footmen, similarly outfitted in peach, were stationed at the ornate doors. They opened them wide at Scarborough's approach. Dani, Lady Aberlie and the duke followed closely behind.

Another servant in peach waited inside the front hall, ready to announce the arrival of the guests for the ball. While he was occupied announcing the couple ahead of them, Dani had time to survey the large room below. On either side of the platform they stood on were stairs that would lead them down into the crowded ballroom. Along each set of stairs were vines of peach flowers all the way down to the floor. From the ceiling hung even more peach flowers. Dani couldn't imagine how they'd placed them up so high.

"Don't announce me," Scarborough said to the servant when the man requested his name. His lip curled up ever-so slightly. He turned to Dani and the duke. "I'm going to find Mama and my sister. I'll see you around."

The duke waved his friend away and slipped past the footman announcing names before he moved on to them. He, Lady Aberlie and Dani weaved their way down the right set of stairs and into the lively ballroom below.

Dani had never seen so many brightly colored dresses. Every shade of blue and yellow was represented and she noted more than one lady dressed in a peach that matched the decor. She wondered at it.

"Come, Miss Crest, I see Lady Berkeley. We shall make the introductions," Lady Aberlie announced. "Your Grace, you needn't come with us if you'd rather mingle."

"No, that is quite all right," Simon replied. "I will pay my respects."

Dani nervously followed the imposing woman in plum. *Please don't let me say anything to embarrass the duke.*

Lady Berkeley stood among a group of colorfully gowned ladies. The hostess herself wore a gown of the same shimmery peach as her footmen. She smiled in their direction and quickly excused herself and walked forward to greet them.

"My, Stratford, what an absolute pleasure and a surprise to have you here," Lady Berkeley, a handsome blonde woman of perhaps thirty, said. "And Lady Aberlie. What a lovely gown." She touched her cheek to Lady Aberlie's before allowing the duke to briefly bow over her gloved hand.

"Lady Berkeley," he murmured.

She glanced at Dani. "And who would this be?"

Lady Aberlie took hold of Dani's hand. "This is Miss Crest. She has arrived from the country to offer comfort and companionship to Lady Norton during this terrible time. As you can imagine, Lady Norton so wished to be here, but she is simply devastated by the untimely passing of her son. She asked me to bring Miss Crest to you."

Lady Berkeley smiled kindly. "What a lovely young lady you are, Miss Crest. I am certain you shall have a wonderful season with Lady Norton and Lady Aberlie sponsoring you."

"I am very pleased to meet you, Lady Berkeley," Dani said slowly and carefully.

Lady Berkeley opened her mouth to speak when a portly gentleman touched her arm. She turned at once.

"My dear, a word."

"Yes, my lord." Lady Berkeley turned to them with an apologetic smile. "I'm so sorry, I'll only be a moment."

Dani blew out a breath, glad the whole business of an introduction had been accomplished.

"My dear Lady Aberlie," the duke spoke from next to Dani. "Is that not Lady Hendricks? I believe she is waving you to her side."

Lady Aberlie glanced where he indicated. "Oh…yes. That is her. Excuse me a moment, will you?"

The duke smiled. "Of course."

He waited for her to disappear in the direction of her friend before he took Dani's hand and put it on his arm. "Come on. Lady Aberlie will surely believe you are safe with Lady Berkeley."

He led her away and toward the entrance. Dani heard a collective gasp around them. A group of young beautiful ladies were staring openly at her and the duke. One, in the middle of the group of about six, raised an elegantly shaped blonde brow in their direction. The woman was dressed in a deep emerald gown with a low-cut bodice. She leaned over and whispered something to the brunette woman next to her, who laughed and then smirked in Dani's direction.

The duke, whose gaze was drifting across the room, did not appear to notice the ladies. Dani was about to comment on them when they approached like a swarm and surrounded both her and the duke.

"Your Grace," the blonde said in a husky voice. "What a delight it is to see you here tonight. I had no idea you would be attending."

"First, His Grace the Duke of Scarborough and now, you," her brunette friend said, giggling. She batted her lashes. "This night is proving to be more interesting than I dared imagine."

The duke favored the gaggle of ladies with a smile. "Miss Morely, Miss Divers."

The blonde, clearly Miss Morely, cast her icy gaze briefly at Dani, before returning her smile to the duke.

"You did promise to dance with me at the next ball you attended." She curved her fingers over his arm. "You do remember, don't you, Your Grace?"

"If you dance with Amanda, you must dance with me," Miss Divers exclaimed, to Dani's surprise, shooting a look of scornful challenge at her friend.

"And me," another of the ladies called out, giggling.

"I'm sorry. My family is still mourning the death of my cousin. There won't be any dancing tonight" the duke said. He gently disengaged Miss Morely's gloved fingers from his arm. "If you will excuse me, Miss Crest and I are looking for someone. I'm afraid I cannot stay long."

"Miss Crest?" Amanda Morely, lifted a looking glass up from around her neck. She peered at Dani coldly. "I don't recall meeting her before."

"She arrived from the country to stay with the family and keep my aunt company. An old family friend," the duke said. "If you will excuse us."

Amanda Morely pouted. "Well, if you must."

"Perhaps the next ball I attend, Miss Morely."

She sniffed. "I hope I will see you at Lady Needham's ball on Saturday."

He inclined his head.

The blonde woman brightened noticeably. "I do so want to ask you about your investigation." She lowered her voice to a husky whisper. "I've heard you mean to find the culprit who murdered your poor cousin."

The duke bade goodbye to the group of ladies and moved further into the room.

"Let's hope we can find Dresden quickly," he said, smiling down at Dani.

Her heart picked up its rapid pace. He was so handsome, it nearly hurt to look at him, Dani thought fancifully. She would remember this wonderful night forever.

"Stratford."

They both turned at the male voice coming from behind them. A pretty young man dressed in dark blue evening clothes with a pale blue shirt and cravat bowed before them.

"I'm Dresden. Scarborough told me you wanted to see me."

The duke nodded. "Yes. Is there somewhere we can speak privately?"

Dresden glanced at Dani. "The card room?"

The duke grimaced. "No, not there." He seemed to consider something. Then he inclined his head toward Dani. "My friend, Miss Crest, will be joining us. If you don't mind."

The tone he used gave Dani the impression that Dresden was not being given the option to argue the point. She held her breath, waiting for the young man to answer.

Dresden stared coldly at the duke, then flicked a glance at Dani. "This is about Douglas Norton, isn't it?"

"Yes."

"What does Miss Crest have to do with this?"

"A friend of the family from the country. She's assisting my aunt during this difficult time and is helping me in my investigation."

Dresden frowned darkly, he brushed at the sleeve of his right arm. "Very well. I'm meeting someone later, so if you don't mind let's make this quick." He scanned the throng of people behind Dani and the duke.

"The library," the duke said, his own voice cool. "Do you know it?"

"Yes," Dresden said, nodding.

"Meet us there in five minutes."

Simon watched Dresden disappear dispassionately. He didn't care for the fop's attitude at all. If Dani were not there with him he would be sorely tempted to extract the information out of Dresden in a different way. Plastering a smile on his face to mask his irritation, he threaded his fingers through hers.

"Shall we head for the library?"

They'd only taken a few steps when Dani saw him. A man standing off to the side of the ballroom, leaning casually against the wall. With dark, nearly black hair streaked with a smattering of gray at his temples, the man was older than the duke by some years but still very handsome in a dark way. His regard, focused on Dani, was intent, unnerving. She missed a step and stumbled against the duke.

"Easy," he said, steadying her, smiling inquiringly.

Dani licked her lip nervously, grasped his hand tight. "Who is that man?"

He frowned. "Man?"

"Over there against that wall." Dani turned to show him who she meant but the space the man had been occupying was empty. Feeling like a dolt, she attempted a smile. "I guess it wasn't anything. Just a man staring at me. He's gone now."

He ran his thumb along her bottom lip. "It would be difficult for any man not to stare at you, sweetheart."

Her heart light, Dani let Simon lead her to the library.

Simon nodded to several peers he knew and shook his head at those who tried to stop him for conversation. On the way through the ballroom to the long hallway that would take them to the Berkeleys' library, he glanced around trying to locate Scarborough.

Almost to the hall, he finally spotted the tall blond duke, leaning over to speak with his young sister, whose face glowed with the excitement of her first season. Satisfied Scarborough would not be leaving soon, he steered Dani through the door that would take them to the library.

Reaching the door, the hair on the back of his neck prickled. Simon hesitated. His senses screamed a warning. Yet he heard no unusual sound coming from inside. Dani looked a question at him. He smiled reassuringly and opened the door.

Dresden had reached the library before them and was sitting in a chair facing the French doors that led out to the garden.

"Dresden?" Simon called out, tugging Dani further into the room with him. He'd been in the Berkeley library once a few years ago with Lady Berkeley herself. He noted the same chaise still sat before the fireplace. The dark wood-paneled room was barely lit by a single candelabrum.

Dresden did not answer. He just stared out the partially open French doors. Simon came round the large chaise and to the front of the chair Dresden sat in.

Dani gasped and buried her face in his neck. Dresden's eyes were wide open but unseeing. His throat had been slit.

Chapter Ten

"Maybe someone's killing all of society's reprobates and fops," Scarborough commented dryly in the carriage some hours later. He smiled wryly into the gloom of the dimly lit vehicle.

"If that were true you might be next," Simon returned, his gaze falling briefly on the carriage window, where the first signs of dawn streaked through, then on the sleeping woman snuggled next to him. He gently brushed Dani's curls. Finding Dresden murdered had been an ordeal for her. Endless questions. No answers.

"I'm far too clever for any murderer," his friend assured him arrogantly. "So Dresden's out, who's next on your list?"

Simon briefly told Scarborough about the note he'd received to meet a mysterious someone at Vauxhall Gardens on Saturday.

"I see." Scarborough's tone was flat.

"You don't approve of my going."

"I'm fairly certain you can handle yourself, Simon," Scarborough told him, steepling his long fingers. "I do urge caution."

Dani murmured softly when the carriage hit a bump in the road. Simon pulled her closer.

"You care to tell me about Miss Crest?"

Simon did not miss the thread of amusement in Scarborough's voice. He decided to choose his words carefully. More to protect Dani than himself.

"She comes from outside our usual circle."

Scarborough snorted. "To put it mildly."

Simon cleared his throat and peered once more at the dawn. "She's not used to society's dictates."

"Hmm. She's more used to the dictates of London's East End, I'd wager," Scarborough said, holding up a hand at Simon's grunt of protest. "I don't care who you choose to play with, Simon, truly, you have always had eccentric tastes, just be certain you know what you're doing. You're too trusting sometimes." His cynical gaze drifted to Dani's peacefully sleeping face. "She's beautiful, yes but what do you really know about her kind?"

His friend's words annoyed Simon. He hadn't known Dani long and he even suspected she twisted the truth about what she'd seen down by The Black Swan but her spirit was truer than many he'd known.

"You said a moment ago you were certain I could handle myself," Simon said coldly.

"Don't ruffle your feathers." Scarborough shifted his large frame on the seat. "Just a little warning."

"Julian..." Simon stopped his own warning to his friend when Dani stirred in his arms. He glanced down at her and smiled when she opened her eyes. For a moment they remained unfocused. The carriage lurched to a stop.

"It appears we've arrived at your home, Stratford," Scarborough said. "Is there anything I can do to assist?"

"Not right now."

Scarborough inclined his head. "I'll call on you later if I learn anything new about Norton or Dresden."

A few minutes later Dani and the duke watched the Duke of Scarborough's carriage roll off down the cobbled lane. The maid who'd accompanied them, and slept all the way, had already made her way toward the servant's entrance. Dani peered at the light reddish sky. The sun had begun its rise over the horizon.

She didn't remember falling asleep or getting into the coach. The duke smiled reassuringly at her and clasped her hand in his. He pulled her toward the door to his home.

"Do you think Grace has been all right since I've been gone?" Dani wondered fretfully. She'd never intended to be away from her friend until dawn. She bit her lip.

"Let's go and see."

The door opened on their approach and a weary-looking Wilkins stood holding the door for them. The sourpuss sneered ever-so slightly in her direction before turning his full attention to his employer.

"Your Grace, I did expect you home some hours ago. It was my understanding that you would be staying at the Berkeley Ball for a short duration." His tone was one of censure. Dani wondered how long the old butler had been getting away with such impertinence.

"There was a bit of excitement at the ball, Wilkins," the duke told him, gently pushing Dani inside in front of him. He handed both his greatcoat and her borrowed wrap to the old butler. He followed her into the foyer and Wilkins shut the door with a click.

"Excitement, Your Grace?" The old buzzard raised a bushy white brow. "What happened? Did Lord Berkeley find out about her ladyship's trysts?"

The duke smirked. "While that might have been entertaining, no. The Earl of Dresden was found murdered in the Berkeleys' library."

"Murdered you say?" exclaimed Wilkins.

"Your Grace, can I go to Grace now?" Dani asked, trying to tamp down her impatience. She did care about the poor man's murder but she wanted to be sure nothing had happened to Grace during her absence.

"Just a moment, Dani." He turned to Wilkins and patted the butler on the arm. "I'll tell you about Dresden later, Wilkins. Has there been any change to Dani's friend?"

"No, Your Grace. Mrs. Martin is with her now."

"Come on, Dani," he snagged her hand once more and towed her to the stairs leading to the upstairs rooms. Wilkins disappeared into the darkness below.

At the top of the stairs, the duke stopped and turned her to face him. "Let's see Grace," he said softly, his lips touching hers in brief contact.

The old buzzard had been right, Dani quickly realized when she hurried into the sickroom. Grace looked no different. Which, though it meant her condition had not improved, she hadn't worsened either. Mrs. Martin rose from her chair by the hearth when Dani and the duke came in.

"She's said a few words," Mrs. Martin told them, her hands on her hips, surveying her charge. "Nothing I could make out though."

"Thank you for watching her, Mrs. Martin," Dani said, smiling gratefully. She sat on the edge of the bed and grasped one of Grace's thin hands. "She's so cold."

"Stoke up the fire some more, Mrs. Martin," Simon ordered his housekeeper. "And add some more bedclothes to the bed. Did you use a warmer?"

"No, Your Grace, but I'll see to it now," Mrs. Martin assured him.

"How long have you been with Grace?"

"Just a few hours. Maggie was watching her before. I've got more left in me."

The duke smiled. "Very good. After Dani has had some rest, I am sure that she will want to stay with her friend for a while."

"I can stay with her now," Dani assured him, her eyes wide. Her grip on her friend's hand was tight.

"No." He came forward and extracted her from Grace's side. "Grace will need you to be strong."

Dani opened her mouth to protest but one look from the duke told her she had better not. She really wasn't sleepy at all. Maybe because she'd slept after they'd found Dresden and then again in Scarborough's coach. But she allowed herself to be led from Grace's sickroom.

Dani swallowed the hard lump that formed in her throat. She owed so much to Grace. She wiped at a tear. "I can stay with her, Your Grace, honest."

"You're obviously exhausted and overwrought. I promise you we are watching Grace around the clock. You can sit with her all the rest of today after your lessons if you like." He led her down the hall to her room and opened her door.

Dani nodded. She knew he was doing all he could to help her and Grace. "Thank you, Your Grace. You must be tired, too."

The duke yawned. "I am a bit." He framed her chin in his hands and looked intently at her. "Dani, I want you to start calling me Simon."

If he'd told her to call him Prinny she couldn't have been more surprised. Call the duke Simon? Could she do that?

"I..."

"I insist, Dani." His thumb stroked her bottom lip. "Say my name."

Her lungs seized momentarily. She swallowed in an attempt to regain her wits. "Simon."

Her reward was a heart-melting smile. Dani blinked against the sheer impact of it.

"Sleep well, Dani."

Chapter Eleven

ಬ

"And off we go," Jack commented to Simon and Dani when the coach began moving away from the St. James Square toward Vauxhall Garden Saturday afternoon.

Simon's brother sat next to him in the carriage, his arms crossed in front of him, the pale yellow cravat he wore slightly askew. His right leg was crossed in front of him, his boot resting on his left knee. Next to Dani was one of the household maids.

"You've made out nicely, haven't you?" Jack asked Dani with a grin.

They'd just come from the dressmaker's. Amélie, the French seamstress was named. Dani still felt annoyed by her near pawing of Simon. Amélie'd been draped all over him.

It had been difficult to enjoy the experience of being measured for all the lovely gowns that Simon had insisted on ordering for her. She'd wanted to wring Amélie's neck.

But Jack was right. Dani had been shocked at how many different gowns Simon had ordered for her. Gown after gown in endless shades of purple. Then gowns in yellow, green, blue, even pink. Her head was still swimming.

According to the evil Amélie, Dani had to have a different gown for every occasion. And the gown one was to wear in the morning was different from what was worn at night. She was to have matching slippers for all the gowns too.

Dani slid a glance at Simon, wondering how much it would all cost him. She couldn't even begin to guess and she supposed asking would be terrible. She licked her bottom lip. Being a man's potential mistress was complicated. Assuming that was what was happening. He was becoming more affectionate with her all the time. Then there was having Lady Norton teach her how to be a proper lady and now all the clothes.

If all the dresses and matching slippers had not been enough, Simon insisted she was to have several wraps and bonnets. She could never repay such overwhelming kindness. And when he got tired of her…

She glanced once more in his direction but he seemed to be paying neither herself nor Jack any attention. He'd been preoccupied since they'd returned to the carriage. Dani hoped she hadn't done anything wrong.

Jack loosened his cravat, causing it to look even more off center. "What did Henning say about your friend, Dani?"

Dr. Henning came by that morning and spent a long time with Grace. As soon as he finished, Simon and Dani spoke to him about her care.

Dani looked to Simon, who feeling her gaze turned from staring out the window.

"Not much improvement since the fever broke," Simon spoke up for the first time since they'd left for Vauxhall. "She still hasn't awakened though she has done some mumbling. He'll stop by this evening to check on her." Simon attempted a smile at Dani but he had a suspicion it fell flat.

"I'm surprised he doesn't want to bleed her." Jack snorted. He leaned his head back in the carriage and closed his eyes.

"That's old medicine," Simon retorted. "Dr. Henning isn't that sort."

"If you say so."

Simon studied Jack silently for a minute. His brother's usual lightly tanned color was absent. Around his lips he was white, his eyes looked vaguely pained. "Are you all right?"

"Never better," his brother muttered.

Simon recalled Wilkins mentioning something about Jack having a dawn appointment. A duel? He frowned darkly. Surely his wayward brother wasn't fighting challenges over some light-skirt?

He opened his mouth to ask his brother when Jack sighed heavily and leaned his head back against the seat wearily. Jack rubbed his temples.

Dani looked quizzically at Simon. "What's the plan?"

Simon grinned nonchalantly. "I don't exactly have one."

Jack's head rose from the seat. He quirked an eyebrow. "You intend to just show up at Vauxhall and hope someone doesn't come up behind you with a knife." His brother shook his head. "Amazing. Do me a favor and stick close to my side. No offense but I'm usually better at the rough stuff than you are."

"Yeah, right," Simon said scornfully. "Care to be reminded of all the scrapes I've rescued you from? Shall we talk about that scuffle with Lord Falhearth? Or the duel you almost were engaged in over Lady Haverly?"

Jack flushed slightly. "I was only jesting."

Simon noticed Dani out of the corner of his eye, smiling. He turned his attention to her.

She looked positively edible, he noted, in the gown Amélie had provided for her right away. It was a shade of lavender that went especially well with her red hair and periwinkle eyes. The maid had dressed her curls in ringlets atop her head. A spray of violets tucked in the knot at her nape completed the look.

"Lucy wanted to come with us."

Jack's casually spoken words drew Simon's sharp attention from the temptress across from him.

"Lucy? How did Lucy even know we're going?" Simon fixed an accusing look on Jack.

"You know how she loves it there," Jack said, grinning sheepishly. "I let it slip."

"It's bad enough I'm taking Dani there with so much uncertainty," Simon said, angrily.

Jack smiled serenely. "Do you happen to see Lucy anywhere in this carriage?"

"You shouldn't have mentioned it." Lord, he sounded pompous. He shifted in his seat, hoping he sounded worse to his own ears that he sounded to Dani. He cleared his throat. "We'll take her there another day."

"I already told her so," Jack advised.

The carriage rumbled to a stop and Simon removed his pocket watch to check the time. They still had half an hour before the appointed time but he wanted to arrive early to have a chance to look around for anything suspicious. He took a deep breath to ready himself. The hairs on his neck stood at attention and he wondered how he let the minx next to him talk him into bringing her along. The situation was even more dangerous now that Dresden had been murdered.

Jack bounded out of the coach much like an eager puppy and Simon had to stop himself from calling out to him to maintain caution. Jack already thought him old before his time.

Instead Simon turned and helped Dani out of the coach. Her gloved fingers wrapped around his palm and a jolt of awareness went through him. She felt it too. Her eyes widened and her lips parted ever-so slightly. The maid dutifully followed them out of the carriage, trained to remain silent and unobtrusive in the background.

He closed his hand around Dani's and followed after his brother, who waited by a rather large flowering bush.

"It just occurred to me that whoever sent you that note didn't tell you exactly where you were supposed to meet him," Jack said, glancing around, occasionally smiling engagingly at passing ladies.

"Or her. We really don't know if it's a man or woman who we're meeting," Simon pointed out.

"Hell," muttered Jack.

"What?" Simon turned around to look in the direction Jack was staring. Coming toward them was their cousin, Lawrence Ashford and on his arm was Margaret Cavendish, Simon's former mistress.

"Quick dash down the next lane," Jack suggested. "Maybe he hasn't spotted us."

"He's waving." Simon squashed both their hopes. Dani shot him a questioning glance but he didn't appear to notice.

Lawrence, of all Simon's relatives, resembled no one in particular in the family. His hair, which was curly, could only be likened to a strawberry and his fair complexion was splattered with freckles. Most of the males of the family on both his mother's and father's side were tall and muscular whereas Lawrence was short and reed thin. He was dressed on this particular occasion in a deep plum shade that contrasted rather badly with the strawberry hair. His cravat, which no doubt he'd taken great pains to have designed, was a slightly paler shade of plum.

Simon's mouth twisted in disdain when his gaze shifted to Margaret Cavendish, the fair widow, who clung to Lawrence's arm with such apparent force it was small wonder his cousin didn't cry out. Her dress was a deep shade of burgundy, her favorite color and wine, he recalled and in her golden hair she wore tiny flowers. Her gloves and parasol matched, of course.

"Stratford," Lawrence called out when the pair neared them. "What a surprise. I didn't think you frequented this place."

"Afternoon, Lawrence, Margaret." He nodded stiffly at her. "I'm meeting someone here."

"An assignation?" Lawrence asked, grinning, then casting his eyes at Dani, inquiringly. "I didn't think you had it in you, old boy."

"Simon," Margaret purred. "How wonderful to see you again. It's been so long, dearest."

"Not long enough," Jack said from beside a flowering bush.

Margaret barely spared him a glare before she turned her adoring eyes back to Simon. She completely ignored Dani.

"Allow me to introduce Miss Crest." Simon indicated Dani. "This is Lawrence Ashford, another of our cousins." He paused, then continued, "And Lady Cavendish."

Lawrence's smile went up a notch and he snagged Dani's hand from Simon's arm. "Miss Crest, what a delight."

Simon noted he held Dani's small hand in his large paw for much too long. He was about to extract it from the popinjay, when Dani managed to free it herself. Simon nodded approvingly.

Lawrence finally looked past Simon to where Jack stood, his hands linked casually behind his back, a bored expression on his face. Simon didn't miss his cousin's sneer.

"Thorndike" Lawrence said, his voice dripping contempt, acknowledging Jack only with obvious reluctance.

"Ashford," Jack returned with equal belligerence. "Incidentally, cousin, you didn't much care for Dresden, I believe. Had a disagreement with him over a woman. Can you account for your whereabouts when he met his untimely death? And Douglas too?"

"Not that I have to answer any questions from either you or Stratford, if it comes to that," Lawrence said, straightening up, "but I assure you I was in bed quite content with a paramour both times."

"Which can all be verified, of course." Jack came closer to Lawrence and peered down at him. That he was attempting intimidation over the much smaller Lawrence was quite obvious.

"Of course," Lawrence retorted, apparently not threatened.

Simon shook his head and tried to ignore Margaret, who had latched onto his arm when Lawrence had hold of Dani's hand. Dani was biting her lip, watching Margaret. His former mistress was now none too subtly blowing in his right ear.

"You were fairly close to Douglas," Simon said, directing his question to Lawrence. "I've heard he had a new mistress. Did you know who his newest mistress was?"

Lawrence grimaced and appeared to give it some thought. After a moment he said, "I think I recall him mentioning a name but I can't quite come up with it. I didn't really think it very important."

"Simon," Margaret said, her hand turning his face to her to get his attention. "Can I have a private word with you?"

"In a minute, Margaret," he answered, removing her hand. "Lawrence, did you sometimes gamble with Douglas at Brooks'?"

"Simon, it's important," Margaret insisted.

"I don't gamble." Lawrence frowned. "I find it immoral. If there's nothing else, I wish to be on my way."

Simon took his own watch out and noted the time was quickly approaching four. "Yes. Good afternoon, Lawrence."

Lawrence nodded stiffly, then looked to Margaret. "Are you coming, Margaret?"

"In a moment, Lawrence," Margaret said, pouting. "I want to speak with Simon. I'll be along."

"As you wish," he said coldly, bowing briefly to Simon, then Dani. "Miss Crest." He completely ignored the mocking bow he received from Jack.

Margaret took hold of Simon's arm again and led him a few steps away from Jack and Dani. Out of the corner of his eye, Simon noted Dani, wringing her hands fretfully. Margaret peered back at them as though to make sure they couldn't listen to their conversation.

"What is it?" Simon demanded, barely holding on to his patience.

"You could be a little more gracious than that," Margaret said, her bottom lip sticking out. "You used to like me once."

"Don't play games with me, Margaret. What do you want?"

"I'm not going to tell you if you're going to be mean," she said, acting very much like a spoiled child. Simon recalled that her behavior was similar during their affair. He realized he much preferred Dani's sweetness to Margaret's manipulations.

"Good, then I can leave. I have an appointment," he said, turning from her.

"I know you have an appointment at four, Simon," her soft voice barely reached his ears.

He froze, slowly turning around to face her. Her expression was crafty. "What do you know, Margaret?"

She smiled, clearly enjoying herself. "I sent you that note."

"You did?"

"Surprised? I thought you might be."

Simon shook his head. "This isn't a game, Margaret. I'm trying to learn who killed Norton. Don't waste my time sending meaningless notes."

Her eyes narrowed and she approached him, taking his hands in hers. "It wasn't meaningless. I meant every word."

"What are you talking about?"

She gave him a smug smile. "Douglas confided in me. I know everything. You see, I was his new mistress."

"You?" He was dumbfounded. It never occurred to him Margaret would bother with someone like Douglas.

"I'm sorry about Douglas. I quite liked him. He was handsome like you but much more fun." She chuckled a little.

"Very well. Tell me what you know."

"Do you think it will be that easy, dearest?" Her eyes gleamed with a calculating glint. "I want to be set up for life."

He frowned. "What are you talking about? Your husband left you with a lot of money."

She smiled almost girlishly. "That's something Douglas and I had in common. We both loved to gamble." She reached into the reticule she carried and pulled out a note. She placed it in his hands. "These are my demands. That idiotic Lawrence is waiting for me. I'll be in touch." She leaned up and kissed his cheek, then followed after Lawrence.

After a brief hesitation Dani and Jack hurried up to him.

Dani, glanced first at Margaret's retreating back and then at the note in his hand, a puzzled look on her face. "What was that?"

Simon briefly glanced at the note. "A calculating woman."

Chapter Twelve

Dani paused in the doorway of Grace's room. Sitting on the side of the bed mopping Grace's brow, was a blonde angel. Simon's sister, Lucy.

Lucy wore her long blonde hair loose about her shoulders and down her back. Though she was still young, the pale green morning gown clinging to her gave her the appearance of being nearly the same age as Dani.

Lucy turned when she noticed Dani and smiled brightly. "I'm not supposed to be here," Lucy said, her voice conspiratorial. "Maggie wanted to meet her young gentleman." Lucy giggled. "He's one of the footmen I think. I told her I'd watch your friend until she got back. Don't tell my governess or Aunt Pen."

Dani smiled in return and came fully into the room. She approached the bed. Her smile faltered when she saw Grace's noticeably gray color.

Lucy sighed. "I'm sorry. She doesn't seem to get any better." She rose from her seat and Dani sat in her place. Lucy stood nearby, her hands clasped behind her back, watching Dani grasp Grace's hand.

"Did Simon call you Dani the other day?" Lucy asked.

Dani shot her a brief glance. Lucy's smile was sunny and welcoming. She nodded.

"That's a man's name." Lucy came around the other side of the bed to view Grace.

"My mother named me after her dad."

Lucy eyed her curiously. "Aunt Pen's been teaching you, hasn't she? I bet she's more strict than my governess. She comes in sometimes to see about my progress."

"She's all right," Dani said. "I've learned quite a lot from her. I've been painting and learning my writing today."

"You went to the Berkeley ball, didn't you?" The young girl's eyes were dreamy.

"Yes." Dani moistened the cloth in the bowl of water on the nearby table.

"I'd love to hear about it," Lucy exclaimed, clapping her hands together enthusiastically. "I can hardly wait for my first season. I heard that the Duke of Scarborough went with you."

Dani glanced at the young girl sharply. She'd spoken the words casually enough but Lucy's face glowed. She shrugged and returned her attention to Grace.

Lucy sighed. "Well, do you think you can tell me all about it later?"

Dani smiled. She wasn't sure if Simon would approve of her befriending Lucy but it was obvious the young girl was eager to have a friend close to her age. "I'd like to talk about it. It was very exciting up until..." She hesitated.

"Yes?" Lucy prompted, her green eyes wide with wonder.

"That will be enough, Lady Lucy," Mrs. Martin said coming into the room, her mouth puckered and as usual her hands on her hips. "Maggie's scheme is up and you've been caught. I believe your governess is waiting for you."

"I don't want to go." Lucy pouted. "Dani was going to tell me about the ball. And I haven't even had a chance to ask her about Vauxhall." She scrunched up her lips. "I know Simon and Jack took her there. It was all very mysterious and I want to know."

Mrs. Martin shrugged her shoulders unsympathetically. "Before I forget," she said to Dani, "His Grace said to tell you you're to attend Lady Needham's ball tonight."

"That's not fair," Lucy protested, stomping her feet. "Dani gets to go to all these balls and I don't."

"You haven't had your season," Mrs. Martin pointed out.

"Well," Lucy said, her expression mutinous. "Neither has she."

Mrs. Martin ignored her and turned back to Dani. "You're to be ready at eight sharp."

Another ball? She wondered why. She wanted to ask Simon but he'd closeted himself off in his study with his man of affairs shortly after they'd returned from Vauxhall. Both she and Jack tried to learn what the note Margaret Cavendish gave him said but he had remained stubbornly close-mouthed.

"A new gown is waiting for you," Mrs. Martin continued.

"A new one? Can't I wear the one from the other night?"

Mrs. Martin and Lucy both laughed at that. "Heavens no!" The housekeeper exclaimed, holding her stomach. "You must wear a new gown for every occasion. His Grace instructed Amélie to have a gown ready for you for this ball. Paid handsomely for it, I'd guess."

Dani shook her head. She would never understand the gentry. Back home she wore the same clothes every day and nobody cared. Grace's murmur drew her attention from the pair and any thoughts of a ball.

"We'll leave you here to sit with Grace for a bit," Mrs. Martin said kindly. "I'll come back when the time comes for you to get dressed. Shall I send up tea?"

Dani smiled gratefully. "That would be just the thing, Mrs. Martin."

Mrs. Martin put an arm around Lucy and steered her toward the stairs.

Dani watched them leave, Lucy all the while glancing back over her shoulders, a frown on her young face. When they were out of sight and she heard the last of their footsteps echoing in the hall, she turned to her pale and lifeless friend.

"I know you probably can't hear me," Dani said. "Just as well too, because you know I've never had anything good to say. You remember when you told me the biggest mistake you ever did was to fall in love with a man you knew you could never have?" Dani sighed. "I wish you could tell me what it's like to be in love. I never have been before so I don't really know. But I think I might love the duke."

Grace moaned a little and Dani leaned closer to peer at her. Was her friend waking up at last? But her eyes were still closed. Pushing aside her disappointment, she dipped the cloth in the basin of water and soothed Grace's brow once more.

"You don't know who the duke is, of course," Dani continued. "But if you would only wake up, you'd get to meet him. He's the most wonderful man. You'd like him. You'd like Jack too. He's...what would you call him?" Dani paused, thinking. "A rake, that's it."

As usual no response came from Grace and Dani was beginning to think her friend would never wake.

An hour later Simon watched Dani from the doorway for several ticks of the nearby clock. Henning would arrive shortly and it was very nearly time for them to dress for the Needham Ball. He intended to seek out Pembroke there. The Earl always attended Lady Needham's affairs because she was Pembroke's mistress. It was the perfect opportunity to question the man. He had planned to bring Dani, but now he wondered if he shouldn't let her rest and then stay with her friend. He could question Pembroke alone.

On her knees beside her friend, her head resting at an awkward angle on Grace's chest, Dani slept. Exhausted and emotionally drained no doubt. Why wasn't Mrs. Martin there?

Simon crossed the room in a few quick strides and picked Dani up, careful not to disturb her and spared a glance at Grace. The woman looked no better. He would have to talk to the physician about her care. His gaze rested on the sleeping woman in his arms. Her white skin was tinged pink at her cheeks and there were tiny freckles on her small, pert nose. The scent of the rose soap she'd been using assailed his nose. He took a deep breath but realized instantly it was a mistake for her essence surrounded him. His body shaking, he carried her from the room and nearly ran into Wilkins.

"Your Grace, what in the world?" Wilkins asked, raising his bushy brows.

"Keep your voice down," Simon whispered, scowling at the butler.

"Is she ill?" Wilkins whispered back.

"No, just exhausted. Where is Mrs. Martin?"

"With Lady Lucy the last I saw."

Simon nodded. "Find her and have her sit with Grace until Dr. Henning arrives."

"Yes, Your Grace."

Simon carried Dani to the room Dani stayed in even though he was frankly tempted to carry her to his. After struggling a bit so he wouldn't jostle Dani too much, Simon twisted the handle and entered the small but sunlit room. He laid her gently down on the bed, then went to the curtains to draw them closed.

"Uh," she moaned from the bed.

Simon stepped over and stared into her now open but confused eyes. "Shh. Go back to sleep," he ordered softly.

"What?" she asked, clearly confused.

Simon sat down on her bed and took possession of her hands. "You fell asleep while watching Grace. I've brought you to your room. Now, sleep."

Her periwinkle eyes focused on his at last. Frowning, she said, "But Grace…"

"I'm having Mrs. Martin stay with her. Dani, you won't do her any good if you become ill yourself. You need your rest."

She struggled to sit up at the same time Simon reached down to try to tuck the covers around her. The top of her head clipped him on the chin.

"Oh, sorry," Dani exclaimed, her expression stricken.

"It's quite all right," Simon assured her, rubbing his chin. He touched the top of her head with his fingertips. They brushed her silky hair. "How's your head?"

"Fine, I think," she said softly.

"Dani, sleep for a while. I was going to have you come with me to Lady Needham's ball later to question Pembroke, but I think it's best you rest and stay with Grace, after all. Would you like that?"

She nodded. "Yes, if it's all right. I would like to stay with her. Thank you, Your Grace."

"Simon," he reminded her.

"Simon," she said softly. Her eyes turned dreamy and she tilted her head up to stare at him.

His gaze dropped to her plump pink lips. *Get out now.* But he ignored his inner voice as he seemed to be doing a lot lately and instead dipped his head down until his mouth covered hers. Her honey-sweet taste mingled with his spice and brandy in a heady mixture. Silk. His fingers threaded through her vibrant locks, bringing her closer to him, until she was pressed so tightly against his chest he felt her breathe.

He didn't quite know how he ended up lying on the bed, next to her, his arms wrapped around her waist. Nor did he remember when her arms had ensnared his neck.

She whimpered low in her throat, the animal sound feeding the heat that threatened to overtake him. Her warm tongue swirled around his, making him quiver like a leaf in the wind.

"Need," he gasped into her mouth.

"W-What?" Dani mumbled, moving her soft, sweet lips away causing pinpricks of pain to slam through him.

"Nothing." He drew her lips back to his, devouring her mouth hungrily. His hand moved to her breast as though it knew better what it wanted than he did. He cupped the soft mound, groaning both with desire and frustration at the material that separated him from his goal. Somehow he was going to have to remove their clothes without breaking away from her delicious mouth.

He struggled out of his coat, trying not to put too much weight on her. He tossed it to the floor without bothering to look. His cravat and shirt soon followed.

He couldn't think what came next so he renewed his fervor in assaulting her mouth. She arched underneath him, reminding him he wanted to rid her of her gown. He pulled back from her, staring at her kiss swollen lips. Beautiful. He had never known anyone so sweet and beautiful.

His eyes met hers. Her incredible eyes sparkled, desire and something more unfathomable shining from within.

The sharp tap on the other side of the door made his racing heart slow abruptly. Lowering his forehead to hers in frustration he waited.

"Your Grace?"

Wilkins. Blast, he was going to sack the old butler. He gritted his teeth.

"Your Grace, are you in there?"

Dani pushed at his shoulders, her cheeks red with embarrassment. He eased his weight off her.

"Yes, yes, Wilkins," Simon said, annoyed. "I'm here."

"Dr. Henning has arrived, my lord," Wilkins said through the door. "He's in with the dock woman and has asked to speak with you."

Simon determined then and there he would have to seek out a new physician. He sat up on the edge of the bed and reached for his shirt. "I'll be down presently."

Dani scrambled out of bed.

"I will see Dr. Henning, sweetheart. I want you to rest."

"I want to know about Grace."

Simon shook his head and stood up. "Take a nap. You aren't used to the demands of society life."

"I'm not tired," Dani said softly.

Finishing with his shirt, Simon grabbed his cravat, and coat. "Don't argue with me, sweetheart. I'll tell you everything the doctor says about Grace," he promised.

Dani frowned, a hesitant look on her beautiful face but she said nothing further. Simon went to the door and stepped out.

Dani waited for him to leave before she pulled the door open. She had every intention of hearing firsthand what the physician had to say about Grace. She didn't doubt that Simon would be honest but he might try to soften the information to spare her.

She paused in front of the mirror and grumbled when she realized her locks were a tangled mess from their tussle on the bed. Brushing her fingers over her tingling lips, Dani took a calming breath. Then she hurried down to Grace's room.

Dr. Henning was just finishing up with Grace and he glanced at Dani when she came in. Standing with him was the duke and Jack. Neither of them had yet noticed she was there.

"I don't understand why she still hasn't regained consciousness," the doctor said. "Her fever has broken but still she does not wake." He sighed. "She may never wake. I recommend an asylum."

"An asylum?" Dani exclaimed, coming forward. The duke, noticing her presence for the first time, frowned at her.

She smiled hesitantly at him, then turned her attention back to the physician. "Grace doesn't belong in a place like that."

"I'm certain that Simon won't allow that, Dani." Jack patted her on her shoulder. He winked at her.

"It's the place for her," Henning said. "She won't be able to care for herself anyway so she will need constant attention. An asylum is best."

"I'll take care of her," Dani promised, hurrying to Grace. She brushed a dirty lock of hair off her friend's forehead.

"No, you will not." Simon shook his head firmly. "I will hire someone."

"But I can…"

"No," he said sharply. "Thank you, Dr. Henning. Jack will see you out."

Jack raised an eyebrow at his brother but otherwise did not comment.

"I will drop by in a few days to see how you're getting along. Have your man of affairs stop by my office, I may be able to recommend someone," Henning said.

"Come on then," Jack said, pointing toward the door. "Maybe you can tell me how someone like you became a physician."

"Have you had anyone look at those cuts and bruises?" Henning asked, following Jack.

"I'll stay with her until you can hire someone," she suggested, hoping to forestall his anger.

"Dani, I'm not trying to be cruel," he said, then he softened his words with one of his heart-melting smiles. "I promise you that Grace will have the care she needs."

"Oh." Dani flushed. She hoped he didn't think her ungrateful. There was so much he'd already done for her.

"I shouldn't have acted as I did," Simon told her. "It was wrong of me to try to keep you from hearing what the doctor said and I apologize."

Dani didn't know what to say, she just stared at him, her heart swelling with emotions she could barely define.

Simon reached for her hand, brought it to his lips. "I'll come and see you after the ball."

Chapter Thirteen

༄

Simon hoped he would locate the Earl of Pembroke quickly so he could question the man about Norton and return home.

He noted Lady Needham herself greeted her arrivals, a smug smile of satisfaction on her regally beautiful face. A widow, Lady Needham, had more power in the *ton* than when her late husband was alive. Simon knew she was delighted with the success of her ball. He also knew she would eat someone as sweet as Dani for lunch. Perhaps it had been a good idea to leave Dani at home, though he had wanted her by his side.

He scanned the crowd around him, spotting Pembroke. He crossed over to the opposite side of the room, stopping in front of a tall, thin man with brown hair and a thin mustache. The man was dressed in the same evening dress as most of the men there. He paused in his conversation with a young buxom woman.

"Stratford?"

"Pembroke. It's time for answers."

"Indeed." Pembroke sniffed and pulled down the bottom of his coat. "Excuse me, dear Miss Haversham." The young woman in question shrugged and moved off.

"There's a balcony over there. After you," Simon said. He wanted to question him before something happened to him.

Pembroke flicked a questioning glance at him but nodded. "Very well. I'd like to get this over with."

"I've heard you've been investigating what happened to Norton, Stratford but I really doubt I have much to tell you."

The Earl of Pembroke spoke as soon as they'd stepped out onto the large balcony overlooking Lady Needham's garden maze. Pembroke headed straight for the railing and leaned against it facing Simon.

"Still, since I have heard you spent part of his last evening in his company I have some questions for you."

"I gamble with a lot of men, Stratford," Pembroke said, evenly. "I cannot be expected to remember every detail concerning the game."

"Since I don't care about the details of the game, Pembroke, there shouldn't be a problem." Simon detested men like Pembroke. An excellent gambler, Pembroke almost always won and he took advantage of weaker, more desperate fools. Simon's father had been of the latter set.

Pembroke sighed dramatically and crossed his arms in front of him, impatient. He fixed his dark stare on Simon. "Well, then, proceed."

The idiot obviously had forgotten that Simon could well afford to ruin two or three Pembrokes. But discovering what the man knew about Norton was more important at the present than bringing the man's pomposity down a peg or two.

The nearby throaty laughter of a lady whispering to a gentleman a few paces from where they stood distracted Simon for a moment. He glanced their way, then gestured Pembroke to a further corner of the balcony.

"I believe that it was you, Carstairs, Dresden and Norton that night."

Pembroke shrugged. "I believe that was the makeup of the room."

"And who won?"

Pembroke looked smug. "I usually win, Stratford and that night, of course, was no exception."

"How often did Norton gamble with you?"

"Not terribly often. Norton was generally a bad card player. He couldn't afford to play with me most times. He started with quite a bit, though." Pembroke's smug smile returned. "He departed considerably less well off."

"Was there anything unusual about his behavior?" Simon asked, deciding to get straight to the point. He didn't want to prolong his interview with Pembroke. He was feeling positively uncharitable and he was anxious to see Dani.

"I couldn't tell you whether Norton's behavior was unusual or not. I didn't know him well enough to distinguish any difference." Pembroke's upper lip curled in disdain. "The few times I played with him he gambled with a desperation that does not bode well for his finances. He was no different that night."

"Very well, Pembroke," Simon said after a moment of studying the other occupants of the balcony. "What about Dresden?"

"What about him?" Pembroke asked impatiently.

"Do you know have any idea why anyone would want him dead?"

"I haven't the faintest notion." Pembroke's sneer was a little less certain. He was worried about his own life, Simon realized.

"Did he gamble often with Norton?"

"Yes, I believe so." Pembroke shrugged as though it were insignificant.

"And Carstairs?"

Pembroke snorted. "Yes, frequently." He straightened from the railing. "If there is nothing else, Stratford, I believe Lady Needham has need of me."

"One other thing, Pembroke. Have you seen Carstairs tonight?"

"No," Pembroke said, curtly. "Excuse me."

Simon watched the earl walk stiffly toward the doors leading to the ballroom. He didn't really feel that Pembroke was holding anything back, which meant he was no closer to discovering anything about Norton's murder. If only he'd been able to learn what Dresden knew before his death. Murder. There was no doubt in his mind that the same culprit who'd killed Norton slit Dresden's throat.

* * * * *

Dani felt a gentle hand touch her cheek. She opened her eyes to see Simon crouched down next to her still dressed in his evening wear.

"Good evening, Dani."

She rubbed her eyes, then straightened in the chair next to Grace's bed. "How was the ball?"

"Tedious, especially without you." He shrugged out of his coat and glanced at Grace. "Her color looks a bit better. Pembroke wasn't much help, I'm afraid."

"I'm sorry."

"Come, Maggie is here to relieve you watching over Grace." He grasped her hand and pulled her up from the chair. He turned to the maid. "If anything changes notify Mrs. Martin at once, Maggie."

"Yes, Your Grace."

Expecting him to bring her to Jessica's room, the one she had been using, Dani was surprised when he walked past the room and down the hall to the door of the room she knew to be his.

Simon pulled her into his arms and gently smoothed her hair. He closed his eyes when the scent of roses assailed his nostrils. There was nothing between them but the gown she wore and his own thin shirt. Her nipples pressed against him.

Tilting her head back, he told himself he just wanted to be sure she was all right. Her lips, full and trembling, were parted just inches from his. Her eyes were filled with dawning passion. He lowered his head and nipped her bottom lip. She did not pull back. Instead, she raised herself up on her toes and met his lips with hers in a searing, staggering kiss.

Closing his fist in her silky locks, he drew her head back, exposing the column of her throat. He slid his mouth from hers to trace the supple line and find the spot where her pulse beat. He kissed it and her breath caught. Her fingers speared through his hair, holding him to her.

"Dani, I don't want you to think…" He broke their kiss on a gasp, shook his head. "I know you must think me a cad for taking you to my room. I didn't think."

"I don't mind," she admitted.

He blew out a breath. "The thing of it is, I've wanted you for days. Since I saw you in the parlor wearing that damn ball gown. Even before that. I haven't stopped thinking of you all night. You're beautiful." He shook his head again, knowing he must sound like a cork-brained idiot.

Dani reeled from the wonderful words that had just come from his incredible lips. He wanted her. He thought she was beautiful. Her. No one in her life had ever said those words to her. And he meant them. Dani was positive he did. Tears of longing pricked her eyes but she blinked them away. She didn't think Simon would understand her tears.

Instead, Dani did something he would understand. She entwined her arms around his neck and pressed her body to his. Her lips claimed his in what she hoped was a provocative kiss.

He groaned in response and wrapped his arms around her. Then he backed up into his room and slammed the door shut behind them.

His hands closed over her firm, swollen breasts, filling his palms through the soft material of her gown. He returned his lips to hers and she kissed him avidly, as ravenous as he.

Trapping Dani's lips with his, Simon urged her to the bed and set his fingers to her laces. When he freed her laces and her gown was loose, he reached for her shoulders and drew her gown down, pushing the sleeves down her arms, freeing her breasts, now covered only by the thin silk of a chemise.

He broke the kiss and undid the tiny buttons that fastened the garment. He ached with need but he wanted to savor every inch of her. Her breasts were beautiful. Firm and full, they filled his hands, hot and heavy. He pushed aside the open halves of her chemise and feasted on one of her erect nipples. She moaned, closing her eyes, her head thrashing from side to side. His erection was hard against her lower belly, her softness surrounding him. She lifted her arms to encircle his shoulders and pulled his head back to hers for another ravenous kiss. Her tongue tangled with his, boldly. Sliding his hands down her hips, he pushed the folds of her gown down until she kicked her legs free from it. Then he lifted her slightly to remove the chemise entirely. He laid her gently on the bed.

Simon knew he had to remove his own clothes soon or die from the want surging through his veins. He tried to slow his reaction, his touch, for in spite of her street upbringing he knew instinctively she was no experienced courtesan. But her generous, open responses drove him insane with lust.

He shrugged out of his cravat and shirt and tossed them on the floor.

Dani watched him, her periwinkle eyes hazed with passion and wonder. She was beautiful and he intended to have her. But was she ready for this? He had to know.

"Dani?"

Dani didn't say a word. But she smiled a glorious smile that reached all the way to his toes. Her eyes were welcoming. He fought to keep from sighing in relief. Simon removed the rest of his clothing and joined her on the bed. Taking possession of her lips once more, Simon was nearly content to fence with her tongue all night. She had the most delicious mouth he'd ever tasted.

The sight of her naked body held him spellbound. She did not cover herself from him, for which he was glad. She merely stared back at him, her periwinkle eyes dreamy, her lips puffy from his kisses. He wondered if he was a cad for his need to possess her but he pushed aside the thought. He couldn't think while looking down at her luscious curves.

His body covered hers. Skin to skin, her heated flesh made him shiver with want. She reached up and stroked his muscled arms with her fingertips. He groaned.

"Don't do that, sweetheart," he said, desperately. Confusion shone in her eyes and he hurried to reassure her. "I'm holding on by a thread. I want you so badly."

They resumed their kissing, both growing hotter, sweeter. He moved to caress her soft, silken skin, stroking her hips, the sweet indentation where her hip met thigh. His fingers brushed the springy curls at the junction of her thighs and her breath hitched. Distracting her with his kiss, his thumb probed her delicate folds, finding her slick with wetness. She arched at the touch.

Parting her legs gently with his own, he moved his erection against her. Her eyes widened but she did not tense or pull back. Holding her hips, he plunged into her. He covered her cry of surprise with his mouth and held still while she adjusted to him filling her.

He reached up and touched her cheek with his hand. "Are you all right, Dani?"

"Y-yes," she said, her voice shaky.

He knew she was not a virgin but the tightness surrounding him gave Simon a good idea that she hadn't been with many men. Her once passion-filled eyes were now tinged with fear.

Though it might be the hardest thing he ever did, he asked, "Would you like to stop, sweetheart?"

For a moment he thought she might say yes but then, her expression very serious, she shook her head. He started to breathe again.

He kissed her hungrily until he was certain she was ready for him to start moving within her. She moaned against his lips when he started thrusting slowly into her. Her fingers gripped his arms, digging in but he didn't mind. She was so sweet and so tight.

His senses were full of her, focused completely where his body joined with hers. The heightened sensations left him reeling. She was very wet, hotter than any woman he'd experienced and her thighs eased about him as he loved her. He pulled her closer to him, loving the feel of her in his arms, his body surging into hers. She had picked up his rhythm and was matching his thrusts with her own. He laced his fingers with hers and kissed her deeply. No woman had ever been as giving as she was, so soft, so sweet.

Her eyes closed, her head thrown back, the passion on Dani's face as she found her release was his undoing. Her legs tightened around him, her moans of pleasure sang through his ears and with a shout of his own, he poured himself into her slick heat.

A long time later, Dani became aware that the duke was crushing her. He had collapsed on her after their passionate lovemaking. She smiled. It seemed absurd to call him the duke now but she didn't think she could call him Simon either. Her prince, maybe?

Though she was loath to dislodge him from the closeness they were sharing, she could not breathe from his weight. She pushed gently at his shoulder. She loved the feel of him. Hot steel. He murmured and rolled off her slowly. She was grateful that he didn't get up from the bed. How long this closeness would last she couldn't guess but it was more wonderful than she could ever have imagined. Especially after… No, she would not spoil this moment with thinking of the other time.

There was a slight chill in the air. She quickly snuggled up to his warmth.

She now had a chance to study his naked chest and tentatively she reached out to stroke it. He caught his breath and clasped her hand in his.

"Easy," he said softly. "I'm only human."

She shook her head, her head angled to look up at him. "No, you're not only anything."

He smiled. "We're both a little too tired right now, Dani. If you keep doing that I won't be able to stop making love to you."

Dani trembled from the emotions his deep voice sent through her. For a moment, she wanted to tell him about her other experience. She knew, somehow, he wouldn't judge her. But doubt crept in. Mary told her never to tell anyone. But being like this with the duke was a dream.

"How do you feel, Dani?" he asked her.

"Wonderful," she said, then blushed.

"It was wonderful."

His agreement pleased her and she happily rested her head on his chest.

"Dani, why were you frightened before?" His voice was whisper soft, a caress almost.

Tears stung her eyes. The duke might despise her if he knew the truth.

"I was raped." She pushed her fist into her mouth, wishing she could take back the blurted words. But she'd said them. The duke stiffened.

"I didn't know. Dani, I'm sorry. I wouldn't have…" His voice trailed off.

She sat up and looked down at him, studying his reaction. If she saw pity in his eyes she would just die. No, not pity. Sympathy and understanding, maybe. A tightening around his jaw too. She traced it with her finger. "I'm not sorry."

"I'm glad you aren't," he said, gently pushing her back to his chest. "Do you want to tell me what happened?"

She shook her head. Her chest hurt. "No," she whispered. "I can't."

Dani felt him nod, his chin touching the top of her head.

"All right. You can tell me when you're ready, if you ever want to. Sleep now, Dani. I'll keep you safe."

Safe? She did feel safe. For the first time ever.

Simon listened to Dani's breathing long after she drifted off to sleep.

Raped. He heard the deep pain in her voice when she'd told him what happened to her. She couldn't talk about it. He would give her time.

Unwittingly, Dani had turned Simon's thoughts to his father once more. His father had shot himself rather than face charges he'd raped a woman. The power of the Stratford line kept the entire affair quiet.

He stroked Dani's silky red locks. He couldn't help but smile at them. Who would have known the little urchin who forced her way into his home would have the most beautiful hair he'd ever seen?

Dani woke to sunlight shining in her eyes. She blinked, groaned and turned away from the open window.

"Good morning, sweetheart," Simon called cheerfully, leaning over her to plant a kiss on the tip of her nose.

How could anyone be so happy so early? She pulled the pillow he'd previously occupied over her head.

Simon chuckled and wrenched it out of her hand, tossing it across the room. She glared through slits at him. His wide grin told her he didn't care.

"Wake up, sleeping beauty. We have much to do today."

Dani stifled a groan. He was washed, dressed and devastating in buckskin breeches, brown coat, ivory shirt and cravat.

"What have we to do?" she asked petulantly.

"Well, I have to stop at my boot makers." Mischief flashed in his eyes.

"Your boot makers? You woke me up at dawn for that?"

He laughed, a deep, booming laugh that warmed her soul. "It's not dawn, sweetheart. It's well past noon. I would have prodded you up earlier but you were awake rather late." He gaze dropped pointedly to her breasts. He raised a brow.

Dani flushed, averted her eyes, focused on his cravat. "Still. You don't need me to go to your boot makers!"

"No, indeed. But there's this wonderful bakery just a few storefronts down and they sell delightful little teacakes."

Dani's stomach growled. She licked her lips. Swallowed. She could almost taste the cakes. Of course he knew she would react that way. She smiled at last.

"But what about my lessons? I'm supposed to start learning French."

"You can have them later this afternoon." Simon curled a lock of her hair around his finger. "You really are amazing. I knew you were clever but even I am surprised at how quickly you are learning everything."

Dani blushed. "Well…I can't hardly pass up an opportunity like this."

"I supposed not." Simon leaned in to kiss her lightly, then stepped back, his expression startlingly serious. "Then too, I thought we might pay a visit to Margaret Cavendish."

Dani almost wished Simon hadn't told her of that particular destination. She hadn't been able to keep her mind off going with him to visit his former mistress. Current and former. When had she ever thought to be in such a position?

Going to the bakeshop for the teacakes was wonderful. Hooked for life, Dani had been thrilled when Simon bought an extra batch of them to take home with them. But all the while, Margaret Cavendish loomed over her head like a black cloud.

Dani sat next to him in the carriage, though the maid Simon had been bringing with them sat on the seat opposite. Both of them had decided there was no point in sitting at a proper distance across from each other. They were beyond that, if they'd ever been there. One hand was laced in his while she stared at the nails of her other. Her stomach lurched in time with each roll and rumble of the carriage.

Simon didn't look forward to seeing the unpleasant woman. What he ever saw in a cold, calculating fish like Margaret he couldn't begin to fathom. Ice. That was what she represented to him now. The sweet, delectable redhead tucked at his side was Fire.

He wrapped his free arm around her shoulder and pulled her even closer. Margaret's tongue could be vicious. He had no intention of letting it lash at Dani.

But he wanted her with him. All the time. Simon told himself he liked the insights Dani sometimes had on people. He'd become jaded toward others, but she viewed everything with a fresh eye. The truth, he was afraid, went much deeper.

The meeting at Vauxhall Gardens had been on his mind though and it was past time he use an iron hand with Margaret. No one was going to blackmail him. The list of her demands was outrageous.

"What does she want?" Dani's soft voice penetrated the silence. Could she read his mind?

Simon freed his hand from hers and pulled out Margaret's note from his coat pocket.

"A monthly allowance for the rest of my life," Simon read out loud, "an all new wardrobe at the start of every season, the lease on my townhouse paid…"

"Why does she need the allowance if you're paying all her expenses?" Dani interrupted, tilting her head back to look at him.

Simon met her eyes. "Clever girl." Shaking his head, he continued, "A box at the opera."

"The opera?"

Simon nodded. "Would you like to go some time? I can take you. I have a box." He didn't add that he hated the opera. Dani might love it. He didn't want to prevent her from having the experience. He flicked the note. "And two new carriages."

"Two?" Dani exclaimed.

Simon shrugged and thrust the note back into his coat. He intended to get the information from Margaret without having to give into even one of her demands.

The coach stopped and Simon opened the door, helped Dani alight.

"Just stay with the carriage," he instructed the maid.

He glanced at Margaret's townhouse with undisguised contempt. He hadn't been to the address on Chancery Lane for a number of months. Most of the homes on this particular street belonged to mistresses of one of his peers.

Margaret's place was small but otherwise unremarkable. It looked like every other townhouse on the street. He noted that except for one room upstairs there was no light glowing from within. Odd. Usually Margaret surrounded herself with servants and activity. The evening was still early. She wouldn't have left for a fête or the opera.

Unable to shake the feeling that something was amiss, Simon tucked Dani's hand in his arm and approached the door. It was slightly ajar. Simon shared a frown with Dani.

"Anyone home?" he called into the dark townhouse. But there was no answering call. No sign of any servants about either. He pushed the door open further and stepped into the foyer. "Margaret?"

Simon told himself she must have just given her staff the night off. That explained why there wasn't anyone to man the door. She probably just forgot to close and lock it. After all hadn't he seen a lit candle through the window of one of the upper rooms? She probably just couldn't hear him from downstairs. Maybe she even entertained some gentleman up in her room. He blanched, not wanting either himself or Dani to witness that eventuality.

Barely able to see the stairs illuminated by the minimal light from the front door he'd left open, he spied a candelabrum set on a small foyer table. Grabbing hold of it, Simon took note just before he lit it that the wax was still soft.

Dani gasped just as Simon's own gaze lit on the prone figure of a well-dressed butler just by the stairs. Tolstoy. Simon remembered him. Simon hurried over to him, hoping it was not too late for him. He crouched down and turned him toward him. Tolstoy's chest rose and fell.

"Thank God," Dani said, her hand resting between her breasts. Her breath was shallow.

Simon knew what they found didn't bode well for Margaret. He looked to the top of the stairs, listening. He heard nothing.

"Dani, stay down here," he ordered. He didn't wait for her nod. Simon pulled the butler out of the direct path of the stairs, then took them two at a time calling Margaret as he went.

Simon stopped at the landing to get his bearings. Not having been to Margaret's home for some time he tried to remember where her room was. The light they'd seen from below came from under a room on the right. The door was partially open and the glow coming from it seemed ominous.

"Margaret?" he called out, moving toward the room more slowly now. It occurred to him that whoever had attacked her butler might be still in the house. He was sorry he hadn't brought Dani up with him.

On the other hand if the intruder stood over Margaret even now doing her some great harm he could hardly stand nearby and let the creature do his worst, could he? He pushed the door open all the way and rushed into the room, his stance one of someone who was prepared to retaliate against anyone attacking him.

"Oh!" Dani's cry came from directly behind him. She clung to the back of his coat.

The intruder, who ever it was, no longer lingered. The room was empty but blood was splattered everywhere.

Chapter Fourteen

"Tolstoy."

Simon patted the old man gently on the cheek. The butler was coming to, slowly. Dani stood nearby while Simon crouched next to the man. Bile rose in her throat. She pushed aside the images of the room upstairs.

"Do you think he'll be all right?" Dani asked softly.

"Yes, I think so." Simon felt the underside of the man's head. "He's got quite a bump."

Dani touched her stomach to ease the sickening lurch. "Should I get a cloth or something?"

"No. I don't want you wandering around this place by yourself." Simon frowned. Tolstoy's eyes opened fully but they remained unfocused.

Tolstoy, a rather portly, balding man, struggled to sit up. Simon helped him.

"Easy. You've had a blow to the head."

Tolstoy's gaze went to Simon's face. "Stratford?"

"Yes."

"But-but Your Grace, you don't come round here anymore." Tolstoy said in apparent confusion.

"Never mind that. How do you feel? Do you know what happened to you?"

Tolstoy shook his head. "I remember answering the door. A man to see Lady Cavendish. I turned round to advise her ladyship." He shook his head again. "I don't recall anything else."

"This man. Did he give you his card?"

"It's on the tray on the table by the door."

Simon's quick glance confirmed that the tray was empty. "Do you remember his name? Had you ever seen him before?"

Tolstoy frowned in consternation. "No, Your Grace. I don't remember."

"Margaret… Lady Cavendish." Simon paused. "Do you know where she is?"

"Upstairs in her room, Your Grace."

Simon shared a glance with Dani. He patted Tolstoy's arm. "Let me help you to a chair."

* * * * *

Later that night in bed, Dani played with the hair on Simon's chest. Simon's bed. She'd spent another night in his room.

They'd returned late from Lady Cavendish's house. Dani barely had a chance to look in on Grace. In the morning she would sit with her.

"Simon?" Dani whispered. If he had fallen asleep she didn't want to disturb him. The day had been an ordeal for both of them.

"Yes?"

He sounded wide awake, so she tilted her head to look at him. He kissed her forehead.

"Lady Cavendish's disappearance." Dani paused. She didn't say murder even though they both suspected it. She exhaled slowly. "It reminded me of Mary. I've been thinking about how she disappeared right after that man's murder."

"You think maybe there's a connection between all of this?"

Dani nodded, brushing his chin with her hair. She raked her nails across his muscled chest. "Do you think you might be able to find out what happened to her?"

Simon dipped his head and claimed her lips for a brief kiss. Moved a lock of her head from her forehead. "I've already hired a runner to see what can be learned."

Dani's heart swelled. Why had God blessed her with him, she touched her lips to his chest and sighed.

"Dani, I want you to tell me about the rape."

His hoarsely whispered words stilled her. Pierced her. Ice closed around her heart.

"If you're not ready," Simon said, his arms tightening around her, pulling her closer, "you don't have to."

Blinking away the tears that speared her lashes, Dani shook her head. She would never be more ready to tell him than she was now.

"It was when I was thirteen." Dani closed her eyes, cleared her throat. The hard lump didn't disappear. "A ship had just docked. Grace and Mary were real busy. All the doxies were."

Simon threaded his fingers through hers, clenched them tight.

Dani licked her dry lips. "I tried to stay out of the way. They came round all the time. I knew how it was. I had a little corner I often hid in. Up until then, I thought no one could find me."

"But someone did?" Simon broke the heavy silence that enshrouded them for a moment.

"Yes." A tear dropped, rested on his chest. Dani concentrated on it. "I'd never seen him before. But he pulled me out of the corner. Leered at me, like a rat eyeing a crust of bread." Bitterness welled inside her. "Told me he was looking for a special girl to pass the time with. Didn't want the usual whores."

Simon's body quaked. "Dani, you don't have to continue if you don't want to."

She shook her head. "I want to say it all."

"All right."

From his tone, Dani didn't know what he thought. She struggled to finish, wanted it over quickly. Never wanted to speak of it again.

"Said he liked them young. He pushed up me skirts and…did it. He raped me." Her tears soaked Simon now. "It hurt so much."

"Dani." Simon's voice was raw, strained. He pulled her so close Dani couldn't tell where her body and his separated.

"When he finished, he threw me a coin. Said I'd make a really good whore." Dani's voice broke. "For a long time I thought that would happen to me. I'd be like all the others. What choice would I have? But I never gave up on thinking, if I just got out of there." She exhaled a shaky breath. "I made sure my hiding place was better next time. I never saw him again."

Rage consumed Simon. Didn't think he'd ever been more full of loathing than for the bastard who'd dared to cause Dani such pain.

"That will never happen again," he promised her. "I'll keep you safe."

Dani nodded her understanding, clinging to him. He kissed the top of her curls.

"My father raped a woman."

Simon hadn't planned to tell her. Hadn't planned on telling anyone. Kept quiet for so long. Dani tensed in his arms.

"A friend of my mother's," Simon explained. "He was drunk. He was nearly always drunk. Shortly after my mother died, her friend came round to go through her belongings. My father came into my mother's room and saw the friend. He claimed he thought she was my mother. He killed himself like the cowardly bastard he was rather than face up to his actions."

Dani reached up and touched his cheek. Their eyes met. Then their lips.

*****

"Your Grace, the Duke of Scarborough is here," Wilkins announced the next morning just as Simon took a large swallow of coffee.

"Ask him if he's breakfasted," Simon said, raising a curious eyebrow. It was not yet noon.

"He hasn't," Scarborough spoke up for himself, brushing past Wilkins. Grinning at Wilkins, he took a plate from the side table and helped himself to the food laid out there.

Simon's lips twitched. "Thank you, Wilkins, that will be all."

The old servant sniffed, turned on his heels and left the breakfast room.

"Where's the delectable Miss Crest?" Simon's friend asked, seating himself. He stabbed into the food with gusto.

"She's still asleep." Simon hid his frown behind his coffee cup. His fingers tightened around it, imagining it was the throat of Dani's rapist.

"Anyone with any sense is abed still," Scarborough said.

"Which brings us to the question of why you're here."

Scarborough smiled wryly, shoveled another forkful of food. "Thought you might be interested in what I learned about Dresden."

Simon lowered his coffee cup, sat back in his chair. "I'm listening."

"My sources were able to locate a witness to the card game Norton engaged in with Dresden, Carstairs and Pembroke."

"A witness?"

Scarborough nodded. "Anonymous, of course. Doesn't want his wife to know he was there. Said Norton wasn't the only one playing and losing a lot of money."

"Dresden?"

"Indeed. The source said Dresden was extremely agitated that night. Overheard him arguing with young Viscount Carstairs." Simon's friend finished the last of his eggs and pushed aside his plate. "Any luck with locating him?"

"None," Simon replied, frustrated. "I've been by his townhouse and his club. Always out."

"Makes you wonder if he's avoiding you." Scarborough pulled his tall frame out of the chair. "Another thing about Dresden. His finances were not good. His gambling was starting to smack of desperation. The wide speculation is that someone he owed money to slit his throat."

"Another pat answer." Simon shook his head. He knew in his gut that Dresden's throat was slit because whoever killed Norton didn't want him to talk. He'd stake his estates on it.

"I'm off," his friend told him. "I've an appointment. I'm not out and about this early just to give you the news and eat your food."

*****

"There you are," Mrs. Martin said, a welcoming smile on her lips, when Dani opened the door to Grace's room early that afternoon. Dani had overslept. "She's much improved and has been asking for you."

"She's awake?" Dani whispered, joy filling her heart. "Why didn't someone tell me?" She hurried to Grace's bedside. Grace still appeared so pale but her eyes were open. Dani's heart thudded. "I'll sit with her now, Mrs. Martin."

Mrs. Martin rose from the chair. "Would you like me to bring in some tea, Dani?"

"Maybe in an hour or so, if you wouldn't mind," Dani said, returning her smile. She sat in the chair recently vacated by Mrs. Martin and reached for Grace's frail hand. Grace stirred and looked directly into Dani's eyes. Grace's brown eyes were remarkably clear considering what she'd been through in the last few days.

"Dani? Dani, is that you?" Grace whispered, shock registering on her face.

"Yes, it's me," Dani told her, squeezing her hand reassuringly.

Her friend smiled wanly, shaking her head. "It sounds sort of like you but you look so different."

"I know." Dani swallowed. Grace's dark hair was as matted and unkempt as her own had once been. Now she longed to wash the soil out and allow Grace to know the way life could be. "How do you feel?"

"Weak as a babe."

"You'll get your strength back," Dani vowed.

Grace slowly turned her head to look around the room. "Where is this place? It looks like a palace."

Dani smiled and shook her head. "No, but almost. This is the Duke of Stratford's house."

"'What are we doing here?" Grace exclaimed.

"The duke helped me get you out of the docks," Dani said. "I'll tell you about him later."

Grace frowned. "You aren't getting yourself mixed up with something unsavory, are you?"

"No."

"I thought you disappeared like Mary," Grace said, her voice tinged with sorrow.

Dani swallowed hard. A silent moment passed between them where they both thought of their missing friend. Dani sighed. "I wanted to tell you I was all right. Tell you about my plans but I couldn't find you."

"I got worried when the man came looking for you," Grace said, licking her dry lips.

"Man?" Dani grabbed the damp cloth next to the bed and dabbed Grace's mouth.

"Right after you disappeared a man came round the docks asking after you." Grace scrunched up her face. "I told 'im I didn't know you."

"Oliver or one of his men?" Dani wondered. Oliver was one of the bullies of the streets around the docks. He fancied himself the lord mayor or something close to it. He forced many of Dani's friends to hand money over to him in exchange for his protection. In the past both Grace and Mary worked for Oliver.

"No," Grace said, sneering. "I'd know Oliver. And 'is 'enchman by their stench too. He wasn't like that."

"Well, what was he like then?"

"Very mysterious. I thought maybe he came by for the thrill, you know. A street girl."

Dani frowned. "A customer?"

Grace nodded. "I thought that was what he wanted but it wasn't. I didn't feel good that day but when 'e came up I thought I'd be stupid to turn him away. So I went into my usual act but 'e made it clear 'e wasn't interested. Too bad 'cause he was a real looker."

"Grace," Dani said, wanting her to stick to the facts. If you didn't try to focus Grace she would tell her story for the next two or three days. "What did he say?"

"He said he came to find a particular girl," Grace said. "Then 'e started to describe you. I got real scared 'cause I didn't know what a man like that would want with you. And since I hadn't seen you, I lied and told him I hadn't ever seen a girl like that. He offered me a lot of money too. Said 'e'd make it worth my while if I remembered seeing you."

Dani's heart thudded wildly in her chest. Who was looking for her? Why would some strange man want to find her?

"What else can you tell me about him?"

Grace shrugged her thin shoulders. "He was someone from the gentry."

"Really?" Dani asked, surprised. Relief flowed through her. It was probably Simon. Grace probably spoke to him the day she, Jack and Wilkins had gone to the docks when he was trying to find them. Everything made sense again. "I wouldn't worry about him."

Grace didn't look convinced. "Well, if you say so, Dani. 'E was real insistent though. And 'e said if ever I was to see you I was to get in touch with him right away. A fortune would be my reward."

That didn't sound like Simon. Dani stared intently at Grace. "What did he look like?"

"Dark hair and blue eyes, a real handsome one, 'e was," Grace said. "Tall with broad shoulders."

Definitely not Simon, Dani realized, her heartbeat racing. Then who? She couldn't imagine why a man of the gentry would be looking for her. Before she'd come to the duke's house she'd never known anyone from that walk of life.

"I don't think I know a man like that," Dani said softly.

"He reminded me o' someone but I can't remember who," Grace said, sighing. "It's right on the tip o' me tongue too."

"Well, don't fret, Grace," Dani said, trying to remain calm herself. "I'm sure it wasn't anything."

"He did give me his name before he left."

Dani's heart stopped for a beat. She swallowed hard. "What was it?"

"Carstairs," Grace said, nodding. "Viscount Carstairs."

Chapter Fifteen

෨

"Wilkins?" Dani called out when the persistent knocker at the front door rapped again. Passing by when the first knock came, she'd been in pursuit of the aged butler since.

"What is it, ma'am?" A young footman walked into the entry hall. "Do you want me to fetch Wilkins?"

"Yes, well, there is someone at the door," Dani said, pointing to the front door.

The footman smiled slightly and went to open it.

Standing there was a handsome, dark-haired young man dressed in brown-colored breeches and an elegantly tailored brown coat. He smiled winningly at her.

"Good afternoon," he said. "I've come to see the Duke of Stratford." He pushed past the fottman and entered the foyer without an invitation.

Dani gave him what she hoped was a reassuring smile. Mrs. Martin informed her of Simon's absence a short time ago.

"His Grace isn't here right now."

"Oh, well," the man said, looking uncertain. He looked up and down at her blue morning dress. "You aren't one of the servants."

That he was perplexed by her status was clear. But how was she to explain it? I'm sleeping with the duke? She didn't think so. Dani bit her lip and tried to think of the proper response.

"Who is this?" Wilkins asked, coming into the entry hall at last. Dani sighed with relief, knowing the butler was as close to a savior right now as she could get.

"What can I do for you, my lord?" Wilkins asked.

The handsome young man smiled easily and handed Wilkins a card, "I've been told that Stratford has been asking for me."

"Viscount Carstairs, is it?" Wilkins asked, reading the card.

The blood rushed out of Dani's head when the identity of the man sunk in. The room became fuzzy. Gripping the wall, she tried to steady herself but it was too late. She fell to the floor and the world turned dark.

Dani heard voices in the distance but she couldn't see anyone. Her head pounded, swirled.

"I say, miss, are you all right?"

Dani opened her eyes slowly, mortified at the realization that the handsome young man—no, Viscount Carstairs—knelt beside her. When had she been moved to the settee in the parlor?

Wilkins came hurrying in with a wet cloth. "Here, I can take care of that, my lord."

Carstairs took the cloth from him. "Nonsense. I can handle reviving a pretty lady." He laid the cool material across Dani's forehead and smiled down at her. "Is that better?"

"Y-yes, thank you," Dani whispered. She struggled to get up. She wanted to put as much distance between herself and Carstairs as possible.

"No," Carstairs said, pushing gently at her shoulders. "Perhaps you should rest a bit." Had he tracked her down here? But how, when no one knew she was here?

"I'm all right, really," she insisted, hoping she kept the fear out of her voice.

The viscount stood up and brushed his breeches. "Since Stratford is out, I will return at another time," he said to Wilkins. "Tell him I was here."

"Of course, my lord," Wilkins agreed.

Carstairs smiled down at Dani once more. "It was a pleasure meeting you, however briefly, Miss…"

"Miss Crest. A friend of the Thorndikes," Wilkins spoke up, using the identity Simon had given Dani as though it had become second nature. The butler stepped forward to break the awkward silence that followed while Carstairs seemed to consider his words. "I'll see you out, my lord."

Dani said a prayer of thanks for Wilkins' intercession. She did not want to spend another moment in the man's too perceptive regard. Though, she was sure she hadn't seen him before, the young viscount reminded her of the man who'd stared at her so intently at the ball. And Grace's words regarding his appearance down by the docks stuck in her mind. Why was he asking around for her?

* * * * *

"Where exactly are we going?" Jack asked that afternoon in the carriage.

Dani had been about to ask the question when Simon's brother beat her to it. She glanced at Simon, who sat beside her, holding her hand. It had become his habit to grab her hand every time they rode in the carriage. She loved it.

Simon was in a solemn mood. After a brief time spent in his study, Simon had come into the parlor and told Dani and Jack, who'd stopped in for a moment, to come with him. "I received another note," Simon told them, his gaze on the window. Though there were hours still of daylight the sky was darkening with clouds. Another storm.

Tension radiated from him. Dani touched his cheek and he turned to meet her eyes. He didn't smile his usual reassuring smile. She wished they were alone so she could ask him what troubled him.

"What did this note say?" Jack asked, reaching across the carriage, his hand out. "Let me see it."

Handing him the note, Simon shrugged. "It doesn't say much."

"Norton's last resting place." Jack frowned at the note. "What's that supposed to mean?"

"Where I found him," Dani whispered. "By The Swan."

"You mean whoever wrote that note wants you to go there? For what purpose?" Jack wanted to know. He handed the note back to his brother.

"That remains to be seen. Dani knows the area better than I do. That's why I brought her along," Simon replied. "I didn't think it wise to bring one of the maids along. This isn't a social visit. I brought you along for extra protection for Dani."

Dani clutched his arm. "Let's not go."

"Dani…"

"I don't have a good feeling about this," Dani pleaded, knowing her pleas would fall on deaf ears. Men could be so stubborn.

Simon frowned.

"Do you think it's Margaret again?" Jack asked from across the carriage.

Simon flicked a glance at his brother and shook his head. "I know what you're thinking but Margaret didn't stage that scene."

Dani shuddered. No, all the blood was real. She was sure of it. Shrinking against Simon's side, Dani tugged his sleeve until he glanced down at her once more.

"It's going to be all right, sweetheart." This time he did give her his reassuring smile. Dani narrowed her eyes. She'd come to realize he used that smile to his advantage against her. "I'll protect you. Jack will be there too."

Conscious of Jack, Dani glanced his way quickly. He stared out the window pretending polite disinterest.

Dani met Simon's gaze. "It's not me I'm worried about."

Simon blinked. His expression blanked. His gold-green eyes hazed. It lasted a moment. Then his face cleared and he smiled again. "You're joking, of course"

Dani shook her head. "No. Someone sent you that note for a reason. They want you there for a purpose. An evil one."

"I can take care of myself," Simon told her, his tone flat. "I'm getting a little tired of everyone doubting me. You do not need to worry about me, Dani."

Stung by his rebuke, Dani lapsed into silence and stared out the window at the gathering storm. The fishy smell invading her nostrils told her they were nearing the docks.

The carriage rolled to a stop some distance away from the tavern. Simon wanted to keep alert before they got to the spot where Dani found Norton. He helped Dani out of the carriage and laced her arm through his.

"First of all," Jack said when followed them out of the carriage, "get rid of that look you always wear."

Simon pulled his greatcoat tight around him. He swore it was several degrees colder than when they'd set out. The fog was rolling in from off the water too. The chill in the air was bone deep. Simon eyed a man nearby who picked through a pile of rubbish, sniffing it as he went.

"What look?" Simon asked, stepping clear away from the refuse picker. He lifted his right boot, then his left to see if he'd stepped in anything.

"That look," Jack said, rolling his eyes, laughing. "You look as though you're the Regent himself, for God's sake. You don't want to stand out."

"There's simply no way the three of us won't stand out."

"Well, any more than necessary then. I'm just telling you to stop looking so superior."

Simon gritted his teeth. It was time to move on. He didn't quite like the way the man pawing through the rubbish kept looking their way. "Let's go."

Simon pulled Dani with him toward the cobbled lane that would take them to The Black Swan.

"Wait," Jack said. He gestured toward a side street just to the left of them. "This way."

Simon raised an eyebrow. "Why?"

"It's a shortcut," Jack said.

Dani snorted. "It might be shorter that way but some of the most unsavory sorts hang out that way."

As if to prove her words, a man turned the corner from the lane fastening up his trousers.

Jack smirked, shrugged sheepishly. "I doubt whoever sent you that note will expect you to go this way."

"Dani is…"

She shook her head and frowned at him, sourly. "I'm from here."

Simon resisted the urge to remind her of what happened to her there. He was with her and could protect her.

"All right," he agreed, allowing Jack to lead the way.

The street Jack led him down was darker and more uneven then the one they'd just left and Simon wondered at the choice. A sudden passing stench burned his nose. He hid his wince.

"I have to admit I'm not too keen on being here after the last time," Jack said cheerfully. "Yell 'run' if you see our old friend Eddie."

Another man who'd tried to get to his Dani. Anger on her behalf spurred him onward. Run from Eddie? It was more likely he'd want to smash his face in.

"Turn right up at the corner," Jack instructed.

Simon watched as a rat scurried across the street just in front of Jack.

"The truth is," Jack was saying over his shoulder, "this is a plot to trap you on this dark street and murder you for your inheritance."

"Very funny," Simon commented absently, looking instead at the figure of a huddled young woman and a small child under the eaves of a nearby building. They reminded him of the woman and child he and Dani had encountered the last time. Probably the way Dani and her own mother were before her death.

They reached the corner and turned onto another street. This one slightly less menacing than the last. Simon checked over his shoulder frequently to make sure no one was in pursuit.

"So why do you think the bastard came down here anyway?" Jack asked.

"I am assuming you mean our cousin."

"Yes. He was more of a fop than Dresden," Jack said, then laughed. "You know what I mean. I just don't see why he would frequent a place like The Black Swan."

"No one said he frequented it," Simon reminded him. "I don't know why he came here. That's what I'm trying to find out."

Jack stopped at a crossroads and looked down both streets.

"You do know which way we're going, don't you?"

"O' course I do," Jack said irritably. "I'm pretty sure it's this way."

Simon stopped him with a hand on his arm. "You're pretty sure?"

"It's this way," Jack said, sounding more certain. He grinned. "Trust me."

Dani, who had up until then, been quiet, shook her head emphatically. "It isn't that way." She pointed with her free hand toward the thicker swirl of fog.

"Oh." Jack shrugged. "I must have gotten turned around"

"Hmm." Simon smiled at Dani. "Thanks, sweetheart."

"While I agree there's definitely something not quite right about all this business," Jack said after a further minute of silence. "I don't think London will particularly miss Norton or Dresden."

"I didn't particularly care for Norton either," Simon told him. "I can't remember the last time I even said two words to him but Pen asked me to help and that counts for something. At least with me."

"I know." Jack nodded. "All right. Now, we just need to go over this wall here and down the next street and we should be at The Black Swan."

"Over the wall?" Simon was appalled. He stared at the dilapidated stone wall Jack suggested they climb. It had been there for years, that much was certain. Moss and spider webs and cracks in its surface covered most of it and Simon wasn't sure they couldn't just push the whole structure down. It was stained with dark red in some spots and a slimy creamy-colored substance he didn't care to inspect.

"No trouble at all," Jack assured him cheerfully. To prove his point he hoisted himself up onto the top of the wall without so much as a grunt of protest. "Come on," he called down encouragingly.

"In case you've forgotten, Dani is with us," Simon said through clenched teeth.

Dani dropped his arm and with her nose in the air, approached the wall. "I can handle myself."

Simon winced. She was obviously still miffed at his earlier words. Sighing, he went to Dani and lifted her up. With Jack's help she reached the top.

Simon swiftly climbed up after them.

"There, that wasn't so bad was it?" Jack grinned innocently.

"You're enjoying this," Simon accused, shaking his head. "Where next?"

Jack pointed. "See that alley down there."

Simon followed his finger to a small, narrow walkway. "Yes."

"We go down there and to the left and the front of The Black Swan will be on the right."

Without another word, Jack jumped down to the cobbled street below. Dani and Simon followed.

Simon blew out a breath and watched the mist curl around the air. "Where's the alley Douglas was found in?"

"That's around the back of The Swan," Dani replied.

Dani led them to an alley Simon remembered from their earlier visit when they'd looked for Grace. The fog swirled around their feet. Simon reached for and caught Dani's hand. If this were some sort of setup, he wanted her close. The hair on the back of his neck stood at attention.

Simon opened his mouth to say something as they stepped into the alley Dani found Douglas Norton in when he spied the prone figure of a woman just ahead. She was dressed in old soiled rags and yet even from where he was there was something oddly familiar about her. Was she sleeping? She seemed preternaturally still.

"Jack…"

"I see her," his brother answered. Jack reached the woman first and he bent a knee beside her. He shook the woman but he received no response. She wore a scarf around her head that partially covered her face and glancing up briefly at Simon and Dani, he pulled aside the woman's scarf.

Jack whistled low in his throat. "It appears we've found Margaret Cavendish. She's dead."

Chapter Sixteen

ಐ

Simon and Dani returned later that night after bringing the authorities to Margaret's body. They'd dropped Jack off at his mistress's home on the way. Simon's head pounded and his stomach growled.

The man in charge of the investigation had looked at Simon with no little suspicion. Three people Simon had been involved with in some way were dead. It was absurd to suspect him, of course, except that he supposed if he were in charge of the investigation he might wonder about himself too.

"I don't understand why she was dressed like that," Dani said while they were headed up the stairs, Simon's arm draped around her back.

"I can only guess, sweetheart but I think the murderer is playing with us." Simon steered her toward his room. "It amuses him to dress Margaret in rags and leave her in the same spot as Norton."

"Do you think she was killed in her home and he took the trouble of moving her?"

"The blood indicated it was so." He reached around her and opened the door to his room. Dani stepped inside.

Dani shuddered and walked to the brightly burning fire to warm herself. Simon locked the door and removed his now stained and tattered coat. He'd torn it going over the wall.

"I'm sorry you had to see that, Dani," Simon said softly. He tossed the coat on a nearby chair and went to Dani. He wrapped his arms around her waist and pulled her close, nuzzling her neck.

She sighed and leaned back against him. "It's all right. I'm glad I went with you. I don't like you going there by yourself."

Simon was conscious of his own sweat and the grime form the East End. When they arrived, he'd instructed a footman to bring a tub and hot water for a bath. It was his intention to introduce Dani to a new experience. Forget what they'd seen at least for a while.

They waited in his chamber, Simon's arms wrapped around Dani. She didn't yet know what he had in mind but he was looking forward to her realization.

Simon released Dani at the hesitant tap on the door. He didn't want her to be embarrassed in front of the serving staff, so Simon waited for Dani to hide behind a wardrobe screen before opening the door to servants who carried the large round tub.

Those servants were followed quickly by still more hefting large pails of hot water. After pouring the steaming liquid in, the servants, turned as one, bowed and left the room.

"Come." Simon held out his hand to her. "Shall we warm up?"

Dani met his gaze and her periwinkle eyes widened in understanding. "Both of us? At the same time?"

"Indeed." He raised an eyebrow suggestively.

Dani took a step forward, her eyes sparkling and enclosed her hand in his. He held her gaze but dropped her hand so both of his hands could remove her gown.

Simon was delighted when Dani reached up to remove his shirt. Her fingers pulled it up over his head. Clenching his teeth against the wave of desire assaulting him, he inched her gown down to the floor.

He never took his eyes away from her face but Simon helped her unfasten his breeches and push them down his hips. Dani laughed, the sound throaty. She glanced down.

"Your boots."

His mouth curved. "I nearly forgot."

His breath seized when she bent down to remove the offending footwear. Her hair brushed his erection on the way down.

Dani noticed too for she tipped her head up and met his eyes. She touched her upper lip with the tip of her tongue. Simon groaned.

But he wanted to prolong their moment. If she touched him now, Simon was certain it would be over and fast. He smiled wryly and backed away from her.

"I'll take them off." Simon sat on the edge of the bed and quickly removed his boots and the breeches. He stood up, completely naked. "Come to the bath. You're cold. I'll warm you."

Flames of desire already heated her blood. The fire in his eyes nearly consumed her. The blazing lust there nearly buckled her knees.

Dani stood naked before him, but she did not feel vulnerable. Instead, Dani raised her arms and, rested them on her head so Simon could see all she had to offer. He seemed intent on seizing it.

Simon growled low in his throat and swooped her up into his arms, his lips claiming hers in a deep, thoroughly satisfying kiss. He took the two steps to the tub.

Dani peered down into the depths of water doubtfully. "Do you think we'll both fit?"

"I'll make us fit," Simon assured her, nibbling her lips, her darting pink tongue.

He carefully lowered her into the warm, soothing water. Her already heated body went up in flames. Dani lowered her gaze to his erection jutting between his legs. He followed her in the tub, enveloping her, surrounding her with his warmth as well as the heat from the water.

"Dani," he said against her lips, his voice hoarse.

She wrapped her arms around his neck and pressed her breasts to his hard, muscular chest. The crisp hair of his chest rubbed on her already aroused nipples. They pebbled.

"Ah." Dani threw her head back, giving him better access to her throat, which he laved hungrily. Distantly she heard the water splashing out of the tub but neither she nor Simon paid any heed.

She felt the press of him between her legs, against her. Widening her legs, Dani instinctively propped each one on either side of the tub. His sensual smile told her he approved.

She thought Simon would fit himself to her then but instead, his head dipped and he snagged one taut nipple in his mouth. Her body tensed, she clung to him, gasping.

Simon feasted on her breast for several beats of her heart, sending waves of ecstasy crashing through her. When Dani was certain she could bear no more, he raised his head and his burning gaze met hers, consumed her, ravaged her with its intensity.

"Please," she whispered. She wanted him. Now.

Simon shook his head. "Not yet, Dani. First, I'm going to wash you."

"What?" Shock coursed through her. Not because he wanted to bathe her but because he didn't want to give them the release they both needed. Immediately.

His lips curving more than usual, he sat up in the tub and reached behind him. When he brought his hand around Simon held a sliver of soap. Dani licked her parched lips.

"First, your feet." Simon bit the tip of her big toe on her right foot. She cried out. He chuckled. "Easy."

Simon rubbed the soap lightly on her foot. Dani felt her eyes go round and she leaned her head back. The sensation was incredibly erotic. Her lungs seized. He brought her foot into the water and rinsed it, then moved on to the other foot.

Next he soaped up each one of her legs but stopped at the knee. She thought she'd died and gone to heaven. Simon was an angel.

She nearly came out of the tub when his fingertips and the soap touched her inner thighs.

"Simon," Dani breathed, her head still flung back, her eyes closed.

"Do you like the way I give baths, sweetheart?"

"Yes." It came out as a moan.

Dani screamed when his fingers found the particular spot between her legs. He spread her wide, massaging her, entering her. She thrashed.

"Easy, love, easy," he murmured.

Easy? She tried to sit up, tried to seize his shoulders, bring him up to engulf her, thrust into with his erection instead of just his fingers but he shook his head.

"Don't, Dani. Lie back and behave yourself or I'll stop."

Dani could do naught but obey his command. She sobbed as his fingers worked their magic on her. His hand cupped her buttocks and lifted her slightly. She tensed, wondering what exquisite torture he planned next.

"Relax, love," Simon commanded. "I will never hurt you."

She forced herself to calm her racing heart, her pulse, which throbbed, as she throbbed where his fingers played.

Simon's mouth was on her. Dani tried to breathe. Amazed she didn't shoot out of the tub, she grasped the sides as he loved her, his tongue flicking her intimately. Moaning low in her throat, every feeling, every movement, emotion was concentrated where his lips were.

Tensing her legs, thrashing, squeezing, she tried not to buck but Simon was surely killing her. Angel? No, devil, surely. Somewhere, she heard a keening cry, realized vaguely it came from her own lips.

Pure male satisfaction flowed through Simon, knowing he was driving Dani insane with his mouth. It thrilled him, drove him nearly as insane as he was driving her. He wanted to be inside her, thrusting, wanting, but first…

Her shout of completion was deafening but he didn't mind. In fact, the sound of her release would be something he remembered forever.

He raised himself up in the tub, water sloshing out all around, his lips claimed hers in a searing, soul shattering kiss. Her eyes widened, no doubt tasting her own essence on his lips. She clung to him, holding him tight, her breathing labored.

Simon kissed her softly, allowed her lungs to function again. She stared at him, her eyes still hazed with passion. Mirrored by his own.

"Simon," she whispered, weakly.

He smiled. "We're not nearly done, sweetheart."

"No?"

"I still need to wash your stomach and your breasts." He smiled, wickedly and soaped her stomach and sensitive breasts with the rose soap. Dani quaked in his arms. Desire, hot and sure, returned fully to her periwinkle blue eyes. He was surprised at how fast she caught fire. Surprised but pleased.

He rinsed her and then set his lips to hers once more, taking her swollen pink lips in a drugging, consuming kiss. She kissed him back wildly, hard, her tongue dancing with his.

"Now, Simon, please," she cried, breaking her mouth from his on a gasp. "I want you now."

With one long, hard, deep thrust, he entered her. It was so intense, they both groaned. He gritted his teeth, to stop himself from pouring his seed instantly. He'd waited almost too long.

Taking a calming breath, Simon leaned his forehead against hers. Concentrated on getting back under control before he dared to move again. When he had his wits about him once more, he slowly withdrew, then thrust in, repeated the motions. Their gaze held, nearly fractured. Nothing had ever been like this. Would ever be, Simon was certain.

Dani arched beneath him, her wet, still somewhat soapy breasts straining toward him. Her body yearning for and meeting each one of his thrusts.

Simon gripped her chin, plundering her mouth in the same way he plundered her body, driving, thrusting, consuming it. He wanted it all. Everything she had to give.

His thrusts became harder, deeper, more desperate but she met each one with the same powerful urgency. She clung to him, clutched, raked her nails along his back. He was vaguely aware she was scoring him but he was mindless to anything but their joined bodies.

His melded with hers, their tongues tangled. Still he drove them on, further than he'd ever taken them. Dani was up to the challenge.

She was coming apart, she was certain. She reveled in it. Her mating with Simon seemed animalistic this time. More intense. After he'd pleasured her with his mouth she couldn't believe she would be able to find release again but her body was screaming for it. Wanting it.

"Simon, yes, Simon," she breathed, her legs clenching, seizing him, driving him on. Dani squeezed and Simon shouted hoarsely. He joined her as they both felt the jolts of their release rushing through them.

"Dani."

"I love you," Dani whispered, closing her eyes, content to hold him all night.

When their breathing calmed and Simon could move again, he roused Dani. "Sweetheart, we're in the tub. We need to move."

Dani blinked, stared, uncomprehending. He fought not to laugh. She was so damned adorable. He unwrapped himself from her and stood up, getting out of the tub. He reached in and pulled her into his arms.

She glanced down at the soaking wet floor. "What a mess." Her voice sounded dreamy.

Simon did laugh then and she joined him, a lilting, soft sound. He carried her still sleepy form to his bed and laid her there, where she belonged. She snuggled up to the pillows and fell asleep immediately, a smile on her lips.

But for Simon, sleep did not come easily. For something extraordinary had just happened. Dani had said she loved him.

* * * * *

"When do I get to meet this duke o' yours?" Grace asked Dani the next afternoon. The two friends were sitting together in the parlor over some tea. Grace was much improved and Dr. Henning had let her out of bed.

"I don't know," Dani admitted. She didn't know when he would return home from whatever business kept him away.

At least Grace looked so much better than when they'd brought her back from the docks. Her cheeks were tinted slightly red with what could be called a healthy glow. She'd hadn't had that in years. She was well fed and clothed at the duke's home. Even her dark hair was freshly washed and pinned in a tight knot at the top of her head. Both she and Grace had been amazed to learn that Grace even had streaks of gray hair running through it. They both laughed about how they thought it had just been dirt.

"Who was that fancy lady I saw you with earlier today?" Grace wondered, smacking her lips after popping a cake into her mouth.

"That's his aunt, his mother's sister," Dani told her. "She's teaching me to be a proper lady."

Grace gazed at her shrewdly, her dark eyes considering. She didn't say anything for several long minutes, just looked thoughtful.

"What?" Dani asked, unable to bear her scrutiny in silence any longer.

"You're sleeping with this duke. When did you start that?"

One thing that Dani had always admired about Grace was her bluntness. But just now Dani wished she weren't quite so forward. Her face heated, she stared down at her fingers. "How did you know?"

Grace snorted. "It's not too hard to figure out. And he wants you to be like them, is that it?"

"I guess so," Dani whispered.

"When did it start?"

Dani wished Wilkins would interrupt them or something. She didn't want to admit the truth to Grace.

"Well," Dani said, pausing to study her hands. "The first time we...it was a couple of nights after we brought you here..."

"I see," Grace said, saving her from having to finish. "I wish you talked to me before you got yourself involved that much."

"I didn't exactly plan it," Dani protested. "It just happened."

"He didn't force himself, did he?" Grace asked, her voice hard, her gaze ruthless.

"No!"

"He seduced you, did he?"

Dani didn't want to say that, even to Grace. She wouldn't make him sound bad. And besides it was a sort of mutual seduction. Dani took a sip of her tea instead, remembering just as she raised the cup to her lips to take only a tiny sip.

Grace grinned. "You do that real nice."

Dani opened her mouth to reply but quickly shut it when the door of the parlor opened. She turned, expecting to see Wilkins or Mrs. Martin.

"Good afternoon, Dani," Simon said, smiling. He came forward and went directly to Grace. "You must be Grace. I was told you were in here."

"Your Grace," Dani's friend said, her cheeks turning a little redder than before. "I-I want to thank you for all you've done for me."

He took hold of her hands. "I was glad to do it. You're looking much better too. I'm sorry I didn't come to meet you sooner."

"Oh, I know you've been busy," Grace said hurriedly.

He released her hands, then cast his eyes to the tea. "Is there enough for me?"

"Yes."

He sat down on the chair across from the settee and went to reach for the teapot.

"I-I'll pour, Simon," Dani said, hurrying to pick up the pot before he did. Her hands were suddenly clammy. She poured the steaming amber liquid into a cup, prepared it the way he liked it, and held it out to him the way Lady Norton told her to, hoping to impress him.

He took the teacup she offered to him and took a sip. Dani wondered why he joined them in the parlor.

"Your Grace, I was just wondering," Grace said, interrupting the awkward silence that descended on the group.

"Yes?"

"Will you be sending me back to the East End now that I'm better?"

Dani winced at her direct question. She didn't want Grace to go back and she had been thinking about how best to broach the subject with him. It was her intention to ask while he was relaxed after making love.

"Well, now, Grace, that's a good question," Simon said, setting down his cup and saucer. "Do you want to go back?"

Grace snorted indelicately. "Nobody in their right mind would want to."

He nodded. "That's what I thought."

"Well?" she persisted.

"Grace…" Dani started to say.

"If I didn't send you back there, what would you do?"

Grace smiled. "I'd like to repay your kindness to me and to Dani. She's as near a daughter as I'll ever get. I want to be sure of her welfare."

"You don't have to worry about her," he said softly.

"Yes, well, anyway, I was thinking, maybe, I could be a member of your staff or something," Grace said, suddenly not as bold as before. She shifted uncomfortably on the settee. "I don't know what I'm good at other than sewing. And um, the other thing, you know. But I'm willing to learn and do whatever I can to help."

"I'll speak to Wilkins and see what we can come up with," he promised.

Grace nodded, pleased. To cover her embarrassment, she popped a cake into her mouth.

"I'm wondering if I could have a moment alone with Dani, Grace, if you wouldn't mind," Simon said.

"Of course not," she said around the mouthful of cake. She scrambled up from the settee. "I'll just go and um, talk to Wilkins for a bit."

Dani watched her friend hurry out of the room and wished she wasn't in quite such a rush. After what she said to Simon last night she was suddenly very nervous. What would she say to him? What would he say to her? Would he pretend she hadn't said it? And would she be unhappy or glad of that?

Simon stood up when Grace closed the door behind her and came over to the settee. He sat down and grasped her hands. She dared not look at him. She knew she was blushing.

"Dani, look at me."

She slowly turned her head to find his lips waiting. The eyes she had come to adore were passion-filled and it occurred to her why he had sent Grace from the parlor. Later she would probably be humiliated in front of Grace if her friend guessed the truth but now she cared not. She opened her lips for his kiss and his mouth descended on hers.

Chapter Seventeen

ஐ

Simon brushed a stray curl from Dani's forehead and smiled down at her. She lay contented on the settee, her periwinkle eyes still dreamy. He kissed the tip of her nose.

"Dani…"

There was a discreet tap on the parlor door. Simon frowned in consternation.

"What is it?"

"The Duke of Scarborough is here, Your Grace," Wilkins voice came through the door.

Scarborough be damned. He glanced down at Dani, whose brow was furrowed and rubbed his temples. Gritting his teeth, he called out, "Have him wait in the library, Wilkins. I'll be there presently."

Dani murmured, her eyes clearing a little. He touched her cheek tenderly and rose from the settee.

"Sweetheart, Scarborough is here."

"Who?" she asked, blankly, struggling to sit up.

"The Duke of Scarborough. You remember him," he teased.

As he knew she would, Dani blushed and stared down at her disheveled appearance, tried to straighten her clothing.

"Do you want to sit in with me?" Simon helped her to stand up and straightened out her gown.

Dani swayed a little. "Yes." She reached up to smooth her hair.

"Let me." Simon tucked two stray curls back into the knot at her nape. He couldn't resist kissing her again before they went to meet Scarborough.

"Well?" Simon wasted no time when they walked into his library a few minutes later. The Duke of Scarborough lounged in a chair by the fire, a brandy already in his hands. He raised a blond eyebrow at Simon's question but otherwise did not respond.

"I've poured you a brandy," Scarborough said, indicating the glass sitting by the chair across from his. Scarborough smiled wolfishly at Dani. "Would you care for some, Miss Crest?"

"No, thank you," Dani murmured, taking the chair next to Simon's.

"Have you learned anything new?" Simon demanded, cupping the brandy glass in his hands. He took a large swallow, the familiar liquid burning his throat.

"You've become decidedly testy lately. I would think the lovely Miss Crest would improve your disposition." Scarborough raised his glass in salute to Dani.

Dani flushed next to Simon but stared fixedly at Scarborough. Simon's jaw tightened, a muscle flexed.

"Do you know anything or not?"

"Carstairs has left London," Scarborough said casually, linking his fingers behind his head.

"What?" Simon shared a quick glance with Dani. Her eyes were wide, her color a pale ghostly white. He wanted to ask her what was wrong but Scarborough spoke again.

"According to Carstairs' father, he was called to the country estate by his grandfather. Apparently they are quite close."

"Hell," Simon muttered. He certainly didn't want to go traipsing to the country just to question Carstairs. But it was damn coincidental at that. Hadn't Wilkins told him Carstairs had come to see him?

"There is more, if you care to hear," Scarborough said, smiling mysteriously.

"I'm listening."

"What was the name of Norton's mistress?"

"I told you Margaret was his most recent mistress."

"Before Margaret."

"Sally. I can't recall her full name. Why?" Simon asked impatiently.

"Would it be Sally Reynolds?" Scarborough's expression was unreadable.

Simon nodded. "Sounds right. What difference does it make?" Norton's former mistress was an aspect of the investigation Simon admittedly had not pursued.

Scarborough smiled thinly. "Carstairs' grandfather, the old duke. His most recent mistress was Sally Reynolds."

The impact of what Scarborough said was slow to sink in. A thousand thoughts entered Simon's head. None of them making sense. "What does it mean?"

"Not sure. But I thought you'd find it interesting."

"Yes," Simon said, nodding. "I'll have to find Sally Reynolds. Perhaps she can provide some information. I suppose I should have followed through with questioning her before."

"Alas, Simon, you won't find Sally very cooperative."

Simon frowned. "You've tried her?"

"Sally hanged herself a fortnight ago."

Simon sat staring into the fireplace for what seemed hours after Scarborough left. The brandy his friend had poured for him lay half finished. Dani had gone to speak with Grace. He needed time to think about his next move, so he was grateful to be alone. Later, he would ask her what was wrong. Before the information from Scarborough had come he'd intended to be out for the evening, hopefully questioning Carstairs. In just a few moments his plans had changed. The Duke of Lindley's country estate was in Portsmouth. It wouldn't take but a day to go there and speak with Carstairs.

He'd never met Lindley but the old duke had quite a reputation. He didn't know Carstairs' father, the Earl of Waltham, well either. He recalled him from a ball or two.

Sally Reynolds. Was there some kind of connection? It wasn't that unusual for a mistress of Sally's caliber to ingratiate herself with a duke. If she had the chance to have a duke it would make perfect sense that she would drop Douglas. He wondered if Lindley would answer questions about Sally. He pulled the rope next to his chair, calling for Wilkins.

The door opened almost instantly. "Your Grace?"

"I leave for Portsmouth. Have my horse readied, Wilkins."

* * * * *

The Duke of Lindley's Portsmouth estate loomed large and shadowy. Standing at the door, Simon brooded over whether it was a mistake to pay a visit to the old man. He'd left Dani behind in London. The decision was a difficult one. She wanted to come, he wanted her with him. But Simon wasn't certain what to expect in Portsmouth and he didn't want to put Dani in any kind of danger. Either of the sinister sort or simply by having her feelings hurt. A wolf like Lindley would devour her.

The doors of the dark manor were opened and Simon handed his card to an elderly man, flawlessly groomed in a pressed black uniform, standing there. "Yes, Your Grace?"

"I understand that Viscount Carstairs is currently in residence here."

The butler smiled vaguely. "Was, Your Grace. He left for London a short time ago."

Simon tamped down his irritation. Would he ever meet with Carstairs? He let out a breath. "I'd like to see the duke, then."

"I'll see if he is receiving. Please wait here in the parlor."

The butler disappeared leaving him in an immaculate room. Above the fireplace hung a painting of a young man with dark hair and light blue eyes. Something about the man struck Simon as familiar. He approached the painting for closer scrutiny.

"That's my son, Brendan. In his youth."

Simon turned to face an older gentleman dressed in a dark blue coat and breeches with an ivory shirt and cravat. "Lindley?"

"I don't believe we've ever met, have we, Stratford?" Lindley's blue eyes, almost a match of those of the young man in the portrait, were shrewd and assessing. He was still a virile man, though Simon guessed he had passed sixty.

"No."

Lindley came to stand by Simon, glancing at the painting himself. "Brendan was just barely of age when he sat for the portrait. You've met him?"

"Waltham? A few times." Most likely why the youth in the painting seemed so familiar and yet, there was something else. Shaking his head, Simon wondered how he could best broach the subject of Sally Reynolds. Or if he even should. The matter would be indelicate at best.

"My man tells me you asked after my grandson." Lindley was now staring at him. His expression was hard, saying without words what a bother this was.

"There is a bit of business I have with him, yes."

Lindley grimaced. "If he owes you money I would prefer you go through my man of affairs. You can contact him in London."

"I'm not here to collect a debt, Lindley. Your grandson had some dealings with my cousin, Douglas Norton. You may have heard of his recent murder."

Lindley shrugged, flicked at the cuffs of his shirt. "The name doesn't sound familiar. I don't spend as much time in London these days as I once did." The older man sighed and went to a side table. "Care for some brandy, Stratford?"

"Yes, thank you."

Lindley poured two glasses of brandy and handed Simon one.

"What does Justin have to do with this Norton's murder anyway?"

"He played cards with Norton the night of his death," Simon said casually. "I'm questioning all those that spent time with my cousin his last few hours."

"Hmm."

Simon took a sip. It was excellent. French brandy, of course. "I actually have some questions for you, if you don't mind."

Lindley raised his right eyebrow, clearly wondering at Simon's arrogance. "Of what nature?"

"Sally Reynolds." Simon watched the old man for his reaction but it became clear quickly that Lindley had spent many a year schooling his face to not give anything away.

"What about her?" he asked simply.

"I understand she was your mistress until her recent passing," Simon ventured.

Lindley inclined his head, his blue eyes turning a darker shade. "I would give care to what you say to me, Stratford."

"Is the information wrong?"

"Sally was my mistress, yes. So?"

Simon swirled the brandy in his glass. "She was Douglas' mistress before that."

"Is there some implication you'd like to make, Stratford? I am growing weary of this conversation."

"You have just said his name was not familiar," Simon pointed out.

Lindley smiled. Simon knew such a smile at one time had set the ladies' hearts to flutter. It just seemed chilling now. "Do you imagine, then, that my mistress called out her previous lover's name while I bedded her?"

Simon shrugged. "I do not imagine anything, Lindley. I just wonder at the connection."

Lindley snorted and put his own brandy down. "There is no connection. If there is nothing else, Stratford, I do have a previous engagement."

"She committed suicide, did she not?" Simon asked softly.

"Who committed suicide? And what a dreadful conversation," an older, very striking woman dressed in a deep shade of ruby, floated into the room. She instantly took Lindley's arm. "Leo, we are expected at Millicent's soirée very shortly." She glanced at Simon, then smiled, offering him her hand. "Who is this?"

"This is my wife," Lindley said coolly, his upper lip curled. "The Duke of Stratford was just leaving."

"Stratford," the duchess said, dimpling prettily. She was still an attractive woman. "These country parties aren't up to London's affairs, of course. But I do so enjoy them, anyway, don't you?"

"I spend most of my time in London," Simon admitted.

"A pity you're leaving then," she said, beaming her dimples at him. "I'm sure we could get you an invitation to this one. Are you sure you wouldn't like to come?"

"I'm certain Stratford wants to hurry back to London, Eleanor," her husband said flatly, his icy blue gaze fixed on Simon.

"Oh, he'll never make it there before morning with weather like this," the duchess said, releasing her husband's arm to take Simon's instead. "You remind me of how long it's been since my Brendan has come to visit. You're a bit younger, true but still. I couldn't convince my grandson to stay but perhaps I can charm you into it, hmm?"

"Eleanor…"

"Please," she said, fluttering her lashes at Simon in such a way as to make it clear that she'd been a great beauty and a great flirt when she'd been young.

"I would be honored, duchess, to attend you…"

"There you see, Leo," Eleanor said, smiling triumphantly at her husband.

"But," he said quickly, "as it happens, I am fatigued from the journey and have decided to go straight to an inn. I mean to make an early start in the morning."

The duchess pouted. "Well, if you're sure."

"He's very sure, Eleanor," Lindley said. He called to his butler. "See the duke out."

* * * * *

The inn in Portsmouth was not far from Lindley's manor but by the time he reached it, Simon felt weary and a little sick to his stomach. He hadn't eaten much the whole day and the brandy Lindley gave to him was not settling well. He barely made it to his bed before he collapsed on it.

He woke to two men going through his clothes. He pushed at them, still groggy and uncertain where he was.

"The bastard's awake!" one of the men yelled.

"We'd better get it done and get out of here," the other one answered.

Simon wasn't sure what they were talking about but it couldn't be good. He struggled to sit up, resisting the urge of his pounding head to sink back into a deep sleep. He grabbed the arm of one of the men and heard a clang as something in the man's hand flew to the floor.

"Let's get out of here now!" the man whose arm he held screamed. He wrenched his arm, trying to get free of Simon's grip but Simon had no intention of letting go. The other man ran from the room leaving behind his friend, who wouldn't stop howling with rage. "I'll get you, Howie!"

Simon pulled the man up and shoved him into the nearest wall. He winced as the effort sailed to his head. "All right, talk," he told the ruffian, his gaze even now taking in the gleam of the knife that lay on the floor.

Chapter Eighteen

ഌ

"Get your hands off me!"

The man Simon held against the wall howled out his protest, his eyes darting wildly.

"Perhaps the local magistrate can get you to talk then," Simon threatened, the fingers of his right hand itching to close around the man's throat.

The thugs had come to murder him.

"I got nothing to hide," his assailant said, licking his lips uncertainly.

"Howie," Simon said, remembering the brigand's accomplice, "has left you to hang."

"Hang?"

"Murder is a hanging offense," Simon assured him. "I'm sure the magistrate will be very interested in how you and Howie got into my room to kill me."

"All right, guvnor," the man said, fearfully. "I'll tell what I know." He winced. "But do you think you might lessen your grip on my throat a bit?"

Simon loosened his grip but did not release his attacker. His reflexes were still not quite what they should be and his head might well explode. What was this strange lightheadedness?

"I'm waiting," he said in a lethally soft voice after a few minutes of the man's silence.

"I don't know much. Howie got the details. I just got my pay."

Simon tightened his hold on the man's throat. "Try again."

"It's true, it's true," the man gasped. "Howie said a man came to him and offered him money to come to the inn and rob a man of the gentry."

"Rob, hmm? Why the knife then?"

"Tools of the trade, guvnor. Howie and me never go nowhere without our knives." The man swallowed hard. "The man told Howie you'd be easy pickin's too."

"Did he say why?"

"Said you were a heavy sleeper."

* * * * *

Lady Norton left the parlor the next day late morning after giving Dani another lesson. Only moments later the door reopened. Dani looked up from the tea she was enjoying on the settee, expecting to see Lady Norton return for something she must have forgotten.

The beat of her heart stilled.

"There you are!" Viscount Carstairs called to her, coming into the room. The handsome dark-haired young man was dressed in fawn breeches and a dark brown coat. He strode over to her, ready to take her hands into an enthusiastic grip.

Dani set the clattering teacup down on the table. If she'd been able to back away from him she would have done so. But her back was flat against the settee.

"I was told you might be in here," Carstairs said, grabbing her hands in his. He frowned slightly. "But, my dear, your hands are so cold."

"Who, who l-let y-you in here?" she stammered, swallowing. She tried to pry her hands from his but he held on tight.

"A footman." Carstairs shrugged. "I came here looking for Stratford again. The man's damn hard to locate."

Dani shook her head. "He isn't here."

"I know. But then I remembered how distressed you were the other day. I thought I'd look in on you." Carstairs smiled, flashing white teeth. "Truth be told, there's something about you, Miss Crest, wasn't it?"

Dani smiled vaguely. Where was Wilkins? Surely the old butler would never have let Carstairs in to see her.

"An old family friend, was that it?"

"Yes."

"I swear I know you from somewhere but I can't think of it," Carstairs said, as though to himself. "Did you go to Lady Hampshire's fête?"

She didn't know what a fête was. "No. I-I'm not from around here."

"So you come from the country? I just came from Portsmouth, myself. M'grandfather has a home there. Duke of Lindley. Hear of him?"

"I, no."

Carstairs frowned. "But everyone knows him. I know I should know you. Those eyes." He broke off, staring at her intently.

"Dani, I saw Lady Norton leave the parlor and I…" Grace, who'd recently been given a maid's uniform of which she was vastly proud, had come into the parlor but she stopped speaking the instant she saw Carstairs. She went white and her jaw dropped.

Carstairs glanced only briefly at Grace before he turned back to Dani. "Dani? Is that your first name?"

"Grace, I thought I told you never to enter a room without knocking. A maid would never just burst in the door." Wilkins now stood behind Grace. He blinked. "Viscount Carstairs?"

Carstairs stood up. "Good day. I've come to see Stratford."

Wilkins cleared his throat and gently pushed a still shocked Grace out of the way. "He's gone to Portsmouth to see you."

Carstairs frowned. "What the devil for?"

"He was told you had gone there, my lord."

"Only briefly," Carstairs said, sighing. He smiled down at Dani. "I decided to check on this lady's welfare while I was here."

"I expect he'll hie back to London once he's learned he's missed you," Wilkins said. "I'll tell him immediately of your visit."

"Do that." Carstairs stared intently at Dani. "My dear, you'll be seeing more of me, I promise."

Dani shrank back but allowed him to press her fingers in his hands before he walked to the door. He stopped next to Grace and also appeared to assess her. Grace looked down at the floor. Dani wrung her hands together.

"My lord?" Wilkins broke the uncomfortable silence.

"You're very familiar. Have I see you somewhere before?" Carstairs stared at Grace shrewdly.

Grace went even paler but she kept her gaze down. "No, my lord."

Carstairs smiled and looked at Dani. "I'll be seeing you, Dani."

"Have you told the duke?" Grace demanded shortly after Wilkins escorted the viscount out. She now stood before Dani, who was shaking uncontrollably.

"No," Dani whispered. *I'll be seeing you.* She couldn't get Carstairs' parting words out of her mind. What had he meant and what did he want from her? She didn't know him. She didn't know anything.

"Why the hell not?" Grace asked, now pacing in front of her.

"I-I haven't had the chance."

"He knew who I was, Dani, I'm sure of it," Grace said, telling her something she already realized. "That means he probably has guessed who you are too."

"Well but, even if he has, what does that mean?" Dani asked fearfully. "Why is he after me?"

"I don't know. But don't you think His Grace ought to know about this?"

This time there was a light tap on the parlor door. She jumped as though it had been on her heart. She touched her hand to her chest and took a calming breath. She wished Simon would come home.

Grace went to the door and opened it to admit Jack and Lucy along with a maid. Lucy's eyes were shining brightly. Her hand was tucked in her brother's arm. Jack grinned very briefly at Grace, a smile that reminded Dani of his brother, then bowed with dramatic emphasis in her direction.

"I'm taking a turn with Lucy in the park," he announced. "Would you care to join us?"

"In-in the park?" Dani asked, all thoughts of Carstairs momentarily set aside by the thrill she felt at his invitation.

"A simple affair. Just a turn in the curricle. You don't have to come if you'd rather not."

"Please," Lucy said, her big eyes pleading. Her cheeks were flushed with excitement.

"Well, I…"

"It's probably completely inappropriate," Jack said, looking very unrepentant. "Simon's not here to say no."

"Go, Dani," Grace suggested, her older face crinkling in a smile. "It's your first chance to ride through Hyde Park."

"I would like to go," Dani agreed, rising from the settee. She enjoyed the times she could pretend, if only for a moment, that she belonged in Simon's world.

* * * * *

Dani was glad the ride through Hyde Park would get her mind off Viscount Carstairs. She rode in a curricle, the maid next to her, Lucy between her and Jack. She had no idea what the others around them must have thought of them. They certainly got a lot of looks.

Dani clutched a pale green parasol that matched the green muslin dress she wore. It was one of her favorites. Lucy also held a parasol but hers was a sunny yellow that went wonderfully with her long golden hair. Jack was dressed rather rakishly with no cravat and his white lawn shirt open at the throat.

The elegantly turned out curricle with the leather seats hadn't seemed very simple to Dani, but when they approached the park she saw so many beautiful, gilded carriages and breathtaking horses her head was spinning. Brightly dressed, beautiful ladies waved at each other and stopped occasionally to speak. Some of them eyed Jack as though he were a teacake, Dani noticed.

Jack kept up a cheerful tale of some of those they passed in the park for most of the trip. Several times he reduced both her and Lucy to helpless giggles. They were thus in the throes of laughter when Jack stopped the curricle. A tall man on horseback had hailed them.

"Who is this?" Dani whispered, her heart torn between racing and stopping altogether. She could not look away from the large, dark-haired muscular man in elegant riding attire. His cheekbones were high and his eyes a periwinkle blue. At his temple was a hint of gray. The man from the ball who stared so intently at her.

"The Earl of Waltham," Jack said. "A passing acquaintance. I'm not sure why he motioned to us."

The earl pushed his horse forward. He barely glanced at either Jack or Lucy. His gaze was fixed on Dani.

"Waltham," Jack called to him.

The earl flicked a glance to Jack. "Thorndike." He returned his scrutiny to Dani. She squirmed uncomfortably. Why was this man once again studying her so?

"The Earl of Waltham, Miss Crest," Jack introduced. "And my sister."

"My lady," the earl acknowledged Lucy with an almost imperceptible nod. Then he refocused on Dani. "Miss Crest," the earl said. "I don't know the name."

"She's from the North country. An old family friend," Jack offered.

"Forgive me for staring, Miss Crest," the earl said, smiling a little. "You remind me very much of someone I once knew."

"Um," Dani said, not sure what to say. She didn't want to say much.

"Where did you say you're from?" Waltham asked, patting the head of his big horse when the horse stomped restlessly.

"She didn't say," Jack said quickly. "Her people are from Northumberland."

Dani nervously twisted her fingers. The earl continued to stare at her more intently than anyone had ever looked at her. Who did she remind him of?

Waltham hesitated, clearly wanting to say more. After a moment, he inclined his head. "It was nice to meet you, Miss Crest. Perhaps I'll see you again." He flicked a glance at Lucy and gave a brief nod. "Thorndike." He waved and rode away from them.

"He sure liked you," Lucy said, poking Dani in the ribs.

"Oh, no, I don't think so," Dani said, biting her lip.

"Well, he stared at you," Lucy insisted.

"He was definitely staring," Jack agreed, thoughtfully. "The question is why."

"She is pretty," Lucy reminded him.

"He's also old enough to be her father," Jack retorted. "Not that it's ever stopped anyone. But no, that wasn't the way he was staring at her. It was something else."

"He did say I reminded him of someone," Dani said softly, still watching the earl and his horse in the distance.

"Hmm." Jack urged the curricle's horses forward. "I did stop by his home the other day looking for his son for Simon. I thought he was stopping us for that."

"Something to do with the murder?" Dani asked before she thought better of it. She realized her mistake when Lucy turned her large shocked gaze to her.

"Murder?" Lucy exclaimed.

Jack winced. "Don't worry your little head over it, sweet pea. Simon's just making inquiries into our cousin's death."

"Douglas was murdered? I didn't know that." Lucy's eyes were as wide as saucers.

"Don't think about it, Lucy."

"I-I'm sorry," Dani said softly. "I didn't think. It didn't occur to me she didn't know."

"Quite all right. Simon and Aunt Penelope thought it best that Lucy didn't know the details of how he died. They didn't want her to become too concerned."

Dani impulsively grasped Lucy's hand in hers. Lucy smiled at her, seeming comforted by the touch.

"Who's the earl's son?" Dani asked Jack as the curricle turned to head back to the townhouse.

"Viscount Carstairs."

Chapter Nineteen

෨

"There you are, Your Grace," Wilkins greeted Simon when he finally arrived home quite a bit later than he intended. He wanted to be back by early evening but it was already past eleven.

A bit unsteady on his feet still from whatever he'd been given in Portsmouth, Simon attempted a smile. After turning the brigand over to the authorities, his stomach emptied itself of most of the contents.

"Anything happen while I was gone, Wilkins?" he asked, handing his greatcoat to the butler. He went through in his mind what he'd partaken of in Portsmouth. He kept going back to the expensive French brandy the Duke of Lindley gave him.

"Viscount Carstairs was by to see you again."

Simon shook his head, winced at the movement. "I missed him in Portsmouth. Anything else?" He never would have guessed Lindley for the obvious type. He hadn't expected Simon to live to wonder at the brandy, maybe.

He glanced at Wilkins when he realized he'd been quiet for a moment. The old servant had a pensive look on his face.

"What?" he urged.

"One doesn't wish to be branded a taleteller, Your Grace," Wilkins said hesitantly.

"A taleteller?"

"Aye, Your Grace. But you have charged me with looking after Miss...er, Crest."

A finger of dread spiked up Simon's spine. "Dani? Is she all right?"

"Yes," Wilkins said quickly. He tugged down the jacket of his uniform. "What I meant to say is that your brother took the curricle and went for a ride in the park with Miss Crest and Lady Lucy."

All sorts of horrible occurrences had entered his mind when Wilkins mentioned Dani. Her being ill, or injuring herself or someone doing harm to her. It took him a moment to adjust to the fact she'd merely gone for a ride in Hyde Park. After a moment his heartbeat slowed its rapid pace.

"I see." He nodded. "Any incidences?"

Wilkins squirmed uncomfortably. "Well, no, Your Grace, not that they mentioned."

He smiled. "No harm done then." He patted Wilkins arm.

"No harm indeed," the butler responded, smiling in return.

"Where is Dani, Wilkins?"

"I believe she has retired for the evening."

Simon nodded, turned to the stairs. "And Jack?"

Wilkins sniffed audibly, his upper lip quivered. "He mentioned spending the night with his friend."

"Close it up, Wilkins." Simon patted the butler's arm again. "I'll see you in the morning."

Dani awakened to the door clicking open. She had no idea what time it was but judging by the surrounding darkness it was very late. For a moment her heart raced, briefly remembering the fright of waiting to see who would find her in her dark corner by the docks. Little by little her limbs relaxed. She was safe in her bed. Which probably meant the door had been opened by Simon. He was home. Her heart raced for a new reason.

"Dani?" his voice whispered in the darkness, confirming her suspicions.

Dani pulled the blankets aside for him when he approached the bed. He was there beside her in an instant. She threw herself into his arms, which he'd obligingly opened. Simon was home. She'd missed him so much and there was so much she wanted to tell him. Opening her mouth to tell him about her day, her words were silenced by his mouth covering hers. His lips were hot and demanding and she had no wish to refuse their demand. There was something a little more urgent about him than usual, his kisses were ravenous, almost too intense.

Dani ensnared his neck with her arms, wanting him as close as possible. She loved him so.

He nibbled her lips, breaking the kiss. "Lord, you're so soft," Simon whispered, dropping his mouth to her neck. He stopped the onslaught on her throat and tipped her face to his. "I've had a rough day."

"Why?" she asked, stiffening. She wished she could see his face, read his eyes. He rolled to his back and took her with him so that she was snug against his side. Her fingers brushed his jaw.

He blew out a long breath. "I shouldn't bother you with this."

Dani reached for his hand, closed around it when she found it. She didn't like the sound of whatever was on his mind. She wanted him to share his thoughts with her.

"I'd like to listen," she said softly.

He was silent for such a long time she almost believed either he wasn't going to tell her what he was thinking or else he'd gone to sleep. Slowly he leaned his head down and kissed the top of her head.

"I don't want you to worry."

A sense of dread washed through her. Worry? She grasped his hand tighter.

"I went to Portsmouth to talk to Lindley about Norton's murder. You remember?"

She nodded to let him know she understood.

"I had a bit of trouble there. I was jumped in my room at an inn."

Dani immediately tilted her head to look up at him. She could only make out his outline. She put their entwined hands to his chest, closing her eyes at the comforting feel of his heartbeat.

"I think someone slipped me something," he continued, "and when I came to there were men going through my coat."

"Are you hurt?" Fearfully, she grasped his face in her hands. If she couldn't see him at least she could feel him.

He kissed her gently. "No, not really. Don't worry about it. It's nothing."

How could he say that? "It's not nothing."

"Well, anyway, there's no point in worrying you over it, is there?" He touched his lips to hers.

"Maybe you should stop," Dani suggested, knowing even while she said it that he wouldn't.

"Stop investigating what happened to Norton?" He shook his head. "I can't do that, Dani. If I weren't getting close, there would be no reason to act against me. Pen is counting on me."

Dani heard the rain hitting the window of her room. But the storm outside was nothing compared to the one raging in her heart. His aunt might be counting on him but Dani needed him. Not because he was her savior, though he was that but so much more.

Simon's lips claimed hers in deep kiss and when his fingers went to the laces on her nightgown she knew he was through discussing it. For now. She didn't plan on dropping it. Dani helped him finish with the laces and then she pulled the gown off and flung it down to the floor. Impulsively, she sat astride him and undid the shirt he still wore. He sat up just enough for her to discard it. She ducked down and flicked his nipple with her tongue.

Simon shivered as her reward, which emboldened her. His fingers threaded through her hair and he pulled her to his kiss, demanding and scalding. Knowing she might never have had this time with him again spurred her on. Dani tore her mouth from his and grazed his throat with her teeth.

He cupped her buttocks and moved her just enough so that he could undo his breeches. He scooted them down and off. Dani felt his hardness underneath her and she undulated against him.

"Dani," he murmured, a bare whisper.

"Simon." He quaked when she said his name. "Kiss me," she commanded.

He grabbed her head in his hands and took possession of her lips. She shifted until she was poised over his erection. She nearly sank down when she changed her mind. She wanted to go slowly. She wanted this to be perfect. Dani moved away.

He groaned in protest but she laughed low in her throat, a little surprised by her own wantonness. She'd overheard Grace and Mary talking about a particular part of coupling men especially liked. She meant to try it on Simon. She inched down his body, trailing kisses on his exposed skin.

"Dani?"

"Shh," she ordered. When she reached him, she hesitated a moment. Suddenly feeling shy, she pulled her hair until it covered her face. He was beautifully made. Dani licked her lips and took him in her mouth.

"Ah," he said, tensing beneath her. "Lord."

She swatted his hands when he tried to pull her away. She touched her tongue to the tip of him, inordinately pleased when he breathed her name. She pleasured him with her mouth for several moments until he gently pushed her away.

"It's my turn," Simon told her. Dani licked her lips in anticipation, knowing what he intended, craving it. He took her nipple in his mouth and sucked. She nearly shot off the bed.

When Dani thought she could stand no more, he moved down her stomach until he reached the sensitive spot between her legs. Throwing her head back, her eyes closed, Dani gave herself up to the wonderful sensations he was giving her with his mouth. A little while later, he swallowed her scream when his lips claimed hers.

Threading his fingers through hers, he rose above her and thrust deeply. She tightened her legs around his, meeting the rhythm he established. Her whole body was alive again, aching and open to his every move.

"Simon," she whispered, still so unaccustomed to the sound of his name on her lips. Still not used to the feel of him, lying across her. His thrusts quickened and she knew they were both close to finding their release. She reached hers first and sank her nails into his back, branding him. He followed shortly after, pouring his seed deep. Unable to stop the words from coming out, she said the words, she thought she'd never say again, "I love you."

A while later, Dani became aware of her surroundings again, of the man who still lay within her. Where before she barely noticed his weight now he was too heavy. She gently prodded his shoulder and with a murmur he rolled off her. He pulled her close to him and only a moment later she heard him softly snoring.

Dani splayed her fingers on his chest. She'd told him she loved him again. What possessed her to do that? She swore to herself she would not. And again he didn't respond in kind. What had Dani expected? It might have been possible the first time that he hadn't heard her. But she wouldn't get lucky both times. She shouted it, didn't she?

Dani loved him with all her heart of course, but she never meant him to know it. She might be naïve but she wasn't stupid and Dani knew she would never be anything but a mistress no matter what Lady Norton taught her. Tears pricked her eyes. She was feeling sorry for herself.

Even if she could stay his mistress forever, Dani snorted at that fanciful thought, Simon would one day marry and have children with some other woman. The thought of him even being with someone else caused her chest to ache unbearably. She wouldn't even think about him having children with someone else. Why had she let herself fall so deeply in love with him?

Dani balled her fist and stuck it in her mouth to stop the sob that threatened. She didn't want to wake Simon with her wailing. If she were really smart, Dani would leave before she had to face him marrying some woman. What if he even fell in love with his wife? Where would she go, if she could tear herself away? Dani didn't want to return to the East End, couldn't return and she didn't think she could fit in as a maid the way Grace was doing. Maybe a seamstress but she had wanted more for herself. She was just a fool that was all there was to it. She brushed at the puddle on his chest that had dripped down from her eyes.

* * * * *

Simon kissed Dani's curl that lay just above her closed eye. She was still sleeping though the sun streamed brightly through the curtains on the window. He wanted to wake her and make love to her all over again. What was he to do with her? For the second time Dani had told him she loved him. He knew it was true. Known it before she said it.

Dani wasn't the kind of woman who slept with just anyone. Simon knew that before she told him of the rape.

How did he feel about her? There was more than just an all-consuming lust, though he could not deny he felt that. Keeping Dani safe, making her happy. All of this he wanted. It was just complicated.

Simon rose from the bed without making a sound. He couldn't afford to dally further. It was past noon as it was and his man of affairs would be arriving shortly to go over the month's accounts.

He quietly closed her door behind him and padded over to his own room, holding his boots in his hands. There was no sign of his valet and he didn't bother to ring for him. He washed up quickly and dressed in dark brown breeches and coat.

Simon was about to head for the door when something on his bed caught his attention. The sun reflected off whatever it was. Frowning, he approached the bed. It lay there in the middle.

Reaching out, his hand closed around it. A pocket watch. Not his.

Grimacing, he turned it over to view the back. There was an inscription on it.

"To my beloved son, Douglas." Next to the inscription were the carved initials D.N.

Douglas Norton. He yanked the bell pull.

"Wilkins!"

"No need to shout, Your Grace, I heard the bell," Wilkins assured Simon coming into his rooms. The butler's gaze went to the pocket watch Simon dangled in front of him.

"Do you know what this is?"

"A pocket watch, Your Grace. Although not yours."

"Indeed not. It belonged to Douglas." Simon fought the urge to gnash his teeth in frustration. What was Norton's watch doing on his bed?

"Ah." Wilkins nodded, though his eyes remained uncertain.

"Aunt Pen gave it to her son last Christmas," Simon explained. "The watch was missing when Douglas' body was found,"

"Then how did you come into possession of it, Your Grace?" The old man was clearly as perplexed as he was.

"I found it just now on my bed. Who has access to my rooms, Wilkins?"

Wilkins thought about it only for a moment. "Myself, your valet, the maid staff. Nearly anyone in the household."

Simon couldn't imagine any of the servants conjuring up Douglas' pocket watch and placing it on his bed. But if not them, then who? He blew out a breath.

"Have you seen anyone lurking about my room?"

"Certainly not," Wilkins said, his nostrils flaring in outrage. He shook his head. "Really, Your Grace, I don't see a member of the staff involved."

"Neither do I." Simon ran his hand through his hair. "But ask them if they saw anything unusual."

"I will." Wilkins bowed. "Will there be anything else?"

"Send a footman with a message to my man of affairs and tell him I'll meet with him another day. I don't think I'll have the concentration for it today."

Chapter Twenty

"You still haven't told him have you?" Grace asked Dani the next afternoon. Dani waited in the parlor for her next lesson with Lady Norton. She'd been told Lady Norton slept late. Grace stood by the mantel, dressed in her new maid's uniform, dusting.

"I wanted to." Dani sipped her tea, being careful to hold her cup as she'd been instructed.

"But?"

"We got involved in other considerations," Dani said, blushing hotly. She did not feel comfortable sharing her intimate moments with Simon even with Grace.

Grace snorted.

"I wanted to bring it up today when I saw him," Dani defended herself.

"And?"

She sighed and put down her teacup. "He distracted me. Told me he was taking me to the opera tonight." Dani reached for the tray of tiny sandwiches. She selected her favorite. "I've never been to an opera. I'm a bit nervous."

Grace grinned. "I been meaning to tell you, you're talking real nice like."

"I've been trying." Dani bit her lip.

Wondered if Simon had noticed. She was very worried about him. Wilkins said something odd had occurred yesterday morning but he would not go into details. Dani wanted to ask Simon about it but after telling her about the opera and planting a very nice kiss on her, he'd said he had to pick up his new pair of boots. She hoped he would be careful.

After hearing what happened to him in Portsmouth, Dani would worry about him every time he left the house.

Dani glanced at Grace, who was busy running a cloth around the mantel. "How about you?"

"Me?" Grace was suddenly wary. The cloth froze in her hand.

"How are you fitting in with the rest of the staff?"

"Oh. I think good," Grace said, smiling once more. She stepped away from the mantel and picked up a large vase.

Dani frowned. "What did you think I meant?"

"What?"

"You thought I was talking about something else, didn't you?"

Grace nearly dropped the vase. She laughed nervously and quickly set the heavy object down.

"Grace? What?"

Her friend looked around the parlor and sighed. "Well, I've been making my play as it were."

"Making your play?" Dani asked perplexed.

To Dani's shock, Grace turned a dark shade of red. She never would have believed it had someone told her the story.

"Wilkins," Grace whispered.

Dani listened and glanced at the door. "No, he isn't coming."

Grace shook her head vehemently. "Wilkins is who I'm making my play for."

"That old rascal?"

Grace grinned. "That's what I like about him."

"I don't believe it!" Grace and Wilkins? She could never see the old butler showing an interest in Grace. "But he doesn't like you, is that it?" Dani popped a tiny sandwich into her mouth. Brushed the crumbs off her skirt.

"I think he does," Grace said.

"Wilkins?"

"Shh!" Grace told her. They both heard the footsteps approaching the door at the same time. The door opened and in walked Wilkins.

He narrowed his eyes at Grace. "Haven't you got something to do?"

"Right you are, Wilkins," Grace said quickly.

"Lady Norton is ready," Wilkins said, stepping aside to let the woman in.

* * * * *

Dani placed her hand in Simon's and stepped down from the carriage. Before them was the opera house. Beaming with anticipation, Dani allowed Simon to tuck her hand in his arm and draw her forward. They had brought along Lucy's governess this time as a chaperone, although Simon had made it clear the woman was to stay in the background as much as possible.

Dani wore one of her finest new gowns. It was a deep burgundy silk with matching gloves. Around her throat was a necklace of garnet beads. Her hair had been dressed in knot on the top of her head but several ringlets draped down to her shoulders in the back.

Simon was immaculately attired in formal black with a crisp white shirt and cravat. The night was warm so neither Dani nor Simon bothered with a wrap or coat.

When they approached the doors to the enormous opera house, Simon paused. He turned to Dani and took her hands in a tight grasp. He smiled down at her.

"You're the most beautiful woman here."

Having seen the brightly adorned women arriving for the opera, Dani knew the truth but she was thrilled by his words. She gave him a radiant smile.

Dani stepped out of the way of an elderly couple heading for the doors.

"It's so crowded. A lot of people must love the opera."

Simon shook his head. "Most don't come for the performance, sweetheart. They're here to be seen. This is the height of the season. Nearly everyone attends the opera at this time."

"Do you attend often?"

"No." Simon sighed. "I don't care for the opera. And really I'm beyond the days when I felt I had to be seen."

Dani frowned, confused. "Then why are we here?"

"I wanted you to experience it."

His simple words warmed her to the bone. Her eyes shining with happiness, Dani said, "Shall we go in, Your Grace?"

"Indeed, Miss Crest."

In his private box, he gestured to a seat overlooking the stage. Taking the seat, Dani turned inquiringly at him. "If you don't attend, why have a box?"

Simon shrugged and took the seat next to her. The governess sat in a chair he pointed out in the back corner. "Everyone has a box. It's what's done."

"Why?"

Simon grinned. "I've no idea."

The curtain behind them opened and they both turned to see the Duke of Scarborough enter. Scarborough's arm was around a strikingly beautiful brunette, whose throat dripped with emeralds, which matched her dark green low-cut gown.

"Stratford, Miss Crest." Scarborough bowed dramatically. "May I present Lady Selby?"

"I believe His Grace and I met once," Lady Selby said, smiling and extending her hand to Simon.

"Indeed you did," Scarborough acknowledged.

"Miss Crest, what a pleasure it is to meet you."

Dani felt three pairs of eyes on her. She prayed she wouldn't embarrass Simon by saying the wrong thing. Tried to remember her lessons.

"It is a pleasure to meet you too, Lady Selby." Dani pronounced each word carefully. It sounded odd to her ears but the other three occupants of the box smiled. She must have said it right.

"Do you mind if Lady Selby and I join you this evening?" Scarborough asked.

"As you wish," Simon replied, his hand waving toward two unoccupied chairs. "I'm surprised to see you here this evening, Scarborough."

"I'm a trifle surprised myself." Scarborough's lips curved.

"Julian is being such a dear escorting me tonight," Lady Selby purred. "Lord Selby had to beg off at the last moment."

"How convenient that Scarborough was available," Simon murmured.

Dani enjoyed the first half of the opera immensely. She knew from what Simon and the others told her that she was not supposed to watch but she could not help it. It mesmerized her. She hung over the side of the box transfixed the entire time. Vaguely, Dani heard the other occupants of the box chattering away behind her. Once in a while Dani noticed other attendees in nearby boxes staring in their direction. She paid them little heed.

Scarborough and Lady Selby left the box at intermission to mingle, they said. Dani and Simon chose to stay behind.

Simon noticed Dani watching Scarborough and Lady Selby leave pensively. When her attention was once more on him, Simon raised an eyebrow.

"What?" Dani asked innocently.

"I saw the way you looked at them. What's on your mind?"

"Well." Dani hesitated. "Do you think that she is his mistress?"

"Hmm. Could be. Why do you care?"

Dani shook her head, her ringlets bobbing. "I don't. Not really. It's just that…" She stopped, sighed.

"What?" For just a moment, Simon wondered if Dani was jealous. Was she attracted to Scarborough? No, it wasn't possible. She loved him. It was something else.

"I think Lucy fancies him a bit, that's all." Dani blushed.

Simon rolled his eyes, snorted. "Is that all? Don't pay any attention to who Lucy fancies, Dani. She changes her mind on a daily basis. And she's got at least one or two more years before her season."

Dani smiled. "I guess you are right. I told you it was nothing."

At that moment a man stuck his head in and asked to speak to Simon for just a moment. Simon excused himself from Dani and went just outside the box.

Dani glanced behind her at the governess who appeared to be dozing off. Lucy must be exhausting her. Smiling a little, her eyes wandered to the other boxes, wondering what was being discussed by other people. Or who, most likely. In her limited experience with the *ton* she knew they all loved to gossip. Sometimes viciously. They were worse than most of the people she grew up with.

Dani stood up from her chair and walked to the edge of the railing. She peered down at the group of musicians below, then past them to the stage. Mary had had a wonderful voice. Dani could almost picture her old friend on that stage singing one of the beautiful tunes. She smiled wistfully. No news of Mary. In her heart, Dani knew Mary was probably dead. She turned her eyes from the stage.

It was then that she saw him.

He was standing in a box almost directly across from Simon's. At first she didn't even realize it was him. Raised to his eyes was some sort of looking device. Her blood froze.

He lowered the device slowly but kept his gaze firmly locked on her. Carstairs.

Dani backed away from the railing. It was mere coincidence he was at the opera. Simon told her many *ton* members attended. Once Carstairs was there anyway, he just happened to see her from across the opera house. That was all there was to it.

But Dani knew she would wonder if the viscount had followed them for the rest of the evening.

Chapter Twenty-One

She'd fallen asleep in the coach.

Dani punched the pillow next to her with frustration the next morning. During the second half of the performance the previous night, Dani had resolved to tell Simon about Viscount Carstairs. Her enjoyment of the performance had been noticeably dimmed. Simon cast more than one glance her way but did not press her.

After the opera was over, they joined Scarborough and Lady Selby in a glass of port. Dani had never tasted it before but it had served to soothe her nerves. Before she knew it, Scarborough had poured her another. She drank that one faster than the first. By the time Simon led her out to the carriage, Dani was very sleepy.

Now, she vaguely remembered Simon carrying her into the house and up the stairs. He'd removed her gown, dressed her in her nightclothes, then stayed with her, wrapping his arms around her for the night. But he was gone this morning.

Raising her head from the pillow, Dani winced.

"Ugh," she said out loud, laying her head back down. It pounded. She touched it gingerly.

Wishing she could stay in bed for the day, Dani forced herself to sit up again. She wasn't exactly sure what time it was but she knew she was due for more lessons from Lady Norton.

* * * * *

"Good afternoon, Dani," Lady Norton called, coming into the room dressed in a gray mourning gown.

Dani's stomach fluttered nervously as it always did every afternoon when Lady Norton came to teach her. Her head still pounded too. Grace informed her it was because of last night's port.

"Tea, your ladyship?"

'Thank you." Lady Norton took her seat on the settee.

Dani poured the tea, her hands shaking. She handed the cup to the woman.

Penelope Norton eyed her shrewdly. "You've learned so much since our lessons began. You speak properly, are reading much better, can paint and draw. You've even picked up your French words quickly. You really are a fast learner, Dani."

"Thank you, my lady."

"But you know, dear, no matter how well you speak and act it isn't quite the same." Lady Norton reached over and took a teacake from the platter of biscuits and cakes.

"The same?"

"Let's be honest with each other, Dani," Lady Norton said with a cool smile. "You are Simon's mistress, aren't you?"

The fluttering in Dani's stomach increased. She pressed a hand to it, hoping the woman could not hear the churning. Her cheeks grew warm. Mistress. Did Lady Norton view her in the same way she viewed Lady Selby last night?

"No one could blame you for it, of course," Lady Norton continued, not waiting for Dani's confirmation. "A rich, handsome duke. You must have thought you were very lucky, indeed, when he took you in. Why don't you tell me about it, dear?"

"Ah," Dani said, warily, biting her lip. What was this?

"Tell me about how you convinced my nephew to make you one of his projects," Penelope Norton urged.

"Projects?" There it was again. Just as Wilkins said. Dani stared down at the cup of tea she held.

"Yes, dear Simon. He's so very kind to the unfortunate. But you know that. You were very smart coming to see him, weren't you?" she asked. "Coming from that part of London. What a killing you've made."

Dani felt the prick of tears. Now, why was she crying? She didn't want to cry in front of the woman. It wasn't like that. Not the way Lady Norton made it sound.

"As kind as Simon is, Dani, you must know that's all it can ever be."

Dani raised her gaze to Lady Norton's. The older woman's smile was kind and sympathetic. Dani swallowed the lump in her throat.

"When Simon marries I imagine his wife will put a stop to a lot of Simon's odd ways."

"Odd ways?" Dani frowned.

Lady Norton sniffed. "You aren't the first, you know."

"I-I know."

"He's always taking in strays. I can't think of any potential wife who will tolerate it," Lady Norton said. "His mother was my dear older sister. Since her death, I feel it is my duty to act in her place. Frankly, I've been telling him it's time he looked to securing a wife. It's his responsibility."

Dani wondered why the older woman felt the need to tell her all this. She knew she didn't exactly fit in with the *ton*.

"I've grown quite fond of you, dear," Lady Norton said, touching Dani's hand with her own. "I don't like the idea of your being hurt. You are in love with Simon, aren't you?"

The question did not help in her desire not to cry in front of Lady Norton. A tear slipped down her cheek.

"Oh, my dear, I didn't mean to upset you so," the older woman said, brushing at the tear. "I just wanted you to realize that you can never be anything to Simon other than his mistress. Surely you must know that."

Dani took a deep breath, then nodded. "Yes." But she didn't want to think about it.

"I'm certain you think you don't want my advice and I probably shouldn't say this but if I were in your place I would put a stop to it."

"A stop to it?"

Lady Norton nodded. "You're already in love with him. I'm certain he feels a certain tenderness for you which only serves to encourage your love but it will no doubt pass. These sorts of affairs always do. The longer you allow it to go on, the harder it will be for you, Dani, when Simon breaks it off."

"What...what do you think I should do?" Dani asked, hating the quaver in her voice.

"First, let me say that I don't mean to be cruel, Dani," Penelope Norton said. "But I know the way things are."

Lady Norton paused took a sip of the hot amber liquid in her cup. "I don't want to see you end up in a situation like Melanie Cross."

"Melanie Cross?"

"A dear old friend of mine back in my youth. The daughter of a baronet. She fell in love with a duke, poor girl, much the same as you have and ended up being his mistress. A baronet's daughter was respectable enough, of course."

The way Lady Norton said the words had Dani thinking she wanted to add the words unlike you. But she did not. Dani waited for her to continue.

"But the duke wanted something more than a baronet's daughter. He felt he was above that. Melanie found herself expecting and planned on begging him to marry her. She found him in the middle of his own wedding to an earl's daughter." Her mouth thinned. "She took her own life when the whole mess ended."

"I-I would never..."

"Of course not, dear," Lady Norton said quickly. She patted Dani's hand. "I don't wish to be indelicate but I am certain you don't wish to become with child, Dani."

Her words nearly pierced Dani's heart. She would have given the world to have a child with Simon. But she knew it was hopeless, had always known. More tears spilled down her cheeks but she ignored them. Her throat hurt.

"I really have upset you, haven't I?" Lady Norton asked mournfully. "Don't let yourself be a victim, dear. It will hurt at first to end it with Simon but far less than it might later." She stood up. "I can see that you're too distraught to have a lesson today."

"Thank you," Dani said, absently. She no longer cared if the woman was even in the room. Her stomach ached nearly as much as her heart.

"Goodbye, Dani," Lady Norton called on her way out of the room.

* * * * *

Simon's carriage rolled along the cobbled streets to Brooks' but in spite of the days he'd spent trying to speak with the young viscount now that he'd received Carstairs' note to meet him at Brooks' the meeting held little interest for him.

Dani's strange mood during the second half of the opera bothered him. She'd almost seemed frightened. He intended to find out what was wrong but Scarborough wanted them to join them in a drink. Damn, his friend. Dani got drunk and fell asleep before he had a chance to ask her.

He could have awakened her before he left in the morning, asked her why she had frozen up. Dani had loved the first part of the opera, Simon was certain. But he didn't want to disturb her rest. She would probably need it after the port.

The coach came to a stop. Stepping down from the carriage, he glanced around at the bustling pedestrian traffic.

He'd lived his life in luxury and thought nothing of it. Taken it all for granted. Dani hadn't had that. He wanted to make sure she lived like a queen.

"Your Grace?" The coachman's brows were furrowed.

"I'm not sure how long I will be," Simon said absently. He headed for the club. The day was bright with sunshine so when he stepped into Brooks' it took a moment for his eyes to adjust to the darker interiors. All around him men spoke in hushed voices, speaking of political intrigues and clandestine affairs no doubt. Neither subject mattered to him. Glancing around the room, his gaze finally rested on a dark-haired young man who gestured to him.

The man he assumed to be Carstairs stood up as he approached. "Stratford?" He pointed to a chair across from him at a table.

"You're hard man to track, Carstairs."

Carstairs smile was disarming. "I don't mean to be. Brandy?"

"Yes."

Carstairs poured the rich amber liquid into a glass and handed it to Simon. He stared at the drink, remembering the brandy he'd recently partaken of in Portsmouth. He lowered the glass and set it down.

"Since I know what you've been seeking me for, I won't bother with the niceties," Carstairs said. His gaze raked the crowd around them before coming to rest once more on Simon. "I liked your cousin. I suppose I was one of the few who did."

"Did you spend a lot of time in his company?"

"Generally, no," the young viscount admitted. His smile was slightly twisted. "Much as I liked Douglas he had a tendency to keep company with some rather unsavory sorts."

"Oh?" Simon raised an eyebrow.

"One doesn't wish to speak ill of the dead, Stratford," Carstairs said musingly. He took a swallow of his brandy. "But the night Douglas was murdered by The Black Swan was not the first time he'd been down to that part of London."

"Go on."

"I'm sure you already know that he played cards too much." Carstairs shook his head. "The times I played with him I don't think he ever won. He told me once that he frequented The Black Swan. Men at places like that aren't always as forgiving of debt as we might be."

"So," Simon said slowly, considering. "You believe that Douglas was the victim of ruffians he gambled with down by the docks, is that it?"

Carstairs tilted his head. "I really couldn't say exactly what happened to him. That last night he arrived with quite a bit of blunt."

"Hmm."

Carstairs shrugged. "He mentioned that he could pay some of the debts he owed with what he had but how much better would it be if he could double his money." The young viscount briefly sneered. "He erred in playing cards with Pembroke. Ruthless."

Simon nodded. "Pembroke won."

"Every hand," Carstairs agreed. "Douglas became more uneasy as the evening progressed. Both Dresden and I urged him to give up for the night. Luck not with him. He didn't want to listen. By the time it was over he'd lost everything he came with and more."

"How did he pay Pembroke?"

"He gave him what he had, of course, then told him he'd get the rest of it to him the next day." The viscount shook his dark head. "The next day, of course, he was found murdered."

"And what did you do afterward, Carstairs?" Simon asked.

"Am I a suspect then?"

"Are you?" Simon countered.

Carstairs smiled and sipped his brandy. "I hate to disillusion you on that point, Stratford but I went to a lady's house after the card game. I was most thoroughly engaged until morning. She can tell you the same if you'd care to know her name."

"No." Simon remembered something Scarborough told him. "What about Dresden?"

Carstairs looked puzzled. "What about him?"

"I've heard you argued with Dresden that night. Also about money."

"Dresden was a nobody." Carstairs shrugged. "Came into the title by some distant relation. Played at being somebody. He cheated most times. I didn't like playing with him."

There was an earnestness about Carstairs that seemed quite genuine but there was something about the Viscount that Simon didn't quite trust. His grandfather was an entirely different story but though he suspected the man drugged his brandy, Simon had trouble believing the old man would be interested enough in Douglas Norton to murder him. But then why had the duke bothered with the whole business in Portsmouth? Little of it made sense.

"That's all the questions I have for you now."

"Are you sure?" Carstairs asked.

"Quite." He stood up and pushed the untouched brandy aside. "I hope you will be somewhat easier to locate should I think of any more questions for you."

"Your servant, Stratford," Carstairs said, lifting his own glass in a salute.

Simon made his way to his carriage and stood at the steps leading into it, thinking. He really wanted to return to Dani and put Douglas Norton's murder far from his mind. He needed a distraction from it. But there was a matter he'd been thinking of more often and it now seemed more important to him than ever.

He glanced up and noticed his coachman was not about. "Richmond?"

Richmond never left his post. Frowning, Simon walked round to the other side of the carriage. There was no sign of him. Though his driver had never once presumed to wait inside the carriage, Simon felt he had to check. He opened the door and peered in. Richmond, blood all over his nose, was slumped on the cushion to the right.

The hair on his nape bristled. Simon turned just as a man to his right wielding an ugly looking knife hurried toward him. Out of the corner of his eye, Simon noted his accomplice coming from the left.

"We've got a message for you, Your Grace," the one with the knife snarled.

"Hell," Simon muttered.

Chapter Twenty-Two

ஐ

"Well, well, well, what 'ave we 'ere, Sammy?" the knife man asked his hulking companion as they boxed Simon in from both sides. The carriage door pressed against Simon's back.

Sammy, a large man with a stomach that hung over his trousers, laughed low in his throat so that it came out sounding more like a growl. He wore a dark brown hat pulled low over one brow and he held up meaty fists.

"You're making a grave error," Simon informed them calmly.

"Oh, I'll just bet we are, guvner," Knife Man said, grinning. He was the smaller, thinner of the two brigands but the wicked, fiendish glint in his eyes also made it clear he was the more dangerous. He waved his weapon. "We gots a message to deliver, don't we, Sammy?"

"That we do, Marty."

"I'm not presently receiving," Simon retorted. He moved his hand up ever-so slightly on his coat but neither man appeared to notice.

"What was the message, Sammy?" Marty asked, chuckling. "Was it break 'is legs?"

"Nah, it were cut off 'is thumbs," Sammy cackled.

"I'm really rather fond of both and would appreciate keeping them, if you don't mind," Simon told the thugs.

Sammy looked momentarily nonplused, not quite understanding the situation. Simon was certain Sammy was the type who was used to men fearing him and Simon's lack of fear confused him.

"I don't know, guvnor," Marty, the man clearly in charge, said with a depraved grin. "I think you might be missing both by the time we get done wiv you."

Simon pulled out the pistol hidden in his coat. "I am afraid I won't tolerate missing anything, gentlemen."

"'Ey, 'e's armed," Sammy yelled, his voice a high-pitched whine. The big man backed up a step.

"So 'e is," Marty said, sneering. "But 'e can't shoot us both."

"True enough, Marty, old boy," Simon said evenly. "But I think I will shoot you." He aimed the pistol at the man with the knife.

"I'm getting outta 'ere." Sammy turned and ran down the alley.

Simon smirked and raised an eyebrow at Marty. "Shall I?"

Marty grimaced and turning on his heels ran down the opposite end of the alley. Simon shrugged and returned his pistol to its place. He was sincerely glad he'd had the presence of mind to bring it with him.

* * * * *

"Are you sure you're all right?" Dani asked him for the fifth time since he'd returned home. She clung to his arm, her extraordinary eyes wide with undisguised fright.

"Quite." Simon smiled reassuringly. He led her to the settee and sat down, pulling her to his side. "Richmond is the one who was injured." Simon glanced at Wilkins who hovered nearby.

"Richmond's being tended to right now, Your Grace."

They were all there in the front parlor. Dani, Wilkins, Jack, Lucy, Mrs. Martin and even Grace.

Simon was warmed by their presence. They'd all insisted on hearing his adventure with Sammy and Marty over and over again. All except Dani. She just wanted to know he was all right.

"Bastards," Jack grumbled from his post by the mantel. "How dare they?"

"Perhaps you'd like some tea?" Dani asked him, her voice barely above a whisper.

"Probably brandy would be more like it." Jack headed for the side table, picked up the decanter.

"No, Jack." Simon shook his head. "I'm off brandy just now. Mrs. Martin, how about some tea, all around?"

"Right away, Your Grace." Mrs. Martin hurried from the parlor.

Lucy moved restlessly by the door drawing Simon's attention. "I have studies I have to get to," she said reluctantly. "If you are sure you are all right?"

"I'm sure, go ahead, sweet pea."

Lucy rushed to him, planted a kiss on his forehead and than to Simon and Dani's mutual surprise, she leaned down and kissed Dani's cheek. Lucy reddened than hurried out the door.

She looked faintly bemused by his sister's action.

"Just what did these bastards want?" Jack asked. He'd begun to pace the room, tension radiating off him. Simon actually believed he was worried about him. Amazing.

Simon shook his head. "I've no idea, but I am sure they were sent by the same person as the pair from Portsmouth. I'd just come from speaking with Viscount Carstairs."

His arm was wrapped around a block of ice. Dani went completely still and very cold. Simon stared down at her. She'd lost all color to her face too.

"Dani, what is it?"

Her eyes were as wide as saucers. He sensed the fear throbbing through her.

"Your Grace, if I may." It was Grace who spoke up.

Simon glanced at her. Grace came toward them, twisting her hands in front of her. She flicked a quick look at Wilkins who nodded encouragingly.

"Before you and Dani found me down by the docks, a man came looking for a young girl. He asked me a lot of questions. A girl with red hair named Dani is who he asked about."

Simon went as cold as Dani. "And?"

"The man were from the gentry. He told me his name was Viscount Carstairs." Grace's eyes crinkled. "I told Dani about him when I came to."

"Did you tell the man anything about Dani?" Simon asked, tightening his hold on Dani, who was still.

"No, of course not. I would never betray her. I didn't know what he wanted."

Simon grasped Dani's chin and forced her to look at him. "Sweetheart, why didn't you tell me about this?"

"I tried to. I mean I wanted to." Her bottom lip trembled.

"All right." Simon pressed his lips to hers lightly. "It's going to be fine."

The door opened to allow Mrs. Martin to come in, pushing the tea tray.

"Wilkins, why don't you and Grace attend to your duties? Mrs. Martin, just leave the tea. I'll pour for us." Simon knew Wilkins would understand he wanted to be alone with Dani. Wilkins quietly ushered Grace and Mrs. Martin out. That left only Jack.

"I know, I know. Get out." Jack held up his hands. "I'm not wanted. I have somewhere to be anyway. Be careful, Simon. I don't like the sound of all this."

"Sweetheart?" Simon turned to Dani. Her eyes were closed. A single tear squeezed out and fell on to her cheek.

She shook her head and buried her face in his collar. He held her with both arms wrapped tightly around her.

"I'm all right, Dani," he assured her again. "I'm not going anywhere."

Dani hiccupped, hesitated, then hugged him tightly. His chest constricted. What was wrong with her? It was more than just concern over what had happened to him today. "Tell me."

Dani tried to push away then but he would not let her. She fought him for a moment but then sighed. "I don't want you."

"You don't?"

"At least I'm trying not to," she said thickly.

Simon breathed again. "Why would you try not to?"

"Lady Norton."

"What has she to do with this?" Simon frowned. "What did she say to you?"

Dani didn't respond for a long time, she just continued to cry softly. He stroked her back soothingly. He would not leave until he got every detail from her.

"She said you and I could never be together and I should stop, well, you..." Dani shrugged.

"You and I should not sleep together?" he guessed. She nodded. Simon wanted to wring the interfering old woman's neck. It was a mistake to allow her to tutor Dani that much was certain. "Dani, I don't want you to listen to her."

"You don't?" Dani hiccupped.

"Sweetheart, whatever she said to you is not how I feel. You told me you loved me. Did you mean it?"

Now she did pull back and she tilted her chin up to look at him. Her eyes sparkled with diamond tears. She nodded slowly. He kissed her lips lightly.

"That's all that matters then, isn't it? She probably meant well, Dani but she doesn't know what's between us. She can't know." He tightened his grip on her. She buried her face against him again. He rested his chin against her fragrant locks.

Simon didn't know how long they stayed that way but after a while he sensed that Dani had fallen into a troubled sleep. He gently eased her down on the settee, being careful not to wake her when he dislodged himself from her. Now was definitely not the time to tell her about the message he'd received from the runner he'd hired to look into Mary's disappearance. He'd found it when he returned home.

Simon stood up and placed a kiss on her forehead.

Simon decided he would talk to Grace about Mary. He wanted to learn a few more details and then he would ask Grace what she thought about breaking the news of Mary's probable murder to Dani. He sought her out and found her in the kitchen alone. He cleared his throat to get her attention.

"Grace, can I have a word with you?"

"Aye, Your Grace," she said, smiling a little warily. "I could use a break."

Simon gestured to the stiff-backed chair by the fire. Grace sat down. "Grace, tell me about you and Mary and Dani."

Grace crossed her arms in front of her. "Mary and I knew her mother before Dani was born. Beautiful she was. Dani looks a lot like her. Rose was Dani's mother. She was the daughter of a baron's son and she became a really good seamstress for the ladies of the *ton*. None of them liked her though."

"Why?"

Grace grinned. "Like I said she was beautiful and a lot of their husbands started coming to their fittings so they could see Rose."

"Of course."

"We started out as her assistants. Mary and I figured it was one of them."

Simon frowned, shaking his head. "One of them?"

"What got Rose in trouble. But Rose seemed happy while she was expecting Dani. While she was expecting, a very handsome man came to the shop and took her away. She disappeared for a while. We didn't know what happened and we struggled to keep the shop going, but we thought maybe he was the one. Didn't see Rose or the child after that."

"And then?" Simon prodded when Grace paused.

"Well, Rose came back with Dani a few years later and she was very ill. She asked us to take care of Dani. She had a terrible cough. She said we had to leave the shop and take Dani with us. We wanted to know, but she just kept saying he was after them. We asked Rose to come with us too, but she refused and then coughed up some blood." Grace sighed sadly. "She died then and we took Dani with us and whatever we could sell from the shop. We had to leave our lives behind. Most people we knew wouldn't help us and we had no where to go. We did the best we could."

"You did a fine job with her too," Simon said, smiling. "Dani's wonderful."

"We were real proud of her," Grace agreed. "But we never wanted her to end up selling herself like we both did. She deserved better."

"You all did. Grace, tell me about Mary's disappearance."

Grace's eyes clouded over, she stared into the fire. There was a single pot on it, probably with soup for the evening meal. She twisted her hands in front of her. "Mary was always cautious. She could smell a bad customer two streets away. She distrusted that man the moment he came."

"What man?" Simon asked sharply.

"Same man what came to talk to me. A young man from the gentry. Dark hair, blue eyes," Grace said. "If you get a customer like that you think it's your lucky day."

"But not Mary?"

"She wanted nothing to do with him. She told him she were busy. Already had a man waiting. All he wanted was time and information, she said. Same as me. Mary didn't tell him anything either and he gave her a shiner." Grace shook her head. "Mary didn't really say what he was after but she was real scared. Started acting real secretive. When she went missing I was sure he was responsible. Who else could it have been?"

"So she didn't tell you what he wanted?"

"No. But she kept looking over her shoulder all the time. I knew she was afraid he might come back." Grace lowered her voice. "And he did." Grace shivered. "Until you brought me here I was afraid he might have taken Dani cause I didn't know you had her. I was so glad when I found out he hadn't."

"Tell me about the man again." Simon wished he had Carstairs in front of him that moment.

"He called to me and I knew he was the same one as had been talking to Mary." She twisted her hands in her lap again, her expression agitated. "He asked me about a young woman he was searching for with red hair and blue eyes. Dani, he called her. I told him nothing, of course."

"And you are sure he said he was Viscount Carstairs?"

Grace snorted. "Aye and even if he hadn't told me I would know. He came by here."

Simon nodded. "Looking for me, I know."

The fire crackled.

"No," Grace said, shaking her head.

"What?"

"The first time he came was to see you, Your Grace. But the second time, he was here looking for Dani."

* * * * *

It still hurt.

Dani woke a short time later on the settee with an empty ache in her heart. Despite his words, Dani knew that she and Simon could never truly be together. She had nothing in common with him except sex. Society would never allow a match between them.

She was torn between so many feelings. Anger because after all this time of trying to avoid being a doxy that was exactly what she had ended up as. It mattered little that it was only for Simon. The end result was the same. She was somebody's plaything.

Sorrow, deep and piercing, for in spite of feeling practically worthless, she still loved him. Still wanted him. Would give just about anything to stay with him. Pathetic, because she had stooped so low as to crave any bit of warmth from him.

Desperation and fear. She was afraid her time with Simon could end any time and she was also afraid that he'd endangered himself with the Norton investigation.

She struggled up into a sitting position and brought her knees up to her chest. She wrapped her arms about them and wondered just what she should do next. Should she distance herself from him as Lady Norton suggested? She didn't think she could do such a painful thing. She wasn't even sure how to stay away from him for she was drawn like a moth to a flame.

She sat like this for so long, lost in thought, she barely registered the click of the door opening. She knew who stood in the threshold without even looking. The door closed softly behind Simon.

"You're awake."

She offered no response, still torn between her conflicting emotions. What did she think she would do? Tell him to take her back to the East End? Never.

"How do you feel?" Simon approached the settee. She felt his gaze on her. She met his concerned eyes. Their gold-green depths nearly overwhelmed her.

"I don't know."

He sank down on his knees in front of her and took her hands in his. He frowned uncertainly.

"Sweetheart, we need to talk about something." His voice was low, gentle.

Dani tensed. Surely he would not tell her their association was over already? That he had changed his mind and he didn't want her around anymore?

"What is it?" she asked.

"I received a message from a runner I hired to look into Mary's disappearance." Simon blew out a breath. "There's a prostitute down by The Black Swan who has some information about Mary. I'm going to go down there tomorrow."

"I see." Her voice sounded hollow to her own ears.

"I'll come back as soon as I can and tell you all about it," he promised.

Dani shook her head quickly. Simon met her gaze, he raised a brow. "No, Simon. I want to go with you."

"Dani."

"Please. I need to do this."

Simon's mouth twisted in a grimace but he nodded. "Very well."

* * * * *

By the time, Simon and Dani headed for the East End it was nearing noon.

Earlier, Simon had sent round a note to Carstairs' home asking to see him again but the footman returned saying the viscount was out.

This time he had the coach drop them near the tavern. The East End of London was a dangerous place for anyone even in the daytime. But his well-tailored black breeches, black coat and pristine white cravat and Dani's yellow muslin gown, with her looking every inch a *ton* beauty, made them instantly stand out. Simon did not intend them to become victims.

A group of men standing near where the coach dropped them off stopped talking and eyed them balefully. Simon met their gaze directly and after a moment they turned back to their conversation.

"It's just a couple streets to the Swan from here," Dani said. She linked her arm with his. Once again Simon had decided it was best for them to come without a maid. He knew a place like this would only frighten them.

While they drew a number of calculating stares from the people on the streets, no one approached them. Simon and Dani rounded a corner that took them into a narrow lane. It was down this alley the runner had informed Simon the doxy usually spent her time. Simon squinted, halted, held Dani's hand tightly. Huddled against one stained wall of the passage was a woman of undeterminable age. She beckoned to them.

"'Ey, now, me luv, care for some company?" She pulled her shawl away to reveal her breasts popping from her tattered gown. The woman eyed Dani saucily. Dani inched closer to the duke.

Simon crouched down next to her, being careful to position himself so that he had a view of each entrance to the alley. "I don't want company but I would like some information."

"Information?" she asked, her inviting eyes now becoming wary.

"I'm willing to pay for it," he assured her. "I imagine you know a lot about what goes on around the docks. I was told you might know something about a doxy named Mary."

She pulled her shawl closed once more and studied him. Now that Simon had a closer look at her face he guessed she was only a few years older than Dani. He pushed aside the relief that Dani had escaped such a fate. He needed to concentrate on their surroundings.

"You ain't Ben."

Ben was the runner Simon had hired. He nodded. "I know. Ben sent me."

"What do you want to know?" she asked after a moment. "I'll let you know 'ow much after you ask."

"Mary disappeared recently, did you know her?"

"Yes."

He nodded, watching out of the corner of his eye a man coming down the alley. There was something oddly familiar about the man. "I need some information on her." He hesitated. "And also a bit on the goings on around The Black Swan." The man continued to pass them and Simon watched him with his other eye.

The prostitute nodded. "I can 'elp you. It'll cost you 'alf a crown, though."

"Very well," Simon agreed solemnly. The man who'd walked past them had now left the alley and he relaxed just a little.

"Up front if you please, guvnor," the young doxy said.

He removed the coin from his coat and placed it firmly in her hand. She glanced and it and nodded, pleased.

"All right, then. Ask me your questions."

"You said you know Mary. How well?"

"We was friendly like. You spend most o' your life with some o' these girls. You gets to know 'em pretty well."

"And you haven't seen Mary since the night she disappeared?"

The light in her brown eyes dimmed. "No. It 'appens sometimes, you know. You gets a bad customer and you ain't 'eard from again."

Dani flinched beside him.

"Is that what happened to Mary?"

She shrugged, causing her shawl to slip from her shoulders a bit. "Don't really know. Mary was experienced, you know. She was always on 'er guard. She knew what men would be trouble and she avoided those mostly."

Simon nodded.

The woman sighed, her eyes darting around the alley for a moment. "It's getting more dangerous all the time around 'ere. Just before Mary went missing she told me about a gentlemen." She paused, looking Simon up and down. "Sort o' like you, 'e was."

"Did she describe him?"

"Yes. She said 'e was from the gentry, real 'andsome. Young. Younger than you, begging your pardon." She grinned, flashing her partially missing teeth at him.

He smiled. "Go on."

"Dark 'air, blue eyes. A real charmer she said. Asking around 'bout one o' the girls."

Carstairs again. He felt Dani's hand against his back. "Did she say who he asked about?"

"No. She said all 'e wanted was information." The young doxy paused. Wariness appeared in her eyes again. "You ain't like 'im, are you?"

"No."

"Well, but you is asking about information." She shook her head. "She didn't tell 'im what 'e wanted to know and 'e got angry. Mary said 'e thought she was lying."

"Did he get rough with Mary?"

The girl nodded. "She 'ad a black eye. It was just a couple days after that she went missing. I've wondered if 'e weren't responsible."

Simon wondered too. The prostitute's story was nearly identical to Grace's.

"I seen me a man that looked just like the one what Mary described."

"The night Mary disappeared?"

"No but a couple days after that. Down by The Black Swan."

Simon opened his mouth to say more when out of the corner of his left eye he noticed the man who'd come down the alley coming toward them once more. He shook his head and pulled out a fistful of coins. He pressed them in the girl's hands. Simon remembered why the man was familiar.

"What's this?" she exclaimed, her eyes wide with shock.

"I know you probably won't listen to me but try to take these coins and make a better life for yourself. You don't deserve this." Simon stood up then. The man was closer now and Simon could clearly see the length of rope he played with. Dani had noticed him too. He heard her gasp. Simon glanced briefly in the other direction and saw the man had an accomplice coming from that way, also. "Run," he urged the doxy.

She stood up and quickly looked both left and right. She bit her lip and decided to go to her left. The men did not stop her because she was clearly not their intended victim.

"Well, if it ain't the Prince Regent," the man with the rope snarled, twirling it round in his meaty paws.

"Nice to see you again too, Eddie," Simon drawled, pushing Dani behind him.

"You got courage coming back 'ere," Eddie acknowledged. He laughed. "I don't admire courage much"

"I'll keep that in mind." Eddie and his friend ran at him. Wanting to keep Dani as far from the trouble as possible, he moved forward to meet them. Wondered briefly why he hadn't thought to bring his walking stick with the rapier in it.

Dani wasn't about to stand by and let the thugs rough up Simon. Not while she could do something about it. How dare they think they could just attack him? Backing away, further down the wall, Dani kept one eye on the action and the other she used to look around for an object she could use.

Wincing when one of Eddie's punches connected with Simon's stomach, Dani spotted a discarded bottle on the other side of the alley. Confirming that Eddie and his fellow attacker at the moment were too interested in pummeling Simon, Dani inched over to the bottle and seized it in her fists.

She turned and watched the fight for a moment or two more, trying to decide whether to take out Eddie or his friend. It appeared, though, that Eddie was the bigger threat. He seemed to be landing punches more accurately than the other man and he was also twice his friend's size. Dani would have to strain on her tiptoes to reach his big fat head.

Simon ducked another fist, this one knocking Eddie slightly off his balance. It was now or never. Dani rushed up to the thug and slammed the bottle down over the crown of his head.

Eddie straightened in surprise, turned abruptly to face Dani, staggered toward her and collapsed onto the ground with a loud thud.

Simon and Eddie's friend stopped to stare at her handiwork. Simon's expression was one of admiration for her feat. The other man was clearly consternated.

Simon then turned to the other man, raised an eyebrow and with a final wallop to the man, knocked him to the ground unconscious.

He held out his hand to Dani. Her nose in the air as she stepped around Eddie, Dani placed her hand in his.

"Thank you, sweetheart."

Chapter Twenty-Three

ಐ

A short while later, Simon and Dani stepped through the doorway of The Black Swan. Immediately every man in the tavern glanced their way. Their expressions ranged from baleful to merely curious to open lust directed at Dani. Simon wondered what he thought he was doing in a place like the Swan. And why he brought Dani with him. Idiot. But they were committed now. The idea had come to Simon to pay another visit to The Black Swan when they'd emerged from the alley after their near miss with his old mate, Eddie. His intention had been to head back to the carriage and make their way home. The wise way to go, no doubt. Then he'd noticed the tall bearded sailor staring at them.

The man looked to be middle-aged with dark hair streaked through with gray but his piercing blue eyes were strangely youthful. For some reason, the man's regard seemed more intent than any others who had yet studied them. He'd spent several minutes regarding Simon and Dani before finally going into the tavern. Simon had followed.

Simon located a table in the back corner of the room. It was the perfect vantage point to view the entire tavern without allowing someone to sneak up on them. He steered Dani toward it and they took their seats.

"I don't know if this is a good idea," Dani whispered.

A buxom blonde came forward and took Simon's order for ale. Dani politely declined. While he waited for the barmaid's return he scanned the crowd of men looking for the strange sailor. Some of the Swan patrons had turned their attention elsewhere but a number of them still stared at him and Dani. He couldn't spot the man among them.

"'Ere you are, luv," the tavern wench said, slamming down his pint.

Simon glanced briefly at the dirty mug of ale then looked up quickly when he saw the tall odd sailor ambling toward their table. The sailor walked with an exaggerated limp.

He shared a quick glance with Dani, who raised her eyebrow in a gesture very similar to his own.

"A wee bit lost, ain't you?" the man asked when he reached them. Without waiting for an invitation, he helped himself to a seat on the bench across from Simon and Dani.

"You've been staring at us. Mind telling me why?" Simon asked.

The sailor, his familiar blue eyes twinkling, rubbed his bristly chin. "Just curious what a pair like you'd be doing down this area. We don't get your kind here so often. You ought to be careful. It can get rough if you don't watch yourself." He inclined his head to Dani. "Watch your lady too."

"Thanks for the warning. Speaking of men like me, would you mind answering some questions now that you've helped yourself to our table?"

"Questions, is it? Well, now, I might be able to but it'll cost you."

Simon nodded. He was used to that. "How much?"

"Depends on what questions you plan on asking."

"I'm interested in a murder that took place a few weeks ago just outside this tavern," Simon told him.

The sailor puckered up his lips, looking thoughtful. After a moment, he shrugged his broad shoulders. "Ask me. I'll tell you me price when we're through."

Simon lifted his pint up, tempted to take a drink, then lowered it just before it reached his lips, remembering the layer of dirt around the rim. He set it back down on the table.

His gaze roamed the crowd but most of the tavern's patrons had lost interest in their table. At least for now.

"Did you hear about the murder?"

"Aye. I hear about most things round here."

"I see. Do you frequent The Black Swan then?"

"Whenever I'm in London."

"And the man who was murdered, had you seen him before?"

The man puckered his lips again. He stared at Simon silently for a few minutes, his youthful eyes darkening a bit, then he shrugged. "I seen him a few times. Sort o' looked like you he did."

"Did you see him around the time of the murder?"

"He was at the Swan the night before if that's what you mean," the sailor said, nodding.

Simon had come by The Black Swan on two other occasions since Douglas' murder but this was the first time he'd actually found anyone willing to speak to him about it. Finally he felt like he was getting somewhere and yet the sailor's answers almost sounded too convenient. The way the man spoke seemed forced, unnatural, as though he was trying to disguise his voice, and he seemed vaguely familiar but Simon couldn't recall ever crossing paths with the sailor before. He eyed the man closely.

"What was he doing here that last night? Do you know?"

"The times I seen him he came to play a bit of cards." The sailor chuckled. "Sort o' like the group what plays at White's I imagine."

"Indeed. Was that night any different?"

He seemed to give it some thought for he was silently pensive for a few moments. Then he glanced at Simon's ale. "You going to drink that?'

Simon pushed it toward him and allowed him to drink it. He waited. Felt Dani's gaze on his face.

"That man," the sailor said, after taking several swallows of the drink, "he wasn't very bright." The sailor's voice dropped conspiratorially. "Reckless with the cards. Always showing a lot of money around to people who shouldn't see it, if you know what I mean."

"Yes."

"He didn't blend in." He eyed Simon, a slight sneer on his whiskered face. "Stuck out worse than you when he came. But he came a few times and so the clientele, as it were, got used to seeing him. But they watched him close, like."

"Did they steal from him?"

"Once or twice they did," the sailor admitted. "Easy pickings. And when they did take his blunt most times he weren't even aware of it."

"Do you know when he first started coming here?"

"A few months." The man shrugged. "At first he came and just played cards."

"How often?"

"A couple of times a week. About the fifth time he came to the Swan he started asking questions."

Simon grimaced. "Of what nature?"

"Something about a missing girl. He asked all kinds of questions about her."

"What sort of missing girl?" Simon froze. He did not glance at Dani, though he felt her reaction, stiffness, radiating from her. Felt her eyes fixed on him.

"Don't know. He ain't never asked me anything. Most of us figured he asked the wrong bloke the question the night he got murdered."

Simon blew out a breath. "So you don't think he was murdered by mere robbers?"

The sailor snickered. "If he was it was someone with a nasty streak. He was too easy to steal from. Weren't no reason to kill him for that. If a robber did him in he enjoyed killing. Ain't your average thief."

Simon had always believed that to be the case also. He was glad for the confirmation of it. But speaking of missing girls. He hesitated a moment, eyed Dani out of the corner of his eye, then plunged on ahead. "Just one other thing if you wouldn't mind."

The older man shrugged.

"Did you know a prostitute around here that goes by the name of Mary?"

"Mary, eh?" The sailor peered curiously at Simon. "You looking for a whore?" His gaze drifted to Dani, questioningly. Dani sniffed.

"Into the whereabouts of one, yes," Simon clarified.

"Begging your pardon, guv but why?"

"For a friend. Do you know her?"

"I know a lot of prostitutes. I ain't acquainted with a lot of their names." He grinned. It occurred to Simon that for a sailor the man had very well cared for teeth. Interesting.

"Mary went missing about the same night Norton was murdered. She frequented the alleys around the Swan."

"Don't know anything about her…" Then the sailor stopped speaking, looking thoughtful for a moment. He puckered his lips. "Well, now, I wonder."

"You wonder what?" Simon prompted.

"Yesterday the body of a woman washed up by the docks. I heard she were a whore. Maybe that's your Mary."

"Did you hear that?" Dani asked. Her eyes were as wide as saucers. She had hold of Simon's hand and she gripped it tightly.

"Of course I heard it, sweetheart." Simon looked grim. They were back in the coach, heading to the magistrate's to ask about the body found.

Dani prayed it wasn't Mary but was afraid it was. "What do you think it means?"

"I suppose we'll find out when we get to the place."

Dani shook her head frantically, her stomach lurching with the movement of the carriage. "Not that. The other."

Simon turned his gold-green eyes to her face at last. She'd been trying to catch his attention since the odd conversation with the sailor in the swan. He'd refused to meet her gaze.

"You mean about Douglas asking after a missing girl?"

Dani nodded. Her mind had been on it ever since the strange man had told them. Dani didn't like the man. She couldn't put her finger on what bothered her.

"I admit to a certain curiosity about it also," Simon said, brushing his lips over hers. "I think I'm going to have to seek out the elusive Carstairs. It's not mere coincidence."

"Be careful."

The coach pulled up before the magistrate's office and Dani's heart plummeted.

"Throat slit, Your Grace," the magistrate told them. He licked his lips, glanced briefly at Dani, considering. "Nearly from ear to ear. Grisly."

"Any ideas what her name was?" Simon asked.

The magistrate, a portly man with a large mustache, shrugged. "To be honest, Your Grace, we can't really keep track of every prostitute in that area. Lots of them get roughed up by their customers too."

"This one was a bit more than merely roughed up," Simon pointed out.

"This one's customer got a bit more rough," the man agreed. His attitude was one of someone who had more important matters to concern himself than the killing of a prostitute.

"So no one recognized her?"

The magistrate chewed his lower lip. "Didn't say that, Your Grace. A few of the men down in the East End and one of the fruit sellers said they thought her name was Mary. Lot of Marys out there." He eyed Simon and Dani speculatively. "Want to see the body?"

Simon glanced at Dani, who nodded slowly. "Yes."

The magistrate sighed. "I was afraid you'd say that."

* * * * *

Dani leaned against Simon in the carriage and cried. He didn't say a word, just stroked her hair.

Suspecting Mary was probably dead had been one thing, knowing for a certainty was something altogether different. She was shattered.

"I can't believe she's really gone," Dani whispered thickly.

Mary had always been so strong. Seeing her dead. It was a mistake. She wished she hadn't wanted to see. Could have kept the image of Mary laughing and talking in her heart. Now she would be haunted by the stiff, cold body Mary had become.

"I'm very sorry, Dani," Simon's deep voice penetrated her haze of grief.

She opened her eyes, tears squeezing from them. Lifted her chin to look at him. He met her eyes. Sorrow filled them. Dani reached up to cup his cheek.

"If I could have done anything to spare you this, I would," he told her.

"I know." Dani squeezed her eyes shut. "I just feel so alone."

His fingers clenched her jaw, tilted her face up further. "Dani, look at me."

Dani opened her eyes. The fire in his eyes was so intense, she blinked. Wondered at it. Her heart started racing.

"You are not alone."

Dani tried to nod that she understood but he held her chin too tightly. "I know. I have Grace." She smiled through her tears. "And you've been so kind. I don't tell you often enough how grateful I am for everything you've done."

"Your gratitude." Simon's tone had softened but was oddly devoid of warmth. "You're still bothered by what Aunt Pen said to you, aren't you, Dani?"

Dani wished she could look away from his too-knowing eyes. But he held her fast. Outside, carriages passed them on their way, shouts from drivers, pedestrians filtered in. The beat of her heart was louder.

"Would you like to talk to me about it?"

Dani sighed. With his other hand, his thumb stroked her palm lightly. How could she put into words what she was thinking? There was so much she had to be grateful for. He'd rescued her from a horrible life of uncertainty. She experienced luxuries and surroundings she never would have if it weren't for him. But she would trade all that if she could be just a seamstress and he just a merchant.

"I'm not sure you would understand," she said finally. "And anyway, I don't think you can do anything to change it."

"I would try."

She studied him, seeing nothing but sincerity. She wished he were less kind and good. She would like to rail at him. But it would seem so unjust.

"I don't like being a whore," Dani said, surprising herself with the words pouring forth from her mouth. She hadn't meant to say them out loud but now she did. She waited for his reaction, looking at him from beneath her lashes.

"You aren't a whore, Dani." Simon's jaw tightened.

"Are you sure?"

He gritted his teeth and released her in agitation. "Of course I am sure. Why would you think that? Do I treat you like that?"

"No," she said honestly. "You have been very kind."

"Then why would you say that?"

"Because that's the way I feel. I'm no better than a street woman," she said.

"Dani…"

"I know you've been kind to me, you've given me everything I could ever hope for," Dani said, her eyes burning with the tears that formed in her eyes. "But it's not enough."

"Dani, listen."

"No, I don't want to listen," she said, now sobbing openly. "You've made me want things I can't have and now I don't know what to do."

Simon blinked. His hand had been raised, reaching out to her but he abruptly lowered it. He stared at her, his expression unreadable. Then he bowed his head for a moment. When he met her gaze again, his eyes had hardened.

"I see," he said quietly. "I guess I hadn't realized you felt that way. I thought I was treating you better than that. I'm sorry. Of course, you are right."

"I am?"

"Yes. You deserve something more than that," he said, his face deadly serious. "I can't…" He shook his head. "Dani, we both need time to think."

"Time?" She was uncertain of his suddenly strange mood.

"Time. We've been rushing this." With the word this, he waved his hand. "I've been rushing this. I see what a mistake that has been."

Mistake? It pierced straight to the heart. She didn't want to be treated like a doxy, true, but she didn't want him to come to the conclusion that they should never have been. Was he regretting it? His beautiful eyes were filled with a sorrow that made her wonder if he regretted making love to her that fateful night.

The carriage pulled to an abrupt stop. It echoed her heart.

Simon took a deep breath, exhaled. "What we need is to step back."

Chapter Twenty-Four

He loved her.

The realization hit Simon when the carriage door opened. He'd never been in love before so he wasn't completely certain that was the emotion he felt these last several days until that moment. It consumed him. Simon wasn't sure what he should do about it.

His hands lingered on Dani's waist, his gaze locked on hers. Now what was he to do about it?

Dani's eyes were full of pain and doubt. Simon knew he'd put it there. He would have to fix it. But the emotions churning his heart were too new, too raw. He needed time to think, as he told her.

Simon broke the spell that held them and with a hand on the small of her back, steered her toward the front door.

Wilkins opened the door on their approach. He appeared to have been waiting for them. The old butler stepped back and allowed them to walk over the threshold.

"There you are, Your Grace." Wilkins wrinkled his nose. "What is that smell?"

"We've been to the East End, old boy."

Wilkins took a step back. Simon expected him to hold a handkerchief over his nose. But the servant just grimaced.

"What is it?" Simon handed his overcoat and Dani's wrap to Wilkins.

"There's a Mr. Reynolds here to see you. He's waiting in the parlor." Wilkins voice had dropped to a conspiratorial whisper.

Simon frowned. "Mr. Reynolds? I don't know any Reynolds. Send him away, Wilkins."

Wilkins cleared his throat. "I would, Your Grace but he did say that it was about Sally Reynolds."

"Who is that?" Dani was in the middle of removing her gloves.

"Douglas Norton's ex-mistress." Simon briefly wondered if he should change his clothes as he had intended but decided against it. "I'll be right in, Wilkins."

"Yes, Your Grace."

When Wilkins' footsteps had retreated, Simon turned to Dani. Hesitated.

"Do you want to come in with me?"

"Yes." She spoke quickly, no uncertainty at all.

Simon nodded. Reached out and took her hand for a moment. He squeezed it then released her.

When Simon and Dani entered the parlor, John Reynolds was nervously pacing the room. He was a young man no older than his early twenties, with thinning blond hair. He turned when he became aware he was not alone. His young face was earnest.

"Your Grace? John Reynolds. Thank you so much for agreeing to see me. I do hope I'm not imposing."

"Not at all," Simon said pleasantly. "This is Miss Crest. She has been invaluable in assisting me with some recent investigations." He gestured to the brandy on the side table. "Care for some refreshment?"

Reynolds frowned, shook his head. "I'm not a drinker, Your Grace." He paused, then looked hopeful. "I'd love some tea, if you wouldn't mind."

Simon ordered the tea and bade Reynolds have a seat on the settee. The young man sat stiffly, his back as straight as a board. He was dressed in a clean, well-kept coat that was several years out of fashion, his cravat slightly askew.

Simon and Dani each took one of the large dark green high-backed chairs that faced the settee.

They waited for the maid to hurry in with the tea before they began their conversation. Simon had the impression that Reynolds did not care for an interruption to whatever prompted his visit.

"I suppose you are wondering why I am here, Your Grace," the young man said, his hands shaking as he took a sip of his tea. He glanced quickly at Dani, blushed. "Miss Crest."

Simon smiled a little. "I admit to being somewhat curious, Mr. Reynolds."

"John, please."

"Very well, John."

John set his teacup down carefully. "I believe you knew my sister."

"Sally?"

John brightened. "Yes, yes, Sally."

"I didn't really know her," Simon admitted. "I knew who she was. I can't say I was ever introduced to her."

"Oh." John's expression turned crestfallen. He shifted nervously on the settee.

"What can I help you with, John?" Simon asked gently.

"Well, Sally was my only sister. She meant the world to me."

"I understand." Simon nodded when the young man paused.

A sneer curled his lips. "I hated that she was the mistress of all those men. She was better than that, you know." John sighed. "She was an actress. That was how Douglas Norton met her."

"I think I've heard that mentioned once or twice."

"She really liked him." John reached for a sandwich on the tea tray.

"Yet she unceremoniously dumped him."

John flushed. "It wasn't personal. The Duke of Lindley wanted her as his mistress. Sally was real proud of that. A duke." John flushed again, seeming to recall Simon was a duke. He cleared his throat. "I didn't like it for a moment."

Simon raised an eyebrow. "Why not?"

"Well, he was too old for her and I never did like the way he treated her." He frowned darkly. "And that's why I'm here."

"Why would that be, John?" Simon shared a quick glance with Dani.

"I figure you and I have something in common."

"Really?" Simon raised a brow at that. What did Reynolds think he had in common with him?

The young man squirmed. "Well, you want to know who murdered your cousin."

"Yes." Simon wondered where this conversation was going.

"I want to know who murdered my sister."

"Indeed?"

"She didn't hang herself, Your Grace," John insisted. "She wouldn't. Somebody killed her and I think I know who."

"Who?"

"The Duke of Lindley." John grimaced.

"And why would Lindley kill Sally?" Simon asked, casually as though merely curious.

"Because she had information about him."

"What information?"

"I don't know," John said, with obvious reluctance. "But I know she had something. She told me she had information that could make her and someone else wealthy for the rest of their lives."

"I see," Simon said, disappointed. "And what do you want me to do?"

"I think Lindley must have killed Douglas Norton too."

"And how did you reach that conclusion?" Simon asked, keeping his tone merely curious. The truth was that he had his own doubts about the autocratic Lindley. But murdering Norton? It seemed far-fetched.

John scowled, his youthful face taking on a menacing look. "I told you, Your Grace, she said that she had information that could make herself and another wealthy."

"I don't follow."

John set down his steaming cup of tea. His voice dropped to a conspiratorial whisper as though Lindley might be in the next room. "She was the duke's mistress."

"Yes?"

"Well, don't you get it?" John was becoming impatient. "How could she be more wealthy than she was simply by being Lindley's mistress? I can assure you, Your Grace, that she wanted for nothing." He flushed. "She even gave me some of the money she received."

"Go on."

"She must have gotten the information on Lindley," the young man said excitedly. "There is no other explanation. He found out and made it look like she hanged herself."

"Even if all you have guessed at," Simon said slowly, "were true, John, what makes you think that has any connection to my cousin?"

The look the young man gave him told Simon he thought him daft. John shook his head and popped a small tea biscuit into his mouth. After chewing and swallowing it, he steepled his fingers and leaned forward.

Simon noticed out of the corner of his eye that Dani leaned forward expectantly at the same moment. She was riveted by the man's words.

"I told you. Sally always liked Douglas. More than any of the others she'd ever been with." John flicked at a crumb of the biscuit. "In fact, I think it was more than just affection she had for him, if you take my meaning."

"You're saying that your sister loved Douglas?" From what Simon knew of the late Sally Reynolds she had been a cool, jaded mistress, not one given to flights of fancy.

"Only Sally could tell you for sure," John said, his voice tinged with sorrow. "But I know she acted differently with him."

Simon shook his head. "Look, John…"

"I know what you're going to say," John cried, interrupting him. "But please, listen to me. I think that whatever information Sally had on Lindley she shared with Norton. It got them both killed."

"You cannot make such accusations against a peer of the realm lightly, John."

"I know but that is why I am coming to you." His young eyes burned bright. "I want you to look into it for me. Sally deserves to be avenged." He picked up his teacup. "Or at least she deserves not to be forgotten. I don't want Lindley to get away with what he did to my sister. He is extremely ruthless and powerful. If he is guilty of the atrocities I believe he certainly would not hesitate to make anyone his next victim."

Simon grimaced. "Damn."

After John Reynolds had gone, Simon left Dani in deep conversation with Grace. She wanted to tell her friend everything she'd learned, including about Mary's death. Deciding to leave the two friends to their grief over Mary, he went to speak to Aunt Pen. He planned to take the interfering woman to task for what she said to Dani.

She received him warmly in the sitting room connected to her room with twin kisses on his cheeks.

"It is wonderful to see you, dear," she said, pointing him toward the large red settee in the room. "Shall I have Mrs. Martin bring you in some tea?"

"No, I'm going out to speak with Carstairs again soon," Simon told her.

"You've news?" The older woman asked hopefully.

"Sit down." Simon patted the spot next to him. "I want to talk to you."

Her eyes troubled, Pen took the seat beside him. "What is it, Simon?"

He blew out a breath. "Two things, actually. Both rather uncomfortable."

The older woman's eyes dimmed. "Tell me straight. It is worse to delay it."

"I have no direct news on Douglas," he said, taking hold of her hands. "But I do have some questions for you regarding his activities. If you know the answers."

"All right." She nodded.

Simon thought about how to word his questions. He doubted she would not know the answer anyway. "How much did you know about his private life?"

She didn't pretend to misunderstand. "You mean his mistress, don't you?"

He inclined his head.

She sighed, then glanced beyond him, her eyes fogging over. "I didn't really know much. He didn't talk to me about anything, let alone that. But I'd heard some things. You know, how it is. I knew he had a mistress named Sally at one time and then later…" She stopped abruptly, her gaze focusing on Simon once more. She blushed.

"You heard he took up with Margaret," he guessed, smiling gently.

She gave a barely perceptible nod. "Not long before his," she paused slightly, "death, Sally came by asking for him. Our butler sent her away. Very strange girl."

"I know I've asked you this before but I want to ask you one more time."

"What?"

"Did Douglas act different in any way? Come into more money than usual? Seem secretive? More secretive."

"I simply don't know." Pen pulled her hands from his grasp. She stood, wringing her hands in agitation. She began to pace the room. "You have no idea, Simon. We had hardly any relationship. He... He hated me, I think."

"I don't believe that's true."

Her eyes filled with tears. "He did. I know it. He blamed me for his father. Somehow he found out about what we were doing when his father died. I never told him but he did. Douglas accused me once of causing his death."

"Pen, he spoke in anger."

"Maybe." She gave him a watery smile. "Is there anything else?"

He was loath to bring up Dani in Pen's present mood but he felt that if he did not address her behavior toward Dani it would be a betrayal of some sort.

"Come sit with me again."

After she had settled down next to him, he said, "I want you to know I am very grateful to you for the lessons you've been giving Dani."

"Oh." She seemed startled by his words. "It's nothing. I was glad to take my mind off Douglas."

"I had hoped that it would do that for you," Simon admitted. "And she has really learned quickly." He smiled. "I knew from the first I met her she was very clever."

"I think I may know where this is leading." Pen looked past him, at some point on the wall. "She told you about our conversation, didn't she?"

"She mentioned it. I don't know everything."

Her mouth thinned. "I was not trying to be deliberately cruel, Simon."

"I would never perceive that you had," he assured her. "I know you think you know what's going on…"

"I do know what is going on," she interrupted rather petulantly.

"You think you know." Simon's tone was sharp. "But Dani means something more to me than you realize."

"I know you think this is none of my business, Simon," Penelope said, sighing heavily. "And you are right. But she is really rather sweet and she's going to be hurt."

"Pen."

"Where is this going, Simon?" It was her turn to speak with a sharp tone. "Ask yourself that. You are the Duke of Stratford and she is a poor young woman from the East End. Taking in strays is one thing but making one of them your mistress is quite another."

"I am not my father."

"And I thank God for that every day," Pen assured him. "But if you continue to keep Dani as your mistress, you know well what may happen. She has grown fond of you, very fond, already. You cannot even conceive that this relationship will ever lead to more than a brief affair."

"Have a care, madam," Simon snapped. "You are overstepping your bounds."

"Am I?" She shot back. "Or are you?"

Simon determined to pay the elusive Carstairs another visit to find out just what Carstairs wanted with Dani.

Everything kept going back to the young viscount and his grandfather.

Simon handed his card to the tall, distinguished butler at the Earl of Waltham's home. He knew that Carstairs was currently in residence with his father.

"Good day to you, Your Grace," the severe butler said, studying the card carefully. "I am afraid the earl and his countess are not in at the moment."

"I have actually come seeking an audience with their son."

The butler's eyes lit with understanding and he set the card down on the table among a large stack of other cards. He shrugged his broad shoulders just a little.

"I am afraid I must disappoint you there also," the butler said gravely. He gestured with his hand at the table. "Viscount Carstairs has not been home for days."

Chapter Twenty-Five

ಬ

"Sorry, Your Grace, I don't understand it," his coachman said a short time later. "I don't know how Willie's foot went lame."

Simon frowned and glanced at the coach. Richmond had just informed him the horse could go no further.

"I've sent James home to fetch help," the coachman continued. "Shall I get you a hackney home?"

"Don't be absurd." Simon shook his head. He glanced up at the clear night sky. "It's a short distance from here. I'll walk it."

"But, Your Grace." Richmond was clearly appalled. "It's gone quite dark."

"I've walked it dozens of times." Simon cast one last look at the injured horse. Too many odd incidences had been occurring. "I don't like this."

"Me either, Your Grace."

Simon nodded and pulled his greatcoat tighter around him. Though the night was a clear one the air was chilled. "Good night."

He began the short walk home. From Waltham's house it was no more than three blocks, a straight walk at that. The area the home was in was really in one of the best parts of London.

In spite of his rational thinking Simon felt uneasy. Horses went lame, there was no mistaking that but the recent attacks in Portsmouth, by his club and by the docks had him leery.

At least there was some activity on the streets. He recognized several carriages that passed by. Lord Wilmot's, Lady Abernathy's. Nothing at all out of the ordinary.

They jumped him less than a block from home. He'd been alert to any noises but they surprised him anyway. He had no idea how many men there were but he saw the shadow of at least two before the attack. One came from the ledge of a wall nearby.

"I have him." The voice was definitely cultured. Simon had barely a moment to reflect on that when he lost consciousness.

* * * * *

"What is it Wilkins?" Dani came down the stairs.

The staid butler stood at the door, his hand posed on the handle, a perplexed expression on his face. He glanced at Dani when she spoke.

"I thought I heard a noise." Wilkins frowned. He made no move to twist the handle.

"Well, why don't you open it and see?" she asked impatiently. She took the last few steps to the floor and then placing her hand over Wilkins' opened the door.

"Your Grace!" Wilkins exclaimed.

Slumped on the threshold was Simon. The sleeve of his coat had been ripped off and the coat was covered in blood and dirt. His cravat was gone. There were cuts and big red and purple bruises all over his face, a large one covering most of his jaw. Blood encrusted his split lip. He didn't move.

Dani fell to the ground next to him. Her heart in her throat, she lifted his head into her lap. "He's still breathing," she said haltingly.

"What's going on?" Jack came into the small hall.

"Jack, help me get him inside," Dani cried, brushing her fingers lightly over his swollen lips.

"Simon, my God, what happened?" Jack's expression was crestfallen.

"I don't know," Dani said. "But that doesn't matter now. We need to get him to a bed. Quickly."

Jack bent down and then lifted Simon into his arms. He headed up the stairs, Dani and Wilkins following closely on his heels. He went straight toward Simon's room and Wilkins hurried in front to open it for him.

"Wilkins, send someone for the physician." Jack set his brother down on the bed.

"Who did this to him?" Dani whispered, watching as Wilkins hurried off. She returned her gaze to Simon. The skin on his face that wasn't covered with the reddish bruises was a sickly white.

"I don't know." Jack sat down on the bed. He gingerly touched his brother's face. "But I mean to find out."

Dani turned when Wilkins rushed back into the room. The butler's face was contorted with anguish.

"I've sent someone round for Dr. Henning."

Dani wanted to be beside Simon and she wished Jack would move. He was his brother, she knew but no one could love Simon more than she did. She bit her lip.

"Uh."

She pushed Jack out of her way when she heard Simon's moan. His eyes blinked rapidly, then he stared at Dani through swollen eyes.

"Dani?"

"Yes, it's me." She edged Jack out even more. "Jack and Wilkins are here too."

"Simon, who did this?" Jack demanded, coming up on the other side of the bed. His expression grave, he loomed over his brother.

"I don't know," he admitted. "I didn't see them clearly."

"Them? So it was more than one? Were you ambushed? Where?" Jack rattled off his questions in quick succession.

"Can't this wait?" Dani frowned at him. Wilkins handed her a damp cloth. She used it to gently wipe the blood from Simon's mouth.

"No, it's all right, Dani," Simon mumbled. "One of the carriage horses went lame. I didn't want to wait nor catch a hackney. Waltham's just a few blocks away."

"The streets of London are no longer safe." Wilkins clucked his tongue.

"I'd have to agree with you, Wilkins," Simon replied, "except that these men were more than just thugs. One of them spoke like a peer. I think I even recognized it, though it escapes me just now."

"Scandalous," murmured the old butler.

"You could have been killed." Dani's fingertips brushed his lips. She couldn't bear to be without him.

The smile he gifted her with was strained. "I don't think that was their intent, love."

"Is this all tied in with Norton?" Jack asked, his voice was low but Dani detected anger in its tone.

"Apparently. I've been attacked several times," Simon admitted.

"What?"

"He was accosted in Portsmouth," Dani explained. "And by his club. This is the third."

"The fourth." Simon winced when Dani pressed the swollen skin around his eye a little too hard.

"Fourth?" Dani clutched one of Simon's hands tightly in hers, her heart in her mouth.

"Down by the docks. We ran into Eddie." Simon paused. "That one might not be connected but it seemed awfully convenient that Eddie happened to show up."

Dani shivered. Four attempts on Simon's life? Four too many as far as she was concerned. If Simon cast her aside because of society's dictates of whom he should want as a wife was one thing. As long as Dani knew he was alive and happy, that would be all that mattered. But she wouldn't survive if something happened to him.

"This is too dangerous. You have to stop," she pleaded. Tears pricked her eyes.

"Dani…"

"Dani is right, Simon," Jack cut in. "I had no idea it had become this bad. Why haven't you told me about it?" His expression was grave but also vaguely insulted by the imagined slight he felt at Simon not sharing what was going on.

"I didn't want to worry anyone," Simon admitted. "I was also certain I could handle it. But it's happening more frequently now."

"You're getting too close." Jack frowned.

"Did that man who came by to see you today have anything to do with this?" Dani wondered.

"Man? What man" Jack asked.

"John Reynolds. Sally Reynolds' brother."

Jack shook his head. "Sally Reynolds?"

"Douglas' former mistress." Simon's hand went to his head and he grimaced. "I don't think I'll ever get rid of this headache."

"Where is that doctor?" Dani fretted.

"I think it's time you left this to a runner." Jack sat down on the edge of the bed on the other side of Dani. "You've got somebody's attention. Leave it to a runner."

"I heartily agree," Wilkins announced from his position by the door.

The door burst open and in walked Mrs. Martin. The housekeeper's face was red and she panted, obviously having run up the stairs.

"Dr. Henning is here," she said, then quickly stood aside to allow the physician access to the room.

*****

Dani slipped back into Simon's room later after Dr. Henning had left. The physician had gone downstairs to speak with Jack. Wilkins had declared his intent to listen in also. She'd been more interested in returning to Simon.

The doctor had shooed all of them out upon his arrival and spent what Dani decided was an absurd amount of time with him. She could barely contain her impatience. She had to reassure herself that Simon would be all right.

If he were asleep, she would just sit on the chair by the side and stay with him all night in case he needed anything. She'd already made up her mind.

"Who's there?" His masculine voice sounded from the bed.

"It's me." She crossed the room and to the bed in just a few short strides. He tried to smile but it came out twisted and with his split lip looked painful.

"Oh, shh," she said softly. She found a fresh cloth that had been set on the table next to a bowl of water and she dabbed it in until it was just damp. Then she crawled onto the bed so she could get as close to him as possible.

"Dani, it's late. Get some sleep."

"I wanted to see you again." Dani bathed his face gently, conscious of the crack in her voice. "I wanted to make sure you'll be all right."

"I'm in one piece." He winced. "Though it doesn't feel like it."

"What did the doctor say?"

He reached a hand out to touch her face. She pressed it to her cheek and held it there.

"I've got mostly bruises and lumps, nothing that will keep me down. I was afraid they'd broken my ribs but they're just badly bruised."

Tears welled in her eyes. "I can't believe they did this to you," she whispered. "You said they must not have intended to kill you. Why do you think that?"

His gaze was intent. "They would have succeeded if that had been their intent. I had no defense. I allowed them to take me by surprise." His voice was filled with self-recrimination.

"Wilkins said the carriage has returned," Dani told him. "The horse slipped a shoe I think it was."

His thumb grazed the wetness on her cheek. "I haven't asked how you're doing. I left you still upset over Mary. I'm sorry I was short with you before."

She shook her head vehemently. "No, don't be. I'm fine. It's you I'm worried about now."

"But Mary…"

"I am sad about Mary," Dani admitted. "I'll always miss her. But you are who I care about."

"Fine mess I'm in when such a beautiful lady has to be concerned about me."

He'd called her a lady. Dani didn't think he'd ever done so before and the word washed over her as though he'd called her a princess. It probably didn't mean the same to him but to Dani it meant everything.

"Come, rest your head on my chest and we'll fall asleep together," Simon urged her, pushing her head downward.

"But I still want to talk to you about the murders." Dani wanted to tell him he couldn't take any more chances.

"Tomorrow." Simon sighed when she laid her head down and brushed her hair lightly. "I love you, Dani."

She stopped breathing. Stopped everything but the beating of her heart. Dani tried to look at him, to determine if he was delirious. But he wouldn't let her tilt her head up to look at him.

"I don't know what we're going to do about it, Dani. But we'll find a way. I promise."

Dani's scream jarred Simon awake and froze his blood. He shot up in bed without thinking, instantly regretting it when searing pain shot through his rib cage and head.

Dani was staring in horror at something that lay across him. His eyes were still filled with sleep so all he could make out was that it was red.

"Dani, what is it?" he asked, trying to force his heart to return to its regular beat. He couldn't imagine what caused such fright. "Did you have a bad dream?"

"No," she exclaimed and buried her face in his shoulder.

Simon rubbed his eyes and reached for the object that had been laid across their bodies. A red wool scarf. He frowned at it. How did it get there?

"Dani, is this why you screamed?" He shook his head. "Sweetheart, I don't know where it came from but it's just a scarf. Nothing to scream about."

She shook her head, then turned her tear-streaked face up to him. Stark terror shone from within the depths of her periwinkle eyes.

"It's Mary's."

Chapter Twenty-Six

ഌ

"I know you're all wondering why I've called you in to the parlor." Simon eyed each of his staff members carefully. He had them lined up in front of the mantel. They stood at attention as though he were some military leader and they his troops. He moved stiffly in front of them, his bodily aches reminding him of his ordeal the day before.

Wilkins, who stood apart from the others, sniffed. "I have informed them, Your Grace, of the appearance of the red scarf."

Simon nodded, his gaze going briefly to Dani, who stood very close to him. A few times she'd rested her hand on his sleeve, then removed it to twist her hands together. Her expressive eyes were still filled with fear. Anger at whoever had played such a nasty trick laced through him.

Jack was there too. His brother leaned against a wall, silent and brooding, his accusing gaze fixed on the household servants.

One of the footmen shuffled his feet, drawing Simon's attention once more.

"Then you know what it is I want to ask." Simon moved along the line, staring at each one as he went. He didn't want to believe that any of them would do something so malicious. They'd all been with him for years. He'd pulled them off the streets, given them their chance, against advice from family and friends. He couldn't have been wrong.

Simon stopped in front of Mrs. Martin. There was simply no way he would believe it of the stern yet kind housekeeper. She gazed back steadily at him, her lips pursed.

"Mrs. Martin, do you know anything about that red scarf?"

"No, Your Grace," she replied, cracking her knuckles. She colored a little when Simon glanced down at her twisted hands. "Sorry."

He smiled a little and moved to the next servant. Every one of them he passed answered no and every one of them seemed sincere. The final servant in the row was a young maid named Anne. Though she was not a pretty woman, she was of pleasant disposition and Simon had always liked her.

"Anne," he said, as he had to all the others, "do you know anything about the scarf?"

When Anne opened her mouth to reply, Simon expected the usual negative response. He was, therefore, startled when instead she let out an ear-shattering wail of anguish. The maid covered her face with her hands and sobbed.

Simon frowned, stepped back and said quickly to the others gathered, "That will be all."

His servants appeared reluctant to leave, all of them staring intently at Anne but after a moment of hesitation, they left the parlor. Wilkins, Dani and Jack remained. Their expressions were all as dumbfounded as he was sure his was.

"Anne?"

"I-I'm sorry, my lord," she wailed, stuffing her fist into her mouth.

"Anne, I don't understand, why?" It was Wilkins who spoke up. The butler prided himself on a loyal, efficient staff.

Anne's lips quivered. "I didn't realize it would be so bad. The man said it was a gift for Dani."

Simon glanced at Dani, who was very white. He took hold of her small hand in his larger one and squeezed.

"What man, Anne?"

"I don't know his name, Your Grace." Anne let out a shattered breath. "He was well dressed, spoke real well.

Young, very handsome. Dark hair, blue eyes." She paused, blushing. "A dimple in his left cheek."

"Carstairs, I'd wager," Jack said, coming away from the wall. His eyes hard, he said, "What did Carstairs give you to deliver this gift?"

"A sovereign." Her whole body shook. "He approached me outside, when I went down to the bakeshop for Mrs. Martin."

"When was this, Anne?" Simon inquired.

"Yesterday afternoon."

"And you innocently put the scarf on the duke and Dani while they slept?" Jack snarled, looking at that moment very pantherlike.

The maid's eyes filled with renewed tears. "The man told me I should try to do that while Dani slept."

"Idiot," Jack said. "His Grace is your employer."

"Jack." Simon waved his hand at his fuming brother. "Anne, is there anything else you can tell us about this man who gave you the scarf?"

Anne shook her head. "No, that's everything."

"Very well," Simon said, then looked to Wilkins, silent communication between them. The old butler nodded solemnly.

"Come with me, Anne." Wilkins came forward to take the maid's arm. She was crying softly as he escorted her from the room.

Jack, looked thoughtful, but remained silent for the moment.

Simon turned to Dani, his hands grabbing her by the shoulders. "Are you all right?" He didn't like her white color.

"Yes." Her eyes were watery.

"Jack, you're right, her description sounds like Carstairs."

"What do you mean to do about it? He's got some fixation with Dani. Hell, he's involved up to his ears." Jack began to pace.

"I went to Waltham's house yesterday before I was attacked. Carstairs was not at home."

"Waltham," Jack said, almost to himself. He narrowed his eyes suddenly. "I took Lucy and Dani riding in the park one day and we ran into him."

"So?"

"Waltham said Dani reminded him of someone. He was very interested in her."

Dani clenched Simon's coat, twisting it in her fingers. "Remember that ball where I said a man kept staring at me?"

Simon nodded.

"It was that man, Waltham. And at the opera, Viscount Carstairs was there." Dani bit her lip. "I should have mentioned it before."

Carstairs and Waltham both after Dani? And Lindley. Duke, Earl, Viscount. Grandfather, father and son. Not coincidental. "I'm going to Waltham's," he announced to Dani and Jack.

"I'm going with you," Jack said quickly.

"Me too."

Both of them turned to Dani in surprise. Her expression was a mixture of determination and defiance. She crossed her arms in front of her and stamped her foot.

"And you won't stop me."

Much of the carriage ride to the Earl of Waltham's home was spent arguing with Dani about her insistence on going with them. Simon didn't like putting her in danger. But he also didn't think she was in immediate danger while he and his brother were with her. Whatever Waltham and Carstairs were up to it involved Dani, that much was clear.

"Did you find something in the refuse you searched through that was connected with Norton?" Simon asked her after a moment of contemplative silence. They had almost reached their destination.

"No." Dani shook her head. She was as perplexed as he was.

"And you didn't see anything involving either man?"

"No, nothing."

"Maybe," said Jack, "she did see something but she doesn't know what she saw."

"What?" Dani twisted her mouth.

"What I mean is that maybe they think you know or saw something but you didn't."

Simon nodded. "That has occurred to me too. But I cannot imagine what either one of them would be doing in that part of London."

"Well, we've only placed Carstairs there," Jack pointed out.

Simon frowned. "What troubles me is Waltham said she reminded him of someone. Besides, a sailor Dani and I question mentioned Norton was also asking around about a missing girl."

The carriage pulled to a stop and the door opened.

"Here we are, Your Grace," the driver announced. Simon helped Dani down and they walked to the door of Waltham's townhouse.

The same severe butler of the day before peered out at Simon and his companions. He stepped aside to let them in but quickly refused Simon's card.

"I remember who you are, Your Grace. Viscount Carstairs is not in."

"What about the earl?" Jack asked.

The butler turned his superior look on Jack. "Who would you be?"

"My brother and this is Miss Crest," Simon explained. "We'd like to see Waltham, if you please."

"Wait here a moment." The somber servant's tone was imperious.

"He'll let us in or by damn I'll break through the door," Jack murmured. Simon decided it was best to ignore him. He could hear whispers down the hall.

Dani studied the walls in the foyer. There were three paintings on the wall, all of men. Simon knew from their dark hair and blue eyes they were probably ancestors of the Dalton family. He came up to stand behind Dani. Her attention was riveted on one painting in particular.

"Leonard Dalton," he read out loud. "The Duke of Lindley when he was a young man."

Dani traced the name with her fingertips, still staring at his likeness. Simon watched her, turned to the painting. Around the eyes. He looked sharply at Dani.

The butler came back down the hall, his stiffly elegant uniform crinkling as he walked. He stood before them.

"The Earl of Waltham has agreed to see you in his study." The servant looked down his long crooked nose at them. "Follow me."

Simon reached for Dani's hand, his mouth in a thin line. He knew a detail he had not realized before and he wanted to throttle himself for not recognizing it sooner.

Dani's eyes while very similar to Lindley's were an exact match for the duke's son.

"The Duke of Stratford, my lord," the butler announced them when they reached Waltham's study.

Brendan Dalton, the Earl of Waltham, stood up, came round the desk and stopped in front of them. He never once looked at Simon or Jack. His gaze was on Dani and hers on him. The silence deepened.

Simon waited for the butler to close the door behind them. "Dani's your daughter, isn't she?"

The Earl of Waltham turned his steely periwinkle gaze on Simon. His look was one of cool appraisal. "What happened to you?"

Simon fingered his still swollen jaw. "I was attacked by thugs." He paused, then met the earl's gaze with a hard look of his own. "Hired thugs."

Dani didn't miss the anger below the surface. Simon radiated tension.

Waltham appeared to be ignoring her for the moment, though he never really took his gaze off her completely. It gave her time to study him. His dark upswept hair was black with silver at the temples. The eye color was nearly an exact match. Her father? Was it possible? He did look like her, now that Simon mentioned it. The earl glanced at Jack, acknowledged him briefly, then turned back to Dani.

"Dani. I remember you from Hyde Park the other day."

"I'm right, aren't I?" Simon demanded, interrupting.

Dani shook her head and backed away from the earl into Simon. He put a hand on her waist to steady her. Waltham frowned at the gesture.

Waltham studied Dani for a moment. "We need to talk, I think. First of all, why are you all here? Brinks said something about Justin."

"We do want to see your son, Waltham." Simon spoke coldly. "But it seems he isn't the only one involved in this."

Waltham indicated several chairs situated around the dark oak study. "Sit down, then. Would you care for refreshment?"

Jack opened his mouth to reply but Simon interrupted. "No. Nothing for any of us."

Waltham turned a questioning look on him but shrugged. Simon squeezed Dani's hand.

Her temples throbbed. The last few days had seen so many shocks. Mary's murder, Simon being attacked. Him saying he loved her. He loved her. Dani still couldn't quite believe it was true. And what did it mean for them? She hadn't had time to talk to Simon. And now, this. Waltham her father?

Waltham stepped around them and went to a bookshelf where a decanter of brandy sat. He poured a glass of it for himself. Such a large man but he moved with an elegant grace. He resumed his seat behind the large desk that dominated the dark oak room.

After taking a sip, Waltham set the glass, which had seemed so tiny in his large hand, down on the desk in front of him.

"You said Justin wasn't the only one involved in this." Waltham peered at them. "Just what is he involved with?"

"I don't know everything he is involved with." Simon rubbed Dani's thumb lightly with his own. It occurred to Dani Simon had grown accustomed to touching her. It was a comfort to him, as it was to her. "But he's been making it his business to locate Dani."

Waltham frowned, looking perplexed. "I don't understand that. Justin doesn't know anything about what happened."

Dani sucked in a breath. So it was true.

"So there is something with you and Dani, isn't there?" Simon asked. "You'd better tell us about it, Waltham."

Waltham took another sip of his brandy. In the meantime, Dani's world spun out of control. When she saw the paintings of Waltham and Lindley it suddenly struck her she bore a striking resemblance to the Dalton men. Especially Waltham. Dani knew her father was a member of the gentry but an earl!

"It was a long time ago." Waltham broke the extended silence. "When I was young I married as my father wanted. I never got on very well with my first wife. Diana and I had very little in common other than our mutually desirable connections. I didn't believe it was possible to defy my father.

"Anyway, we both did our duty and Diana gave birth to Justin. After that we went our separate ways. The usual *ton* marriage. I kept a mistress, an actress, and one day I went with her to the shop of a seamstress."

Dani stiffened, her heart dropping to her stomach. "My mother?"

"Yes," Waltham agreed. "Her name was Rose. She was the daughter of a baron's son, and she was so beautiful." He paused and stared into the amber liquid in front of him. "The actress noticed my interest right away but I know she assumed it was just a passing matter. It wasn't. I went back alone to see Rose many times after that. At first we just talked but it soon became much more."

"Did you love her?" Dani had to know. Had wondered for so long if her mother ever had any happiness.

Waltham met her gaze and smiled. "Yes. She loved me too. We were very happy for many months. I had intended to buy her a townhouse and set her up as my permanent mistress but then I decided Rose deserved something more. I wanted her as my wife." He shook his head. "You can imagine how well that would go over. I was trying to work up the nerve to tell my father I intended to divorce my wife when Diana had an accidental fall from her horse. She broke her neck and died only a few days later. It was very difficult for Justin losing his mother. He was quite young." He sighed. "But it also gave me my chance with Rose, who had just told me she was carrying my child."

He paused. During that time Dani tried to take in the meaning of the earl's story. Her mother had been in love with an earl. Just as she now loved a duke. Their lives were so similar. It was hard to believe. She was staring at the man who had sired her.

Chapter Twenty-Seven
ಐ

Waltham smiled a little wryly.

"That settled it for me. I went to Rose's shop and took her away. We were married in secret at Gretna Green, for I didn't want to speak a word of it to my father until we had it all settled. Not far from our home in Portsmouth I purchased a little cottage for Rose to live in. I knew I would eventually have to admit to my father we had married, but I thought if I waited until the child was born... I visited with Rose as often as I could. One day, as Rose's time to have the baby drew closer, my father grew suspicious and followed me. He found out everything. He wanted to have the marriage annulled and Rose sent away. We had a very unpleasant argument.

When I thought he'd calmed down I went back and spoke to him. He was very reasonable and calm at that point. I thought we would work it all out. I went back to the cottage to tell Rose, but she was gone. My father told me he had gone to her and offered her a large sum of money for her to leave me and our family alone. I was furious with my father for his interference, but also surprised and horrified. I didn't hear from Rose again."

Hot tears stung Dani's eyes. Her stomach hurt too. "Didn't you go and look for her? For us?"

"Of course I did," Waltham assured her. "I didn't want to believe my father for I knew he would lie if it suited his purposes. I went to Rose's shop and it all seemed true. She was gone and the women there said they hadn't seen her in months. Still I searched. I asked around. Nobody knew anything." Waltham sighed and tugged at his cravat. "I never found her or you. Until I saw you recently. But I've never forgotten Rose."

"It's a lie." Dani clenched her fists.

"What?" Waltham looked surprised.

"It's a lie!" Dani exclaimed louder this time. She removed her hand from Simon's grasp. "My mother didn't take money from your father to forget you."

"Dani…" Simon spoke up.

"You believe it too, don't you?" Dani accused him. She returned her glare to Waltham. "Well, it isn't true. She had no money."

Waltham shrugged at that statement. "She must have spent it."

"She did not," Dani insisted. "We were practically starving and Mother was sick all the time. She had a terrible cough. We had to hide and she worked for almost nothing for strangers. When I was five she got too sick to manage any longer, she brought me back to the seamstress shop and Mary and Grace cared for me. She died on the streets, my lord."

Sorrow filled his eyes but Dani didn't care. Her own eyes were flowing with scalding tears.

"She's dead no thanks to you or your father. And I was left alone."

"Which brings me back to your son, Waltham," Simon said, reaching for Dani's hands again. "Dani, calm down, sweetheart.

"I don't want to calm down," she snapped.

"I don't understand what Justin has to do with Dani." Waltham frowned. "He was just a child when I met Rose."

"He's been asking around for her," Jack cut in. "Down by the docks."

"The docks?" Waltham frowned.

"Dani was raised for much of her life in the East End of London by the seamstresses who worked with Rose." Simon put his arm around Dani.

Waltham appeared stunned. "I had no idea."

"I'll just bet you didn't," Dani said, "because you didn't care. You probably tried to give my mother money and she wouldn't take it."

Waltham shook his head sadly. "I loved your mother, Dani."

"What I would like to know," Simon said slowly, "is why Carstairs is involved. You say he was just a child and you claim not to know that Dani was raised by the docks."

"Are you calling me a liar?" Waltham's blue eyes narrowed.

"Yes." Dani shook with anger and betrayal. Of her, yes, but mostly of her mother.

"Shh," Simon said, rubbing her wrist with his thumb. "No one is calling you a liar, Waltham. But your son has been asking questions about her and he's been by my home seeking her out too. You must have mentioned Rose and Dani's existence at some point."

"Until I saw her at that ball and again Hyde Park I didn't even know if the babe Rose had was a boy or a girl," Waltham insisted. "And then, I thought that she might be mine but I couldn't imagine how she could be. Rose left London years ago."

"And yet your son knows about Dani and even had a description of her," Jack pointed out.

"I have no idea how Justin could have learned about her." Waltham drummed his long fingers thoughtfully on the desk in front of him. "Unless..."

"Unless what?" Simon prompted.

"Well, there is another who knows about Rose, of course but I don't believe he knew any specifics about Dani" Waltham's mouth twisted.

"Your father, the Duke of Lindley."

"Yes." Waltham nodded. "But he paid off Rose before Dani was born."

Simon rubbed Dani's wrist a little harder when she stiffened. She was about to protest her mother's innocence again.

"Lindley could have found out the information easily enough, I'd wager," Simon said ruefully. "I'm told he has sources everywhere."

"True but to what purpose?" Waltham raised a brow.

"You'd know the workings of Lindley's mind better than me."

Waltham lowered his gaze to Dani's wrist, taking in the intimate gesture from Simon. "You said Justin sought Dani out at your house, Stratford."

"That's right."

"Just what is your relationship with my daughter?" The earl raised an eyebrow.

"It's a little late for the protective father act, Waltham." Simon's tone was even, casual.

Dani trembled, surprised by the earl's remark herself. She'd just found out he was her father. Now he jumped ahead to a completely different relationship. She didn't know him. Would never know him but for a few fateful moments by the docks. He thought he could just ask about Simon in that accusing voice?

The door of the study opened suddenly just as Dani opened her mouth to make a comment about the man's nerve. He might have sired her but by God, he was not her father.

"Brendan, I couldn't find Brinks so I thought I'd just come right in. Oh." A strikingly beautiful golden-haired woman stood just inside the doorway. Dressed in a light green morning dress with matching bonnet and gloves, her mouth had pursed into a shocked circle. "I'm sorry, I didn't realize you had guests."

The Earl of Waltham stood up and smiled, coming around the desk to take the woman's hand in his.

"It's all right, Josie," he assured her. "Let me introduce you. Darling, this is the Duke of Stratford and his brother, Lord Thorndike. This is my wife, Lady Dalton."

The Countess of Waltham extended her hand to Simon. "Your Grace, nice to meet you."

"Lady Dalton." Simon rose and pressed her hand.

Lady Dalton greeted Jack, then turned her curious gaze to Dani. Dani had never seen a more beautiful woman. The earl's wife had light green eyes that matched her lovely dress. Dani felt clumsy and awkward next to her.

She smiled warmly before turning to her husband, a questioning look on her face. Waltham kept smiling and tucked her hand into the crook of his arm.

"This is Dani." Waltham paused. "My daughter."

Lady Dalton blinked, studied Dani.

"Nice to meet you, ma'am." Dani was at a loss. He'd just blurted out to his wife that she was his daughter. No preamble. No preparation. Her stomach gurgled nervously. What was she supposed to say? She did not know many of the social graces and what she did know she'd only recently learned from Lady Norton.

"Rose had a daughter?" Lady Dalton exclaimed. To Dani's surprise, Waltham's wife came forward and reached for Dani's hands. She clasped them. "You do look like Brendan!" Her eyes shining brightly, she glanced at her husband. "How did you finally find her?"

Finally? Had the earl been looking for her? Had he actually told his wife about her? Uncertain, Dani bit her lip.

She had been so sure his association with Rose had been nothing but an embarrassment for him.

"She found me actually or rather Stratford did," Waltham said. He returned his hard gaze to Simon. "Stratford was just about to tell me of his relationship to Dani when you came in. I'm still waiting for his answer."

"She's my fiancée." Simon's tone was serious, his expression unreadable.

Lightheaded, Dani turned sharply to look at Simon. What was he thinking to tell the earl and his wife that? It wasn't true. She wished with all her heart it was. Their love was impossible. Wasn't it?

Dani sank her teeth harder into her lip to concentrate on the pain in her mouth rather than the sharp one in her heart. Her pulse racing, she turned her attention back to the woman who still held her hands.

"Well." Lady Dalton watched Dani's face. "That's simply wonderful. I'd love the chance to plan a large wedding." She beamed at Waltham. "Our own children are still so young."

"I don't think…" Dani panicked.

"We haven't planned the date yet and under the circumstances a large affair wouldn't be agreeable," Simon interrupted, encircling Dani's waist with his hands. "Anyway, Lady Dalton, while we appreciate your kind words, we've a few other matters to settle involving your husband and stepson right now."

"Oh?" Lady Dalton glanced at her husband, a troubled look on her face.

Waltham shook his head. "I'll tell you later, Josie."

Dani was grateful, though confused, for Simon's hands holding her up. She trembled, blackness threatening to overwhelm her. She was nauseated too.

"I was about to invite Brendan to ride in the park with me but I can do that any time." Lady Dalton smiled at Dani again. "I'd much rather get to know my new daughter better."

Jack cleared his throat and shifted in his chair.

Dani's hand went to her throat. The earl's wife seemed so genuine. She wanted to like her. She even wanted to like the handsome earl. But how could she? Her mother and she had nothing. Her mother had been left to die.

"We can't stay, Lady Dalton," Simon spoke up again. His gaze hardened when he looked toward the earl.

"I'd really rather my daughter moved her belongings here, Stratford." Waltham returned Simon's look with a challenging one of his own.

Dani shook her head vehemently. She tipped her head to give Simon a pleading look. He wasn't looking at her.

But there was no need. "I don't think so, Waltham."

Lady Dalton went to her husband's side and placed a restraining hand on his arm. "She needs time to adjust to finding you." She turned to Dani and Simon. "We ask only, my lord, that you bring Dani back to spend more time with us. We are anxious to know her better."

"I promise nothing," Simon retorted coolly. He reminded Dani of a restless panther. His hands had tightened possessively around her waist. "We'll take our leave now. And should you find out where your son is, Waltham, I would appreciate hearing from you."

The three occupants of the Stratford carriage were silent. Shortly after declaring it was time for them to depart, Simon informed them there was something he needed to attend to. His cool distance since leaving her father's home alarmed her.

She's my fiancée. Why in the world had Simon called her that? Why not admit the truth? Dani still didn't understand his motives but she was afraid to ask. Instead of sitting next to her, as he always did, he now sat next to Jack and across from her. He stared out the window, brooding. She had no idea what his mood meant?

"The driver will drop me off on the way," Simon explained, breaking the silence at last.

"Whatever this is, can't it wait, Simon?" Jack flicked a glance at his brother. He looked as dumbfounded as she felt.

"No, the sooner it is taken care of, the better," Simon said vaguely, his attention once more to the streets of London.

"Well." Jack smiled cheerfully at Dani in an obvious attempt to lighten the dark mood that descended over them all. "I think we'll make a stop of our own then."

"Where?" Simon turned his smoldering eyes to his brother.

"Nowhere ominous I assure you." Jack held up his hands briefly. The carriage bounced over a rock. He steadied himself by grabbing the side. "Just to the bakeshop on the way. I thought we'd get some of Dani's favorite teacakes."

Simon narrowed his eyes, then appeared thoughtful. "I suppose there's no harm in that." He nodded. "Very well."

"Thanks for your approval." Jack smirked.

Dani twisted her hands in her lap nervously. She paid little attention to the banter that continued between the two.

"I can't believe I've found my father after all these years." Dani broke the silence that had overcome them once more.

All her life she'd dreamed of something like this. Near to it anyway. In her dreams she'd pretended to be a princess but an earl's daughter wasn't bad either. And one day, when the Duke of Lindley died, her father would be a duke. She shook her head at that notion. That was practically royalty.

He claimed to have loved her mother and that he had married her. She wanted more than anything to believe her mother had some happiness before her rotten life and death on the streets. It would be nice to believe that Rose's eyes glowed with love for the handsome Waltham. But somehow it seemed to Dani that to believe such would only be dreaming again.

"I'm not sure any good will come of it." Simon was stoic. "I don't trust him. Any of the Daltons."

"I'd like to see them again." Dani did not look at him. She kept her eyes on her lap. Her heart still raced from the confrontation at Waltham's home.

"No." Simon spoke flatly, his voice indicating he brooked no argument. Then she did glance up at him. His face was an impassive mask. "At least not for a while," he amended.

The carriage jolted to a stop and Simon got up from his seat. She thought he would just leave but instead he bent over her, kissed the tip of her nose and stroked her cheek.

"We'll talk later. This won't take long." He hesitated, his eyes troubled. "It's something I should have taken care of before. Remember what I said before. It's true. Wait for me." Then he was gone from the carriage.

When their coach was moving again, Jack was quiet and contemplative for a while.

"Is there anything you want to know about the Daltons?" Jack asked eventually.

Dani looked up from her twisting hands. "You'd tell me about them?"

Jack shrugged. "What I know. I run in different circles from Lindley and Waltham. And Carstairs, well, I've never been a close companion of his. I've played cards with him a time or two. Been a while, though."

"Is he a good man?" Dani asked softly.

Jack didn't pretend not to know which of the Daltons she inquired about.

"Probably the best of the three from what I've heard. He was a bit of a rake when he was married to the first wife."

"Diana?"

Jack nodded. Voices drifted in occasionally from the streets outside but neither of them paid much attention.

"I doubt he mourned her much. Most say she wasn't a very nice woman. But from everything I've heard he's completely devoted to his current wife, Josephine Dalton."

"She's beautiful."

"No more so than you." Jack grinned.

Dani smiled a little at his kind words. She took a deep breath. What else did she want to know? Children. Waltham said he had more with Lady Dalton.

"Do you know about their children?"

"They have five," Jack said.

"Viscount Carstairs is the heir, right?"

Jack grimaced and crossed his arms. "Yeah."

"You don't like him much," Dani said. "But you didn't before you found out that he was looking for me, did you?"

"He's dirt as far as I'm concerned." Jack sneered. "Yes, he came from so-called good blood. Both of his parents were of noble birth. He was raised with all the privileges of a peer. But it doesn't take away the fact that he's low. Snakelike, I guess."

The carriage rolled to a stop and the door popped open. The coachman stood aside.

"We've arrived at the bakeshop, my lord."

"Ah, excellent." Jack took Dani's hand and helped her out of the coach.

* * * * **

They stood on a street Dani was not that familiar with because it was in the good part of London. The air was even breathable and she couldn't detect even a hint of fish.

All around shoppers bustled by. Most of them were dressed in beautiful bright dresses and striking coats with perfectly placed top hats. The day was brisk but those on the street were cheerful. She took a deep breath and inhaled the scent of freshly baking bread.

"The shop is over here." Jack offered her his arm and led her to the very place the wonderful smells came from. Dani remembered it from the time Simon took her there.

There was a huge line at the counter. An indication the shop did very well. The noise from the patrons talking among themselves was nearly overwhelming to her ears.

Jack saw her wince. "A little much, eh? We don't have to stay, if you don't want."

Dani hesitated, biting her lip. She did want more of the wonderful cakes.

"Don't worry, I'm only joking." Jack laughed. "Why don't you stand outside? I'll wait at the counter. The line moves fast."

Dani stepped outside gratefully. She could still smell the wonderful bakery but she was also able to smell the fresh air. Next to the bakeshop was a flower shop and the scent of the posies drifted over. There was a gentle breeze too.

"Well, fancy running into you here."

Dani stiffened. She turned to her right to see Viscount Carstairs coming toward her at a rapid pace. The handsome young man wore a smile as he reached her but it did not reach his cold eyes. His hand abruptly closed around her wrist.

"Come with me, Dani." His voice was hard.

"No, I won't." She struggled to free her hand.

"I think you'd better." All trace of the charming young man she'd met before in Simon's parlor was gone. A chill came off him. She shivered.

"I'll call for Jack," she vowed, still trying to break free of his grip. She prayed that Jack had noticed Carstairs standing outside with her. She glanced back at the shop but saw that several patrons in line blocked her from his view.

"If you get Thorndike's attention." Carstairs inclined his head toward a carriage nearby. "What will happen to her?"

Peering from the window of the carriage, her eyes wide with terror, was Lucy. Panic clawed at Dani's stomach.

"What have you done to Lucy?"

Carstairs' cold, calculating smile returned. "Nothing yet, Sister, but that may change very soon. She's young but a pretty bit o' fluff just the same."

Dani gasped at the implication of his words. Lucy was still two years shy of her first season. She couldn't bear the thought of the sweet girl in Carstairs' clutches.

"You're wasting my time," Carstairs growled. "Get in the carriage now. Or Lucy dies."

"Lucy, are you all right?" Dani asked quickly when Carstairs shoved her into the carriage.

"Just shut up and sit down." Carstairs pushed her into the seat across from Lucy. He leaned out the window and ordered the coachman to go forward.

Lucy, her golden curls askew, stared wildly at him. Her bottom lips trembled. Finally she turned her wide gold-green eyes, so like Simon's, to Dani. Tears streamed down her slightly pink cheeks.

"I-I'm sorry," Lucy wailed.

Carstairs shut the curtains of the carriage and sat down next to the frightened girl. Heart in her mouth, Dani watched him thread his fingers through her pretty hair and yank until her head snapped back.

"Ah," Lucy cried.

"Stop it," Dani pleaded. "I'll do whatever you want. Leave her alone."

Carstairs' handsome face twisted with his maniacal laugh. "You will do whatever I want, Sister. Whether I leave Lucy alone or not." Stilling holding Lucy's hair in his grip, he sneered down at the girl. "She's my prize for what her damn brother has put me through."

"She has nothing to do with this." Dani swallowed the lump that formed in her throat. It would be all her fault if something happened to Lucy.

"Be quiet," Carstairs snarled. "You're so annoying. Whatever was my father thinking of when he bedded your mother?"

Waltham. Was he in on this too? Dani hoped not. Her heart twisting painfully, she had to know. "Your father...did he put you up to this?"

The young viscount tore his heated gaze away from Lucy for a moment to glare at Dani. "My father is a fool."

But that wasn't quite clear enough for her. "So, then you are doing this on your own?" At least her questions distracted him from pawing at Lucy. He still held her hair in one hand but the hand that was creeping toward the bodice of her gown had stopped its progress.

"No, but not with him."

For some strange reason, relief flooded Dani at the admission from Carstairs that her father was not a part of his nefarious doings. She wished he hadn't pulled the curtains closed. She wanted to be able to see where they were going. If she could only recognize the area...

"Justin." Dani hoped his more familiar name would soothe him. "I'd really like to help you. You don't need Lucy. We could stop somewhere and leave her. Whatever you want or need, I'm sure that we can get it for you."

"Bah, you'd like me to let her go, wouldn't you?" Carstairs moved his free hand once more to Lucy's bodice. He dipped his hand inside and fondled her breast. Lucy whimpered.

Dani winced. Mentioning Lucy again had been a mistake. She wished Simon were with her. Of course she wouldn't be in this predicament if he had been. Where had he gone?

"Justin, who is acting with you in this?" His eyes were glazing over with lust.

"You ask too many questions." Carstairs frowned. "You're giving me a headache."

"But you've been so clever, haven't you?" Men liked to have their egos stroked, didn't they? She would appeal to Justin's.

"I have been clever." Justin's smile was triumphant. His fingers stilled on Lucy's flesh. "And I will continue to be so. I've already left a note for Stratford."

"What sort of note, Justin?"

"I told him to come alone to meet with us." He laughed. "At first I thought I'd just take you but then I realized he wouldn't care enough about his whore to bother." He yanked on Lucy's hair. "But his sister…how could he resist saving her?"

"Why do you want Simon to come, Justin?" Dani's head pounded. Fear gripped her stomach. She had to hold on. For Lucy.

He glared at her again, his blue eyes clouding over. "I told you to stop asking me questions. Leave me alone."

"Justin…"

"You'll know when the bastard gets there, all right? Now, for the last time shut up and let me think."

Viscount Carstairs shoved at Lucy suddenly, pushing the cowering girl into the corner of her seat. Lucy bent her head and cried into her hands. Dani wished she could go to the frightened girl and offer her comfort but she dared not.

* * * * *

Jack burst through the door just as Wilkins handed Simon a message that a small boy had just delivered. Simon looked up, surprised.

"What's wrong with you?" Simon set the message down on the table. He'd just come in the door himself and was about to ask Wilkins where Dani was when his brother burst in the door.

"Is Dani here?" Jack was out of breath. His hair was standing on end and his eyes were wide almost crazed.

"What do you mean is she here?" Simon demanded, confused. "She was with you."

Jack ignored his remark and turned to Wilkins. "Did she come back here, Wilkins?"

"No." Wilkins shook his head.

"Damn." Jack muttered.

Fear gnawed at Simon. "What the hell is going on, Jack? What happened to Dani?"

"I don't know," Jack admitted. "I went into the bakeshop. When I came out, she was gone."

"You left her alone?" Simon roared, angrier with his brother than he had ever been before. He took a lethal step forward.

"She was just outside and the coach was there," Jack said. "I don't know. I looked around for her but she wasn't anywhere and the driver said he thought she got into another coach."

"Why would she do that?" Simon wanted to shove his fist into Jack's face. Dani was gone. "Goddamn it, Jack."

"I'm sorry. I thought maybe, there was some way she came back here. She got tired of waiting or something."

"Where's the coachman? Get him in here now!"

Carstairs, it had to be him. And Waltham. They'd just been there with him. Did he have them followed?

His gaze fell on the message he had placed on the table. Simon grasped it in his hand and tore it open, his eyes raking over the contents.

You're really not very clever, Stratford. I've been several steps ahead of you the entire time. Enjoyed our conversation at The Swan. But enough of how much better I am than you. I have two precious belongings of yours. One is my sister, the other yours. Come to the old Fremont Warehouse by the Priorman Pier. Same place I killed that whore, Mary. Come alone. Not that I think that useless brother of yours can help. Be there at eleven. You might get your sister back but I think I'll keep mine.

Jack came hurrying back, the coachman in tow. He took one look at Simon's face, then glanced at what he held in his hand. "Oh, God. Carstairs, isn't it?"

"Yes." An odd calmness came over Simon. He supposed it was better than to let the rage and anguish over power him. That wouldn't help Dani or Lucy.

"Where?" Jack wondered.

"An old abandoned warehouse down by the docks." Simon's lip curled. "I'm sure he sees the irony in that."

"When do we go?"

"He says to come alone."

Jack snorted. "I'm sure he does, the coward. Abducting a woman. Very brave."

"It's worse than you know." Now he knew why the sailor in The Black Swan had seemed so convenient and familiar. *Enjoyed our conversation at the Swan.* Simon crumpled the note in his hand. He imagined it was Carstairs' head. "He has Lucy too."

Jack eyes widened, his nostrils flared. "I'm going, Simon," Jack vowed. "If you stop me, I'll follow."

"I have no intention of stopping you." Simon's hand rested briefly on the special license in the pocket of his coat. It would be a little longer before he and Dani would be able to use it but he took comfort in its presence. "But I will go alone. Follow me with Scarborough."

Jack nodded. "I think we should involve Waltham too."

"I don't trust him."

"And maybe that's wise but I don't think he's involved in this, Simon. Call it instinct. And Carstairs is his son."

"And Dani his daughter."

"Exactly."

Simon grimaced. He didn't trust Waltham but he didn't get the same evil feeling he got from the Duke of Lindley. The old man was involved, Simon was sure of it. Carstairs was too young and too stupid to act on his own. Whatever it was. Simon wasn't entirely sure but he suspected even Douglas Norton's murder all went back to the powerful duke.

"All right, Jack. Get Waltham too."

Chapter Twenty-Eight

೫

Drip…Drip…Drip…

The sound was enough to make anyone crazed. Dani hugged her knees and peered around the scarcely lit room in the warehouse where Carstairs had taken her and Lucy. He'd closed them in this tiny cramped room when they first arrived. However long ago that was now. She had no way of knowing.

Lucy had fallen into a fitful sleep but Dani dared not succumb. She wanted to watch over Simon's young sister.

Somewhere nearby the water continued to drip and the noise was one of the few sounds she could hear from their location. The roof of the warehouse was high above even though Carstairs dragged them up a rickety set of wooden stairs. The old building was enormous. And Dani recognized it the moment Justin had pulled them out of the carriage in front of it. It was just a few hundred yards from The Black Swan.

At least he'd left them with a small lamp. She shuddered at the notion of having to sit in the tiny space in total darkness. Besides the incessant sound of dripping water, there was one other distinct sound penetrating Dani's ears. Scuffling, rustling. She knew the warehouse was infested with an enormous army of rats. She'd met many a rat in her days of living in the East End but she'd made friends with none.

Only one door in the room. And Carstairs had locked it. She'd heard the key click in the lock. No windows either. The air was heavy and musty. If she ever got out of here, Dani thought, she didn't think she could bear to be in a room without windows again.

If… She closed her eyes against the unbidden thought. When she got out, of course. That was what she meant. She knew, after all, Simon would come. She didn't doubt him for an instant. And yet, she dreaded his arrival. She would do anything to save him. She would rather he did not come and stay safe.

Of course, Dani wanted him to rescue Lucy. Her gaze fell on the sleeping blonde girl. She deserved better than to be in the clutches of evil. How could Carstairs involve poor, sweet Lucy who had never hurt anyone?

What did he plan for Lucy? For her? For Simon? Justin was surely mad. She'd caught the desperation in his eyes in the carriage and when he'd tossed them into this room. His mind had snapped. Dani had no doubts.

Dani found herself feeling sorry for the earl, her father, while she sat in the cramped space. She was sure he loved his son. Sensed it in their conversation earlier that day, in spite of the fact he had never loved Justin's mother. How had the earl sired such a madman?

As if on cue, the key clicked in the door and it swung open. Lucy woke abruptly and scooted back against the wall. Her arms lay across her breasts as though she would be able to protect them.

Dani had never known such fear when she lifted her head up to meet the cold ice in Justin's eyes. His lips curled into a vicious sneer and in his right hand he held a pistol. He raised it until it pointed at Dani's chest.

"It's time, get up." His voice was filled with loathing, dark and dismal in its hollowness. He flicked a glance at the cowering Lucy. "You too. Up."

Dani scrambled up from the floor, grabbing onto the wall to steady herself as she rose. She took hold of Lucy's hand to assist her up too. Lucy clung to her and tried to hide her face in Dani's shoulder, as she trembled. Dani patted her back gently.

"How touching," Carstairs sneered. With his free hand he grabbed Lucy's tresses and yanked her with him.

"Ah," Lucy yelped.

"Let's go." Carstairs indicated the door to Dani with his pistol. His other hand still held Lucy's hair. Dani flew through the door quickly and Carstairs dragged Lucy out with him. He kicked the door closed.

He led them down the same suspended wooden slat floor he'd taken them on when they'd first arrived. There were large holes and missing slats in the floor and Dani had to walk carefully. Carstairs didn't seem to notice the state of disrepair.

"Stop there," he yelled to Dani when she'd reached a wall on the south side of the empty warehouse. She stared at a large gaping hole that went to the floor below. A long way down.

Carstairs reached her with his captive. He was breathing heavily, as though he had exerted himself and each breath was an effort. "All right. He should be arriving any time."

Dani noticed he had stopped them by an old, partially broken railing. If she stretched on her tiptoes she could see down into the main room below, including the front door that led into the building. Her heart in her mouth, her pulse racing, she wondered when Simon would walk through the door.

"Why are you doing this?" Lucy wailed. "What has Dani ever done to you?"

"She was born," Carstairs spat venomously. "Bitch! I hate her. My bastard father. He had to bed her whore mother and look at the result. She will rot in Hell by the time I am done with her."

Dani looked away, unable to bear the loathing that burned in his eyes. He was not merely mad, as she guessed but seemed to exude evil and rancor.

"My mother," Carstairs ranted, "wasn't good enough. She wanted him to love her but he wouldn't because he loved Rose. She killed herself because of him. They said she had an accident and fell from her horse but I know better." He peered over the railing. "Where is he? It's time, by God."

"Justin, this isn't about me or even about Rose." Dani crept closer to him. He was standing very close to the edge of the railing and he still had Lucy. If he should slip, she didn't want Lucy going with him. "It's about Waltham. He is the one you hate."

"I do hate him," he agreed. "He ruined everything. And now Stratford is trying to do the same. Why did he have to get involved?"

Dani turned to face the front door of the warehouse when they all heard the click of it opening. Squelching her sense of panic, she bit her lip to keep from crying out. Simon walked in slowly, his footsteps echoing loudly on the floor.

"Carstairs?" Simon called out.

Justin did not move. From where Simon stood it would be hard for him to see them standing on the second floor in the darkness. Carstairs no doubt planned it that way. Did he intend to aim for Simon in the darkness?

"Simon!" It was Lucy who yelled his name.

Simon turned sharply at the sound of his sister's voice and the quick turn probably saved his life for Justin had aimed his pistol at the same time Lucy cried out. Carstairs dropped his arm and swore.

"Stupid bitch," Carstairs snarled and shoved the young girl with all his might.

"No." Dani lurched forward to try to catch the falling girl. She was heading straight for the broken railing. Dani barely had time to notice the sound of a door opening below from another direction and the sound of running boots.

Carstairs grabbed Dani and pulled her hard against him. He put the pistol to her head.

"Scarborough, get Lucy!" Simon yelled.

Lucy went flying over the railing and Dani moaned low in her throat. She knew Simon was too far away to save her from the fall.

"Damn." Carstairs scooted closer to the railing to peer down. His movement gave Dani a chance to see what was going on too. The Duke of Scarborough had caught Lucy. She lay in his arms in a dead faint but she would be safe. Dani started weeping with relief. "I told him to come alone, damn!"

As Justin moved away from the railing once more Dani caught a glimpse of Jack and the Earl of Waltham. They'd all come.

"Justin!"

His father's voice caused Carstairs to freeze in his tracks. The veins in his neck strained and for the first time Dani noticed beads of sweat on the young man's forehead.

"Justin, let's talk about this," Waltham said from below. "Release Dani."

Carstairs returned to the railing with lightning speed. His grip on both Dani and the pistol had tightened. His eyes were wild. His breath came in short gasps.

"Father, I don't know what you're doing here but you can't stop me."

"Whatever this is all about, I am sure that your grandfather and I can fix it."

Carstairs laughed a crazed, high-pitched squeal. "Grandfather? Ha, you idiot, who do you think got me into this?"

Silence greeted Carstairs' words for nearly a moment. All she could hear was the thundering of Justin's heart. It threatened to deafen her.

"Justin…" The earl's voice was weary. "What has he done? Tell me?"

"He didn't buy off Rose, Father," Carstairs called down. "It was a lie." He chuckled. "I guess maybe he intended to but the stupid whore refused him. He told me he couldn't believe she had the nerve to turn down money from him. Said that you'd married her, she knew that you loved her. You've never loved anyone!"

"That's not true, Justin. I love you." Waltham stood on the floor below next to Simon and Jack. Apparently Scarborough had taken Lucy somewhere safe.

"Don't lie," Carstairs snarled. "If he couldn't get rid of her that way though, he decided to kill her and her unborn child." With that statement, Carstairs shook Dani. "Too bad he didn't succeed. The whore got away. Grandfather kept trying to find her but she disappeared. Always one step ahead of him. He finally gave up then because that was what he wanted all along."

Carstairs had loosened his grip on the pistol slightly. Just a little more and Dani might be able to wrestle it away from him. If she could work up the courage.

"But then Grandfather fell victim to a schemer."

"Who was it, Justin?" This time the question was asked by Simon. His voice sounded distant to Dani but still welcome. She said a silent prayer to keep him safe no matter what else happened.

"His mistress. Old fool. In his cups one night he bragged to her about how he saved his family from the terrible scandal."

"Sally Reynolds"

"Yes, it was Sally. She demanded money from him to keep quiet. Threatened to go to you, Father. And then there was the pending engagement between the Duke of Shelton's daughter and me. Shelton hates scandal of any kind and if that kind of gossip got around…that you'd married a shop girl and had a child, I'd never see his daughter again." Carstairs' voice was strained, whiny, as though he'd reached the end of his rope.

"Grandfather decided we needed to kill Sally," Carstairs explained. "Then we found out she wasn't working alone. She'd given the information to someone else."

"Douglas Norton," Simon said.

"Scheming bastard." Carstairs turned a dark shade of red. Rage thrummed through him. "He approached me. Didn't have what it takes to approach Grandfather. But Norton didn't just hold the information about Rose over our heads. He found out about Rose's daughter. He started asking questions and found out where she was. Knew she lived as a strumpet by the docks."

The chill in his voice froze her blood. Fueled by his rage, his grip on the pistol had tightened once more and he held it to her, pushed it between her breasts.

"I killed Norton myself. And Dresden. He was going to talk. He saw me paying Norton. Grandfather took care of that incredibly vapid Margaret Cavendish too. Norton couldn't keep his mouth shut and he told her." Justin laughed. "I enjoyed dressing her in those rags. She thought she was so much better than me. Grandfather took care of Sally Reynolds himself too. But," And he pushed the pistol hard against Dani. "I am going to kill my sister."

She was going to die.

Dani didn't know how else the standoff between her captor, Viscount Carstairs, and the men below would end. The pistol was poised between her breasts and the young man's eyes, so like her own, glinted with madness.

"Justin." Waltham's voice sounded from below. There was an urgent plea to the tone from the earl. Dani trembled.

Carstairs glanced over the rail when his father spoke, frowning darkly. "What do you want now?"

"If there is someone you should kill, it is not Dani. She has never done anything to hurt you," his father said slowly.

"She was born." The young man stared hard at Dani, his blue eyes somehow cold and feverish at the same time. The hand that held the pistol shook.

"That's not Dani's fault but mine," the earl continued. "I could have prevented it and didn't. I am the one who should pay for your pain, not her."

Justin blinked uncertainly. He inched closer to the edge, both of the floor and his sanity. Dani licked her lips.

"It is Mother who bore the most pain from your actions," Carstairs said. "She wanted you to love her but instead you loved that whore, Rose."

"It was a mistake, I know. I realized I loved your mother too late. After the accident."

"You didn't love her." Carstairs shook his head in denial. "She was always crying."

"I did, only I was too blind to see it," the earl argued. "I loved both of you so much. I never meant to cause you any pain. Come down from there and we'll talk about it."

The laugh that came from Carstairs was hollow and without mirth. "It's too late. There's no point in talking now."

"It's not too late. I'll help you, Justin. We all will. You trusted your grandfather. That was a mistake."

"He loves me."

"No, Justin. He only used you. Let me help you."

"I don't need the kind of help that comes from our family." Carstairs went cold. Still. Dani sensed the abrupt change in him. The sorrow that seeped through his bones. "I went to Grandfather for help and look what happened. You're right. He doesn't love me either. He just wants to use me for his schemes. Nobody cares about me."

"Justin..."

"Be quiet." Carstairs grimaced, tightened his grip on Dani and dragged her away from the edge. "I don't want to listen to you anymore. She has to die."

Dani and her captor heard the footsteps at the same time. Carstairs wheeled to face the stairs. Standing on the top step was Simon.

No, go away, please. She wouldn't be able to bear it if Justin shot Simon. Her heart thundered so loudly she thought her ears would explode from the deafening noise. Her stomach gurgled.

"Get away!" Carstairs moved the pistol from Dani's chest to Simon. "Don't come any closer."

Dani, eyes wide, noticed the pistol Simon held in his hand. It was larger and more deadly looking than Carstairs' small dueling pistol. Simon held it steady.

"Let her go, Justin," Simon said, coolly. "You won't get away from here. Let her go and we'll help you."

"You don't want to help me." There was a curious quaver in Justin's voice. "You just want your whore back."

"Give me the pistol, Justin." Simon held out his other hand. He stepped two steps closer.

Dani closed her eyes. Justin was shaking uncontrollably now.

Simon he stepped much closer to Carstairs. Dani felt the viscount raise his pistol arm. She knew Justin would shoot. She also knew he was paying absolutely no attention to her anymore. He was entirely focused on Simon. Her only chance was now.

She opened her eyes and stared down at his trembling right arm. Without further hesitation, she sank her teeth through his coat into the fleshy part of his arm above the elbow.

"Bitch!" Carstairs dropped his arm and held it, angry pain coloring his face.

"Dani, down!" Simon yelled.

Justin had released her when she bit his arm, so she quickly hunkered down onto the floor at Simon's command.

"Stay away from me." Justin's tone was stiff, icy.

Dani tucked her head underneath her arms and winced when she heard the firing of a pistol. She prayed that Simon was not hit.

"Sweetheart, are you all right? Are you hurt?"

It was Simon. The most wonderful sound in the world. She peeked up, surprised at the wetness on her own cheeks. He was whole. He kneeled down next to her and pulled her into his arms.

"Are you injured?" he demanded, kissing her face.

"No, no." Dani shook her head. She reached up to frame his face in her hands. "You?"

"No." He glanced behind her.

Dani tried to follow his gaze but he quickly shielded her.

"Don't look, sweetheart." He pushed her head down, to rest on his chest. She could hear the distant sound of running.

"Is he dead?"

"I'm afraid so."

"I'm sorry. You killed him?" Her tears soaked his shirt but he didn't seem to mind.

"No." After a brief hesitation, Simon said, "He put the pistol to his temple and shot himself, Dani."

"Oh." Dani swallowed the bile that rose in her throat.

"Not that I wasn't about to shoot him." Simon stroked her hair gently. "I want to take you home."

"I want to go home." She tilted her head to look up at him. "Lucy?"

"She's fine. Shaken up and a bit hysterical," Simon told her.

Footsteps came up the stairs and they both glanced that way. Waltham and Scarborough had come up the stairs. Waltham, looking ashen, immediately hurried to his son's side.

"I'm taking Dani home," Simon said to Scarborough.

The duke nodded. "Jack took Lucy home. There's a carriage waiting for you."

Simon helped Dani stand up but he still held her close to him. Dani was glad because she doubted she could stand on her own.

"There's still Lindley to deal with," Scarborough commented.

"I know." Simon nodded. "As soon as I take Dani home I'm going to see him."

"I'm coming too," Waltham said from his position by his son. His tone was filled with bitter anger.

Dani closed her eyes. "Me too."

"I'll take care of matters here," Scarborough promised.

Chapter Twenty-Nine

Waltham took his own conveyance to his father's.

Simon held Dani close on his lap the entire carriage ride to Portsmouth. Her arms clung to his neck and she rested her head against his chest, listening to his heartbeat return to normal. She doubted hers ever would.

"I was so afraid for you," she whispered.

"Afraid for me?" He laughed hoarsely. "It's you I was worried about."

"He was mad, you know."

"Yes. One so young as he, what a waste."

Dani nodded against him. She tightened her hold on his neck and was silent for a moment, listening to their breathing and the night sounds outside the carriage—other coaches riding by, voices in the darkness.

"He killed so many. Ruined so many lives."

"Yes. All on orders from Lindley."

Dani shuddered. "What an evil, vile man. He chased my mother away too. I hate him."

"He'll pay for what he's done to everyone, Dani," Simon vowed, kissing the top of her head.

"Be careful. I don't want you to get hurt, even if it means he gets away."

"I'll be careful. You be careful too." Simon stroked her cheek. "Against my better judgment I'm letting you come. You deserve to be there, I know."

"I love you." She brushed her lips on his.

"I love you too." He looked toward the window. "It's late and we still have some hours ahead of us. Rest for now."

*****

"We have to be prepared for anything, Waltham." Simon, Dani and Waltham stood outside their carriages, watching the dark, foreboding mansion of the Duke of Lindley.

"I am the last person you have to warn to be wary of my father," Waltham said in a detached voice.

"Yes, I suppose that's true." Simon felt Dani shiver from the frothy air. The night had become cold and wicked.

"Are you really going to marry my daughter?"

Waltham's soft question startled Simon for a moment. It took him some time to adjust to the topic. He supposed he owed the earl that much.

"I was securing a special license this afternoon when your son abducted her."

Dani gasped, pulled away to stare at him, her jaw dropped.

Waltham flicked a glance to his daughter.

"And she agrees?"

His question took Simon aback. It did not occur to him that Dani could or would have any objection. She loved him, damn it. He frowned crossly.

"Of course she agrees."

Dani's lips curved slightly but Simon knew from the light in her eyes that he was right. He had nothing to fear.

Waltham was quiet for several more minutes. It was a heavy, burdensome silence. Simon couldn't imagine what he was feeling. He could try but somehow any words he could think of to say seemed small when faced with a man who learned he had a daughter and whose oldest son confessed to murder and then turned the pistol on himself in the same day.

And now they faced the mastermind of the crimes, Waltham's father.

"I want Dani to move in with me and Josie for a while." His tone was one of autocratic command. Challenging and yet full of a silent threat. Under normal circumstances Simon would have scoffed immediately at it for the Stratford title was older than even Lindley's title. But these were not ordinary times for either of them and he did not want to make light of Waltham's concerns.

"I intend the wedding to take place rather quickly."

"I understand that. I do not object, exactly. I have barely met my daughter and you would carry her off already. I only want the opportunity to know her. Josie is anxious too. We talked about it at length this evening after you left."

Dani stared at Waltham, clearly surprised by his words.

"How long are you thinking, Waltham?" Simon refused to wait for months at a time. He was willing to have some patience. But the sooner he married Dani the sooner they could both be assured the other wasn't going anywhere.

"A month," he said slowly, "or two. My family will be in mourning for Justin for some time."

"Dani is not a substitute for Justin," Simon pointed out.

"I know that." Waltham's voice hardened. "What I meant is that we will not be attending any more affairs for the season and will have more time to devote to knowing Dani. It will take some time for the *ton* to become used to who Dani is. How her mother and I were married."

Simon's mouth thinned. A month or two? He wanted her as his wife now. Part of the reason he'd gotten the special license was the fear that Waltham and his family would try to sink their claws into his Dani. He didn't think Dani wanted to wait that long either.

"Sir." Dani put a hand on Waltham's sleeve. The earl smiled tenderly at her.

"You remind me so much of your mother." Waltham straightened and pulled his coat down. "We'll speak about it later, Stratford, Dani. Now, I think it's time to face the lion. On your guard." They stepped forward as one.

The courtyard surrounding the duke's manor was well lit and buzzing with footmen scurrying about. At the sight of their master's son, their excited agitation increased.

"Milord, welcome, we had no idea you were coming," a footman cried, biting his lip fretfully.

Lindley Manor stood dark and imposing in front of them. Waltham narrowed his eyes and refused the offer of assistance given him by another footman.

"I assume His Grace is in residence?" He asked.

"Yes, milord." The footman bowed.

Simon recalled Lindley Manor from his previous visit searching for Carstairs. One half of the house appeared ancient, hundreds of years old, but the rest of the house had been built since and it exuded wealth and extravagance. At the entrance to the manor were two gold lions on either side. The same lions graced the double front doors. Two footmen scrambled to open them for Waltham's entrance.

"Milord, how delightful to see you," a butler exclaimed, clapping his hands and hurrying forward. The butler was much younger than Wilkins, perhaps only in his early thirties and he wore his hair powdered and tied back with a gold bow. His uniform was also made up of matching gold knee breeches and a gold coat. "Her Grace will be positively thrilled."

"This is not exactly a social visit, Milo. I don't wish to disturb Her Grace. Where is my father?" Waltham demanded coldly.

"In his study, I believe." Milo cleared his throat. "I shall announce you." He glanced at Simon and Dani. "And you are?"

"No need," Waltham said. "I will announce us. You have the rest of the evening off, Milo."

"But milord..." It was clear the butler was at a complete loss to explain Waltham's odd behavior.

They ignored the servant and headed down the hall to the Duke of Lindley's study.

Leonard Dalton, the Duke of Lindley, looked up quickly when the door of his study opened with a distinct thud. His expression one of extreme irritation, he opened his mouth to say something to the intruder. His eyes instantly lit up when he saw Waltham. Simon guessed he hadn't noticed himself and Dani behind his son yet.

"Brendan!" Lindley exclaimed, rising from his chair behind the enormous cherrywood desk. The duke was dressed casually, his shirt open at the throat and without a coat. On the desk in front of him was a ledger book. Next to it a glass, a brandy bottle and a box of snuff.

Waltham accepted his effusive embrace without enthusiasm. He stood stiff, unyielding. When his father stepped back, a questioning frown on his face, Waltham stared back blankly. It was then that Lindley noticed Simon and Dani. His gaze flicked briefly on Dani, his eyes widening almost imperceptibly, then moved on to Simon, darkening, turning angry and fierce. Lindley turned back to his son.

"Why are Stratford and this woman with you? What is this about?"

"Sit down, Father." He said it distastefully, as though the bitterness of it was hard to swallow. Simon had some experience with wretched fathers.

If Lindley had been a horse, steam would have come from his nostrils. But he was a man, albeit a dangerous one and he made his way to the seat behind his desk. He gestured to the chairs that faced his desk and Simon and Dani took the pair closest together. Simon pulled them even closer.

Waltham refused to sit and instead moved over to the bookcase on the right side of the luxuriously furnished study.

The chair Simon sank into was extraordinarily comfortable and made of rich leather.

Lindley flicked a cold glance at Simon and Dani, barely acknowledging them, before turning to look at his son. His hands were crossed in front of him on the desk.

"What is this about, Brendan?"

"Justin is dead," Waltham said bluntly. His face expressionless he stared at his father.

"What? Dead? How?" To his credit, the old man acted as though he actually cared about the fate of his eldest grandson. His upper lip quivered just a little and the malevolent sparkle in his eyes gave a tiny hint of dimming. His hands clenched together tightly. Then he turned abruptly to look at Simon, as though something had occurred to him. "Are you responsible for my grandson's death?"

"Justin is responsible for is own death," Waltham said quietly. "His death was self-inflicted."

Lindley's white eyebrows furrowed together. The very idea was alien to him. He shook his head. "Impossible. I won't believe it."

"It's true." Waltham glared. "But there are others who bear some responsibility for it, nonetheless."

This time Lindley scowled at his son. "Well, why are these people here? This is obviously a private family moment."

Waltham smiled, raised an eyebrow. A wild animal closing in on its prey. Lindley should have known better. He'd raised Brendan himself.

"Ah but Father, Stratford is very nearly family after all."

"What are you talking about?" Lindley snarled.

"He's about to marry my daughter." Waltham glanced quickly at Dani. Lindley followed his gaze.

The old man gave away nothing. An excellent gambler, Simon was sure. He had his own words to say to the old shark but for now he was content to let his son handle him.

"Your daughters are a little young for marriage." Lindley licked his lips.

"Most of them yes," Waltham agreed. "But my daughter with Rose is of age to marry."

"Brendan, I don't know what game you are playing…"

"I play no game, Father." Waltham laughed. "How despicable you are. I bear some responsibility for the way Justin turned out, it's true. I should have paid more attention to the time he was spending with you but in truth I had no real notion of what a true serpent you are."

"I don't like the way you are speaking to me." Lindley slammed his fist onto the desk. "I am your father!"

"Justin is dead because of you. I would that it was you instead." Waltham took a step closer to his father, his hands clenched at his side. "You think to control everyone and everything don't you? You bastard. Rose was my wife and you offered her money and when she refused to take it you chased her down until she had no choice but to disappear. You knew how I felt about her and you didn't care."

"She was trash, Brendan." Lindley's jaw tightened.

Dani visibly flinched.

"She would have destroyed us. You. She was a conniving little fortune hunter. We are Daltons. We don't settle for seamstresses, for God's sake. You weren't thinking clearly. I had to do it for you."

The look Lindley turned on Dani was contemptuous. "Is this trollop trying to claim she's Rose's daughter by you?" He wagged a finger. "Nobody gets away with trying to suck money from a Dalton."

Dani raised her chin and met the old man's eyes. "I am your son's daughter by Rose. And I'm not trying to suck anything from anyone."

Simon noticed Lindley's hand slide from the desk to open a drawer at the front of his desk. He reached in. Alarms went off in Simon's head.

"No!" Dani noticed it too.

"Waltham! He's got a pistol!" Simon went to throw his body across Dani's protectively.

A shot rang out.

Simon reached for his own pistol, then his gaze focused on Lindley, slumped over his desk. Blood oozed out of a rather large wound in his forehead. Lindley's hand was wrapped around a pistol but it was not in a firing position. Stunned, Simon looked at Waltham, expecting to see the earl holding a pistol of his own. He was not. Waltham stared past Simon to the door of the study. The earl's expression was one of pure disbelief.

Simon pulled away from Dani and they both followed Waltham's gaze. Standing in the doorway holding a still smoking pistol was the Duchess of Lindley. Waltham's mother, dressed in an elegantly tailored dark blue ball gown and matching gloves up to her elbows, appeared satisfied with her handiwork. She stared long and hard at her husband. Upon her lips was a small triumphant smile. This was the family his beautiful Dani belonged to?

"Bastard," cried the duchess, waving the pistol in her husband's direction. "Tries to kill my son, does he?"

Waltham, coming to life once more, cleared his throat and walked over to his mother. He gently removed the pistol from her grasp and set it down on a nearby bookcase.

"Mother, what have you done?"

Simon noticed that when she turned her eyes to Waltham at last her eyes were filled with unshed tears. She held his hands in hers.

"I couldn't let him hurt you, Brendan, not any more," she whispered. "He was going to kill you."

Brendan nodded. "He was ill. Justin too."

"Then it's true? Justin killed himself?"

Waltham blew out a breath. "Yes. I'll tell you all about it too. Only now, I think I'd better take care of…" He stopped, raised his hand to gesture to his father but thought better of it. He shrugged. "Perhaps we need some tea."

"I need something a great deal stronger then tea." The duchess eyed Simon and Dani. "What about you?"

"Definitely stronger, madam," Simon agreed. He grabbed Dani's trembling hand and together they walked over to the duchess.

"Perhaps you'll tell me some of what's happened while Brendan sees to his father." She reached up and stroked the cheek of her son with her gloved hand. "You're the Duke of Lindley, now, Brendan."

The duchess would not sit still. She paced back and forth in front of the elaborate gold settee in the gold-colored parlor where she'd brought Simon and Dani. He guessed the duchess was very fond of gold.

"I had no idea," the duchess kept repeating in between rather large sips of port.

"Yes, Your Grace."

"Leo always tried to keep me out of important matters. He thought women shouldn't know anything. But if I had known what he'd been doing." She clucked her tongue. "I had no idea." She downed her port and went to the side table to pour herself another. She glanced at Simon. "How is your drink, young man?"

"Fine, madam," Simon assured her.

She smiled kindly at Dani who nearly sat in his lap she was so close. Dani stared wide-eyed at the woman who had shot her own husband.

"You, dear?"

Dani shook her head.

"I keep talking, you know, because it just hasn't sunk in yet," the duchess said, pacing once more. "My God, Justin. He was just a b-baby." Her voice broke a little, new tears streaming down her face. "Do you know why it is that an old lady like me outlives her grandson?"

They said nothing, just let her talk.

"I killed my own husband." Her bottom lip quivered. She wrung her hands. "I didn't know what else to do. I couldn't let him kill Brendan. You understand, don't you?"

"Yes. I'm very sorry, Your Grace. Do you need anything? Shall I get Brendan for you?" Simon asked.

She shook her head just a little. "You're very kind." She caught her breath. "So, this young lady is my Brendan's?"

"Yes."

The duchess came toward Dani. She took hold of her hands. "Let me look at you, dear. Oh, no need to shake so. I'm your grandmother, after all." She glanced shrewdly at Simon. "You're going to marry her?"

"I hope to." Simon smiled reassuringly at Dani.

The duchess smiled. "You're quite smitten with her, aren't you?"

He nodded.

"I once loved Leo," she said, sadly. "I don't know if he changed or if I did. Maybe it was both of us. I was so naïve and full of love when we married but he started...well, he had so many mistresses, you see. It was hard to love him after that." She frowned. "You won't do that to your wife, will you, young man?"

"No."

"I didn't know about Brendan and Rose. I knew he was miserable in his marriage to Diana. Never did like that woman," the duchess said disapprovingly. "She was a fortune hunter. I told Leo that but..." She stopped. "I caught them together, you know."

"Who, madam?" Dani asked, her eyes wide.

"Leo and Brendan's wife, Diana." Her tone was bitter. "I think that is why he pushed Brendan into marrying her. So he could take up with her." She smiled a cool smile. "I was so happy when she died."

Dani and Simon shared a quick horrified glance.

* * * * *

"She's sleeping now," Brendan said coming into the parlor later. "I gave her something to help her sleep." He ran his hand through his hair. "I'm ready to go back to London. There's so much that has to be done for both of them. But I want to be with Justin now."

"I understand. We're ready, too." Simon stood up, stretched his stiff legs. "I don't relish the carriage ride home, though." He pulled Dani up from the settee.

Brendan nodded. "I know. I have to return here tomorrow."

"Brendan?"

"Hmm?"

Simon opened his mouth to say something about the duchess but changed his mind. He shrugged. "Nothing."

Simon and Dani followed Waltham out to the hall of Lindley Manor. "It's amazing."

"What is?" Brendan asked, stopping before the front door.

"That you're the only one in your family that turned out normal, I guess," Simon said a bit sheepishly.

Brendan raised an eyebrow and opened the door. "How do you know I'm normal?" He stepped outside.

Simon breathed the fresh air outside the front entrance. Somehow the air inside the manor was still, stuffy. He didn't get a good feeling there at all.

"About your mother..."

Brendan pulled his greatcoat close about him to block the chill wind that blew. "I know what you're going to say. Don't worry, she'll stay here in Portsmouth until her death."

Simon didn't really believe the now dowager duchess would harm Dani or probably anyone else but he didn't want to take any chances. For the first time since he met Dani she was out of danger. They could start their lives together without fear. He didn't want anything that might threaten Dani in any way. It would be hard enough for her trying to adjust to life among the cutthroats of the *ton*.

Brendan stopped when he reached the bottom of the outside stairs and he turned to gaze at him. His frown was dark, considering.

"I think when my mother dies, I'll close this up until one of my sons is old enough to do with it as he pleases."

"It's a magnificent house," Simon commented, choosing not to comment on the cold feel of it. He had a feeling Brendan knew that all too well himself.

"It's a façade," Brendan replied. "Let's go to London."

* * * * *

It was nearly late morning by the time Simon and Dani arrived home. Dani's father advised Simon that he and his wife would be by in the afternoon to meet with Dani.

Wilkins opened the front door of Simon's townhouse immediately, as though he'd been standing guard watching for them. Simon suspected he had.

"Everyone's waiting for you in the front room, Your Grace." Wilkins smiled in Dani's direction. "Dani."

Simon raised an eyebrow, then frowned. "Everyone?" He didn't want to see everyone. He wanted to be alone with Dani.

"Yes, Your Grace. The Duke of Scarborough is here. And Lady Lucy has recovered enough from her fright to come downstairs. And Lord Jack."

Simon handed his greatcoat to Wilkins. He supposed they were all going to want to know what happened in Portsmouth.

"Tea, Wilkins?"

"Already waiting for you, Your Grace." Wilkins hesitated. He wanted to say more, no doubt.

Simon smiled and patted the old man on his shoulder. "You may come in and hear this as well, Wilkins."

The butler brightened. "Thank you, sir."

"And bring Grace in too."

Wilkins was positively beaming. "I will fetch her immediately."

Her heart floating, Dani entered the room on Simon's arm to find all the people they cared most about gathered around. Jack gestured to two chairs by the fire with a flourish. The chairs looked like thrones to Dani.

When they were seated, Simon leaned over and kissed her. "Are you all right?"

"Yes, I'm better than all right." She let her love shine through her eyes.

Simon turned to face the group when Wilkins entered with Grace in tow. Wilkins looked well pleased and Grace had a rather shy smile on her face. Simon had a feeling they would have an announcement of their own soon.

Jack stood up — he never seemed content to sit idly by — near the windows. His arms were crossed in front of him, his face solemn.

And finally Lucy and Scarborough sat together on the small green settee. Simon frowned. Lucy was staring at Scarborough with nothing less than hero worship. Simon did not care for it at all.

"I'm sure you all have a dozen questions." He drew their attention to him. "Not the least of which how it turned out at Lindley Manor."

"Did the bastard admit his part?" Jack growled.

"Not exactly," Simon murmured. "He didn't really get the chance."

"You and Waltham didn't make him?" Jack was incredulous.

Simon squeezed Dani's hand. "The old duke is dead, Jack. That's all that matters now. Waltham is now the Duke of Lindley."

"Heavens," Lucy exclaimed, her large green eyes wider than usual.

"So Brendan Dalton is Dani's father?" Scarborough asked. The question gained him a radiant smile from Lucy.

"Yes, when he was young he fell in love with Dani's mother, Rose, and married her," Simon explained. "Leonard Dalton was furious his son would marry so far beneath him. Lindley insisted his son annul the marriage. When Brendan refused to listen to his father, the duke took the matter into his own hands."

"He chased my mother away," Dani whispered.

"Yes." Simon looked over at her. "His intent was to pay her off but she couldn't be bought."

"She loved my father."

"To her detriment," Simon agreed. "I believe Lindley intended to kill Rose but she somehow managed to escape him. She left her shop and everything she ever had behind. She dared not return."

"And when she got sick and died, Mary and I took care of her," Grace spoke up from beside Wilkins.

"Yes, exactly." Simon rubbed his thumb along Dani's wrist. He could feel the tension in here. This would be difficult for her and he still wanted to get her alone so he could hear her say she loved him again. "I suppose after all these years Lindley put the matter out of his mind but not entirely. While in his cups he said a little bit too much to his mistress, Sally Reynolds one day."

"And always the schemer, Sally thought she found the perfect way to make her fortune." Jack shook his head. "Only she included Norton in that."

"Likewise to his detriment," Scarborough commented.

Simon nodded. "He was losing money in card games all the time. He must have thought this was his chance at good fortune. But Douglas didn't stop there. He decided he wanted more to hold over the duke's head and he went looking for information."

Dani shook her head. "And then Carstairs? Did he follow him?"

"Norton probably told him his plans. He never could keep his mouth shut." He paused, considering. "The night Douglas was murdered, Mary must have seen it happen and so Carstairs had to kill her too."

"Poor Mary," Dani whispered brokenly.

"And then you got in the way, Simon," Jack said. "Both with looking into Norton's murder and bringing Dani into your home."

"He was so frightening," Lucy said softly. "I thought he would hurt me." Scarborough patted her hand.

"He was a bit of a victim himself." Dani shook her head. "I felt kind of sorry for him. His grandfather misled him. And he lived with such hate."

Simon was surprised at the depth of her understanding. He shook his head. "I'll have to talk to Aunt Pen about all this tomorrow. She's resting now."

There would be more time for talking over events later. For now he was out of patience.

"Wilkins, see the Duke of Scarborough to the door, please."

Scarborough raised a blond brow but then shrugged nonchalantly. He got up from the settee, taking Lucy's hand. He bent over it. "I hope you will feel better, Lucy."

Lucy blushed and stammered, "T-thank you, Your Grace."

"You and Jack can see him to the door too," Simon called out. Everyone in the room, including his Dani, turned to stare at him. He ignored their curious glances. He only had eyes for Dani.

Jack grinned. "Let's go, sweet pea," He said to Lucy. "We know when we're not wanted."

Dani watched everyone but Simon leave the front room.

She supposed Simon wanted to discuss the problems associated with their love and his wanting to marry her.

Simon turned to her now that everyone had left and her heart skipped a beat. He was more handsome now than when she'd first met him. It seemed so long ago now but really she'd only been with him a few weeks. How her life had changed.

"Dani..."

"Simon..."

They both spoke at the same time. Dani blushed, laughed. He smiled and told her to go first.

"I love you."

"I love you too. More than I ever imagined was possible." His gold-green eyes were intense. He'd come to stand by her. He reached down and helped her up from the chair. "You consume me."

She could have wept with happiness at his words but not yet. There was so much more she needed to hear from him.

"And what you told the earl about marrying me. I... Are you certain marriage is what you want? I wouldn't want to cause you harm because of my love." She bit her lip, suddenly shy. She looked down at their feet. She looked up at him when he pulled papers out of his coat.

"This is a special license," Simon said, holding up the papers for her to see. "What it means is that we can get married whenever we want."

Her breath caught in her throat. For several moments she couldn't even speak. Tears streamed out of her eyes but she resisted the urge to wipe at them. "You really want to marry me?"

"Yes." Simon brushed a tear with his finger. "If you'll have me."

"But, I'm from the streets," Dani said.

"No, you're the daughter of the new Duke of Lindley and his late wife, Rose, who was the daughter of a baron's son."

"It will be an awful scandal, though," she whispered.

"There won't be any scandal. Well, that's not entirely true. But your parents were married and together with your father and your stepmother we'll work out the rest. Some story to explain where you've been all this time." He smiled gently. "I'm very grateful to Mary and Grace for saving you, but you'll not be able to talk about that time spent in the East End now. It has to stay our secret."

"Yes, I know, but..."

"You say you love me, Dani"

"Of course I love you," she exclaimed and was rewarded with a hard kiss.

"Than you will say yes?" he prompted.

"How can I refuse?" She laughed, a joyful sound that went straight to both their hearts.

Also by Sharon Lanergan

ಸಾ

eBooks:
Duke Pretender
Duke's Project

About Sharon Lanergan

ಸಾ

Sharon Lanergan has been writing since childhood when she first fell in love with ancient legends and romances of bygone eras. Though fascinated by those days of old, Sharon is grateful to live with her family in California in the twenty-first century.

ಸಾ

The author welcomes comments from readers. You can find her website and email address on her author bio page at www.ellorascave.com.

Tell Us What You Think

We appreciate hearing reader opinions about our books. You can email us at Service@ellorascave.com (when contacting Customer Service, be sure to state the book title and author).

Why an electronic book?

We live in the Information Age—an exciting time in the history of human civilization, in which technology rules supreme and continues to progress in leaps and bounds every minute of every day. For a multitude of reasons, more and more avid literary fans are opting to purchase e-books instead of paper books. The question from those not yet initiated into the world of electronic reading is simply: *Why?*

1. **Price.** An electronic title at Ellora's Cave Publishing runs anywhere from 40% to 75% less than the cover price of the exact same title in paperback format. Why? Basic mathematics and cost. It is less expensive to publish an e-book (no paper and printing, no warehousing and shipping) than it is to publish a paperback, so the savings are passed along to the consumer.
2. **Space.** Running out of room in your house for your books? That is one worry you will never have with electronic books. For a low one-time cost, you can purchase a handheld device specifically designed for e-reading. Many e-readers have large, convenient screens for viewing. Better yet, hundreds of titles can be stored within your new library—on a single microchip. There are a variety of e-readers from different manufacturers. You can also read e-books on your PC or laptop computer. (Please note that Ellora's Cave does not endorse any specific brands.

You can check our website at www.elloracave.com for information we make available to new consumers.)

3. *Mobility.* Because your new e-library consists of only a microchip within a small, easily transportable e-reader, your entire cache of books can be taken with you wherever you go.

4. *Personal Viewing Preferences.* Are the words you are currently reading too small? Too **large**? Too... ANNOYING? Paperback books cannot be modified according to personal preferences, but e-books can.

5. *Instant Gratification.* Is it the middle of the night and all the bookstores near you are closed? Are you tired of waiting days, sometimes weeks, for bookstores to ship the novels you bought? Ellora's Cave Publishing sells instantaneous downloads twenty-four hours a day, seven days a week, every day of the year. Our webstore is never closed. Our e-book delivery system is 100% automated, meaning your order is filled as soon as you pay for it.

Those are a few of the top reasons why electronic books are replacing paperbacks for many avid readers.

As always, Ellora's Cave welcomes your questions and comments. We invite you to email us at Service@ellorascave.com or write to us directly at Ellora's Cave Publishing Inc., 1056 Home Avenue, Akron, OH 44310-3502.

Discover for yourself why readers can't get enough of the multiple award-winning publisher Ellora's Cave. Be sure to visit EC on the web at www.ellorascave.com to find erotic reading experiences that will leave you breathless. You can also find our books at all the major e-tailers (Barnes & Noble, Amazon Kindle, Sony, Kobo, Google, Apple iBookstore, All Romance eBooks, and others).

www.ellorascave.com

CPSIA information can be obtained at www.ICGtesting.com
Printed in the USA
BVOW031321060513

319994BV00001B/3/P